BORDERS.
CLASSICS

DANTE ALIGHIERI

The Divine Comedy

Translated by A. S. Kline

BORDERS.

CLASSICS

CONTENTS

INFERNO

1

In the middle of the journey of our life, I came to myself in a dark wood, where the direct way was lost. It is a hard thing to speak of—how wild, harsh, and impenetrable that wood was—so that thinking of it recreates the fear. It is scarcely less bitter than death; but in order to tell of the good that I found there, I must tell of the other things I saw there.

I cannot rightly say how I entered it. I was so full of sleep at that point where I abandoned the true way. But when I reached the foot of a hill, where the valley, which had pierced my heart with fear, came to an end, I looked up and saw its shoulders brightened with the rays of that sun that leads men rightly on every road. Then the fear, which had settled in the lake of my heart through the night that I had spent so miserably, became a little calmer. And as a man who, with panting breath, has escaped from the deep sea to the shore turns back towards the perilous waters and stares, so my mind, still fleeing, turned back to see that pass again, which no living person ever left.

After I had rested my tired body a while, I made my way again over open ground, always bearing upwards to the right. And behold, almost at the start of the slope, a light swift leopard with spotted coat. It would not turn away from me, and so obstructed the path that I often turned in order to go back.

The time was at the beginning of the morning, and the sun was mounting up with all those stars that were with Him when Divine Love first moved all delightful things, so that the hour of day, and the sweet season, gave me fair hopes of that creature with the bright pelt. But not so fair that I could avoid fear at the sight of a lion that appeared, and seemed to come at me with raised head and rabid hunger, so that it seemed the air itself was afraid; and a she-wolf that looked full of craving in its leanness, and, before now, has made many men live in sadness. She brought me such heaviness of fear from the aspect of her face that I lost all hope of ascending. And as one who is eager for gain weeps, and is afflicted in his thoughts if the moment arrives when he loses, so that creature, without rest, made me like him: and coming at me, little by little, drove me back to where the sun is silent.

While I was returning to the depths, one appeared in front of me who seemed hoarse from long silence. When I saw him, in the great emptiness, I cried out to him, "Have pity on me, whoever you are, whether a man, in truth, or a shadow!" He answered me: "Not a man, but a man I once was, and my parents were Lombards, and both of them, by their native place, Mantuans.

"I was born *sub Julio* though late, and lived in Rome under the good Augustus, in the age of false, deceitful gods. I was a poet, and sang of Aeneas, that virtuous son of Anchises, who came from Troy when proud Ilium was burned. But you, why do you turn back towards such pain? Why do you not climb the delightful mountain that is the origin and cause of all joy?"

I answered him with a humble expression: "Are you then that Virgil, and that fountain, that pours out so great a river of speech? O, glory and light to other poets, may that long study, and the great love that made me search your work, be worth something now. You are my master, and my author: you alone are the one from whom I learned the high style that has brought me honor. See the creature that I turned back from: O sage, famous in wisdom, save me from her, she that makes my veins and my pulse tremble."

When he saw me weeping, he answered: "You must go by another road if you wish to escape this savage place. This creature that distresses you allows no man to cross her path, but obstructs him, to destroy him, and she has so vicious and perverse a nature that she never sates her greedy appetite, and after food is hungrier than before.

"Many are the creatures she mates with, and there will be many more until the Greyhound comes who will make her die in pain. He will not feed himself on land or wealth, but on wisdom, love, and virtue, and his birthplace will lie between Feltro and Montefeltro. He will be the salvation of that lower Italy for which virgin Camilla died of wounds, and Euryalus, Turnus, and Nisus. He will chase the she-wolf through every city until he has returned her to Hell, from which envy first loosed her.

"It is best, as I think and understand, for you to follow me, and I will be your guide and lead you from here through an eternal space where you will hear the desparate shouts, will see the ancient spirits in pain, so that each one cries out for a second death; and then you will see others at peace in the flames, because they hope to come, whenever it may be, among the blessed. Then if you desire to climb to them, there will be a spirit, fitter than I am, to guide you, and I will leave you with her when we part, since the Lord who rules above does not wish me to enter his city because I was rebellious to His law. He is lord everywhere, but there He rules, and there is His city, and His high throne. O happy is he whom He chooses to go there!"

And I to him: "Poet, I beg you, by the God you did not acknowledge, lead me where you said so that I might escape this evil or worse, and see the Gate of Saint Peter, and those whom you make out to be so saddened."

Then he departed and I followed behind him.

2

The day was ending and the dusky air was freeing the creatures of the earth from their labors, and I, one alone, prepared myself to endure the inner war of the journey and its pity that the mind, without error, shall recall.

O Muses, O high invention, aid me, now! O memory, which has engraved what I saw, here your nobility will be shown.

I began: "Poet, you who guides me, examine my virtue, see if I am fitting before you trust me to the steep way. You say that Aeneas, the father of Sylvius, while still corruptible flesh, went to the eternal world, and in the flesh. But if God, who opposes every evil, was gracious to him, thinking of the noble consequence, of who and what should derive from him, then that does not seem unreasonable to a man of intellect, since he was chosen to be the father of benign Rome and of her empire. Both of them were founded as a sacred place, where the successor of the great Peter is enthroned. By that journey, by which you graced him, Aeneas learned things that were the source of his victory and of the papal mantle. Afterwards Paul, the chosen vessel, went there to bring confirmation of the faith that is the entrance to the way of salvation.

"But why should I go there? Who allows it? I am not Aeneas; I am not Paul. Neither I, nor others, think me worthy of it. So if I resign myself to going, I fear that going there may prove foolish: you know, and understand, better than I can say." And I rendered myself, on that dark shore, like one who unwishes what he wished, and changes his purpose after changing his mind, so that he leaves off what he began completely, since in thought I consumed action that had been so ready to begin.

The ghost of the generous poet replied: "If I have understood your words correctly, your spirit is attacked by cowardly fear, which often weighs men down so that it deflects them from honorable action, like a creature seeing phantoms in the dusk. That you may shake off this dread yourself, I will tell you why I came, and what I heard at the first moment when I took pity on you.

"I was among those in Limbo, in suspense, and a lady called to me: she so beautiful, so blessed, that I begged her to command me. Her eyes shone more brightly than the stars, and she began to speak, gently, quietly, in an angelic voice, in her language: 'O noble Mantuan spirit, whose fame still endures in the world, and will endure as long as time endures, my friend, not fortune's friend, is so obstructed in his way along the desert strand that he turns back in terror, and I fear he is already so far lost and that I have started too late to his aid, from what I heard of him in Heaven. Now go, and help him so with your eloquence, and with whatever is needed for his relief, that I may be comforted. I am Beatrice who asks you to go: I come from a place I long to return to: love moved me and made me speak. When I am before my Lord, I will often praise you to Him.'

"Then she was silent, and I began: 'O lady of virtue, in whom, alone, humanity exceeds all that is contained in the lunar Heaven, which has the smallest sphere, your command is so pleasing to me that, obeying, were it done already, it were done too slow; you have no need to explain your wishes further. But tell me why you do not hesitate to descend here, to this center below, from the wide space you burn to return to.'

"She replied: 'Since you wish to know, I will tell you this much, briefly, of why I do not fear to enter here. Those things that have the power to hurt are to be feared; not those other things that are not fearful. I am made such, by God's grace, that your suffering does not touch me, nor does the fire of this burning scorch me.

"'There is a gentle lady in Heaven, who has such compassion for this trouble I send you to relieve that she overrules the strict laws on high. She called Lucia to carry out her request, and said: "Now, he who is faithful to you needs you, and I commend him to you." Lucia, who is opposed to all cruelty, rose and came to the place where I was, where I sat with that Rachel of antiquity. Lucia said: "Beatrice, God's true praise, why do you not help him, who loved you so intensely he left behind the common crowd for you? Do you not hear how pitiful his grief is? Do you not see the spiritual death that comes to meet him, on that dark river, over which the sea has no power?"

"'No one on earth was ever as quick to search for their good, or run from harm, as I to descend from my blessed place after these words were spoken, and place my faith in your true speech, which honors you and those who hear it.' She turned away, with tears in her bright eyes, after saying this to me, and made me, by that, come here all the quicker: and so I came to you, as she wished, and rescued you in the face of that wild creature that denied you the shortest path to the lovely mountain.

"What is it then? Why do you hold back? Why? Why let such cowardly fear into your heart? Why, when three such blessed ladies, in the courts of Heaven, care for you, and my words promise you so much good, are you not free and ardent?"

As the flowers, bent down and closed by the night's cold, erect themselves, all open on their stems, when the sun shines on them, so I rose from weakened courage; and so fine an ardor coursed through my heart that I began to speak like one who is freed: "O she who pities, who helps me, and you, so gentle, who swiftly obeyed the true words she commanded, you have filled my heart with such desire, by what you have said, to go forward that I have turned back to my first purpose. Go now, for the two of us have but one will, you, the guide, the lord, the master." So I spoke to him, and he moving on, I entered on the steep, tree-shadowed way.

3

THROUGH ME THE WAY TO THE INFERNAL CITY,
THROUGH ME THE WAY TO ETERNAL SADNESS,
THROUGH ME THE WAY TO THE LOST PEOPLE.

JUSTICE MOVED MY SUPREME MAKER:
I WAS SHAPED BY DIVINE POWER,
BY HIGHEST WISDOM, AND BY PRIMAL LOVE.

BEFORE ME, NOTHING WAS CREATED
THAT IS NOT ETERNAL, AND ETERNALLY I ENDURE.
ABANDON ALL HOPE, YOU THAT ENTER HERE.

These were the words that I saw written in dark letters above the gate, at which I said: "Master, their meaning is not clear to me." And he replied to me, as one who knows: "Here, all uncertainty must be left behind; all cowardice must be dead. We have come to the place where I told you that you would see the sad people who have lost the benefit of the intellect." And placing his hand on mine, with a calm expression that comforted me, he led me towards the hidden things.

Here sighs, complaints, and deep groans sounded through the starless air, so that it made me weep at first. Many tongues, a terrible crying, words of sadness, accents of anger, voices deep and hoarse, with sounds of hands amongst them making a turbulence that turns forever in that air, stained, eternally, like sand spiralling in a whirlwind. And I, surrounded by the horror, said: "Master, what is this I hear, and what race are these that seem so overcome by suffering?"

And he to me: "This is the miserable mode in which those exist who lived without praise, without blame. They are mixed in with the despised choir of angels, who were not rebellious, not faithful to God, but for themselves. Heaven drove them out to maintain its beauty, and deep Hell does not accept them, lest the evil have glory over them." And I: "Master, what is so heavy on them that makes them moan so deeply?" He replied: "I will tell you, briefly. They have no hope of death, and their darkened life is so mean that they are envious of every other fate. Earth allows no mention of them to exist; mercy and justice reject them; let us not talk of them, only look and pass."

And I, who looked back, saw a banner that, twirling around moved so quickly that it seemed to me scornful of any pause, and behind it came so long a line of people I never would have believed that death had undone so many.

When I had recognized some among them, I saw and knew the shade of him who from cowardice made "the great refusal." Immediately I understood that this was that despicable crew hateful to God and his enemies. These wretches, who never truly lived, were naked, and goaded viciously by hornets and wasps there, making their faces stream with blood that, mixed with tears, was collected at their feet by loathsome worms.

And then, as I looked onwards, I saw people on the bank of a great river, at which I said: "Master, now let me understand who these are, and what custom makes them so ready to cross over, as I can see by the dim light." And he to me: "The meaning will be explained to you when we halt our steps, on the sad strand of Acheron." Then, fearing that my words might have offended him, I stopped myself from speaking, with eyes ashamed and downcast, till we had reached the flood.

And look, an old man with white hoary locks came towards us in a boat, shouting: "Woe to you, wicked spirits! Never hope to see Heaven; I come to carry you to the other shore, into eternal darkness, into fire and ice. And you there, a living spirit, depart from those who are dead."

But when he saw that I did not depart, he said: "By other ways, by other means of passage, you will cross to the shore: a swifter boat must carry you." And my guide said to him: "Charon, do not vex yourself: it is willed *there*, where what is willed is done: ask no more." Then the bearded mouth of the ferryman of the livid marsh, who had wheels of flame round his eyes, was stilled.

But those spirits, who were naked and weary, changed color and gnashed their teeth when they heard his earlier cruel words. They blasphemed against God, and their parents, the human species, the place, time, and seed of their conception, and against their birth. Then all together, weeping bitterly, they neared the cursed shore that waits for everyone who has no fear of God.

Charon, the demon, with eyes of burning coal, beckoning, gathers them all: and strikes with his oar whoever lingers. As the autumn leaves fall, one after another, till the branches see all their spoilage on the ground, so, one by one, the evil seed of Adam threw themselves down from the bank when signaled, like the falcon at its call. So they vanish on the dark water, and before they have landed over there, over here a fresh crowd collects.

The courteous Master said: "My son, those who die subject to God's anger all gather here, from every country, and they are quick to cross the river, since divine justice goads them on, so that their fear is turned to desire. This way no good spirit ever passes, and so if Charon complains at you, you can well understand now the meaning of his words."

When he had ended, the gloomy ground trembled so violently that the memory of my terror still drenches me with sweat. The weeping earth gave vent and flashed with crimson light, overpowering all my senses, and I fell, like a man overcome by sleep.

4

A heavy thunder shattered the deep sleep in my head so that I came to myself, like someone woken by force, and standing up, I opened my eyes, now refreshed, and looked around steadily to find out what place I was in. I found myself, in truth, on the brink of the valley of the sad abyss that gathers the thunder of an infinite howling. It was so dark and deep and clouded that I could see nothing by staring into its depths.

The poet, white of face, began: "Now, let us descend into the blind world below. I will go first, and you go second." And I, who saw his altered color, said: "How can I go on if you are afraid, who are my comfort when I hesitate?" And he to me: "The anguish of the people here below brings that look of pity to my face, which you mistake for fear. Let us go, for the length of our journey demands it." So he entered, and so he made me enter, into the first circle that surrounds the abyss.

Here there was no sound to be heard except the sighing that made the eternal air tremble, and it came from the sorrow of the vast and varied crowds of children, of women, and of men, free of torment. The good Master said to me: "You do not demand to know who these spirits are that you see. I want you to learn, before you go further, that they had no sin, yet, though they have worth, it is not sufficient, because they were not baptised, and baptism is the gateway to the faith that you believe in. Since they lived before Christianity, they did not worship God correctly, and I myself am one of them. For this defect, and for no other fault, we are lost, and we are tormented only in that without hope we live in desire."

When I heard this, great sadness gripped my heart, because I knew of people of great value who must be suspended in that Limbo. Wishing to be certain in that faith that overcomes every error, I began: "Tell me, my Master, tell me, sir, did anyone ever go from here, through his own merit or because of others' merit, who afterwards was blessed?"

And he, understanding my veiled question, replied: "I was new to this state, when I saw a great one come here crowned with the sign of victory. He took from us the shade of Adam, our first parent, of his son Abel, and that of Noah, of Moses the lawgiver, and Abraham, the obedient patriarch, King David, Jacob with his father Isaac, and his children, and Rachel, for whom he labored so long, and many others, and made them blessed, and I wish you to know that no human souls were saved before these."

We did not cease moving, though he was speaking, but passed the wood meanwhile, the wood, I say, of crowded spirits. We had not gone far from where I slept when I saw a flame that overcame a hemisphere of shadows. We were still some way from it, but not so far that I failed to discern in part what noble people occupied that place.

"O you who value every science and art, who are these, who have such honor that they stand apart from all the rest?" And he to me: "Their fame, which resounds for them in that life of yours, also brings them Heaven's grace, which advances them." Meanwhile I heard a voice: "Honor the great poet: his departed shade returns."

After the voice had paused and was quiet, I saw four great shadows come towards us, with faces that were neither sad nor happy. The good Master began to speak: "Take note of him with a sword in hand, who comes in front of the other three, as if he were their lord: that is Homer, the sovereign poet; next Horace, the satirist; Ovid is the third, and last is Lucan. Because each is worthy, with me, of that name the one voice sounded, they do me honor, and in doing so, do good."

So I saw gathered together the noble school of the lord of highest song, who soars like an eagle above the rest. After they had talked for a while amongst themselves, they turned towards me with a sign of greeting, at which my Master smiled. And they honored me further still, since they made me one of their company, so that I made a sixth among the wise.

So we went onwards to the light, speaking of things about which it is best to be silent, just as it was best to speak of them where I was.

We came to the base of a noble castle, surrounded seven times by a high wall, and defended by a beautiful, encircling stream. This we crossed as if it were solid earth. I entered through seven gates with the wise; we reached a meadow of fresh turf. The people there were of great authority in appearance, with calm and serious demeanors, speaking seldom, and then with soft voices. We moved to one side, into an open space, bright and high, so that every one of them could be seen.

There, on the green enamel, the great spirits were pointed out to me, directly, so that I feel exalted inside at having seen them.

I saw Electra with many others, amongst whom I recognized Hector, Aeneas, and Caesar, armed, with his eagle eye. I saw Camilla and Penthesilea on the other side, and Latinus, the king of Latium, with his daughter Lavinia. I saw that Brutus who expelled Tarquin, Lucretia, Julia, Marcia, and Cornelia, and I saw Saladin, apart by himself.

When I lifted my eyes a little higher, I saw the Master of those who know, Aristotle, sitting amongst the company of philosophers. All gaze at him: all show him honor. There I saw Socrates, and Plato, who stand nearest to him of all of them; Democritus, who ascribes the world to chance, Diogenes, Anaxagoras, and Thales; Empedocles, Heraclitus, and Zeno; and I saw the good collector of the qualities of plants, I mean Dioscorides: and saw Orpheus, Cicero, Linus, and Seneca the moralist; Euclid the geometer, and Ptolemaeus; Hippocrates, Avicenna, and Galen; and Averroes, who wrote the vast commentary.

I cannot speak of them all in full, because the great theme drives me on, so that the word often falls short of the fact. The six companions reduce to two: the wise guide leads me, by another path, out of the quiet, into the trembling air, and I come to a region where nothing shines.

5

So I descended from the first circle to the second, which encloses a smaller space, and so much more pain it provokes howling. There Minos stands, grinning horribly, examines the crimes on entrance, judges, and sends the guilty down as far as is signified by his coils: I mean that when the evil-born spirit comes before him, it confesses everything, and that knower of sins decides the proper place in hell for it, and makes as many coils with his tail as the circles he will force it to descend. A multitude always stand before him and go in turn to be judged, speak and hear, and then are whirled downwards.

When Minos saw me, passing by the activity of his great office, he said: "O you who come to the house of pain, take care how you enter, and in whom you trust; do not let the width of the entrance deceive you." To which my guide replied: "Why do you cry out? Do not obstruct his destined journey: so it is willed, where what is willed is done: demand no more." Now the mournful notes begin to reach me: now I come where much sorrowing hurts me.

I came to a place devoid of light that moans like a tempestuous sea when it is buffeted by warring winds. The hellish storm that never ceases drives the spirits with its force, and, whirling and striking, it molests them. When they come to the ruins there are shouts, moaning and crying, where they blaspheme against divine power. I learnt that the carnal sinners are condemned to these torments, they who subject their reason to their lust.

And, as their wings carry the starlings in a vast, crowded flock, in the cold season, so that wind carries the wicked spirits, and leads them here and there, and up and down. No hope of rest, or even lesser torment, comforts them. And as the cranes go, making their sounds, forming a long flight of themselves in the air, so I saw the shadows come, moaning, carried by that war of winds, at which I said: "Master, who are these people that the black air chastises so?"

He replied: "The first of those you wish to know of was empress of many languages, so corrupted by the vice of luxury that she made promiscuity lawful in her code to clear away the guilt she had incurred. She is Semiramis, of whom we read that she succeeded Ninus, and was his wife: she held the countries that the sultan rules.

"The next is Dido, who killed herself for love, and broke faith with Sichaeus's ashes; then comes licentious Cleopatra. See Helen, for whom, so long, the mills of war revolved: and see the great Achilles, who fought in the end with love, of Polyxena. See Paris, Tristan . . ." and he pointed out more than a thousand shadows with his finger, naming, for me, those whom love had severed from life.

After I had heard my teacher name the ancient knights and ladies, pity overcame me, and I was as if dazed. I began: "Poet, I would speak willingly to those two who go together and seem so light upon the wind." And he to me: "You will see, when they are nearer to us, you can beg them, then, by the love that leads them, and they will come."

As soon as the wind brought them to us, I raised my voice: "O weary souls, come and talk with us, if no one prevents it." As doves, claimed by desire, fly steadily with raised wings through the air to their sweet nest, carried by the will, so the spirits flew from the crowd where Dido is, coming towards us through malignant air, such was the power of my affecting call.

"O gracious and benign living creature that comes to visit us through the dark air, if the universe's king were our friend, we who tainted the earth with blood would beg Him to give you peace, since you take pity on our sad misfortune. While the wind, as now, is silent, we will hear you and speak to you of what you are pleased to listen to and talk of.

"The place where I was born is by the shore, where the river Po runs down to rest at peace, with his attendant streams. Love, which is quickly caught in the gentle heart, filled him with my fair form, now lost to me, and the nature of that love still afflicts me. Love, which allows no loved one to be excused from loving, seized me so fiercely with desire for him it still will not leave me, as you can see. Love led us to one death. Caïna, in the ninth circle waits for him who quenched our life."

These words carried to us from them. After I had heard those troubled spirits, I bowed my head, and kept it bowed, until the poet said: "What are you thinking?" When I replied, I began: "O, alas, what sweet thoughts, what longing, brought them to this sorrowful state?" Then I turned to them again, and I spoke, and said: "Francesca, your torment makes me weep with grief and pity. But tell me, in that time of sweet sighs, how did love allow you to know these dubious desires?"

And she to me: "There is no greater pain than to remember happy times in times of misery, and this your teacher knows. But if you have so great a yearning to understand the first root of our love, I will be like one who weeps and tells. We read one day to our delight of Lancelot and how love constrained him; we were alone and without suspicion. Often those words urged our eyes to meet, and colored our cheeks, but it was a single moment that undid us. When we read how that lover kissed the beloved smile, he who will never be separated from me kissed my mouth all trembling. That book was a pandering Galeotto, as is he who wrote it: that day we read no more."

While the one spirit spoke, the other wept, so that I fainted out of pity and, as if I were dying, fell as a dead body falls.

6

When my senses return, which closed themselves off from pity of those two kindred, who stunned me with complete sadness, I see around me new torments, and new tormented souls, wherever I move, or turn, and wherever I gaze. I am in the third circle, of eternal, accursed cold and heavy rain: its kind and quality is never new. Large hail, tainted water, and sleet pour down through the shadowy air: and the earth that receives it is putrid.

Cerberus, the fierce and strange monster, triple-throated, barks dog-like over the people submerged in it. His eyes are crimson, his beard is foul and black, his belly vast, and his limbs are clawed: he snatches the spirits, flays and quarters them. The rain makes them howl like dogs: they protect one flank with the other, often writhing, the miserable wretches.

When Cerberus, the great worm, saw us, he opened his jaws and showed his fangs: not a limb of his remained still. My guide, stretching out his hands, scooped up earth and hurled it in fistfuls into his ravening mouth. Like a dog that whines for food, then grows quiet when he eats it, only fighting and struggling to devour it, so did demon Cerberus's loathsome muzzles, which bark like thunder at the spirits so that they wish they were deaf.

We passed over the shades, which the heavy rain subdues, and placed our feet on each empty space that seems a body. They were all lying on the ground but one, who sat up immediately when he saw us cross in front of him. He said to me: "O you who are led through this Inferno, recognize me if you can: you were made before I was unmade." And I to him: "The anguish that you suffer conceals you perhaps from my memory, so that it seems as if I never knew you. But tell me who you are, lodged so sadly, and undergoing such punishment that though there are others greater, none is so unpleasant."

And he to me: "Your city, Florence, so full of envy it overflows, held me in the clear life. You citizens called me Ciacco, and for the damnable sin of gluttony I languish, as you see, beneath the rain. Nor am I the only wretched spirit, since all these are punished likewise for the same sin." I answered him: "Ciacco, your affliction weighs on me, inviting me to weep, but tell me if you can what the citizens of that divided city will come to; if any there are just; and the reason why such discord tears it apart."

And he to me: "After long struggle, they will come to blood, and the Whites, the party of the woods, will throw out the Blacks, with great violence. Within three years, then, it must happen: the Blacks will conquer, with the help of him who now manuevers around. That party will hold its head high for a long time, weighing the Whites down under heavy oppression, however they weep and however ashamed they are. Two men are just, but are not listened to. Pride, Envy, and Avarice are the three burning coals that have set all hearts on fire."

Here he ended the mournful prophecy, and I said to him: "I want you to instruct me still, and grant me a little more speech. Tell me where Farinata and Tegghiaio are, who were worthy enough, and Jacopo Rusticucci, Arrigo, Mosca, and the rest who set their minds to doing good: let me know of them, for a great longing urges me to discover whether Heaven soothes them, or Hell poisons them."

And he to me: "They are among the blackest spirits, for another crime weighs them to the bottom: if you descend deep enough, you may see them. But when you are back again in the sweet world, I beg you to recall me to other minds: I tell you no more, and no more will I answer." At that he turned his fixed gaze askance, and looked at me a while, then bent his head and lowered himself, and it, among his blind companions.

And my guide said to me: "He will not stir further until the angelic trumpet sounds, when the power opposing evil will come: each will revisit his sad grave, resume his flesh and form, and hear what will resound through eternity." So we passed over the foul brew of rain and shadows, with slow steps, speaking a little of the future life.

Of this I asked: "Master, will these torments increase after the great judgment, or lessen, or stay as fierce?" And he to me: "Remember your science, which says that the more perfect a thing is, the more it feels pleasure and pain. Though these accursed ones will never achieve true perfection, they will be nearer to it after than before."

We circled along that road, speaking of much more than I recount, then came to the place where the descent begins; there we found Plutus, the god of wealth, the great enemy.

7

"Pape Satan, pape Satan aleppe," Plutus began to croak, and the gentle sage, who understood all things, comforted me, saying: "Do not let fear bother you, because despite whatever power he has, he will not prevent you descending this rock." Then he turned to that swollen face and said: "Peace, evil wolf! Devour your own insides, in your rage. Our journey to the depths is not without reason: it is willed on high, there where Michael made war on the great dragon's adulterating pride."

Like a sail bellying in the wind that falls in a heap if the mast breaks, so that cruel creature fell to earth. In that way we descended into the fourth circle, taking in a greater width of the dismal bank that encloses every evil of the universe.

O Divine Justice! Who can tell the many new pains and troubles that I saw, and why our guilt so destroys us? As the wave over Charybdis strikes against the wave it counters, so the people here are made to dance around. I found more people here than elsewhere, on the one side and on the other rolling weights by pushing with their chests with loud howling. They struck against each other, and then each wheeled around where they were, rolling the reverse way, shouting: "Why do you hold?" and "Why do you throw away?"

So they returned along the gloomy circle, from either side to the opposite point, shouting again their measure of reproach. Then each one, when he had reached it, wheeled through his half circle onto the other track. And I, who felt as if my heart were pierced, said: "My Master, show me now who these people are, and whether all those with tonsures on our left were churchmen."

And he to me: "They were so twisted in their minds in their first life that they made no balanced expenditure. Their voices bark this out most clearly when they come to the two ends of the circle, where opposing sins divide them. These were priests who are without hair on their heads, and popes and cardinals, in whom avarice does its worst."

And I: "Master, surely, amongst this crowd, I ought to recognize some of those tainted with these evils."

And he to me: "You link idle thoughts: the life without knowledge, which made them ignoble, now makes them incapable of being known. They will go on butting each other to eternity; and these will rise from their graves with grasping fists, and those with shorn hair. Useless giving, and useless keeping, has robbed them of the bright world, and set them to this struggle; what struggle it is, I do not amplify. But you, my son, can see now the vain mockery of the wealth controlled by Fortune, for which the human race fight with each other, since all the gold under the moon that ever was could not give peace to one of these weary souls."

I said to him: "Master, now tell me as well about Fortune, that subject you touched on: who is she, who has the wealth of the world in her arms?"

And he to me: "O blind creatures, how great is the ignorance that surrounds you! I want you now to hear my judgement of her. He whose wisdom transcends all things made the Heavens, and gave them ruling powers so that each part illuminates the others, distributing the light equally. Similarly, He put in place a controller and a guide for earthly splendor, to alter from time to time idle possession between nation and nation, and from kin to kin, beyond the schemes of human reason. So one people commands, another wanes, obeying her judgement, she who is concealed like a snake in the grass. Your wisdom cannot comprehend her: she furnishes, adjudicates, and maintains her kingdom as the other gods do theirs. Her permutations never end: necessity makes her swift; thus often someone comes who creates change. This is she: so often reviled even by those who ought to praise her but wrongly blame her with malicious words. Still, she is in bliss, and does not hear: she spins her globe, joyfully, among the other primal spirits, and tastes her bliss.

"Now let us descend to greater misery: already every star is declining that was rising when I set out, and we are not allowed to stay too long."

We crossed the circle to the other bank, near a spring that boils and pours down through a gap that it has made. The water was darker than a dark blue-grey, and we entered the descent by a strange path, in company with the dusky waves. This woeful stream forms the marsh called Styx when it has fallen to the foot of the grey malignant walls. And I who stood there, intent on seeing, saw muddy people in the fen, naked and all with the look of anger. They were striking each other, not only with hands, but head, chest, and feet, mangling each other with their teeth, bite by bite.

The kind Master said: "Now, son, see the souls of those overcome by anger, and also, I want you to know, in truth there are people under the water who sigh and make it bubble on the surface, as your eye can see whichever way it turns. Fixed in the slime they say: 'We were sullen in the sweet air that is gladdened by the sun, bearing indolent smoke in our hearts; now we lie here, sullen, in the black mire.'"This measure they gurgle in their throats, because they cannot utter it in full speech."

So we covered a large arc of the loathsome swamp between the dry bank and its core, our eyes turned towards those who swallow its filth, and came at last to the base of a tower.

8

I say, pursuing my theme, that long before we reached the base of the high tower, our eyes looked upwards to its summit, because we saw two beacon-flames set there, and another, from so far away that the eye could scarcely see it, gave a signal in return. And I turned to the fount of all knowledge, and asked: "What does it say? And what does the other light reply? And who has made the signal?" And he to me: "Already you can see what is expected, coming over the foul waters, if the marsh vapors do not hide it from you."

No bowstring ever shot an arrow that flew through the air so quickly as the little boat that I saw coming towards us through the waves, under the control of a single steersman, who cried: "Are you here, now, fierce spirit?" My Master said: "Phlegyas, Phlegyas, this time you cry in vain: you shall not keep us longer than it takes us to pass the marsh."

Phlegyas, in his growing anger, was like someone who listens to some great wrong done him, and then expands with resentment. My guide climbed down into the boat, and then made me board after him, and it only sank in the water when I got in. As soon as my guide and I were in the craft, its prow went forward, ploughing deeper through the water than it does carrying others.

While we were running through the dead channel, one rose up in front of me, covered with mud, and said: "Who are you, that come before your time?" And I to him: "If I come, I do not stay here: but who are you, who are so mired?" He answered: "You see that I am one who weeps." And I to him: "Cursed spirit, remain weeping and in sorrow! For I know you, muddy as you are."

Then he stretched both hands out to the boat, at which the cautious Master pushed him off, saying: "Away there, with the other dogs!" Then he put his arms around my neck, kissed my face, and said: "Blessed be she who bore you, soul, who are rightly indignant. He was an arrogant spirit in your world; there is nothing good with which to adorn his memory, so his furious shade is here. How many up there think themselves mighty kings that will lie here like pigs in mire, leaving behind them dire condemnation!"

I said to him: "Master, I would very much like to see him drowned in this mire before we leave these waters."

And he to me: "You will be satisfied before the shore is visible to you: it is right that your wish should be gratified." Not long after this I saw the muddy people make such a rending of him that I still give God thanks and praise for it. All shouted: "At Filippo Argenti!" That fierce Florentine spirit turned his teeth in vengeance on himself.

We left him there, so I can say no more of him, but a sound of wailing assailed my ears so that I turned my gaze in front, intently. The kind Master said: "Now, my son, we approach the city they call Dis, with its grave citizens, a vast crowd." And I: "Master, I can already see its towers, clearly there in the valley, glowing red, as if they issued from the fire." And he to me: "The eternal fire that burns them from within makes them appear reddened, as you see, in this deep Hell."

We now arrived in the steep ditch that forms the moat to the joyless city; the walls seemed to me as if they were made of iron. Not until we had made a wide circuit did we reach a place where the ferryman said to us: "Disembark: here is the entrance."

I saw above the gates more than a thousand of those angels that fell from Heaven like rain, who cried angrily: "Who is this, that without dying goes through the kingdom of the dead?" And my wise Master made a sign to them of wishing to speak in private. Then they furled their great disdain, and said: "Come on alone, and let him go who enters this kingdom with such audacity. Let him return alone on his foolish road—see if he can—and you remain, who have escorted him through so dark a land."

Think, Reader, whether I was not disheartened at the sound of those accursed words, not believing I could ever return here. I said: "O my dear guide, who has ensured my safety more than seven times, and snatched me from certain danger that faced me, do not leave me this helpless: and if we are prevented from going on, let us quickly retrace our steps." And that lord who had led me there said to me: "Have no fear, since no one can deny us passage, it was given us by so great an authority. But you, wait for me, and comfort and nourish your spirit with fresh hope, for I will not abandon you in the lower world."

So the gentle father goes and leaves me there, and I am left in doubt, since "yes" and "no" war inside my head. I could not hear what terms he offered them, but he had not been standing there long with them when, each vying with the other, they rushed back. Our adversaries closed the gate in my lord's face, leaving him outside, and he turned to me again with slow steps. His eyes were on the ground, and his expression devoid of all daring, and he said, sighing: "Who are these who deny me entrance to the house of pain?" And to me he said: "Though I am angered, don't you be dismayed: I will win the trial, whatever obstacle those inside contrive. This insolence of theirs is nothing new, for they displayed it once before, at that less secret gate we passed that has remained unbarred. Over it you saw the fatal writing, and already on this side of its entrance one is coming down the slope, passing the circles unescorted, one for whom the city shall open to us."

9

The color that cowardice had printed on my face, seeing my guide turn back, made him repress his own heightened color more swiftly. He stopped, attentive, like one who listens, since his eyes could not penetrate far through the black air and the thick fog. "Nevertheless we must win this struggle," he began, "if not . . . then help such as this was offered to us. O how long it seems to me that other's coming!" I saw clearly how he hid the meaning of his opening words with their sequel, words differing from his initial thought. Nonetheless his speech made me afraid, perhaps because I took his broken phrases to hold a worse meaning than they did.

"Do any of those whose only punishment is deprivation of hope ever descend into the depths of this sad chasm from the first circle?" I asked this question, and he answered me: "It rarely happens that any of us make the journey that I go on. It is true that I was down here once before, conjured to do so by that fierce sorceress Erichtho, who recalled spirits to their corpses. My flesh had only been stripped from me a while when she forced me to enter inside that wall to bring a spirit out of the circle of Judas. That is the deepest place, and the darkest, and the furthest from that Heaven that surrounds all things: I know the way well, so be reassured. This marsh that breathes its foul stench circles the woeful city round about, where we also cannot enter now without anger."

And he said more that I do not remember, because my eyes had been drawn to the high tower with the glowing crest, where, in an instant, had risen three hellish Furies, stained with blood, that had the limbs and aspects of women, covered with a tangle of green hydras, their hideous foreheads bound with little adders, and horned vipers. And Virgil, who knew the handmaids of the queen of eternal sadness well, said to me: "See, the fierce Erinyes. That is Megaera on the left; the one that weeps, on the right, is Alecto; Tisiphone is in the middle." Then he was silent. Each one was tearing at her breast with her claws, beating with her hands, and crying out so loudly that I pressed close to the poet, out of fear. "Let Medusa come," they all said, looking down on us, "so that we can turn him to stone: we did not fully revenge Theseus's attack."

"Turn your back," said the Master, and he himself turned me around. "Keep your eyes closed, since there will be no return upwards if she were to show herself and you were to see her." Not leaving it to me, he covered them too with his own hands.

O you, who have clear minds, take note of the meaning that conceals itself under the veil of clouded verse!

Now over the turbid waves there came a fearful crash of sound, at which both shores trembled; a sound like a strong wind, born of conflicting heat, that strikes the forest remorselessly, breaks the branches, and beats them down, and carries them away, advances proudly in a cloud of dust, and makes wild creatures and shepherds run for safety. Virgil uncovered my eyes, and said: "Now direct your vision to that ancient marsh, there where the mists are thickest." Like frogs that all scatter through the water in front of their enemy the snake until each one squats on the bottom, so I saw more than a thousand damaged spirits scatter in front of one who passed the Stygian ferry with dry feet. He waved that putrid air from his face, often waving his left hand before it, and only that annoyance seemed to weary him. I well knew he was a messenger from Heaven, and I turned to the Master, who made a gesture that I should stay quiet and bow to him.

How full of indignation he seemed to me! He reached the gate, and opened it with a wand: there was no resistance. On the vile threshold he began to speak: "O outcasts from Heaven, why does this insolence still live in you? Why are you recalcitrant to that will whose aims can never be frustrated, and that has often increased your torment? What use is it to butt your heads against the Fates? If you remember, your Cerberus still shows a throat and chin scarred from doing so."

Then he returned, over the miry pool, and spoke not a word to us, but looked like one preoccupied and driven by other cares than of those who stand before him. And we stirred our feet towards the city, in safety, after his sacred speech.

We entered Dis without trouble, and I gazed around as soon as I as was inside, eager to know what punishment the place enclosed, and saw on all sides a vast plain full of pain and vile torment.

As at Arles, where the Rhone stagnates, or Pola, near the Gulf of Quarnaro, which confines Italy and bathes its coast, where the sepulchers make the ground uneven, so they did here, all around, only here the nature of it was more terrible.

Flames were scattered amongst the tombs, by which they were made so red-hot all over that no smith's art needs hotter metal. Their lids were all lifted, and such fierce groans came from them that, indeed, they seemed to be those of the sad and wounded.

And I said: "Master, who are these people, entombed in those vaults, who make themselves known by tormented sighing?" And he to me: "Here are the arch-heretics, with their followers, of every sect; and the tombs contain many more than you might think. Here like is buried with like, and the monuments differ in degrees of heat." Then after turning to the right, we passed between the tormented and the steep ramparts.

10

Now my Master goes, and I behind him, by a secret path between the city walls and the torments. I began: "O summit of virtue, who leads me around through the circles of sin as you please, speak to me and satisfy my longing. Can those people who lie in the sepulchers be seen? The lids are all raised, and no one keeps guard." And he to me: "They will all be shut when they return here from Jehoshaphat with the bodies they left above. In this place Epicurus and all his followers are entombed, who say the soul dies with body. Therefore, you will soon be satisfied with an answer to the question that you ask me, and also the longing that you hide from me here inside." And I: "Kind guide, I do not keep my heart hidden from you, except by speaking too briefly, something to which you have previously inclined me."

"O Tuscan, who goes alive through the city of fire, speaking so politely, may it please you to rest in this place. Your speech shows clearly you are a native of that noble city that I perhaps troubled too much." This sound came suddenly from one of the vaults, at which, in fear, I drew a little closer to my guide. And he said to me: "Turn aound, what are you doing: look at Farinata, who has raised himself: you can see him all from the waist up."

I had already fixed my gaze on him, and he rose expanding his chest and brow as if he held the Inferno in great disdain. The spirited and eager hands of my guide pushed me through the sepulchers towards him, saying: "Make sure your words are measured." When I was at the base of the tomb, Farinata looked at me for a while, and then almost contemptuously, he demanded of me: "Who were your ancestors?"

I, desiring to obey, concealed nothing, but revealed the whole to him, at which he raised his brows a little. Then he said: "They were fiercely opposed to me, and my ancestors and my party, so that I scattered them twice." I replied: "Though they were driven out, they returned from wherever they were, the first and the second time, but your party have not yet learnt that skill."

Then, a shadow rose behind him from the unclosed space, visible down to the tip of its chin: I think it had raised itself onto its knees. It gazed around me, as if it wished to see whether anyone was with me, but when all its hopes were quenched, it said, weeping: "If by power of intellect you go through this blind prison, where is my son, and why is he not with you?" And I to him: "I do not come through my own initiative: he that waits there, whom your Guido disdained perhaps, leads me through this place."

His words and the nature of his punishment had revealed his name to me, so that my answer was a full one. Suddenly raising himself erect, he cried: "What did you say? *Disdained?* Is he not still alive? Does the sweet light not strike his eyes?" When he saw that I delayed in answering, he dropped supine again, and showed himself no more.

But the other one, at whose wish I had first stopped, generously did not alter his aspect or move his neck, or turn his side. Continuing where he left off, he said: "And if my party have learnt that art of return badly, it tortures me more than this bed, but the face of the moon-goddess Persephone, who rules here, will not be crescent fifty times before you learn the difficulty of that art. And as you wish to return to the sweet world, tell me why that people is so fierce towards my kin, in all its lawmaking?" At which I answered him: "The great slaughter and havoc that dyed the Arbia red is the cause of those indictments against them in our churches."

Then he shook his head, sighing, and said: "I was not alone in that matter, nor would I have joined with the others without good cause, but I was alone there, when all agreed to raze Florence to the ground, and I openly defended her."

"Ah, as I hope your descendants might sometime have peace," I begged him, "solve the puzzle that has entangled my mind. It seems, if I hear right, that you see beforehand what time brings, but have a different knowledge of the present."

"Like one who has imperfect vision," he said, "we see things that are distant from us: so much of the light the supreme Lord still allows us. But when they approach, or come to be, our intelligence is wholly void, and we know nothing of your human state, except what others tell us. So you may understand that all our knowledge of the future will end from the moment when the Day of Judgment closes the gate of futurity."

Then, as if conscious of guilt, I said: "Will you therefore tell that fallen one, now, that his son is still joined to the living? And if I was silent before in reply, let him know it was because my thoughts were already entangled in that error you have resolved for me."

And now my Master was recalling me, at which I begged the spirit with more haste to tell me who was with him. He said to me: "I lie here with more than a thousand: here inside is Frederick the Second, and Cardinal Ubaldini, but of the rest I am silent." At that he hid himself, and I turned my steps towards the poet of antiquity, reflecting on the words that boded ill for me.

Virgil moved on, and then, as we were leaving, said to me: "Why are you so bewildered?" And I satisfied his question. The sage exhorted me: "Let your mind retain what you have heard of your fate, and note this," and he raised his finger: "When you stand before the sweet rays of that lady, whose bright eyes see all, you will learn of the journey of your life from her."

Then he turned his feet towards the left: we abandoned the wall and went towards the middle, by a path that makes its way into a valley that, even up there, forced us to breathe its foulness.

11

On the edge of a high bank made of great broken rocks in a circle, we came above a still more cruel crowd, and here, because of the repulsive, excessive stench that the deep abyss throws up, we approached it in the shelter of a grand monument, on which I saw an inscription that said: "I hold Pope Anastasius, whom Photinus drew away from the true path."

The Master said: "We must delay our descent until our sense of smell is somewhat used to the foul wind, and then we will not notice it." I said to him: "Find us something to compensate, so that the time is not wasted." And he: "See, I have thought of it."

He began: "My son, within these walls of stone are three graduated circles like those you are leaving. They are all filled with accursed spirits; but so that the sight of them may be enough to inform you, in future, listen how and why they are constrained. The outcome of all maliciousness, which Heaven hates, is harm; and every such outcome hurts others, either by force or deceit. But because deceit is a vice peculiar to human beings, it displeases God more, and therefore the fraudulent are placed below, and more pain grieves them. The whole of the seventh circle is for the violent, but since violence can be done to three persons, it is constructed and divided in three rings. I say violence may be done to God, or to oneself, or one's neighbor, and their person or possessions, as you will hear in clear discourse. Death or painful wounds may be inflicted on one's neighbor; and devastation, fire, and pillage, on his substance. Therefore the first ring torments all homicides; everyone who lashes out maliciously; and thieves and robbers, in their various groups. A man may do violence to himself and to his property, and so, in the second ring, all must repent, in vain, who deprive themselves of your world; or gamble away and dissipate their wealth; or weep there, when they should be happy. Violence may be done against the Deity, denying Him and blaspheming in the heart, and scorning Nature and her gifts, and so the smallest ring stamps with its seal both Sodom and Cahors, and those who speak scornfully of God in their

hearts. Human beings may practice deceit, which gnaws at every conscience, on one who trusts them, or on one who places no trust. This
latter form of fraud only severs the bond of love that Nature created,
and so in the eighth circle are nested hypocrisy, sorcery, flattery, cheat-
ing, theft, and selling of holy orders; pimps, corrupters of public office, and similar filth. In the previous form, that love that Nature creates
is forgotten, and also that which is added later, giving rise to special
trust. So, in the ninth, the smallest circle, at the base of the universe,
where Dis has his throne, every traitor is consumed eternally."

And I said: "Master, your reasoning proceeds most clearly, and lays
out excellently this gulf, and those that populate it, but tell me why
those of the great marsh, those whom the wind drives, and the rain
beats, and those who come together with sharp words, are not punished in the burning city, if God's anger is directed towards them? And
if not, why they are in such a state?"

And he to me: "Why does your mind err so much more than usual,
or are your thoughts somewhere else? Do you not remember the words
with which your Aristotle's *Ethics* speaks of the three natures that Heaven
does not will—incontinence, malice, and mad brutishness—and how
incontinence offends God less and incurs less blame? If you consider
this doctrine correctly, and recall to mind those who suffer punishment out there above, you will easily see why they are separated from
these destructive spirits, and why divine justice strikes them with less
anger."

I said: "O Sun that heals all troubled sight, you make me so content
when you explain things to me that to question is as delightful as to
know. Go back a moment to where you said that usury offends divine
goodness, and unravel that knot."

He said to me: "To him who attends, philosophy shows in more
than one place how nature takes her path from the Divine Intelligence
and its arts, and if you note your *Physics* well, you will find, not many
pages in, that art follows her as well as it can, as the pupil does the
master, so that your art is, as it were, the grandchild of God. By these
two, art and nature, man must earn his bread and flourish, if you recall
to mind Genesis, near its beginning. Because the usurer holds to another course, he denies nature, in herself, and in that which follows
her ways, putting his hopes elsewhere. But follow me now, by the path
I choose, for Pisces quivers on the horizon, and all Boötes covers Caurus,
the northwest wind, and over there, some ways off, we descend the
cliff."

12

The place we reached to climb down the bank was craggy, and because of the creature there, also a path that every eye would shun. The descent of that rocky precipice was like the landslide that struck the left bank of the Adige, this side of Trento, caused by an earthquake or a faulty buttress, since the rock is so shattered, from the summit of the mountain where it started to the plain, that it might form a route for someone above; and at the top of the broken gully lay stretched out the infamy of Crete, the Minotaur, conceived on Pasiphaë in the wooden cow.

When he saw us he gnawed himself, like someone consumed by anger inside. My wise guide called to him: "Perhaps you think that Theseus, the Duke of Athens, is here, who brought about your death in the world above? Leave here, monstrous creature. This man does not come here, aided by your sister Ariadne, but passes through to see the punishments."

Like a bull breaking loose at the moment when it receives the fatal blow, and cannot go forward but plunges here and there, so acted the Minotaur, and my cautious guide cried: "Run to the passage: while he is in a fury, it is time for you to descend."

So we made our way downwards over the landslide of stones, which often shifted beneath my feet from the unaccustomed weight. I went lost in thought, and he said: "Perhaps you are contemplating this fallen mass of rock, guarded by the bestial anger that I quelled a moment ago. I would have you know that the previous time I came down here to the deep Inferno, this spill had not yet fallen. But if I discern the truth, the deep and loathsome valley shook not long before He came to take the great ones of the highest circle, so that I thought the universe thrilled with love, by which as some believe the world has often been overwhelmed by chaos. In that moment ancient rocks, here and elsewhere, tumbled. But fix your gaze on the valley, because we near the river of blood in which those who injure others by violence are boiled."

O blind desires, evil and foolish, which so goad us in our brief life, and then, in the eternal one, ruin us so bitterly! I saw a wide canal bent in an arc, looking as if it surrounded the whole plain, from what my guide had told me. Centaurs were racing, one behind another, between it and the foot of the bank, armed with weapons, as they were accustomed to hunt on earth.

Seeing us descend they all stood still, and three, elected leaders, came from the group, armed with bows and spears. And one of them shouted from the distance: "What torment do you come for, you that descend the rampart? Speak from there; if not, I draw the bow." My Master said: "We will make our reply to Chiron, who is there nearby. Sadly, your nature was always rash." Then he touched me, and said: "That is Nessus, who died because of his theft of the lovely Deianira, and, for his blood, took vengeance, through his blood. The one in the middle whose head is bowed to his chest is the great Chiron, who nursed Achilles; the other is Pholus, who was so full of rage. They race around the ditch, in thousands, piercing with arrows any spirit that climbs further from the blood than its guilt has condemned it to."

We drew near the swift creatures. Chiron took an arrow and pushed aside his beard from his face with the notched flight. When he had uncovered his huge mouth, he said to his companions: "Have you noticed that the one behind moves whatever he touches? The feet of dead men do not usually do so."

And my good guide, who was by Chiron's front part where the two natures join, replied: "He is truly alive, and I alone have to show him the dark valley. Necessity brings him here, not desire. She who gave me this new duty came from singing Alleluiahs; he is no thief, nor am I a wicked spirit. But, by that virtue, by means of which I set my feet on so unsafe a path, lend us one of your people whom we can follow, so that he may show us where the ford is, and carry this one over on his back, since he cannot fly as a spirit through the air."

Chiron twisted to his right, and said to Nessus: "Turn, and guide them, then, and if another crew meet you, keep them off."

We moved onwards with our trustworthy guide along the margin of the crimson boiling, in which the boiled were shrieking loudly. I saw people immersed as far as the eyebrows, and the great Centaur said: "These are tyrants who indulged in blood and rapine. Here they lament their offenses, done without mercy. Here is Alexander, and fierce Dionysius of Syracuse, who gave Sicily years of pain. That head of black hair is Azzolino, and the other, which is blond, is Obizzo da

Este, whose life was quenched, in truth, by his stepson, up in the world." Then I turned to the poet, and he said: "Let him guide you first for now, and I second."

A little further on, Nessus paused next to people who seemed to be sunk in the boiling stream up to their throat. He showed us a shade, apart by itself, saying: "That one, Guy de Montfort, in God's church pierced that heart that is still venerated by the Thames."

Then I saw others who held their heads and their chests likewise free of the river, and I knew many of these. So the blood grew shallower and shallower, until it only cooked their feet, and here was our ford through the ditch.

The Centaur said: "As you see the boiling stream continually diminishing on this side, so on the other it sinks more and more till it comes again to where tyrants are doomed to grieve. Divine Justice here torments Attila, the scourge of the earth; and Pyrrhus, and Sextus Pompeius; and for eternity milks tears, produced by the boiling, from Rinier da Corneto, and Rinier Pazzo, who made war on the highways." Then he turned back, and recrossed the ford.

13

Nessus had not yet returned to the other side when we entered a wood unmarked by any path. The foliage was not green, but a dusky color; the branches were not smooth, but warped and knotted; there were no fruits there, only poisonous thorns. The wild beasts that hate the cultivated fields in the Tuscan Maremma, between Cecina and Corneto, have lairs less thick and tangled. Here the brutish Harpies make their nests, they who chased the Trojans from the Strophades with dismal pronouncements of future tribulations. They have broad wings, and human necks and faces, clawed feet, and large feathered bellies, and they make mournful cries in that strange wood.

The kind Master said: "Before you go further, be aware you are in the second ring, and will be until you come to the dreadful sands. So look carefully, and you will see things that might make you mistrust my words."

Already I heard sighs on every side, and saw no one to make them, at which I stood totally bewildered. I think that he thought that I was thinking that many of those voices came from among the trees, from people who hid themselves because of us. So the Master said: "If you break a little twig from one of these branches, the thoughts you have will be seen to be in error."

Then I stretched my hand out a little, and broke a small branch from a large thorn, and its trunk cried out: "Why do you tear at me?" And when it had grown dark with blood, it began to cry out again: "Why do you splinter me? Have you no breath of pity? We were men, and we are changed to trees; truly your hand would be more merciful if we were merely the souls of snakes."

Just as a green branch burning at one end spits and hisses with escaping air at the other, so from that broken wood blood and words came out together, at which I let the branch fall and stood like a man afraid. My wise sage replied: "Wounded spirit, if he had only believed before what he had read in my verse, he would not have lifted his hand to you, but the incredible nature of the thing made me urge him to do what grieves me. But tell him who you were, so that he might make you some amends, and renew your fame up in the world, to which he is allowed to return."

And the tree replied: "You tempt me so with your sweet words that I cannot keep silent, but do not object if I am expansive in speech. I am Pier delle Vigne, who held both the keys to Frederick's heart, and employed them, locking and unlocking, so quietly that I kept almost everyone else from his secrets. I was so faithful to that glorious office that through it I lost my sleep and my life. The whore that never turned her eyes from Caesar's household, Envy, the common disease and vice of courts, stirred all minds against me, and being stirred they stirred Augustus, so that my fine honors were changed to grievous sorrows. My spirit, in a scornful mode, thinking to escape scorn by death, made me, though I was just, unjust to myself. By the strange roots of this tree, I swear to you I never broke faith with my lord, so worthy of honor. If either of you return to the world, raise and cherish my memory, which still lies low from the blow Envy gave me."

The poet listened for a while, then said to me: "Since he is silent, do not lose the moment, but speak and ask him to tell you more." At which I said to him: "You ask him further about what you think will interest me, because I could not, such pity fills my heart." So he continued: "That the man may do freely what your words request from him, imprisoned spirit, be pleased to tell us further how the spirits are caught in these knots; and tell us, if you can, whether any of them free themselves from these limbs."

Then the trunk blew fiercely, and the breath was turned to words like these: "My reply will be brief. When the savage spirit leaves the body from which it has ripped itself, Minos sends it to the seventh gulf. It falls into this wood, but no place is set for it: wherever chance hurls it, there it sprouts like a grain of German wheat, shoots up as a sapling, and then as a wild tree. The Harpies feeding then on its leaves hurt it, and give an outlet to its hurt. Like others we shall go to our corpses on the Day of Judgment, but not so that any of us may inhabit them again, because it would not be just to have what we took from ourselves. We shall drag them here, and our bodies will be hung through the dismal wood, each on the thorn tree of its tormented shade."

We were still listening to the tree, thinking it might tell us more, when we were startled by a noise, like those who think the wild boar is nearing where they stand and hear the animals and the crashing of branches. Behold, on the left, two naked, torn spirits, running so hard they broke every thicket of the wood. The leader, cried: "Come Death, come now!" and the other, Jacomo, who felt himself to be too slow cried: "Lano, your legs were not so swift at the jousts of Toppo." And since perhaps his breath was failing him, he merged himself with a bush. The wood behind them was filled with black bitch hounds, eager and quick as greyhounds that have slipped the leash. They clamped their teeth into Lano, who squatted, and tore him bit by bit, then carried off his miserable limbs.

My guide now took me by the hand and led me to the bush, which was grieving in vain through its bleeding splinters, crying: "O Jacomo da Sant' Andrea, what have you gained by making me your screen? What blame do I have for your sinful life?"

When the Master had stopped next to it, he said: "Who were you that breathe out your mournful speech with blood through so many wounds?

And he to us: "You spirits, who have come to view the dishonorable mangling that has torn my leaves from me, gather them around the foot of this sad tree. I was of Florence, that city which changed Mars, its patron, for Saint John the Baptist, because of which that God, through His powers, will always make it sorrowful. Were it not that some fragments of his statue remain where Ponte Vecchio crosses the Arno, those citizens who rebuilt it on the ashes Attila left would have worked in vain. I made a gibbet for myself, from my own roofbeam."

14

As the love of my native place stirred in me, I gathered up the scattered leaves and gave them back to him who was already hoarse. Then we came to the edge where the second round is divided from the third, where a fearsome form of justice is seen. To make these new things clear, I say we reached a plain, where the land repels all vegetation. The mournful wood makes a circle around it, as the ditch surrounds the wood; here we stepped close to its very rim.

The ground was dry, thick sand, no different in form than that which Cato once trod. O God's vengeance, how what was shown to my sight should be feared by all who read! I saw many groups of naked spirits who were all moaning bitterly, and there seemed to be diverse rules applied to them. Some were lying face upward on the ground; some sat all crouched; and others roamed around continuously.

Those who moved were more numerous, and those that lay in torment fewer but uttering louder cries of pain. Dilated flakes of fire, falling slowly like snow in the windless mountains, rained down over all the vast sands. Like the flames that Alexander saw falling in the hot zones of India over all his army until they reached the ground, fires that were more easily quenched while they were separate, so that his troops took care to trample the earth—like those fell this eternal heat, kindling the sand like tinder beneath flint and steel, doubling the pain. The dance of their tortured hands was never still, now here, now there, shaking off the fresh burning.

I began: "Master, you who overcome everything except the obdurate demons that came out against us at the entrance to the gate, who is that great spirit who seems indifferent to the fire, and lies there, scornful, contorted, so that the rain does not seem to deepen his repentance?"

And he himself, noting that I asked my guide about him, cried: "What I was when I was living, I am now I am dead. Though Jupiter exhausts Vulcan, his blacksmith, from whom he took, in anger, the fierce lightning bolt that I was struck down with on my last day, and though he exhausts the others, the Cyclopes, one by one, at the black forge of Aetna, shouting: 'Help, help, good Vulcan,' just as he did at the battle of Phlegra between the gods and giants, and hurls his bolts at me with all his strength, he shall still not enjoy a true revenge."

Then my guide spoke, with a force I had not heard before: "O Capaneus, you are punished more in that your pride is not quenched: no torment would produce pain fitting for your fury, except your own raving." Then he turned to me with gentler voice, saying: "That was one of the seven kings who laid siege to Thebes: and he held God, and seems to hold Him, in disdain, and value Him lightly, but as I told him, his spite is an ornament that fits his breast. Now follow me, and be careful not to place your feet yet on the burning sand, but always keep back close to the wood."

We came in silence to the place where a little stream gushes from the wood, the redness of which still makes me shudder. Like the rivulet that runs sulphur-red from the Bulicame spring near Viterbo, which the sinful women share among themselves, so this ran down over the sand. Its bed and both its sloping banks were petrified, as were its nearby borders, so that I realized our way lay there.

"Among all the other things that I have shown you since we entered though the gate, whose threshold is denied to no one, your eyes have seen nothing as noteworthy as this present stream, which quenches all the flames over it." These were my guide's words, at which I begged him to grant me food for which he had given me the appetite.

He then said: "There is a deserted island in the middle of the sea named Crete, under whose king Saturn the world was pure. There is a mountain there called Ida, which was once gladdened with waters and vegetation, and now is abandoned like an ancient spoil heap. Rhea chose it, once, as the trusted cradle of her son, and the better to hide him when he wept, causing loud shouts to echo from it. Inside the mountain, a great Old Man stands erect with his shoulders turned towards Egyptian Damietta, and looks at Rome as if it were his mirror. His head is formed of pure gold, his arms and his breasts are refined silver; then he is bronze as far down as the thighs. Downwards from there he is all of choice iron, except that the right foot is baked clay, and more of his weight is on that one than the other. Every part, except the gold, is cleft with a fissure that sheds tears, which collect and pierce the grotto. Their course falls from rock to rock into this valley. They form Acheron, Styx, and Phlegethon, then, by this narrow channel, go down to where there is no further fall and form

Cocytus: you will see what kind of lake that is, so I will not describe it to you here."

I said to him: "If the present stream flows down like that from our world, why does it appear to us only on this bank?"

And he to me: "You know the place is circular, and though you have come far, always to the left, descending to the depths, you have not yet turned through a complete round, so that if anything new appears to us, it should not bring an expression of wonder to your face."

And I again: "Master, where are Phlegethon, and Lethe found, since you do not speak of the latter, and say that the former is created from these tears?"

He replied: "You please me, truly, with all your questions, but the boiling red water might well answer to one of those you ask about. You will see Lethe, but above this abyss, there, on the Mount, where the spirits go to purify themselves when their guilt is absolved by penitence." Then he said: "Now it is time to leave the wood; see that you follow me: the borders that are not burning form a path, and over them all the fire is quenched."

15

Now one of the solid banks takes us onwards, and the smoke from the stream makes a shadow above, so that it shelters the water and its borders. Just as the Flemings between Bruges and Wissant make their dykes to hold back the sea, fearing the flood that beats against them; and as the Paduans do along the Brenta, to defend their towns and castles before Carinthia's mountains feel the thaw; so those banks were similarly formed, though their creator, whoever it might be, made them neither as high or as deep.

Already we were so far from the wood that I was unable to see where it was, unless I turned back, when we met a group of spirits coming along the bank, and each of them looked at us just as, at twilight, men look one another over under a crescent moon, peering at us as an old tailor does at the eye of his needle. Eyeballed thus by that tribe, I was recognized by one who took me by the skirt of my robe and said: "How *wonderful!*"

And I fixed my eyes on his baked visage so that the scorching of his aspect did not prevent my mind from knowing him, and bending my face to his I replied: "Are *you* here, Ser Brunetto?"

And he: "O my son, do not be displeased if Brunetto Latini tarries a while with you, and lets the crowd pass by."

I said: "I ask it with all my strength, and if you want me to sit with you, I will, if it pleases him there whom I go with.'

He said: "O my son, whoever of the flock stops for a moment must lie there for a hundred years afterwards, without cooling himself when the fire beats on him. So go on, I will follow at your heels, and then I will rejoin my crew again, who go mourning their eternal loss."

I did not dare leave the road to be level with him, but kept my head bowed like one who walks reverently. He began: "What fate, or chance, brings you down here before your final hour? Who is this who shows you the way?"

I replied: "I lost myself, in the clear life up above, in a valley, before my years were complete. Only yesterday morning I turned my back on it; he appeared to me as I was returning to it, and guides me back again, but by this path."

And he to me: "If you follow your star, you cannot fail to reach a glorious harbor, if I judged clearly in the sweet life. If I had not died before you, I would have supported you in your work, seeing that Heaven is so kind to you. But that ungrateful, malignant people, who came down from Fiesole to Florence in ancient times and still have something of the mountain and the rock, will be hostile to you for the good you do, and with reason, since it is not fitting for the sweet fig tree to blossom among the sour crab-apples. Past report on earth declares them blind, an envious, proud, and avaricious people; make sure you purge yourself of their faults. Your fate prophesies such honor for you that both parties will hunger for you, but the goat will be far from the grass. Let that herd from Fiesole make manure of themselves, but not touch the plant in which the sacred seed of those Romans revives, who stayed when that nest of malice was created, if any plant still springs from their ordure."

I answered him: "If my wishes had been completely fulfilled, you would not have been separated yet from human nature, since in my memory the dear, and kind, paternal image of you is fixed, and now goes to my heart; how when in the world, hour by hour, you taught me the way man makes himself eternal; and it is fitting my tongue should show what gratitude I hold, while I live. What you tell me of my fate, I write, and retain it with an earlier text for a lady who will know how to comment on it if I reach her. I would make this much known to you: I am ready for whatever Fortune wills, as long as conscience does not hurt me. Such prophecies are not new to my ears: so let Fortune turn her wheel as she pleases, and the peasant wield his mattock."

At that, my Master, looked back, on his right, and gazed at me, then said: "He listens closely who notes it."

I went on speaking nonetheless with Ser Brunetto, asking who are the most famous and noblest of his companions. And he replied: "It is good to know of some; of the rest it would be praiseworthy to keep silent, as the time would be too little for such a speech. In short, know that all were clerks, and great scholars, and very famous, tainted with the same sin on earth. Priscian belongs with that miserable crowd, and Francesco d'Accorso; and if you had any desire for such scum, you might have seen Andrea di Mozzi there, who was translated by 'the Servant of Servants' from the Arno to Vicenza's Bacchiglione, where he departed from his ill-strained body. I would say more, but my speech and my departure must not linger, since there I see new smoke rising from the great sand. People come that I cannot be with: let my *Treasure* be commended to you, in which I still live: more I ask not."

Then he turned back, and seemed like one who runs through the open fields for the green cloth at Verona, and seemed one of those who wins, not one who loses.

16

I was already in a place where the booming of the water that fell into the next circle sounded like a beehive's humming when three shades, running together, left a crowd that passed under the sharp, burning rain. They came towards us, and each one cried: "Wait you, who seem to us by your clothes to be someone from our perverse city."

Ah me, what ancient, and recent, wounds I saw on their limbs, scorched there by the flames! It saddens me now when I remember it. My teacher listened to their cries, turned his face towards me, and said: "Wait now: courtesy is owed them, and if there were not this fire that the place's nature rains down, I would say that you were more hasty than they are."

As we rested, they started their former laments again, and when they reached us, all three of them formed themselves into a circle. Wheeling around, as do champion wrestlers, naked and oiled, looking for a hold or an advantage before they grasp and attack one another, each directed his face at me so that his neck turned continuously in an opposite direction to his feet.

And one of them began: "If the misery of this sinful place and our scorched, stained look renders us and our prayers contemptible, let our fame influence your mind to tell us who you are that move your living feet safely through Hell. He, in whose footsteps you see me tread, all peeled and naked as he is, was greater in degree than you would think. His name is Guido Guerra, grandson of the good lady Gualdrada, and in his life he achieved much in council, and with his sword. The other that treads the sand behind me is Tegghiaio Aldobrandi, whose words should have been listened to in the world. And I, placed with them in torment, am Jacopo Rusticucci, and certainly my fierce wife injured me more than anything else."

If I had been sheltered from the fire, I would have dropped down among them below, and I believe my teacher would have allowed it, but as I would have been burned and baked myself, my fear overcame the goodwill that made me eager to embrace them. Then I began:

"Your condition stirred sadness, not contempt, in me, so deeply it will not soon be gone, when my guide spoke words to me by which I understood such men as yourselves might be approaching. I am of your city, and I have always heard, and repeated, your names and your deeds with affection. I leave the gall behind, and go towards the sweet fruits promised me by my truthful guide, but first I must go downwards to the center."

He then replied: "That your soul may long inhabit your body, and your fame shine after you, tell us if courtesy and courage still live in our city as they used to, or if they have quite forsaken it? Gugliemo Borsiere, who has been in pain with us a little while, and goes along there with our companions, torments us greatly with what he says."

"New men and sudden wealth have created pride and excess in you, Florence, so that you already weep for it!" I cried with lifted face, and the three, who took this for an answer, gazed at one another, as one gazes at the truth. They replied together: "Happy are you if, by speaking according to your will, it costs so little for you to satisfy others! So, if you escape these gloomy spaces, and turn and see the beauty of the stars again, when you will be glad to say: 'I *was*,' see that you tell people of us." Then they broke up their circle, and, as they ran, their swift legs seemed wings. An *Amen* could not have been said as quickly as their vanishing took, at which my Master was pleased to depart. I followed him.

We had gone only a little way when the sound of the water came so near us that if we had been speaking we would hardly have heard each other. Like that river (the first that takes its own course to the eastern seaboard, south of Monte Veso, where the Po rises, on the left flank of the Apennines, and is called Acquacheta above, before it falls to its lower bed and loses its name to become the Montone, at Forlì) which, plunging through a fall, echoes from the mountain above San Benedetto, where there should be refuge for a thousand, so down from a steep bank we found that tainted water re-echoing, so much so that, in a short while, it would have dazed our hearing.

I had a cord tied around me, and with it I had once thought to catch the leopard with the spotted skin. After I had completely unwound it from myself, as my guide commanded, I held it out to him, gathered up and coiled. Then he turned towards the right and threw the end of it away from the edge a little down into the steep gulf. I said to myself: "Surely something strange will follow this new sign of our intentions, which my master tracks with his eyes as it falls."

Ah, how careful men should be with those who not only see our actions but, with their understanding, see into our thoughts! He said to me: "That which I expect will soon ascend, and the object of your speculatations will soon be apparent to your sight."

A man should always keep quiet, as far as he can, when facing a truth that seems like a lie, since he incurs reproach, though he is blameless, but I cannot be silent here; and Reader, I swear to you by the words of this *Comedy*, that they may not fail to find lasting favor, that I saw a shape, marvelous to every unshaken heart, come swimming upwards through the dense, dark air, just as a man rises who has gone down, sometime, to free an anchor, caught on a rock or something else hidden in the water, who spreads his arms out and draws up his feet.

17

"Behold the savage beast with the pointed tail that crosses mountains and pierces walls and armour: behold the polluter of the whole world." So my guide began to speak to me, and beckoned to him to land near the end of our rocky path, and that vile image of Fraud came on, and grounded his head and chest, but did not lift his tail onto the cliff.

His face was the face of an honest man, it had so benign and outward aspect; all the rest was a serpent's body. Both arms were covered with hair to the armpits; the back and chest and both flanks were adorned with knots and circles. Tartars or Turks never made cloths with more color, background, and embroidery; nor did Arachne spread such webs on her loom. As boats rest on the shore, part in water and part on land, and as the beaver, among the guzzling Germans, readies himself for a fight, so that worst of savage creatures lay on the cliff that surrounds the great sand with stone. The whole of his tail darted into space, twisting the venomous fork upwards that armed the tip, like a scorpion.

My guide said: "Now we must direct our path somewhat towards the malevolent beast that rests there." Then we went down on the right, and took ten steps towards the edge so that we could fully avoid the sand and flame, and when we reached him, I saw people sitting near the empty space, a little further away, on the ground.

Here my Master said: "Go and see the state of them, so that you may take away a complete knowledge of this round. Talk briefly with them: I will speak with this creature until you return, so that he might carry us on his strong shoulders." So, still on the extreme edge of the seventh circle, I went all alone to where the sad crew were seated.

Their grief was gushing from their eyes; they kept flicking away the flames and sometimes the burning dust, on this side or on that, with their hands, no differently than dogs do in summer, now with their muzzle, now with their paws, when they are bitten by fleas, or gnats, or horse-flies. When I set my eyes on the faces of several of them on whom the grievous fire falls, I did not recognize any, but I saw that a pouch hung from the neck of each that had a certain color, and a certain seal, and it seemed their eye was feeding on it. And as I came among them, looking, I saw on a golden-yellow purse an azure seal that had the look and attitude of a lion.

Then my gaze continuing on its path, I saw another, red as blood, showing a goose whiter than butter. And one who had his white purse stamped with an azure, pregnant sow, said to me: "What are you doing in this pit? Now go away, and since you are still alive, know that my neighbor, Vitaliano, will come to sit here on my left. I, a Paduan, am with these Florentines. Many a time they deafen my ears, shouting: 'Let the noble knight come who will carry the purse with three eagles' beaks!'" Then he distorted his mouth, and thrust his tongue out, like an ox licking its nose, and I, dreading lest a longer stay might anger him who had warned me to make a brief stay, turned back from those weary spirits.

I found my guide, who had already mounted the flank of the savage creature, and he said to me: "Be firm and brave. Now we must descend by means of these stairs; you climb in front: I wish to be in the center so that the tail may not harm you."

Like a man whose fit of the quartan fever is so near that his nails are already pallid and he shakes all over by keeping in the shade, so I became when these words were said; but his reproof roused shame in me, which makes the servant brave in the presence of a worthy master. I set myself on those vast shoulders. I wished to say: "See that you clasp me tight," but my voice did not come out as I intended. He who helped me in other difficulties, at other times, embraced me as soon as I mounted, and held me upright. Then he said: "Now move, Geryon! Make large circles, and let your descent be gentle; think of the unusual burden that you carry."

As a little boat goes backwards, backwards, from its mooring, so the monster left the cliff, and when he felt himself quite free, he turned his tail around to where his chest had been, and stretching, flicked it like an eel, and gathered the air towards him with his paws. I do not believe the fear was greater when Phaëthon let slip the reins and the sky was scorched, as it still appears to be; or when poor Icarus felt the feathers melt from his arms as the wax was heated, and his father Daedalus cried "You are going the wrong way!" as mine was when I saw myself surrounded by the air on all sides, and saw everything vanish except the savage beast.

He goes down, swimming slowly, slowly, wheels and falls; but I do not see it except by the wind on my face and from below. Already I heard the cataract on the right, make a terrible roaring underneath us, at which I stretched my neck out, with my gaze downwards. Then I was more afraid to dismount, because I saw fires, and heard moaning, so that I cowered, trembling all over. And then I saw what I had not seen before, our sinking and circling through the great evils that drew close on every side.

As the falcon that has been long on the wing descends wearily, without seeing bird or lure, making the falconer cry: "Alas, you stoop!" and settles far from his master disdainful and sullen, so Geryon set us down at the base, close to the foot of the fractured rock, and relieved of our weight, shot off like an arrow from the bow.

18

There is a place in Hell called Malebolge, all of stone, and colored like iron, as is the cliff that surrounds it. Right in the center of the malignant space a well yawns, very wide and deep, whose structure I will speak of in due place.

The belt that remains between the base of the high rocky bank and the well is circular, and its floor is divided into ten moats. Like the form the ground reveals, where successive ditches circle a castle to defend the walls, such was the layout displayed here. And as there are bridges to the outer banks from the thresholds of the fortress, so from the base of the cliff causeways ran, crossing the successive banks and ditches, down to the well that terminates and links them. We found ourselves there, shaken from Geryon's back, and the Poet kept to the left, and I went on, behind him.

On the right I saw new pain and torment, and new tormentors, with which the first chasm was filled. In its depths the sinners were naked; on our inner side of its central round they came towards us, on the outer side, with us, but with larger steps. Thus the people of Rome, in that year of the Jubilee, because of the great crowds, initiated this means to move the people over the bridge: those on the one side all had their faces towards Castello Sant' Angelo, and went to Saint Peter's, those on the other towards Monte Giordano. On this side and on that, along the fearful rock, I saw horned demons with large whips who struck them fiercely from behind. Ah, how it made them quicken their steps at the first stroke! Truly none waited for the second or third.

As I went on, my eyes encountered one of them, and instantly I said: "This shade I have seen before." So I stopped to scrutinize him, and the kind guide stood still with me, and allowed me to tarry a little. And that scourged spirit thought to hide himself, lowering his face, but it did not help, since I said: "You who cast your eyes on the ground, if the features you display are not an illusion, you are Venedico Caccianimico; but what led you into such a biting pickle?"

And he to me: "I tell it unwillingly, but your clear speech, which makes me remember the former world, compels me. It was I who seduced the fair Ghisola into doing the Marquis of Este's will, however unpleasant the story sounds. And I am not the only Bolognese that weeps here; there are so many of us here that fewer tongues are taught to say 'yes' Bolognese-style between the Savena and the Reno. If you want assurance and testimony of it, recall to mind our avaricious hearts." And as he spoke, a demon struck him with his whip and said: "Away, you pimp, there are no women here to sell."

I rejoined my guide, and within a few steps we came to where a causeway ran from the cliff. This we climbed very easily, and turning to the right on its jagged ridge, we moved away from that eternal round. When we reached the arch where it yawns below to leave a path for the scourged, my guide said: "Wait, and let the look of those other ill-born spirits strike you, whose faces you have not yet seen since they have been going in our direction."

We viewed their company from the ancient bridge, traveling towards us on the other side, chased likewise by the whip. Without my asking, the kind Master said to me: "Look at that great soul who comes, and seems not to shed tears of pain; what a royal demeanor he still retains! That is Jason, who, by wisdom and courage, robbed the Colchians of the Golden Fleece. He sailed by the Isle of Lemnos, after the bold, merciless women there had put all their males to death. There with gifts and sweet words he deceived the young Hypsipyle, who had saved her father by deceiving all the rest. He left her there, pregnant and alone—such guilt condemns him to such torment—and revenge is also taken for his abandoning Medea. With him go all who practice such deceit, and let this be enough for knowledge of the first chasm, and those whom it swallows."

We had already come to where the narrow causeway crosses the second bank and forms a buttress to a second arch. Here we heard people whining in the next chasm, and blowing with their muzzles, and striking themselves with their palms. The banks were crusted with a mold from the fumes below that condenses on them and attacks the eyes and nose. The floor is so deep that we could not see any part of it except by climbing to the ridge of the arch, where the rock is highest. We arrived there, and from it I saw people in the ditch below immersed in excrement, which looked as if it flowed from human privies. And while I was searching down there with my eyes, I saw one with a head so smeared with shit that it was not clear if he was clerk or layman.

He shouted at me: "Why are you so keen to gaze at me more than the other befouled ones?" And I to him: "Because if I remember rightly, I have seen you before with a dry head, and you are Alessio Interminei of Lucca; so I eye you more than all the others." And he then, beating his forehead: "The flatteries of which my tongue never wearied brought me down to this!"

At which my guide said to me: "Advance your head a little so that your eyes can clearly see, over there, the face of that filthy and disheveled piece, who scratches herself with her soiled nails, now crouching down, now rising to her feet. It is Thais, the whore, who answered her lover's message, in which he asked: 'Do you really return me great thanks?' with 'No, *wondrous* thanks.' And let our looking be satisfied with this."

19

O Simon Magus! O you, his rapacious, wretched followers, who prostitute for gold and silver the things of God that should be wedded to virtue! Now the trumpets must sound for you, since you are in the third chasm.

Already we had climbed to the next arch onto that part of the causeway that hangs right over the center of the ditch. O Supreme Wisdom, how great the art is that you display in the Heavens, on earth, and in the underworld, and how justly your virtue acts. On the sides and floor of the fosse, I saw the livid stone full of holes, all of one width, and each one rounded. They seemed no narrower or larger, than those in my beautiful Baptistery of Saint John's, made as places to protect those being baptized, one of which I broke, not many years ago, to aid a child inside: and let this be a sign of the truth to end all speculation. From the mouth of each hole, a sinner's feet and legs emerged, up to the calf, and the rest remained inside. The soles were all on fire, so that the joints quivered so strongly that they would have snapped grass ropes and willow branches. As the flame of burning oily liquids moves only on the surface, so it was in their case, from the heels to the legs.

I said: "Master, who is that, who twists himself about, writhing more than all his companions, and licked by redder flames?" And he to me: "If you will let me carry you down there by the lower bank, you will learn from him about his sins and himself." And I: "Whatever pleases you pleases me: you are my lord and know that I do not deviate from your will; also you know what is not spoken."

Then we came onto the fourth buttress: we turned and descended on the left down into the narrow and perforated depths. The kind master did not let me leave his side until he took me to the hole occupied by the one who so agonized with his feet.

I began to speak: "O unhappy spirit, whoever you are, who have your upper parts below, planted like a stake, form words if you can." I stood like the friar who gives confession to a treacherous assassin who, after being fixed in the ground, calls the confessor back, and so delays his burial. And he cried: "Are you standing there already, Boniface, are you standing there already? The book of the future has deceived me by several years. Are you sated so swiftly with that wealth for which you did not hesitate to seize the Church, our lovely lady, and then destroy her?"

I became like those who stand, not knowing what has been said to them, and unable to reply, exposed to scorn. Then Virgil said: "Quickly, say to him, 'I am not him, I am not whom you think.'" And I replied as I was instructed.

At that the spirit's legs writhed fiercely; then, sighing, in a tearful voice, he said to me: "Then what do you want of me? If it concerns you so much to know who I am that you have left the ridge, know that I wore the Great Mantle, and truly I was son of the Orsini she-bear, so eager to advance her cubs that I pursed up wealth above, and here myself. The other simonists who came before me are drawn down below my head, cowering inside the cracks in the stone. I too will drop down there when Boniface comes, the one I mistook you for when I put my startled question. But the length of time in which I have baked my feet and stood like this, reversed, is already longer than the time he shall stand planted in turn with glowing feet, since after him will come Clement, the lawless shepherd of uglier actions, fit indeed to cap Boniface and me. He will be a new Jason, the high priest whom we read about in Maccabees; and as his king Antiochus was compliant, so will Philip be, who rules France."

I do not know if I was too foolhardy then, but I answered him in this way: "Ah, now tell me how much wealth the Lord demanded of Peter before he gave the keys of the Church into his keeping? Surely he demanded nothing, saying only, 'Follow me.' Nor did Peter or the other Apostles ask gold or silver of Matthias, when he was chosen to fill the place that Judas, the guilty soul, had forfeited. So remain here, since you are justly punished, and keep well the ill-gotten money that made you so bold against Charles of Anjou. And were it not that I am still restrained by reverence for the great keys that you held in your hand in the joyful life, I would use even more forceful words, since your avarice grieves the world, trampling the good, and raising the wicked. John the Evangelist spoke of shepherds such as you when he saw 'the great whore that sitteth upon many waters, with whom the kings of the earth have committed fornication,' she that was born with seven heads and, as long as virtue pleased her spouse, drew strength from the ten horns. You have made a god for yourselves of gold and silver, and how do you differ from the idolaters, except that he worships one image and you a hundred? Ah, Constantine, how much evil you gave birth to, not in your conversion, but in that Donation that the first wealthy pope received from you!"

And while I sang this song to him, he thrashed violently with both his feet, either rage or conscience gnawing him. I think it pleased my guide greatly, he had so satisfied an expression, listening to the sound of the true words I spoke. So he lifted me with both his arms, and when he had me quite upon his breast, climbed back up the path he had descended, and did not tire of carrying me clasped to him till he had borne me to the summit of the arch that crosses from the fourth to the fifth rampart. Here he set his burden down, lightly—light for him, on the rough steep cliff that would be a difficult path for a goat. From there another valley was visible to me.

20

I must make verses of new torments, and give matter for this twentieth canto of the first book, which treats of the damned.

I was now quite ready to look into the ditch, bathed with tears of anguish, which was revealed to me: I saw people coming, silent and weeping, through the circling valley, at a pace which processions that chant litanies take through the world. When my eyes looked further down on them, each of them appeared strangely distorted between the chin and the start of the chest, since the head was reversed towards the body and they had to move backwards, since they were not allowed to look forwards. Perhaps one might be so distorted by palsy, but I have not seen it, and do not credit it.

Reader, as God may grant that you profit from your reading, think now yourself how I could keep from weeping when I saw nearby our image so contorted that the tears from their eyes bathed their hind parts at the cleft. Truly, I wept, leaning against one of the rocks of the solid cliff, so that my guide said to me: "Are you like other fools as well? Pity is alive here where it is best forgotten. Who is more impious than one who bears compassion for God's judgment? Lift your head, lift it and see him for whom earth opened, under the eyes of the Thebans, at which they all shouted: 'Where are you rushing, Amphiaräus? Why do you quit the battle?' And he did not stop his downward rush until he reached Minos, who grasps every sinner. Note how he has made a chest of his shoulders; because he willed to see too far beyond him, he now looks behind and goes backwards. See Tiresias, who changed his form when he was made a woman, all his limbs altering; and later he had to strike the two entwined snakes with his staff a second time before he could resume a male aspect. That one is Aruns, who has his back to Tiresias's belly, he who in the mountains of Tuscan Luni, where the Carrarese hoe, who live beneath them, had a cave to live in among the white marble, from which he could gaze at the stars and the sea, with nothing to spoil his view. And she that hides her breasts, which you cannot see, with her flowing tresses, and has all hairy skin on the other side, was Manto, who searched through many lands, then settled where I was born, about which it pleases me to have you listen to me speak a while.

"After her father departed from life, and Thebes, the city of Bacchus, came to be enslaved, she roamed the world a long time. A lake, Lake Garda, lies at the foot of the Alps, up in beautiful Italy, where Germany is closed off beyond the Tyrol. Mount Apennino, between the town of Garda and Val Camonica, is bathed by the water that settles in the lake. In the middle there is a place where the bishops of Trent, Brescia, and Verona might equally give the blessing if they went that way. A strong and beautiful fortress stands where the shoreline is lowest, to challenge the Brescians and Bergamese. There, all the water that cannot remain in the breast of Lake Garda has to descend through the green fields and form a river. As soon as the water has its head, it is no longer Garda but Mincio, down to Governolo where it joins the Po. It has not flowed far before it finds the level on which it spreads and makes a marsh there, and in summer tends to be unwholesome. Manto, the wild virgin, passing that way, saw untilled land empty of inhabitants among the fens. There, to avoid all human contact, she stayed with her followers, to practice her arts, and lived there until she left her empty body. Then the people who were scattered around gathered together in that place, which was well defended by the marshes on every side. They built the city over those dead bones, and without other augury called it Mantua, after her who first chose the place. Once there were more inhabitants, before Casalodi was foolishly deceived by Pinamonte. So, I charge you, if you ever hear another story of the origin of my city, do not let falsehoods destroy the truth.'

And I said: "Master, your speeches are so sound to me, and so inspire my belief that any others are like spent ashes. But tell me about the people who are passing, if you see any of them worth noting, since my mind returns to that alone."

Then he said to me: "That one, whose beard stretches down from his cheeks over his dusky shoulders, was an augur when Greece was so emptied of males, for the expedition against Troy, that there were scarcely any left, even in their cradles. Like Calchas at Aulis, he set the moment for cutting loose the first cable. Eurypylus is his name, and my high poem sings of it in a certain place: you know it well, who know the whole thing. The other, so thin about the flanks, is Michael Scott, who truly understood the fraudulent game of magic. See Guido Bonatti, see Asdente, who wishes now he had attended more to his shoemaker's leather and cord, but repents too late. See the miserable women who abandoned needle, shuttle, and spindle, and became prophetesses: they practiced witchcraft, using herbs and images. But come now, for Cain with his bundle of thorns, that Man in the Moon, reaches the western confines of both hemispheres, and touches the waves south of Seville, and already, last night, the moon was full: you must remember it clearly, since she did not serve you badly in the deep wood." So he spoke to me, and meanwhile we moved on.

21

So from bridge to bridge we went, with other conversations which my comedy does not choose to recall, and were at the summit arch when we stopped to see the next cleft of Malebolge, and more vain grieving, and I found it marvelously dark.

As in the Venetian Arsenal, the glutinous pitch boils in winter that they use to caulk the leaking boats they cannot sail; and so, instead one man builds a new boat, another plugs the seams of his that has made many voyages, one hammers at the prow, another at the stern, some make oars, and some twist rope, one mends a jib, the other a mainsail; so, a dense pitch boiled down there, not melted by fire but by divine skill, and glued the banks over on every side.

I saw it, but nothing in it except the bubbles that the boiling caused and the heaving of it all, and the cooling part's submergence. While I was gazing fixedly at it, my guide said: "Take care. Take care!" and drew me towards him, from where I stood. Then I turned around, like one who has to see what he must run from, and who is attacked by sudden fear, so that he dare not stop to look: and behind us I saw a black demon come running up the cliff.

Ah, how fierce his countenance was! And how cruel he seemed in action, with his outspread wings and nimble legs! His high-pointed shoulders carried a sinner's two haunches, and he held the sinews of each foot tight.

He cried: "You, Malebranche, see here is one of the Ancients of Santa Zita: push him under while I go back for the rest, back to that city which is well provided with them: everyone there is a swindling barrator, except Bonturo; there they turn 'no' into 'yes' for money."

He threw him down, then wheeled back along the stony cliff, and never was a mastiff loosed so readily to catch a thief. The sinner plunged in, and rose again writhing, but the demons under cover of the bridge, shouted: "Here the face of Christ, carved in your cathedral, is of no avail; here you swim differently than in the Serchio; so unless you want to try our grapples, do not emerge above the pitch." Then they struck at him with more than a hundred prongs, and said: "Here you must dance, concealed, so that you steal in private, if you can." No different is it than when cooks make their underlings push the meat down into the depths of the cauldrons with their hooks, to stop it floating.

The good master said to me: "Cower down behind a rock so that you have a screen to protect yourself, and so that it is not obvious that you are here, and whatever insult is offered to me, have no fear, since I know these matters, having been in a similar danger before." Then he passed beyond the bridgehead, and when he arrived on the sixth bank, it was necessary for him to present a bold front.

The demons rushed from below the bridge, and turned their weapons against him with the storm and fury with which a dog rushes at a poor beggar who suddenly seeks alms when he stops. But Virgil cried: "None of you commit an outrage. Before you touch me with your forks, one of you come over here, to listen, and then discuss whether you will grapple me." They all cried: "You go, Malacoda," at which one moved while the others stood still, and came towards Virgil, saying: "What good will it do him?"

My Master said: "Malacoda, do you think I have come here without the Divine Will and propitious fate, safe from all your obstructions? Let me pass by, since it is willed in Heaven that I show another this wild road."

Then the demon's pride was so disappointed that he let the hook drop at his feet, and said to the others: "Now do not hurt him!"

And my guide to me: "O you who are sitting, crouching, crouching amongst the bridge's crags, return to me safely now!" At which I moved, and came to him quickly, and the devils all pressed forward so that I was afraid they would not hold to their orders. Thus once I saw the infantry marching out under treaty of surrender from Caprona, afraid at finding themselves surrounded by so many enemies. I pressed my whole body close to my guide, and did not take my eyes away from their countenances, which were hostile.

They lowered their hooks, and kept saying to one another: "Shall I touch him on the backside?" and answering, "Yes, see that you give him a nick." But that demon who was talking to my guide turned around quickly and said: "Be quiet, be quiet, Scarmiglione." Then he said to us: "It will not be possible to go any further along this causeway, since the sixth arch is lying broken at the base; but if you desire still to go forward, go along this ridge, and nearby is another cliff that forms a causeway. Yesterday, five hours later than this hour, 1,266 years were completed since this path here was destroyed. I am sending some of my company here to see if anyone is out for an airing: go with them, they will not commit treachery." Then he began speaking: "Advance, Alichino and Calcabrina, and you, Cagnazzo: let Barbariccia lead the ten. Let Libicocco come as well, and Draghignazzo, tusked Ciriatto, Grafficane, Farfarello, and Rubicante the mad one. Search around the boiling glue: see these two safely as far as the other cliff that crosses the chasms completely, without a break."

I said: "Ah me! Master, what do I see? Oh let us go alone, without an escort, if you know the way; as for me, I would prefer not. If you are as cautious as usual, do you not see how they grind their teeth, and darken their brows, threatening us with mischief?" And he to me: "I do not want you to be afraid: let them grin away at their will, since they do it for the boiled wretches."

They turned by the left bank; but first, each of them had stuck his tongue out between his teeth towards their leader for a signal, and he had made a trumpet of his ass.

22

I have seen cavalry moving camp, before now, starting a foray, holding muster, and now and then retiring to escape; I have seen war-horses on your territory, O Aretines, and seen the foraging parties, the clash of tournaments, and repeated jousts; now with trumpets, now with bells, with drums and rampart signals, with native and foreign devices, but never have I seen infantry or cavalry, or ship at sight of shore or star, move to such an obscene trumpet.

We went with the ten demons: ah, savage company! But as they say: "In church with the saints, and in the tavern with the drunkards." But my mind was on the boiling pitch, to see each feature of the chasm, and the people who were burning in it. Just as dolphins, arching their backs, tell sailors to get ready to save their ship, so now and then, to ease the punishment, some sinner showed his back, and hid as quick as lightning. And as frogs squat at the edge of the ditchwater, with only mouths showing, so that their feet and the rest of them are hidden, so the sinners stood on every side; but they instantly shot beneath the seething pitch as Barbariccia approached.

I saw (and my heart still shudders at it) one linger, just as one frog remains when the others scatter; and Graffiacane, who was nearest him, hooked his pitchy hair and hauled him up, looking to me like an otter. I already knew the names of every demon, so I noted them well as they were called, and listened when they shouted to each other. "Hey Rubicante, see you get your clutches in him, and flay him," all the accursed tribe cried together. And I: "Master, make out if you can who that wretch is who has fallen into the hands of his enemies."

My guide drew close to him, and asked him where he came from, and he answered: "I was born in the kingdom of Navarre. My mother placed me as a servant to a lord, since she had borne me to a scurrilous waster of himself and his possessions. Then I was of the household of good King Thibaut, and there I took to selling offices, for which I serve my sentence in this heat."

And Ciriatto, from whose mouth a tusk like a boar's projected on each side, made him feel how one of them could rip. The mouse had come among malicious cats, but Barbariccia caught him in his arms, and said: "Stand back while I fork him!" And turning to my Master, he said: "Ask away if you want to learn more from him, before someone else gets at him."

So my guide said: "Now say, do you know if any of the other sinners under the boiling pitch are Italian?" And Ciampolo replied: "I separated just now from one who was a neighbor of theirs over there, and I wish I were still beneath him, since I should not then fear claw or hook!" And Libicocco cried: "We have endured this too long!" and grappled Ciampolo's arm with the prong, and, mangling it, carried away a chunk. Draghignazzo too wanted a swipe at the legs below, at which their leader twisted around on them with an evil frown.

When they had settled down a little, without waiting my guide asked Ciampolo, who was still gazing at his wound: "Who was he from whom you say you unluckily separated to come on land?"

He replied: "It was Friar Gomita, from Gallura in Sardinia, the vessel of every fraud, who held his master's prisoners in his hands and treated them so that they all praise him for it, taking money for himself, and letting them go, quietly; and in his other roles, he was a high, and not a low, barrator. With him, Don Michel Zanche of Logodoro keeps company, and their tongues never tire of speaking of Sardinia. O me! See that other demon grinning: I would speak more, but I fear he is getting ready to claw my skin." And their great captain, turning to Farfarello, who was rolling his eyes to strike, said: "Away with you, cursed bird."

The scared sinner then resumed: "If you want to see or hear Tuscans or Lombards, I will make them come, but let the Malebranche hold back a little, so that the others may not feel their vengeance, and sitting here, I, who am one, will make seven appear by whistling, as we do when any of us gets out." Cagnazzo raised his snout at these words, and, shaking his head, said: "Hear the wicked scheme he has contrived to plunge back down." At which Ciampolo, who had a great store of tricks, replied: "I would be malicious indeed if I contrived greater sorrow for my companions."

Alichino could contain himself no longer, and contrary to the others, said to him: "If you run, I will not charge after you but beat my wings above the boiling pitch; forget the cliff, and let the bank be a course and see if you alone can beat us." O you that read this, hear of this new sport! They all glanced towards the cliff side, he above all

who had been most unwilling for this. The Navarrese picked his moment well, planted his feet on the ground, and in an instant plunged,
and freed himself from their intention.

Each of the demons was stung with guilt, but Alichino most who
had committed the mistake, so he started up and shouted: "You are
caught!" But it did not help him much, since wings could not outrun
terror; the sinner dived down, and Alichino, flying, lifted his chest.
The duck dives like that when the falcon nears, and the hawk flies
back up, angry and thwarted.

Calcabrina, furious at the trick, flew on after him, wanting the
sinner to escape in order to quarrel. And when the barrator had vanished, he turned his claws on his friend and grappled with him above
the ditch. But the other was sparrow hawk enough to claw him thor-
oughly, and both dropped down into the center of the boiling pond.

The heat instantly separated them, but they could not rise, their
wings were so glued up. Barbariccia, lamenting with the rest, made
four fly over to the other bank with all their grappling irons, and they
dropped rapidly on both sides to the shore. They stretched their hooks
out to the trapped pair, who were already scaled by the crust, and we
left them, like that, embroiled.

23

Silent, alone, and free of company, we went on, one in front, and the other behind, like Friars Minor journeying on their way. My thoughts were turned by the recent quarrel to Aesop's fable of the frog and mouse, since "dusk" and "twilight" are not better matched than the one case with the other, if the thoughtful mind couples the beginning and end. And as one thought springs from another, so another sprang from that, redoubling my fear. I thought of this: "Through us, the evil-winged are mocked, and with a kind of hurt and ridicule that I guess must annoy them. If anger is added to their malice, they will chase after us, fiercer than snapping dogs that chase a leveret." I felt my hair already lifting in fright, and was looking back intently as I said: "Master, if you do not hide us both, quickly, I fear the Malebranche—they are already behind us—I imagine I can hear them now."

And he: "If I were made of silvered glass, I could not take up your image from outside more rapidly than I fix that image from within. Even now your thoughts were entering mine, with similar form and action, so that, from both, I have made one decision. If the right bank slopes enough that we can drop down into the next chasm, we will escape this imaginary pursuit . . ." He had not finished stating this resolve when I saw them, not far off, coming with extended wings with a desire to seize us.

My guide suddenly took me up like a mother who, wakened by a noise, seeing flames burning in front of her eyes, takes her child and runs, and caring more about him than herself, does not even wait to look around her. Down from the ridge of the solid bank he threw himself forward onto the hanging cliff that dams up the side of the next chasm. Water never ran as fast through the conduit, turning a mill-wheel on land when it reaches the paddles, as my Master down that bank, carrying me against his breast like a son, not a companion.

His feet had hardly touched the floor of the depth below before the demons were on the heights above us, but it gave him no fear, since the high Providence that willed them to be the guardians of the fifth moat also deprives them of the power to leave it.

Down below we found a metal-coated tribe, weeping, circling with very slow steps, and weary and defeated in their aspect. They had cloaks with deep hoods over the eyes, in the shape they make for the monks of Cologne. On the outside they are gilded so it dazzles, but inside all is leaden, and so heavy that compared to them Frederick's were made of straw. O weary mantle for eternity! We turned to the left again, beside them who were intent on their sad weeping, but those people, tired by their burden, came on so slowly that our companions changed at every step. At which I said to my guide: "Make a search for someone known to us, by name or action, and gaze around as we move by." And one of them who understood the Tuscan language called after us: "Rest your feet, you who speed so fast through the dark air, maybe you will get from me what you request." At which my guide turned around and said: "Wait, and then go on, at his pace."

I stood still and saw two spirits, who were eager in spirit to join me, but their burden and the narrow path delayed them. When they arrived, they eyed me askance for a long time without speaking a word, then they turned to one another and said: "This one seems alive by the movement of his throat, and if they are dead, by what grace are they moving free of the heavy cloaks?"

Then they said to me: "O Tuscan, you have come to the college of sad hypocrites: do not scorn to tell us who you are." And I to them: "I was born, and I grew up, by Arno's lovely river, in the great city; and I am in the body I have always worn. But you, who are you, from whom such sadness is distilled, as I see, coursing down your cheeks? And what punishment is this that glitters so?"

And one of them replied: "Our orange mantles are of such dense lead that weights made of it cause the scales to creak. We belonged to that Bolognese order called the 'Jovial Friars': I am Catalano, and he is Loderingo, chosen by your city, as usually only one is chosen, to keep the peace, and we did can still be seen around your district of Gardingo."

"O Friars, your evil . . ." I began, but said no more because I then came across one crucified on the ground with three stakes. When he saw me he writhed all over, puffing into his beard, and sighing, and Friar Catalano, who saw this, said to me: "That one you look at, who is transfixed, is Caiaphas, the high priest who counseled the Pharisees that it was right to martyr one man for the sake of the people. Crosswise and naked he lies in the road, as you see, and feels the weight of everyone who passes; and his father-in-law Annas is racked in this chasm and the others of that council that was a source of evil to the Jews."

Then I saw Virgil wonder at him, stretched out on the cross so vilely, in eternal exile. He then addressed these words to the Friars: "If it is lawful for you, may it not displease you to tell us if there is any gap on the right by which we might leave here, without forcing any of the black angels to come and extricate us from this deep."

He replied: "There is a causeway that runs from the great circular wall and crosses all the cruel valleys, nearer at hand than you think, except that it is broken here and does not cover this one; you will be able to climb up among its ruins that slope down the side and form a mound at the base."

Virgil stood for a while with bowed head, then said: "Malacoda, who grapples sinners over there, told us the way wrongly." And the Friar said: "I once heard the Devil's vices related at Bologna, amongst which I heard that he is a liar, and the father of lies." Then my guide went striding on, his face somewhat disturbed by anger, at which I parted from the burdened souls, following the prints of his beloved feet.

24

In that part of the new year when the sun cools his rays under Aquarius, and the nights already shorten towards the equinox, when the hoarfrost copies its white sister the snow's image on the ground but the hardness of its tracery lasts only a little time, the peasant, whose fodder is exhausted, rises and looks out, and sees the fields all white, at which he strikes his thigh, goes back into the house, and wanders to and fro, lamenting, like a wretch who does not know what to do; then comes out again, and regains hope, seeing how the world has changed its aspect in a moment, and takes his crook and drives his lambs out to feed; so the Master made me disheartened when I saw his forehead so troubled, but the plaster arrived quickly for the wound.

For when we reached the shattered arch, my guide turned to me with that sweet countenance that I first saw at the base of the mountain. He opened his arms, after having made some plan in his mind, first looking carefully at the ruin, and took hold of me. And like one who prepares and calculates, always seeming to provide in advance, so he, lifting me up towards the summit of one big block, searched for another fragment, saying: "Now clamber over that, but check first if it will carry you."

It was no route for one clothed in a cloak of lead, since we could hardly climb from rock to rock, he weighing little, and I pushed from behind. And if the ascent were not shorter on that side than on the other, I would truly have been defeated, I do not know about him. But as Malebolge all drops towards the entrance to the lowest well, the position of every valley implies that the one side rises, and the other falls; at last, we came, however, to the point at which the last boulder ends.

The breath was so driven from my lungs when I was up that I could go no further; in fact, I sat down when I arrived. The Master said: "Now you must free yourself from sloth: men do not achieve fame sitting on down, or under coverlets; fame, without which whoever consumes his life leaves only such traces of himself on earth as smoke does in the air, or foam on water. So arise, and overcome weariness with spirit that wins every battle, if it does not lie down with the gross body. A longer ladder must be climbed; to have left these spirits behind is not enough; if you understand me, act now so it may profit you."

I rose then, showing myself to be better filled with breath than I thought, and said: "Go on, I am strong again and ardent."

We made our way along the causeway, which was rugged, narrow, difficult, and much steeper than before. I spoke as I went so that I might not seem weak, at which a voice came from the next moat, inadequate for forming words. I do not know what it said, though I was already on the summit of the bridge that crosses there, but he who spoke seemed full of anger. I had turned to look downwards, but my living eyes could not see the floor for the darkness, so that I said: "Master, make sure you get to the other side, and let us climb down the wall, since as I hear sounds from below, but do not understand them; I see down there, but can make out nothing." He said: "I'll answer you with action, since a fair request should be followed in silence by the work."

We went down the bridge to the head of it, where it meets the eighth bank, and then the seventh chasm was open to me. I saw a fearful mass of snakes inside, and of such strange appearance that even now the memory freezes my blood. Let Libya no longer vaunt its sands: though it engenders chelydri, and jaculi, phareae, and cenchres with amphisbaena, it never showed pests so numerous or dreadful, nor did Ethiopia, nor Arabia, the land that lies along the Red Sea. Amongst this cruel and mournful swarm, people were running, naked and terrified, without hope of concealment, and lacking that stone, the heliotrope, that renders the wearer invisible. They had their hands tied behind them with serpents that fixed their head and tail between the loins and were coiled in knots in front.

Now look, a serpent struck at one who was near our bank, and transfixed him, there, where the neck is joined to the shoulders. Neither "o" nor "i" was ever written as swiftly as he took fire, and burned, and dropped down, transformed to ashes; and after he was heaped on the ground, the powder gathered itself together, and immediately returned to its previous shape. So, great sages say, the phoenix dies, and then renews when it nears its five-hundredth year. In its life it does not eat grass or grain, but only tears of incense, and amomum; and its last shroud is nard and myrrh.

When the sinner rose he was like one who falls and does not know how, through the power of a demon that drags him down to the ground, or through some other affliction that binds men, and, when he rises, gazes around himself, all dazed by the great anguish he has suffered, and as he gazes, sighs. O how heavy the power of God that showers down such blows in vengeance!

The guide then asked him who he was, at which he answered: "I rained down from Tuscany into this gully a short while back. Animal life, not human, pleased me, mule that I was: I am Vanni Fucci, the wild beast, and Pistoia was a fitting den for me." And I to the guide: "Tell him not to move, and ask what crime sank him down here, since I knew him as a man of blood and anger."

And the sinner, who heard me, did not pretend but turned his face and mind on me, and gave a look of saddened shame. Then he said: "It hurts me more for you to catch me, trapped in the misery you see me in, than the moment of my being snatched from the other life. I cannot deny you what you ask. I am placed so deep down because I robbed the sacristy of its fine treasures, and it was once wrongly attributed to others. But so that you might not take joy from this sight if you ever escape the gloomy regions, open your ears, and hear what I declare: Pistoia first is thinned of the Black party, then Florence changes her people and her laws. Mars brings a vapor from Valdimagra cloaked in turbid cloud, and a battle will be fought on the field of Piceno in an angry and eager tempest that will suddenly tear the mist open, so that every member of the White party is wounded by it. And I have said this to give you pain."

25

At the end of his speech, the thief raised his hands, making the fig with thumb between fingers, shouting: "Take this, God, I aim it at you." From that moment the snakes were my friends, since one of them coiled itself round his neck, as if hissing: "You will not be able to speak again." Another around his arms tied him again, knotting itself so firmly in front that he could not even shake them.

Ah, Pistoia, Pistoia, why do you not order yourself to be turned to ash so that you may remain no longer, since you outdo your seed in evil-doing? I saw no spirit so arrogant towards God through all the dark circles of the Inferno, not even Capaneus, who fell from the wall at Thebes. Vanni Fucci fled, saying not another word, and I saw a centaur full of rage come shouting: "Where is he, where is the bitter one?"

I do not believe Maremma has as many snakes as he had on his haunches, there where the human part begins. Over his shoulders, behind the head, lay a dragon with outstretched wings, and it scorches everyone he meets. My Master said: "That is Cacus, who often made a lake of blood below the rocks of Mount Aventine. He does not go with his brothers on the same road above because of his cunning theft from the great herd of oxen, pastured near him, for which his thieving actions ended under the club of Hercules, who gave him a hundred blows perhaps with it, and he did not feel a tenth."

While he said this, the centaur ran past, and three spirits went by too beneath us, whom neither I nor my guide saw until they cried: "Who are you?" Our words ceased then, and we gave our attention to them, alone. I did not know them, but it happened, as it usually does for some reason, that one had to call the other, saying: "Where has Cianfa gone?" At which I placed my finger over my mouth in order to make my guide stop and wait.

Reader, if you are slow to believe now what I have to tell, it will be no wonder, since I who saw it scarcely believe it myself. While I kept looking at them, a six-footed serpent darted in front of one of them and fastened itself on him completely. It clasped his belly with its middle feet, seized his arms with the front ones, and then fixed its teeth in both his cheeks. It stretched its rear feet along his thighs and put its tail between them, and curled it upwards round his loins behind. Ivy was never rooted to a tree as much as the foul monster twined its limbs around the other. Then they clung together as if they were melted wax and mixed their colors: neither the one nor the other seemed what it had at first, just as in front of the flame on burning paper, a brown color appears, not yet black, and the white is consumed.

The other two looked on, and each cried: "Ah me, Agnello, how you change! See, you are already not two, not one!" The two heads had now become one, where two forms seemed to us merged in one face, and both were lost. Two limbs were made of the four forearms, the thighs, legs, belly and chest became such members as were never seen before. The former shape was all extinguished in them; the perverse image seemed both, and neither, and like that it moved away with slow steps.

Just as the lizard in the great heat of the dog days appears like a flash of lightning, scurrying from hedge to hedge if it crosses the track, so a little reptile came towards the bellies of the other two, burning with rage, black and livid as peppercorn. And it pierced that part in one of them where we first receive our nourishment from our mothers, then fell down, stretched out in front of him. The thief, transfixed, gazed at it but said nothing, but with motionless feet only yawned, as if sleep or fever had overcome him. He looked at the snake; it looked at him; the one gave out smoke, violently, from his wound, the other from its mouth, and the smoke met.

Let Lucan now be silent about Sabellus and Nasidius and wait to hear that which I now tell. Let Ovid be silent about Cadmus and Arethusa; if he in poetry changes one into a snake and the other into a fountain, I do not envy him, since he never transmuted two natures, face to face, so that both forms were eager to exchange their substance. They merged together in such a way that the serpent split its tail into a fork, and the wounded spirit brought his feet together. Along with them, the legs and thighs so stuck to one another that soon the join left no visible mark. The cleft tail took on the form lost in the other, and its skin grew soft, the other's hard. I saw the arms enter the armpits, and the two feet of the beast that were short lengthened themselves by as much as the arms were shortened. Then the two hind feet

twisted together and became the organ that a man conceals, and the
wretch, from his, had two pushed out. While the smoke covers them
both with a new color, and generates hair on one part and strips it
from another, the one rose up, erect, and the other fell, prostrate, not
by that shifting their impious gaze beneath which they mutually exchanged features. The erect one drew his face towards the temples,
and from the excess of matter that swelled there, ears emerged out of
the smooth cheeks. That which did not slip back but remained formed
a nose from the superfluous flesh, and enlarged the lips to their right
size. He that lay prone thrust his sharpened visage forward and drew
his ears back into his head, as the snail does its horns into its shell,
and his tongue, which was solid before and fit for speech, splits itself.
In the other the forked tongue melds, and the smoke is still.

The soul that had become a beast sped hissing along the valley,
leaving the other, speaking and spluttering, behind him. Then the
second turned his new-won shoulders towards him, and called to the
other: "Buoso shall crawl, as I did, along this road." So I saw the seventh chasm's bodies mutate and transmutate, and let the novelty of it
be the excuse, if my pen has gone astray.

Though my sight was somewhat confused, and my mind dismayed,
they could not flee so secretly but that I clearly saw Puccio Sciancato;
and it was he alone of the three companions who had first arrived
who was not changed. One of the others was he who caused you, the
people of Gaville, to weep.

26

Rejoice, Florence, that since you are so mighty you beat your wings over land and sea, and your name spreads through Hell itself. So, among the thieves, I found five of your citizens, at which I am ashamed, and you do not rise to great honor by it either. But if the truth is dreamed, as morning comes you will soon feel what Prato and others wish on you. And if it were come already, it would not be too soon; would it were so, now, as indeed it must come, since it will trouble me more the older I get.

We left there, and my guide remounted by the stairs that the stones had made for us to descend and drew me up; and, following our solitary way among the crags and splinters of the cliff, the foot made no progress without the hand. I was saddened then, and sadden again now, when I direct my mind to what I saw, and rein in my intellect more than I am used so that it does not run where virtue would not guide it, and so that, if a good star, or some truer power, has granted me the talent, I may not abuse the gift.

The eighth chasm was gleaming with flames, as numerous as the fireflies the peasant sees as he rests on the hill when the sun, who lights the world, hides his face least from us, and the fly gives way to the gnat down there, along the valley, where he gathers grapes, perhaps, and ploughs.

As soon as I came to where the floor showed itself, I saw them, and just as Elisha, avenged by bears after he had been mocked by children, saw Elijah's chariot departing, when the horses rose straight to Heaven and could not follow it with his eyes except by the flame alone, like a little cloud, ascending, so each of those flames moved along the throat of the ditch, for none of them show the theft, but every flame steals a sinner.

I stood on the bridge, having so risen to look that if I had not caught hold of a rock I should have fallen in without being pushed. And the guide, who saw me so intent, said: "The spirits are inside those fires: each veils himself in that which burns him." I replied:

"Master, I feel more assured from hearing you, but had already seen that it was so, and already wished to ask you who is in that fire that moves, divided at the summit, as if it rose from the pyre where Eteocles was cremated with his brother Polynices?"

He answered me: "In there, Ulysses and Diomede are tormented, and so they go, together in punishment, as formerly in war; and in their fire, they groan at the ambush of the Trojan horse, which made a doorway by which Aeneas, the noble seed of the Romans, issued out. In there they lament the trick by which Deidamia, in death, still weeps for Achilles, and there, for the Palladium, they endure punishment."

I said: "Master, I beg you greatly, and beg again so that my prayers may be a thousand, if those inside the fires can speak, do not refuse my waiting until the horned flame comes here; you see how eagerly I lean towards it." And he to me: "Your request is worth much praise, and so I accept it, but hold your tongue. Let me speak, since I conceive what you wish, and since they were Greeks they might disdain your Trojan words."

When the flame had come, where the time and place seemed fitting, to my guide, I heard him speak, so: "O you who are two in one fire, if I was worthy of you when I lived, if I was worthy of you, greatly or a little, when on earth I wrote the high verses, do not go, but let one of you tell where he, being lost through his own actions, went to die."

The greater horn of the ancient flame started to shake itself, murmuring, like a flame struggling in the wind. Then moving the tip, as if it were a tongue speaking, gave out a voice, and said: "When I left Circe, who held me for more than a year near Gaeta, before Aeneas named it, not even my fondness for my son Telemachus, my reverence for my aged father Laërtes, nor the debt of love that should have made Penelope happy could restrain in me the desire I had to gain experience of the world, and of human vice and worth. I set out on the wide, deep ocean with only one ship, and that small company that had not abandoned me. I saw both shores, as far as Spain, as far as Morocco, and the isle of Sardinia, and the other islands that the sea washes. My companions and I were old and slow when we came to that narrow strait where Hercules set up his pillars to warn men from going further. I left Seville to starboard: already Ceuta was left behind on the other side.

"I said: 'O my brothers, who have reached the west through a thousand dangers, do not deny the brief vigil your senses have left to them, experience of the unpopulated world beyond the Sun. Consider your origin: you were not made to live like brutes, but to follow virtue and knowledge.' With this brief speech I made my companions so eager for the voyage that I could hardly have restrained them, and turning the prow towards morning, we made wings of our oars for that foolish flight, always turning south.

"Night already saw the southern pole, with all its stars, and our northern pole was so low it did not rise from the ocean bed. Five times the light beneath the moon had been quenched and rekindled since we had entered on the deep pathways, when a mountain appeared to us, dim with distance, and it seemed to me the highest I had ever seen. We rejoiced, but soon our joy was turned to grief when a tempest rose from the new land and struck the prow of our ship. Three times it whirled her around, with all the ocean; at the fourth, it made the stern rise and the prow sink as it pleased another till the sea closed over us."

27

The flame was now erect and quiet, no longer speaking, and was going away from us, with the permission of the sweet poet, when another that came behind forced us to turn our eyes towards its summit, since a confused sound escaped there.

As the Sicilian bull that first bellowed with the groans of Perillus, who had smoothed it with his file (and that was right), bellowed with the sufferer's voice so that, although it was bronze, it seemed pierced with agony, so here, the dismal words having at their source no exit from the fire, were changed into its language. But when they had found a path out through the tip, giving it the movement that the tongue had given in making them, we heard it say: "O you at whom I direct my voice, and who but now was speaking Lombard, saying: 'Now go— no more, I beg you,' let it not annoy you to stop and speak with me, though perhaps I have came a little late: you see it does not annoy me, and I burn. If you are only now fallen into this blind world from that sweet Italian land from which I bring all my guilt, tell me if Romagna has peace or war, for I was of the mountains there, between Urbino and Monte Coronaro, the source from which the Tiber springs."

I was still leaning downwards eagerly when my leader touched me on the side, saying: "Speak, this is an Italian."

And I who had my answer ready began to speak then without delay: "O spirit, hidden there below, your Romagna is not, and never has been, without war in the hearts of her tyrants: but I left no open war there now. Ravenna stands as it has stood for many years: Guido Vecchio da Polenta's eagle broods over it so that it covers Cervia with its claws. Forlì, the city that withstood so long a siege and made a bloody pile of Frenchmen, finds itself again under the paws of Ordelaffi's green lion. Malatesta, the old mastiff of Verruchio, and the young one, Malatestino, who made bad jailors for Montagna, sharpen their teeth where they used to do. Faenza, on the Lamone, and Imola on the Santerno, those cities lead out Pagano, the lion of the white lair, who changes sides when he goes from south to north, and Cesena, that city whose walls the Savio bathes, where it lies between the mountain and the plain, likewise lives between freedom and tyranny. Now I beg you, tell us who you are: do not be harder than others have been to you, so that your name may keep its luster on earth."

When the flame had roared for a while as usual, it flickered the sharp point to and fro, and then gave out this breath: "If I thought my answer was given to one who could ever return to the world, this flame would flicker no more, but since, if what I hear is true, no one ever returned alive from this deep, I reply without fear of defamation. I, Guido da Montefeltro, was a man of arms, and then became a Cordelier of Saint Francis, hoping to make amends, so habited; and indeed my hopes would have been realized in full but for the Great Priest—may evil befall him—who drew me back to my first sins: and how and why, I want you to hear from me. While I was in the form of bones and pulp that my mother gave me, my actions were not those of the lion but of the fox. I knew all the tricks and coverts and employed the art of them so well that the noise went out to the ends of the earth. When I found myself arrived at that point of life when everyone should furl their sails and gather in the ropes, what had pleased me before now grieved me, and with repentance and confession I turned monk. Ah misery! Alas, it would have served me well. But the Prince of the Pharisees—that Pope waging war near the Lateran, and not with Saracens or Jews, since all his enemies were Christians, and none had been to conquer Acre or been a merchant in the Sultan's land—had no regard for the highest office, nor holy orders, nor my habit of Saint Francis, which used to make those who wore it leaner; but as the Emperor Constantine sought out Saint Sylvester on Mount Soracte to cure his leprosy, so this man called me as a doctor to cure his feverish pride. He demanded counsel of me, and I kept silent, since his speech seemed drunken.

"Then he said to me: 'Do not be doubtful, I absolve you beforehand; and you, teach me how to act so that I may raze the fortress of Palestrina to the ground. As you know, I can open and close Heaven with the two keys that my predecessor, Celestine, did not prize.' Then the weighty arguments forced me to consider silence worse, and I said: 'Father, since you absolve me of that sin into which I must now fall, large promises to your enemies, with little delivery of them, will give you victory from your high throne.'

"Afterwards, when I was dead, Saint Francis came for me, but one of the Black Cherubim said to him: 'Do not take him: do not wrong me. He must descend among my servants, because he gave a counsel of deceit, since when I have kept him fast by the hair; he who does not repent cannot be absolved, nor can one repent a thing and at the same time will it, since the contradiction is not allowed.' O miserable self! How I started when he seized me, saying to me: 'Perhaps you did not think I was a logician.' He carried me to Minos, who coiled his tail eight times around his fearful back, and then, biting it in great rage, said: 'This sinner is for the thievish fire,' and so I am lost here, as you see, and clothed like this go inwardly grieving."

When he had thus ended his speech, the flame went sorrowing, writhing and flickering its sharp horn. We passed on, my guide and I, along the cliff, up to the other arch that covers the next ditch, in which the reward is paid to those who collect guilt by sowing discord.

28

Who could ever fully tell, even with repeated unimprisoned words, the blood and wounds I saw now? Every tongue would certainly fail, since our speech and memory have too small a capacity to comprehend so much. If all the people too were gathered who once grieved for their blood in the fateful land of Apulia by reason of the Samnite War of the Romans, of Trojan seed; and those from that long Punic War that, as Livy (who does not err) writes, yielded so great a wealth of rings from Cannae's battlefield; and those who felt the pain of blows by withstanding Robert Guiscard; and the rest, whose bones are still heaped at Ceperano, where all the Apulians turned traitor for Charles of Anjou; and there at Tagliacozzo, where old Alardo's advice to Charles conquered without weapons—and some were to show pierced limbs, and others severed stumps, it would be nothing to equal the hideous state of the ninth chasm.

Even a wine-cask that has lost a stave in the middle or the end does not yawn as widely as a spirit I saw, cleft from the chin down to the part that gives out the foulest sound: the entrails hung between his legs, the organs appeared, and the miserable gut that makes excrement of what is swallowed.

While I stood looking wholly at him, he gazed at me, and opened his chest with his hands, saying: "See how I tear myself: see how Mahomet is ripped! In front of me, Ali goes, weeping, his face split from chin to scalp, and all the others you see here were sowers of scandal and schism in their lifetimes: so they are cleft like this. There is a devil behind who tears us cruelly like this, reapplying his sword blade to each of this crowd when they have wandered round the sad road, since the wounds heal before any reach him again. But who are you, who muse there on the cliff, maybe to delay your path to punishment in sentence for your crimes?"

My Master replied: "Death has not come to him yet, nor does guilt lead him to torment, but it is incumbent on me, who am dead, to grant him full experience, and lead him through the Inferno, down here, from circle to circle, and this is truth that I tell you." When they heard him, more than a hundred spirits in the ditch halted to look at me, forgetting their agony in their wonder.

After lifting up one foot to leave, Mahomet said to me: "Well now, you who will perhaps soon see the sun, tell Fra Dolcino of the Apostolic Brothers, if he does not wish to follow me quickly down here, to furnish himself with supplies so that the snowfalls may not bring a victory for the Novarese that otherwise would be difficult to achieve." Then he strode forward to depart.

Another, who had his throat slit and nose cut off to the eyebrows and had only a single ear, standing to gaze in wonder with the rest, opened his windpipe that was red outside all over, and said: "You that no guilt condemns, and whom I have seen above on Italian ground, unless resemblance deceives me, remember Pier della Medicina, if you ever return to see the gentle plain that slopes down from Vercelli to Marcabò. And make known to the worthiest two men in Fano, Messer Guido and Angiolello too, that unless our prophetic powers here are in vain, they will be cast out of their boat and drowned near Cattolica by treachery. Neptune never saw a greater crime between the isles of Cyprus and Majorca, not even among those carried out by pirates, or by Greeks. Malatestino, the treacherous one, who sees with only one eye, and holds the land, that one who is here with me wishes he had never seen, will make them come to parley with him, then act so that they will have no need of vow or prayer to counter Focara's winds."

And I said to him: "If you would have me carry news of you above, show me and explain who he is that rues the sight of it."

Then he placed his hand on the jaw of one of his companions and opened the mouth, saying: "This is he, but he does not speak. This outcast quelled Caesar's doubts at the Rubicon, saying that delay always harms men who are ready." O how dejected Curio seemed to me, with his tongue slit in his palate, who was so bold in speech!

And one who had both hands severed, lifting the stumps through the dark air so that their blood stained his face, said: "You will remember Mosca too, who said, alas, 'A thing done has an end,' which was seed of evil to the Tuscan race."

"And death to your people," I added, at which he, accumulating pain on pain, went away like one sad and mad. But I remained behind to view the crowd, and saw something that, without more proof, I would be afraid to even tell, except that conscience reassures me: the good companion that strengthens a man under the armor of his self-respect. I saw clearly, and still seem to see, a headless trunk that goes on before, like the others, in that miserable crew, and holds its severed head by the hair, swinging like a lantern in its hand. It looked at us, and said: "Ah me!" It made a lamp of itself, to light itself, and there were two in one, and one in two: how that can be He knows who made it so.

When it was right at the foot of our bridge, it lifted its arm high, complete with the head, to bring its words near to us, which were: "Now you see the grievous punishment, you who go alive and breathing to see the dead; look if any are as great as this. And so that you may carry news of me, know that I am Bertrand de Born, he who gave evil counsel to the young king. I made the father and the son rebel against each other: Ahithophel did no more for Absalom and David by his malicious stirrings. Because I parted those who were once joined, I carry my intellect, alas, split from its origin in this body. So, in me, is seen just retribution."

29

The multitude of people and the many wounds had made my eyes so tear-filled that they longed to stop and weep, but Virgil said to me: "Why are you still gazing? Why does your sight still rest down there, on the sad, mutilated shadows? You did not do so at the other chasms. Think, if you wish to number them, that the valley circles twenty-two miles, and the moon is already underneath our feet. The time is short now that is given us, and there are other things to view than those you see."

I then replied: "Had you noticed the reason why I looked, perhaps you might still have allowed me to stay." Meanwhile, the guide was moving on, and I went behind him, making my reply, and adding now: "In the hollow where I held my gaze, I believe a spirit of my own blood laments the guilt that costs so greatly here."

Then the Master said: "Do not let your thoughts be distracted by him; attend to something else: let him stay there. I saw him point to you at the foot of the little bridge, and threaten angrily with his finger; and I heard them call him Geri del Bello. You were so entangled then with him who once held Altaforte that you did not look that way, so he departed."

I said: "Oh, my guide, his violent murder made him indignant, not yet avenged on his behalf by any that shares his shame; therefore, I guess, he went away without speaking to me, and by that has made me pity him the more."

So we talked, as far as the first place on the causeway that would have revealed the next valley right to its floor if it had been lighter. When we were above the last cloister of Malebolge, so that its lay brothers could be seen, many groans pierced me whose arrows were barbed with pity, at which I covered my ears with my hands. Such pain there was as there would be if the diseases in the hospitals of Valdichiana, Maremma, and Sardinia, between July and September, were all rife in one ditch: a stench arose from it such as issues from putrid limbs.

We descended on the last bank of the long causeway, again on the left, and then my sight was clearer, down to the depths where infallible Justice, the minister of the Lord on high, punishes the falsifiers that it accounts for here. I do not think it would have been a greater sadness to see the people of plague-ridden Aegina, when the air was so malignant that every animal, even the smallest worm, was killed, and afterwards, as poets say for certain, the ancient race was restored from the seed of ants, than it was to see the spirits languishing in scattered heaps through that dim valley. This one lay on its belly, that on the shoulders of the other, and some were crawling along the wretched path.

Step by step we went without a word, gazing at and listening to the sick who could not lift their bodies. I saw two sitting, leaning on each other, as one pan is leant to warm against another: they were marked with scabs from head to foot, and I never saw a stable lad his master waits for, or one who stays awake unwillingly, use a currycomb as fiercely as each of these two clawed himself with his nails, because of the intensity of their itching that has no other relief.

And so the nails dragged the scurf off, as a knife does the scales from bream, or other fish with larger scales. My guide began to speak: "O you who strip your chain-mail with your fingers and often make pincers of them, tell us if there are any Italians among those here inside—and may your nails be enough for that task for eternity." One of them replied, weeping: "We are both Italians whom you see so mutilated here, but who are you who inquire of us?" And the guide said: "I am one who with this living man descends from steep to steep and mean to show him Hell."

Then the mutual prop broke, and each one turned, trembling, towards me, along with others that heard him, by the echo.

The good Master addressed me directly, saying: "Tell them what you wish," and I began as he desired: "So that your memory will not fade from human minds in the first world but will live for many suns, tell us who you are, and of what race. Do not let your ugly and revolting punishment make you afraid to reveal yourselves to me."

The one replied: "I was Griffolino of Arezzo, and Albero of Siena had me burned, but what I died for did not send me here. It is true I said to him, jesting, 'I could lift myself into the air in flight,' and he who had great curiosity but little sense, wished me to show him that art; and only because I could not make him Daedalus, he caused me to be burned by one who looked on him as a son. But to the last chasm of the ten, Minos, who cannot err, condemned me, for the alchemy I practiced in the world."

And I said to the poet: "Now was there ever a people as vain as the Sienese? Certainly not the French, by far." At which the other leper, hearing me, replied to my words: "What of Stricca, who contrived to spend so little? and Niccolo, who first discovered the costly use of cloves, in that garden, Siena, where such seed takes root? and that company in which Caccia of Aciano threw away his vineyard, and his vast forest, and the Abbagliato showed his wit? But so that you may know who seconds you like this against the Sienese, sharpen your eye on me so that my face may reply to you: so you will see I am Capocchio's shadow, who made false metals by alchemy, and you must remember, if I know you rightly, how well I aped nature."

30

At the time when Juno was angry, as she had shown more than once, with the Theban race, because of Jupiter's affair with Semele, she so maddened King Athamas that, seeing his wife Ino go by carrying her two sons in her arms, he cried: "Spread the hunting nets so that I can take the lioness and her cubs, at the pass," and then stretched out his pitiless talons, snatching the one named Learchus and, whirling him around, dashed him against the rock; and Ino drowned herself and her other burden, Melicertes. And after fortune had brought down the high Trojan pride that dared all, so that Priam the king and his kingdom were destroyed, Queen Hecuba, a sad, wretched captive, having witnessed the sacrifice of Polyxena, alone on the seashore, when she recognized the body of her Polydorus, barked like a dog, driven out of her senses, so greatly had her sorrow racked her mind.

But neither Theban nor Trojan Furies were ever seen embodied so cruelly in stinging creatures, or even less in human limbs, as I saw displayed in two shades, pallid and naked, that ran, biting, as a hungry pig does, when he is driven out of his sty. The one came to Capocchio, and fixed his tusks in his neck so that, dragging him along, it made the solid floor rasp his belly. And the Aretine, Griffolino, who was left, said to me, trembling: "That goblin is Gianni Schicci, and he goes rabidly mangling others like that." I replied: "Oh, be pleased to tell us who the other is, before it snatches itself away and may it not plant its teeth in you."

And he to me: "That is the ancient spirit of incestuous Myrrha, who loved her father Cinyras with more than lawful love. She came to him and sinned, under cover of another's name, just as the one who is vanishing there undertook to disguise himself as Buoso Donati so as to gain the mare, called the Lady of the Herd, by forging a will and giving it legal form."

When the furious pair on whom I had kept my eye were gone, I turned to look at the other spirits, born to evil. I saw one who would have been shaped like a lute if he had only had his groin cut short, at the place where a man is forked. The heavy dropsy that swells the limbs with its badly transformed humors so that the face does not match the belly made him hold his lips apart, as the fevered patient does who, through thirst, curls one lip towards the chin, and the other upwards.

He said to us: "O you who are exempt from punishment in this grim world (and why, I do not know), look and attend to the misery of Master Adam. I had enough of what I wished when I was alive, and now, alas, I crave a drop of water. The little streams that fall from the green hills of Casentino down to the Arno, making cool, moist channels, are constantly in my mind, and not in vain, since the image of them parches me far more than the disease that wears the flesh from my face. The rigid justice that examines me takes its opportunity from the place where I sinned to give my sighs more rapid flight. That is Romena, where I counterfeited the coin of Florence, stamped with the Baptist's image; for that, on earth, I left my body, burned. But if I could see the wretched soul of Guido here, or Alessandro, or Aghinolfo, their brother, I would not exchange that sight for Branda's fountain. Guido is down here already, if the crazed spirits going around speak truly, but what use is it to me, whose limbs are tied? If I were only light enough to move, even an inch, every hundred years, I would already have started on the road to find him among this disfigured people, though it winds around eleven miles, and is no less than half a mile across. Because of them I am with such a crew; they induced me to stamp those florins that were adulterated with three carats alloy."

I said to him: "Who are those abject two, lying close to your right edge, and giving off smoke like a hand bathed in winter?"

He replied: "I found them here when I rained down into this trough, and they have not turned since then, and may never turn I believe. One is the false wife who accused Joseph. The other is lying Sinon, the Greek from Troy. A burning fever makes them stink so strongly." And Sinon, who perhaps took offense at being named so rudely, struck Adamo's rigid belly with his fist so that it resounded like a drum; and Master Adam struck him in the face with his arm, which seemed no softer, saying to him: "I have an arm free for such a situation, though I am kept from moving by my heavy limbs." At which Sinon answered: "You were not so ready with it, going to the fire, but as ready, and readier, when you were coining." And he of the dropsy: "You speak truth in that, but you were not so truthful a witness there, when you were questioned about the truth at Troy."

"If I spoke falsely, you falsified the coin," Sinon said, "and I am here for the one crime, but you for more than any other devil." He who had the swollen belly answered: "Think of the Wooden Horse, you liar, and let it be a torment to you that all the world knows of it." The Greek replied: "Let the thirst that cracks the tongue be your torture, and the foul water make your stomach a barrier in front of your eyes." Then the coiner: "Your mouth gapes wide as usual, to speak ill. If I have a thirst, and moisture swells me, you have the burning, and a head that hurts you; and you would not need many words of invitation to lap at the mirror of Narcissus."

I was standing, all intent on hearing them, when the Master said to me: "If you keep gazing much longer I will quarrel with you!" When I heard him speak to me in anger, I turned towards him with such a feeling of shame that it comes over me again, as I only think of it. And like someone who dreams of something harmful to them, and dreaming, wishes it were a dream, so that they long for what is, as if it were not; that I became, who, lacking power to speak, wished to make an excuse, and all the while did so, not thinking I was doing it.

My Master said: "Less shamefacedness would wash away a greater fault than yours, so unburden yourself of sorrow and know that I am always with you, should it happen that fate takes you where people are in similar conflict, since the desire to hear it is vulgar."

31

One and the same tongue at first wounded me, so that it painted both my cheeks with blushes, and then gave out the ointment for the wound. So I have heard the spear of Achilles, and his father Peleus, was the cause first of sadness, and then of a healing gift.

We turned our back on the wretched valley, crossing without a word, up by the bank that circles around it. Here was less darkness than night and less light than day, so that my vision showed only a little in front: but I heard a high-pitched horn sound so loudly that it would have made thunder seem quiet; it directed my eyes, which followed its passage back, straight to a single point. Roland did not sound his horn so fiercely after the sad rout, when Charlemagne had lost the holy war at Roncesvalles.

I had kept my head turned for a while in that direction, when I seemed to make out many high towers, at which I said: "Master, tell me what city this is?" And he to me: "Because your eyes traverse the darkness from too far away, it follows that you imagine wrongly. You will see quite plainly when you reach there how much the sense is deceived by distance, so press on more strongly." Then he took me lovingly by the hand, and said: "Before we go further, so that the reality might seem less strange to you, know that they are giants, not towers, and are in the pit from the navel downwards, all of them, around its bank."

As the eye when a mist is disappearing, gradually recreates what was hidden by the vapor thickening the air, so while approaching closer and closer to the brink, piercing through that gross, dark atmosphere, error left me, and my fear increased. As Montereggione crowns its round wall with towers, so the terrible giants, whom Jupiter still threatens from the Heavens when he thunders, turreted with half their bodies the bank that circles the well.

And I already saw the face of one, the shoulders, chest, the greater part of the belly, and the arms down both sides. When nature abandoned the art of making creatures like these, she certainly did well by removing such killers from warfare, and if she does not repent of making elephants and whales, whoever looks at the issue carefully considers her more prudent and more right in that, since where the instrument of mind is joined to ill will and power, men have no defense against it.

His face seemed to me as long and large as the bronze pine-cone in front of Saint Peter's in Rome, and his other features were in proportion, so that the bank that covered him from the middle onwards revealed so much of him above that three Frieslanders would have boasted in vain of reaching his hair, since I saw thirty large hand-spans of him down from the place where a man pins his cloak. The savage mouth, for which no sweeter hymns were fit, began to rave: "*Rafel may amech zabi almi*." And my guide turning to him, said: "Foolish spirit, stick to your hunting-horn, and vent your breath through that when rage or some other passion stirs you. Search around your neck, O confused soul, and you will find the belt where it is slung, and see that which arcs across your huge chest." Then he said to me: "He declares himself. This is Nimrod, through whose evil thought one language is no longer used throughout the whole world. Let us leave him standing here, and not speak to him in vain, since every language to him is like his to others, which no one understands."

So we went on, turning to the left, and a crossbow-shot away we found the next one, far larger and fiercer. Who and what the power might be that bound him, I cannot say, but he had his right arm pinioned behind, and the other in front, by a chain that held him tight from the neck down and, on the visible part of him, reached its fifth turn. My guide said: "This proud spirit had the will to try his strength against high Jupiter, and so has this reward. Ephialtes is his name, and he made the great attempt when the giants made the gods fear, and the arms he shook then, now he never moves."

And I said to him: "If it were possible, I would wish my eyes to light on vast Briareus." To which he replied: "You will see Antaeus, nearby, who speaks and is unchained, and will set us down in the deepest abyss of guilt. He whom you wish to see is far beyond, and is formed and bound like this one, except he seems more savage in his features." No huge earthquake ever shook a tower as violently as Ephialtes promptly shook himself. Then I feared death more than ever, and the fear alone would have been enough to cause it had I not seen his chains.

We then went further on and reached Antaeus, who projected

twenty feet from the pit, not including his head. The Master spoke: "O you who of old took a thousand lions for your prey in the fateful valley, near Zama, that made Scipio heir to glory when Hannibal retreated with his army; you, through whom it might still be believed the giant sons of Earth would have overcome the gods if you had been at the great war with your brothers; set us down, and do not be shy to do it, where the cold imprisons the river Cocytus, in the Ninth Circle. Do not make us ask Tityos or Typhon. Bend, and do not curl your lips in scorn; this man can give that which is longed for, here: he can refresh your fame on earth, since he is alive and still expects long life, if grace does not call him to her before his time." So the Master spoke, and Antaeus quickly stretched out both hands from which Hercules of old once felt the power, and seized my guide. Virgil, when he felt his grasp, said to me: "Come here, so that I may carry you." Then he made one bundle of himself and me.

To me, who stood watching to see Antaeus stoop, he seemed as the leaning tower at Bologna appears to the view, under the leaning side, when a cloud is passing over it, and it hangs in the opposite direction. It was such a terrible moment I would have wished to have gone by another route, but he set us down gently in the deep that swallowed Lucifer and Judas, and did not linger there, bent, but straightened himself, like a mast raised in a boat.

32

If I had words rough and hoarse enough to fit the dismal chasm on which all the other rocky cliffs weigh and converge, I would squeeze out the juice of my imagination more completely; but since I have not, I bring myself, not without fear, to describe the place: to tell of the pit of the Universe is not a task to be taken up lightly, nor in a language that has words like "mommy" and "daddy." But may the Muses, those ladies who helped Amphion shut Thebes behind its walls, aid my speech so that my words may not vary from the truth.

O you people, created evil beyond all others, in this place that is hard to speak of, it were better if you had been sheep or goats here on earth! When we were down inside the dark well, beneath the giants' feet, and much lower, and I was still staring at the steep cliff I heard a voice say to me: "Take care as you pass, so that you do not tread with your feet on the heads of the wretched, weary brothers." At which I turned, and saw a lake in front of me and underneath my feet that, because of the cold, appeared like glass not water.

The Danube in Austria never formed so thick a veil for its winter course, nor the Don, far off under the frozen sky, as was here: if Mount Tambernic in the east, or Mount Pietrapana had fallen on it, it would not have even creaked at the margin. And as frogs sit croaking with their muzzles above water at the time when peasant women often dream of gleaning, so the sad shadows sat in the ice, livid to where the blush of shame appears, chattering with their teeth like storks. Each one held his face turned down; the cold is witnessed amongst them by their mouths, and their sad hearts by their eyes.

When I had looked around awhile, turning to my feet I saw two so compressed together that the hair of their heads was intermingled. I said: "Tell me, you who press your bodies together so: who are you?" And they twisted their necks up, and when they had lifted their faces towards me, their eyes, which were only moist, inwardly, before, gushed at the lids, and the frost iced fast the tears between them, and sealed them up again. No vise ever clamped wood to wood as firmly, so that they butted one another like two he-goats, overcome by such rage. And one, who had lost both ears to the cold, with his face still turned down, said: "Why are you staring at us so fiercely? If you want to know who these two are, they are the degli Alberti, Allesandro and Napoleone: the valley where the Bisenzio runs down was theirs and their father Alberto's. They issued from one body, and you can search the whole Caïna and will not find shades more worthy of being set in ice; not even Mordred, whose chest and shadow were pierced at one blow by his father King Arthur's lance; nor Focaccia; nor this one, who obstructs my face with his head so that I cannot see further, who was named Sassol Mascheroni. If you are a Tuscan, now you know truly what he was. And so that you do not put me to more speech, know that I am Camicion de' Pazzi and am waiting for Carlino, my kinsman, to outdo me."

Afterwards I saw a thousand faces, made doglike by the cold, at which a trembling overcomes me, and always will, when I think of the frozen fords. And whether it was will, or fate, or chance, I do not know, but walking among the heads I struck my foot violently against one face. Weeping, it cried out to me: "Why do you trample on me? If you do not come to increase the revenge for Montaperti, why do you trouble me?"

And I: "My Master, wait here for me now, so that I can rid myself of a doubt concerning him, then you can make as much haste as you please." The Master stood, and I said to that shade that still reviled me bitterly: "Who are you, who reproach others in this way?"

"No, who are you," he answered, "who go through the Antenora striking the faces of others, in such a way that if you were alive, it would be an insult?"

I replied: "I am alive, and if you long for fame, it might be a precious thing to you if I put your name among the others."

And he to me: "I long for the opposite: take yourself off, and annoy me no more since you little know how to flatter on this icy slope."

Then I seized him by the back of the scalp, and said: "You need to name yourself before there is not a hair left on your head!"

At which he said to me: "Even if you pluck me, I will not tell you who I am, nor demonstrate it to you, though you tear at my head a thousand times."

I already had his hair coiled in my hand, and had pulled away more than one tuft of it while he barked and kept his eyes down when another spirit cried: "What is wrong with you, Bocca, is it not enough that you chatter with your jaws, but you have to bark too? What devil is at you?"

I said: "Now, accursed traitor, I do not want you to speak, since I will carry true news of you, to your shame." He answered: "Go, and say what you please, but if you get out from here, do not be silent about him who had his tongue so ready just now. Here he regrets taking French silver. You can say, 'I saw Buoso de Duera, there where the sinners stand caught in the ice.' If you are asked who else was there, you have Tesauro de' Beccheria, whose throat was slit by Florence. Gianni de' Soldanier is further on, with Ganelon, and Tribaldello, who unbarred the gate of Faenza while it slept."

We had already left him when I saw two spirits frozen in a hole, so close together that the one head capped the other, and the uppermost set his teeth into the other, as bread is chewed, out of hunger, there where the back of the head joins the nape. Tydeus gnawed the head of Menalippus, no differently, out of rage, than this one the skull and other parts.

I said: "O you who in such a brutal way inflict the mark of your hatred on him, whom you devour, tell me why—on condition that, if you complain of him with reason, I, knowing who you are, and his offense, may repay you still in the world above, if the tongue I speak with is not withered."

33

That sinner raised his mouth from the savage feast, wiping it on the hair of the head he had stripped behind. Then he began: "You wish me to renew desperate grief that wrings my heart at the very thought, before I even tell of it. But if my words are to be the seed that bears fruit in the infamy of the traitor whom I gnaw, you will see me speak and weep together. I do not know who you are, nor by what means you have come down here, but as I hear you, you seem to me, in truth, a Florentine. You must know that I am Count Ugolino, and this is the Archbishop Ruggieri. Now I will tell you why I am a neighbor such as this to him. It is not necessary to say that, confiding in him, I was taken through the effects of his evil schemes, and afterwards killed. But what you cannot have learnt—how cruel my death was—you will hear, and know if he has injured me.

"A narrow hole inside that tower that is called Famine, from my death, and in which others must yet be imprisoned, had already shown me several moons through its opening when I slept an evil sleep that tore the curtain of the future for me. This man seemed to me the lord, and master, chasing the wolf and its whelps on Monte di San Guiliano, which blocks the view of Lucca from the Pisans. He had the Gualandi, Sismondi, and Lanfranchi running with him, with hounds slender, keen, and agile. After a short chase the father and his sons seemed weary to me, and I thought I saw their flanks torn by sharp teeth. When I woke, before dawn, I heard my sons, who were with me, crying in their sleep, and asking for food. You are truly cruel if you do not sorrow already at the thought of what my heart presaged, and if you do not weep, what do you weep at? They were awake now, and the hour nearing at which our food used to be brought to us, and each of us was anxious from dreaming, when below I heard the door of the terrible tower locked up, at which I gazed into the faces of my sons, without saying a word. I did not weep: I grew like stone inside; they wept, and my little Anselm said to me: 'Father you stare so, what is wrong?' But I shed no tears, and did not answer, all that day, or the next night, till another sun rose over the world. When a little ray of light was sent into the mournful jail, and I saw in their four faces the aspect of my own, I bit my hands from grief. And they, thinking that I did it from hunger, suddenly stood, and said: 'Father, it will give us less pain if you gnaw at us; you put this miserable flesh on us, now strip it off again.'

"Then I calmed myself, in order not to make them more unhappy; that day and the next we all were silent. Ah, solid earth, why did you not open? When we had come to the fourth day, Gaddo threw himself down at my feet, saying: 'My father, why do you not help me?' There he died, and even as you see me, I saw the three others fall one by one, between the fifth and sixth days, at which, already blind, I took to groping over each of them, and called out to them for three days, when they were dead: then fasting, at last, had power to overcome grief."

When he had spoken this, he seized the wretched skull again with his teeth, which were as strong as a dog's on the bone, his eyes distorted. Ah Pisa, shame among the people, of the lovely land where "sì" is heard, let the isles of Caprara and Gorgona shift and block the Arno at its mouth, since your neighbors are so slow to punish you, so that it may drown every living soul. Since if Count Ugolino had the infamy of having betrayed your castles, you ought not to have put his sons to the torture. Their youth made Uguccione and Brigata, and the other two my words above have named, innocents, you modern Thebes.

We went further on, where the rugged frost encases another people, not bent down but reversed completely. The very weeping there prevents them weeping, and the grief that makes an impediment to their sight turns inward to increase their agony since the first tears form a knot, and like a crystal visor, fill the cavities below their eyebrows. And though all feeling had left my face, through the cold, as though from a callus, it seemed to me now as if I felt a breeze, at which I said: "Master, what causes this? Is the heat not all quenched here below?" At which he said to me: "Soon you will be where your own eyes will answer that, seeing the source that generates the air."

And one of the sad shadows in the icy crust cried out to us: "O spirits, so cruel that the last place of all is reserved for you, remove the solid veils from my face that I might vent the grief a little that chokes my heart, before the tears freeze again." At which I said to him: "If you would have my help, tell me who you are, and if I do not disburden you, may I have to journey to the depths of the ice."

He replied to that: "I am Friar Alberigo, I am he of the fruits of the evil garden, who here receive dates made of ice, to match my figs."

I said to him: "O, are you dead already?"

And he to me: "How my body stands in the world above, I do not know, such is the power of this Ptolomaea, that the soul often falls down here before Atropos cuts the thread. And so that you may more willingly clear the frozen tears from your face, know that when the soul betrays, as mine did, her body is taken from her by a demon, there and then, who rules it after that, till its time is complete. She falls, plunging down to this well, and perhaps the body of this other shade that winters here behind me is still visible in the world above. You must know it, if you have only now come down here: it is Ser Branca d'Oria, and many years have passed since he was imprisoned here."

I said to him: "I believe you are lying to me: Branca d'Oria is not dead, and eats and drinks, and sleeps, and puts on his clothes."

He said: "Michel Zanche had not yet arrived in the ditch of the Malebranche above, there where the tenacious pitch boils, when this man left a devil in his place in his own body, and one in the body of his kinsman who committed the treachery with him. But reach your hand here: open my eyes." But I did not open them for him, for it was a courtesy to be rude to him.

Ah, Genoese, men divorced from all morality and filled with every corruption, why are you not dispersed from the earth? I found the worst spirit of Romagna was one of you, who for his actions even now bathes as a soul, in Cocytus, and still seems alive on earth, in his own body.

34

"*The banners of the King of Hell advance toward us*, so look in front of you to see if you can see him," said my Master. I seemed to see a tall structure, like a mill the wind turns seems from a distance when a dense mist breathes, or when night falls in our hemisphere, and I shrank back behind my guide because of the wind, since there was no other shelter.

I had already come, and with fear I put it into words, where the souls were completely enclosed, and shone through like straw in glass. Some are lying down, some stand upright, one on its head, another on the soles of its feet, another bent head to foot, like a bow.

When we had gone on far enough that my guide was able to show me Lucifer, the monster who was once so fair, he removed himself from me and made me stop, saying: "Behold Dis, and behold the place where you must arm yourself with courage." Reader, do not ask how chilled and hoarse I became then—I do not write it since all words would fail to tell it. I did not die, yet I was not alive. Think yourself, now, if you have a grain of imagination, what I became, deprived of either state.

The emperor of the sorrowful kingdom stood, waist upwards, from the ice, and I am nearer to a giant in size than the giants are to one of his arms: think how great the whole is that corresponds to such a part. If he was once as fair as he is now ugly, and lifted up his forehead against his Maker, well may all evil flow from him. O how great a wonder it seemed to me when I saw three faces on his head! The one in front was fiery red; the other two were joined to it, above the center of each shoulder, and linked at the top, and the righthand one seemed whitish-yellow; the left was black to look at, like those who come from where the Nile rises. Under each face sprang two vast wings, of a size fit for such a bird: I never saw ship's sails as wide. They had no feathers, but were like a bat's in form and texture, and he was flapping them so that three winds blew out away from him, by which all Cocytus was frozen. He wept from six eyes, and tears and bloody spume gushed down three chins.

He chewed a sinner between his teeth with every mouth, like a grinder, so in that way he kept three of them in torment. To the one in front, the biting was nothing compared to the tearing, since at times, his back was left completely stripped of skin. The Master said: "That soul up there that suffers the greatest punishment, he who has his head inside and flails his legs outside, is Judas Iscariot. Of the other two who have their heads hanging downwards, the one who hangs from the face that is black is Brutus—see how he writhes and does not utter a word—and the other is Cassius, who seems so long in limb. But night is ascending, and now we must go, since we have seen it all."

I clasped his neck as he wished, and he seized the time and place, and when the wings were wide open, grasped Satan's shaggy sides, and then from tuft to tuft, climbed down, between the matted hair and frozen crust. When we had come to where the thigh joint turns, just at the swelling of the haunch, my guide, with effort and difficulty, reversed his head to where his feet had been, and grabbed the hair like a climber, so that I thought we were dropping back to Hell. "Hold tight," said my guide, panting like a man exhausted, "since by these stairs, we must depart from all this evil." Then he clambered into an opening in the rock, and set me down to sit on its edge, then turned his cautious step towards me.

I raised my eyes, thinking to see Lucifer as I had left him, but saw him with his legs projecting upwards, and let those denser people, who do not see what point I had passed, judge if I was confused then, or not.

My Master said: "Get up on your feet; the way is long, and difficult the road, and the sun already returns to dawn." Where we stood was no palace hall, but a natural cell with a rough floor, and short of light. When I had risen, I said: "My Master, before I leave the abyss, speak to me a while, and lead me out of error. Where is the ice? And why is this monster fixed upside-down? And how has the sun moved from evening to dawn in so short a time?"

And he to me: "You imagine you are still on the other side of the earth's center, where I caught hold of the Evil Worm's hair, he who pierces the world. You *were* on that side of it, as long as I climbed down, but when I reversed myself, you passed the point to which weight is drawn, from everywhere, and are now below the hemisphere opposite that which covers the wide dry land, and opposite that under whose zenith the Man was crucified who was born, and lived, without sin. You have your feet on a little sphere that forms the other side of the Judecca. Here it is morning, when it is evening there, and he who made a ladder for us of his hair is still as he was before. He fell from Heaven on this side of the earth, and the land that projected here before veiled itself with the ocean for fear of him, and entered our hemisphere; and that which now projects on this side left an empty space here, and shot outwards, maybe in order to escape from him."

Down there is a space, as far from Beelzebub as his cave extends, not known by sight, but by the sound of a stream falling through it along the bed of rock it has hollowed out, into a winding course, and a slow incline. The guide and I entered by that hidden path, to return to the clear world; and, not caring to rest, we climbed up, he first, and I second, until, through a round opening, I saw the beautiful things that the sky holds, and we issued out from there to see again the stars.

PURGATORY

1

The little boat of my intellect now sets sail to course through gentler waters, leaving behind her a sea so cruel. And I will sing of that second region, where the human spirit is purged and becomes fit to climb to Heaven. But since I am yours, O sacred Muses, here let dead poetry rise again, and here let Calliope sound for a moment, accompanying my words with that mode that so overwhelmed the Pierides they despaired of pardon.

The sweet color of eastern sapphire that gathered on the sky's clear forehead, pure as far as the first sphere, restored delight to my eyes as soon as I had issued from the dead air, which constrained my eyes and heart. The lovely planet that encourages us to love was making the whole east smile, veiling the Fishes that escorted her. I turned to the right and fixed my mind on the southern pole, where I saw four stars never seen until now, except by the first peoples. The sky seemed to be joyful at their fires. O widowed northern region, denied the sight of them!

When I had finished gazing at them and turned a little towards the other pole, there where Boötes had already vanished, I saw a solitary old man, with a face worthy of such great reverence that no son owes his father more. He wore his beard long, flecked with white like his hair, of which a double strand fell to his chest. The rays of the four sacred stars filled his face with such brightness that I saw him as if the sun were in front of him.

Stirring that noble plumage, he said: "Who are you, who have fled the eternal prison against the dark stream? Who has led you, or who was a light to you, issuing out of that profound night that always blackens the infernal valley? Are the laws of the abyss shattered, or is there some new counsel taken in Heaven that you come to my mountain, being damned?"

Then my leader took hold of me and made me do reverence with my knees and forehead, using his words and hand. Then he replied: "I did not come of my own will. A Lady came down from Heaven and, because of her prayers, I helped this man with my companionship. But since it is your wish that more be told about our true state, it cannot be my wish to deny you. He has never witnessed the last hour, but, because of his folly, was so near it that there was little time left for him to alter. As I said, I was sent to rescue him, and there was no other path but this, along which I have come. I have shown him all the sinful people, and now intend to show him those spirits that purge themselves in your care. It would be a long tale to tell, how I have brought him here: virtue descends from above, which helps me to guide him, to see and to hear you. Now, let it please you to grace his coming here: he seeks freedom, which is so dear to us, as he knows who gives his life for it. You know, since death was not bitter to you in Utica for its sake, where you left the body that will shine so bright at the great day. The eternal law is not violated by us, since he lives, and Minos does not bind me; but I am of the circle where the chaste eyes of your Marcia are, who in her aspect begs you, O sacred one, to hold her as your own: lean towards us, for love of her. Allow us to go through your seven regions. I will report to her our gratitude to you if you deign to be mentioned there below."

He then replied: "Marcia was so pleasing to my eyes while I was over there that I performed every grace she asked of me. Now that she is beyond the evil stream, she can move me no longer, by the law that was made when I issued out. But there is no need for flattery; if a Heavenly lady moves and directs you, let it be sufficient that you ask me in her name. Go, and see that you tie a smooth rush round this man, and bathe his face so that all foulness is wiped away, since it is not right to go in front of the first minister of those who are in Paradise with eyes darkened by any mist. This little island nurtures rushes in the soft mud all around it, from deep to deep, where the wave beats on it. No other plant that puts out leaves or stiffens can live there, because it would not give way to the buffeting. Then, do not return this way; the sun that is now rising will show you where to climb the mountain in an easier ascent."

So he left: and I rose without speaking, and drew back towards my leader, and fixed my eyes on him. He began: "Son, follow my steps: let us turn back, since the plain slopes down this way to its low shore." The dawn was vanquishing the breath of morning, which fled before her so that, from afar, I recognized the tremor of the sea.

We walked along the solitary plain, like those who turn again towards a lost road and seem to wander in vain until they reach it. When we came where the dew fights with the sunlight, being in a place where it disperses slowly in the cool air, my Master gently placed both outspread hands on the sweet grass, at which I, apprehending his intention, raised my tear-stained face towards him: there he made my true color visible, which Hell had hidden.

Then we came to the deserted shore that never saw a man sail its waters who could afterwards experience his return. There he tied the rush around me, as the other wished. Miraculous to tell, as he pulled out the humble plant it was suddenly replaced where he tore it.

2

The sun had already reached the horizon, whose meridian circle at the zenith covers Jerusalem, and night, which circles opposite him, was rising out of Ganges with the Scales, which fall from night's hand when the days shorten, so that where I was the pale and rosy cheeks of beautiful Aurora, through age, were turned deep orange.

We were still near the ocean, like people who think about their journey, leaving in spirit while remaining in body, and behold, as Mars reddens through the heavy vapours low in the west over the waves at the coming of dawn, so a light appeared (and may I see it yet) coming over the sea, so rapidly that no flight equals its movement, and when I had taken my eyes from it for a moment to question my guide, I saw it once more grown bigger and brighter. Then something white appeared on each side of it, and little by little another whiteness emerged from underneath it.

My Master still did not say a word until the first whitenesses were discovered to be wings; then, when he recognized the pilot clearly, he cried: "Kneel, bend your knees: behold the Angel of God. Clasp your hands: from now on you will see such ministers. See how he disdains all human mechanism, not needing oars or any sails but his wings between such far shores. See how he has them turned towards the sky, beating the air with eternal plumage that does not moult like mortal feathers."

Then as the divine bird approached nearer and nearer to us, it appeared much brighter—my eyes could not sustain its closeness so I looked down—and it came towards the shore in a vessel so quick and light that it skimmed the waves. At the stern stood the celestial steersman, who seemed to have blessedness written in his features, and more than a hundred souls sat inside. They all sang, together with one voice: "*When Israel went out of Egypt . . .*" and the rest of the psalm that comes after. Then he made the sign of the sacred cross towards them, at which they all flung themselves on shore, and as quickly as he came, he departed.

The crowd that was left behind seemed unfamiliar with the place, looking around like those who experience something new. The sun, which had chased Capricorn from the height of Heaven with his bright arrows, was shooting out the light on every side when the new people raised their faces towards us, saying: "If you know, show us the way to reach the mountain." And Virgil answered: "You may think we know this place, but we are strangers, as you are. We came just now, a little while before you, by another route so difficult and rough that the climbing ahead us will seem like play to us."

The spirits, who had noticed I was still alive by my breathing, grew pale with wonder, and as the crowd draws near the messenger who carries the olive-branch and no one is wary of trampling on others, so those spirits, each one fortunate, fixed their gaze on my face, almost forgetting to go and make themselves blessed. I saw one of them move forward to embrace me with such great affection that he stirred me to do the same. O vain shades, empty except in aspect! My hands met three times behind him, and returned as often empty to my breast. I paled with wonder, I believe, at which the shade smiled and drew back, and I hurried forward, following. It asked me gently to pause; then I knew who it was and begged him to stop a while and speak to me. He replied: "Just as I loved you in the mortal body, so I love you freed; so I stay, but you, where are you going?"

I said: "My dear Casella, I make this journey in order to return here again, where I am; but how have so many hours been stolen from you?"

And he to me: "If he who carries whom he pleases when he pleases has denied me this crossing many times, no wrong is done to me, since his will is full of justice. In truth, for three months past, since the beginning of the Jubilee, he has taken in all peace those who wish to enter. So I, who was on the shore where Tiber's stream becomes saltwater, was accepted by him, in kindness. He has set his winged course to that river-mouth now, because those who do not sink to Acheron are always gathering there."

And I: "If some new law has not taken your memory or your skill in that song of love that used to calm all my desires, may it please you to console my spirit a while with it, my spirit that, coming here in its own person, suffers so." He then began to sing: "*Love that in my mind reasons with me*," so sweetly that the sweetness of it sounds in me yet.

My Master and I, as well as the people who were with him, seemed so delighted that they thought of nothing else. We were all focused and intent on his notes when, behold, the venerable old man cried: "What is this, tardy spirits? What negligence, what idling is this? Run to the mountain, and strip the scales from your eyes that prevent God being revealed to you."

As doves gathering corn or seeds, collected at their meal, quietly and without their usual pride stop pecking instantly if anything frightful appears, since they are troubled by a more important concern, so I saw that new crowd abandon the singing and move towards the hillside like those who leave without knowing where they will wind up; nor was our departure slower.

3

Although their sudden flight was scattering them over the plain, turning toward the mountain where reason examines us, I drew close to my faithful companion; and how would I have fared without him? Who would have brought me to the mountain?

He seemed to me to be gnawed by self-reproach. O clear and noble conscience, how sharply a little fault stings you! When his feet had slowed from that pace that spoils the dignity of every action, my mind, which was inwardly focused before, widened its intent as if on a quest, and I set my face to the hillside that rises highest towards Heaven from the water. The sunlight that flamed red behind us was broken in front of me in that shape in which I blocked its rays. I turned aside from fear of being abandoned, seeing the earth darkened only in front of me.

But my comforter began speaking to me, turning straight around: "Why so mistrustful? Do you think you are not with me, or that I do not guide you? It is already evening there, where the body with which I cast a shadow lies buried: Naples has it, and it was taken from Brindisi. If no shadow goes before me now, do not wonder at that any more than at the Heavenly spheres, where one does not hide the light of any other. That power, which does not will that its workings should be revealed to us, disposes bodies such as these to suffer torments, fire and ice. He is foolish who hopes that our reason may journey on the infinite road that one substance in three persons owns. Stay content, human race, with the '*what*': since if you had been able to understand it all, there would have been no need for Mary to give birth, and you have seen the fruitless desire, granted to them as an eternal sorrow, of those whose desire would have been quenched—I mean Aristotle, Plato, and many more." And here he bent his head, and said nothing more, remaining troubled.

Meanwhile we reached the mountain's foot; there we found the cliff was so steep that even nimble feet would be useless. The most desolate, and the most solitary track, between Lerici and Turbia in

Liguria is a free and easy stair compared to that. My Master, halting his feet, said: "Now who knows which way the cliff slopes, so that he who goes without wings may climb?" And while he kept his eyes downwards, searching out the way in his mind, and while I was gazing up across the rocks, a crowd of spirits appeared to me on the left, who moved their feet towards us but did not seem to, they came so slowly.

I said: "Master, look up, behold one there who will give us advice, if you cannot give it yourself." He looked at them, and with a joyful face answered: "Let us go there, since they come slowly, and confirm your hopes, kind son." That crowd was still as far off, after a thousand paces of ours I mean, as a good thrower would reach with a stone when they all pressed close to the solid rock of the high cliff and stood motionless together, as people who travel in fear stop to look around.

Virgil began: "O spirits who ended well, already chosen by the same peace that, I believe, is awaited by you all, tell us where the mountain slopes allow us to go upwards, since lost time troubles those most who know most." As sheep come out of their pen in ones, twos, and threes, and others stand timidly with eyes and nose towards the ground, and what the first does, the others also do, huddling to her if she stands still, foolish and quiet, and not knowing why, so I saw then the head of that fortunate flock, of modest aspect, and dignified movement, make a move to come forward.

When those in front saw the light on the hillside broken on my right by my shadow falling from me as far as the rock, they stopped and drew back a little, and all the others that came after them did the same, not understanding why. My Master said: "Without your asking, I admit to you that this is a human body that you see, by which the sunlight is broken on the ground. Do not wonder, but believe that he does not try to climb this wall without the help of power that comes from Heaven." And the worthy people said: "Turn, then, and go in front of us," making a gesture with the backs of their hands.

And one of them began to speak: "You, whoever you are, turn your face as we travel, and think if you ever saw me over there." I turned towards him, and looked hard: he was blond and handsome, and of noble aspect, but a blow had split one of his eyebrows. When I had humbly denied ever seeing him, he said: "Now look," and he showed me a wound at the top of his chest. Then, smiling, he said: "I am Manfred, grandson of the Empress Constance, and I beg you, when you return, go to my lovely daughter, Costanza, mother of James and Frederick, Sicily's and Aragon's pride, and tell her this truth, if things are said differently there. After my body had been pierced by two mortal wounds, I rendered my spirit to Him who pardons willingly. My sins were terrible, but infinite goodness has such a wide embrace it accepts all those who turn to it. If the bishop of Cozenza, who was set on by Clement to hound me, had read that page of God's rightly, the bones of my corpse would still be at the bridgehead by Benevento, under the guardianship of the heavy cairn. Now the rain bathes them and the wind moves them, beyond the kingdom, along the river Verde, where he carried them with quenched tapers. But no one is so lost by the malediction of that excommunication that eternal love may not turn back to him, as long as hope is green. It is true that those who die disobedient to the Holy Church, even though they repent at the end, must remain outside this bank for thirty times the duration of their life of insolence, unless such decree is shortened by the prayers of the good. See now if you can give me delight by telling my good Costanza how you saw me, and also of my ban, since much benefit arises here through the prayers of those who are still over there."

4

When the soul is wholly centered on one of our senses, because of some pleasure or pain that it comprehends, it seems that it pays no attention to its other powers, and this contradicts the error that one soul is kindled on another, inside us. So when something is seen or heard that holds the soul's attention strongly fixed, time vanishes and man is unaware of it, since one power notices time, and another occupies the entire soul: the former is as if constrained, the latter free. I had a genuine experience of this while listening to that spirit and marveling, since the sun had climbed fully fifty degrees and I had not noticed it when we came to where those souls, with a single voice, cried out to us: "Here is what you wanted."

When the grape is ripening, the peasant often hedges up a larger opening with a little forkful of thorns than the gap through which my leader climbed, and I behind him, two alone, after the group had parted from us. You can walk at Sanleo, near Urbino, and descend to Noli, near Savone; you can climb Mount Bismantova, south of Reggio, up to the summit, on foot; but here a man had to fly—I mean with the feathers and swift wings of great desire, behind that leader who gave me hope and made himself a light.

We were climbing inside a rock gully where the cliff pressed against us on either side, and the ground under us needed hands as well as feet. Once we were on the upper edge of the high wall, out on the open hillside, I said: "My Master, which way should we go?" And he to me: "Do not let your steps drift downward, always wind your way up the mountain behind me, until some wise escort appears to us."

The summit was so high it was beyond my sight, and the slope far steeper than the forty-five degrees a line from mid-quadrant makes with the circle's radius. I felt weary, and began to say: "O sweet father, turn and see how I am left behind if you do not stop." He said: "My son, make yourself reach there," showing me a terrace a little higher up that goes around the whole mountain on that side. His words

spurred me on greatly, and I forced myself on, so far creeping after
him that the ledge was beneath my feet.

There we both sat down, turning towards the east, from which we
had climbed, since it often cheers men to look back. I first fixed my
eyes on the shore below, then raised them to the sun, and wondered
at the fact that it struck us on the left side. The poet saw clearly that I
was totally amazed at that chariot of light rising between us and the
north, at which he said to me: "If that mirror, the sun, which reflects
the light from above downwards, were in Castor and Pollux you would
see the Zodiac, glowing around him, circle still closer to the Bears,
unless it wandered from its ancient track. If you wish the power to see
that for yourself, imagine Mount Zion, at Jerusalem, and this mountain placed on the globe so that both have the same horizon, but are
in opposite hemispheres, by which you can see, if your intellect understands quite clearly, that the sun's path, which Phaëthon sadly did not
know how to follow, has to pass to the north here when it passes Zion
on the south."

I said: "Certainly, Master, I never saw as clearly as I now discern
there, where my mind seemed at fault, that the median circle of the
Heavenly motion that is called the Equator in one of the sciences, and
always lies between the summer and the winter solstice, is as far north
here for the reason you say as the Hebrews saw it, towards the hot
countries. But if it please you, I would willingly like to know how far
we have to go, since the hillside rises higher than my eyes can reach."

And he to me: "This mountain is such that it is always trouble-
some at the start, below, but the higher one climbs, the less it wearies.
So you will feel at the end of this track, when it will seem so pleasant
to you, that the ascent is as easy as going downstream in a boat. Hope
to rest your weariness there. I answer you no more, and this I know is
true."

And when he had his say, a voice sounded nearby: "Perhaps, before
then, you may have need to sit." At the sound of it, we each turned
around and saw a great mass of rock on the left that neither he nor I
had noticed before. We drew near it, and there were people lounging
in the shade behind the crag, just as one settles oneself to rest out of
laziness. And one of them, who seemed weary to me, was sitting and
clasping his knees, holding his head down low between them.

I said: "O my sweet sire, set your eyes on that one, who appears
lazier than if Sloth were his sister." Then he turned to us and listened,
lifting only his face above his thigh, and said: "Now go on up, you

who are so steadfast." Then I knew who he was, and that effort, which still constrained my breath a little, did not prevent me going up to him; when I had reached him, he hardly lifted his head to say: "Have you truly understood why the sun drives his chariot to the left?" His indolent actions and the terse words moved me to smile a little, then I began: "Belacqua, I do not grieve for you now, but tell me why you are sitting here? Are you waiting for a guide, or have you merely resumed your former habit?"

And he: "Brother, what use is it to climb? God's winged angel, who sits at the gate, will not let me pass through to the torments. First the sky must revolve around me outside for as long a time as it did in my life, because I delayed my sighs of healing repentance to the end—unless, before then, some prayer aids me that might rise from a heart that lives in grace; what is the rest worth if it is not heard in Heaven?"

And the poet was already climbing in front of me, saying: "Come on now, you see the sun touches the zenith, and night's feet have already run from the banks of the Ganges to Morocco."

5

I had already parted from those shadows and was following my leader's footsteps when someone behind me, pointing his finger, called out: "See, the light does not seem to shine on the left of him, below, and he seems to carry himself like a living man." I turned my eyes at the sound of these words and saw them all gazing in wonder, at me alone, at me alone and at the broken sunlight.

My Master said: "Why is your mind so ensnared that you slacken your pace? What does it matter to you what they whisper here? Follow me close behind, and let the people talk; stand like a steady tower that never shakes at the top in the blasts of wind, since the man in whom thought rises on thought sets himself back, because the force of the one weakens the other." What could I answer, except: "I come?" This I said, blushing a little, with that color that often makes someone worthy of being pardoned.

Meanwhile, across the mountain slope, a crowd a little in front of us came chanting the *Miserere*, alternately, verse by verse. When they saw I allowed no passage to the sun's rays because of my body, they changed their chant to a long, hoarse "Oh!" and two of them ran to meet us as messengers and demanded: "Inform us of your state." And my Master said: "You can go back and tell those who sent you that this man's body is truly flesh. If they stopped at seeing his shadow, as I think, that answer is enough: let them honor him and he may be precious to them."

I never saw burning mists at fall of night, or August clouds at sunset split the bright sky so quickly, but they in less time returned up the slope and arrived there while the others wheeled around us, like a troop of cavalry riding with loosened reins. The poet said: "This crowd that presses us is large, and they come to beg you, but go straight on, and listen while you go."

They came, crying: "O spirit who goes to joy with the limbs you were born with, tarry a while. Look and see if you ever knew one of us, so that you can bear news of him, over there. Oh, why are you leaving?

Oh, why do you not stay? We were all killed by violence, and were sinners till the last hour; then light from Heaven warned us, so that, repenting and forgiving, we left life reconciled with God, who fills us with desire to see Him."

And I: "However much I gaze at your faces, I recognize no one; but if I can do anything to please you, spirits born for happiness, speak and I will do it, for the sake of that peace that makes me chase after it, from world to world, following the steps of such a guide."

And one began to speak: "Each of us trusts in your good offices, without your oath, if only lack of power does not thwart your will. So I, who merely speak before others do, beg you to be gracious to me in your prayers at Fano, if ever you see that country again that lies between Romagna and Charles the Second's Naples, so that the good may be adored through me and I can purge myself of grave offense. I sprang from there, but the deep wounds from which the blood flowed that bathed my life were dealt me in the embrace of Paduans, those Antenori there, where I thought that I was safest. Azzo of Este had it done, he who held a greater anger against me than justice merited. Though, if I had fled towards La Mira, when I was surprised at Oriaco, I would still be over there, where men breathe. I ran to the marshes, and the reeds and mire swamped me so that I fell, and there I saw a pool grow on the ground from my veins."

Then another said: "Oh, so the desire might be satisfied that draws you up the high mountain, aid mine with kind pity. I was from Montefeltro, I am Buonconte; Giovanna has no care for me, nor the others, so I go among these, with bowed head."

And I to him: "What violence or mischance made you wander so far from Campaldino that your place of burial was never known?"

He replied: "Oh, at the foot of Casentino, a stream crosses it called the Archiano, which rises in the Apennines, above the Monastery of Camoldoli. There, at Bibbiena, where its name is lost in the Arno, I arrived, pierced in the throat, fleeing on foot, and bloodying the plain. There I lost my vision, and ended my words on Mary's name, and there I fell, and only my flesh was left. I will speak truly, and do you repeat it among the living: the angel of God took me and one from Hell cried: 'O you from Heaven, why do you rob me? You may carry off the eternal part of this man from here because of one little teardrop of repentance that snatches him from me, but I will deal differently with the other part.' You well know how damp vapor collects in the air, which turns to water again when it rises where the cold condenses it. He joined that evil will, which only seeks evil, with intelligence, and stirred the wind and fog by the power his nature gives him. Then, when day was done, he covered the valley from Pratomagno to the great Apennine chain with mist, and made the sky above it so heavy that the saturated air turned to water: rain fell, and what the earth did not absorb came to the fosses; and as it merged into vast streams, it ran with such speed towards the royal river that nothing held it back. The raging Archiano found my body near its mouth and swept it into the Arno, and loosed the cross that my arms made on my chest when pain overcame me. It rolled me along its banks and through the depths, then covered me, and closed me in its spoil."

A third spirit followed on the second: "Ah, when you return to the world and are rested after your long journey, remember me who am La Pia: Siena made me, Maremma undid me. He knows, who having first pledged himself to me, wed me with his ring."

6

When the gambling game breaks up, the one who loses stays there grieving, repeating the throws, saddened by experience; the crowd all follows the winner: some go in front, some snatch at him from behind, or at his side recall themselves to his mind. He does not stop, and attends to this one and that one. Those to whom he stretches out his hand cease pressing on him, and thus he saves himself from the crush. Such was I in that dense throng, turning my face towards them, now here, now there, and freeing myself from them by promises.

There was Benincasa, the Aretine, who met his death by Ghin di Tacco's ruthless weapons, and the other Aretine, Guccio de' Tarlati, who was drowned as he ran in pursuit at Campaldino. Federigo Novello was there, praying with outstretched hands, and Farinata Scornigiani, he of Pisa, whose father Marzucco showed such fortitude on his behalf. I saw Count Orso, and the spirit severed from its body through envy and hatred, and not for any sin committed, or so it said: Pierre de la Brosse, I mean. And here let Lady Mary of Brabant take note, while she is still on earth, so that she does not end with the viler crowd for it.

When I was free of all those shades, whose only prayer was that others might pray so that their path to blessedness might be quickened, I began: "O you who are a light to me, it seems that you deny in a certain passage of your *Aeneid* that prayer can alter Heaven's decree, and yet these people pray only for this. Can it be they hope in vain? Or is your meaning not clear to me?"

And he to me: "My writing is clear, and if you think about it rationally, their hopes are not deceptive, since the nobility of justice is not lessened because a moment of love's fire discharges the debt each one here owes, and in my text, where I affirmed otherwise, faults could not be rectified by prayer because prayer then was divorced from God. Truly, you must not suffer such deep anxiety unless she tells you otherwise—she who will be the light, linking truth to intellect. I am not sure you understand; I speak of Beatrice. You will see her above, on this mountain's summit, smiling, blessed.

And I said: "My lord, let us go with greater speed, since I am already less weary than before, and look, the hillside casts a shadow now." He replied: "We will go forward with this day as far as we still can, but the facts are other than you think. Before you are on the summit, you will see the sun return, which is hidden now by the slope such that you do not break his light. But see there, a soul set solitary, alone, gazes at us: it will show us the quickest way." We reached him. O Lombard spirit, how haughty and scornful you were, how majestic and considered in your manner! He said nothing to us, but allowed us to go by, only watching like a couchant lion. But Virgil drew towards him, begging him to show us the best ascent, though the spirit did not answer his request but asked us about our country and our life.

And the gentle guide began: "Mantua . . ." and the spirit all preoccupied with himself surged towards him from the place where it first was, saying: "O Mantuan, I am Sordello, of your city." And the one embraced the other.

O Italy, you slave, you inn of grief, ship without helmsman in a mighty tempest, mistress not of provinces but of a brothel! That gentle spirit was quick, then, to greet his fellow-citizen at the mere mention of the sweet name of his city, yet now, the living do not live there without conflict, and of those that one wall and one moat shuts in, one rends the other. Wretched country, search the shores of your coastline, and then gaze into your heart to see if any part of you is at peace. What use is it for Justinian to have renewed the law, the bridle, if the saddle is empty? The shame would be less if it were not for that. Ah, race, which should be obedient and let Caesar occupy the saddle if only you understood what God has told you! See how vicious this creature has become through not being corrected by his spurs, since he has set his hand to the bridle. O Albert of Germany, you abandon her, she who has become wild and wanton, you who should straddle her saddle-bow: may just judgment fall on your blood from the stars, and let it be strange and obvious, so that your successor may learn to fear it, since you and your father, held back by greed over there, have allowed the garden of the Empire to become a wasteland. Careless man, come and look at the Montagues and Capulets, the Monaldi and Filippeschi: those who are already saddened, and those who fear to be. Come, cruel one, come and see the oppression of your nobles, and tend their sores, and you will see how secure Santafiora of the

Aldobrandeschi is. Come and see your Rome, who mourns, widowed and alone, crying night and day: "My Caesar, why do you not keep me company?" Come and see how your people love each other; and if pity for us does not stir you, come and be ashamed for the sake of your fame. And if it is allowed for me to say, O highest Jupiter, who was crucified on earth for us, are Your just eyes turned elsewhere, or are you preparing some new good that is completely hidden from our sight? For the cities of Italy are full of tyrants, and every peasant that comes to take sides becomes a Marcellus, against the Empire. My Florence, you may well rejoice at this digression, which does not affect you, thanks to your populace that reasons so clearly. Many people have justice in their hearts, but they let it fly slowly, since it does not come to the bow without much counsel; yet your people have it always at their lips. Many people refuse public office, but your people answer eagerly without being called, and cry: "I bend to the task." Now be glad, since you have good reason for it: you who are rich, at peace, full of wisdom. If I speak truly, the fact will not belie it. Athens and Sparta, which framed the ancient laws and were so rich in civic arts, gave a mere hint of how to live well compared to you, who makes such subtle provision that what you spin in October does not last till mid-November. How often in the time you remember you have altered laws, money, offices, and customs, and renewed you limbs! And if you consider carefully, and see clearly, you will see yourself like the sick patient who finds no rest on the bed of down, but by twisting about escapes her pain.

7

After the noble and joyful greetings had been exchanged three or four times, Sordello drew himself back and said: "Who are you?" My leader answered, then: "Before those spirits worthy to climb to God were turned towards this mountain, my bones had been buried by Octavian. I am Virgil, and I lost Heaven for no other sin than for not having faith."

Sordello seemed like someone who suddenly sees something in front of him that he marvels at, and believes, but does not believe, saying: "It is, is not," and he bent his forehead and turned back humbly towards my guide, and embraced him as the inferior person does. He said: "O Glory of Latin, through whom our language showed its power, O eternal praise of the place from which I sprang, what merit or favor will you show me? If I am worthy to hear your words, tell me if you come from Hell, and from what circle."

He answered him: "I came here through all the circles of the mournful kingdom. Virtue from Heaven moved me, and with that I come. Not for the done, but for the undone I lost the vision of the high Sun you seek, and who was known too late by me. Down there, there is a place not saddened by torment but only by darkness, where the grief does not sound as moaning, only sighs. There I am, with the innocent babes who were bitten by the teeth of death before they were baptized and exempt from human sin. There I am, with those who did not clothe themselves with the three holy virtues, Faith, Hope, and Charity, but without sin knew the others and followed them all. But if you know, give us some indication of how we might come most quickly to the place where Purgatory has its true beginning."

He answered: "No fixed place is set for us: I am allowed to go up and around. I act as guide, beside you, as far as I may go. But see now how the day is declining, and we cannot climb by night, therefore it would be well to think of a good place to rest. Here are some spirits, on the right, apart: if you allow me I will take you to them, and they will be known to you, not without joy."

Virgil replied: "How is that? Would he who wished to climb by night be prevented by others, or would he not climb because he could not?" And the good Sordello drew his finger along the ground, saying: "See, you could not even cross this line after sunset, not because anything other than the darkness of night hinders you from going upwards, which obstructs the will through the will's powerlessness. Truly, you could return downwards at night, and walk, straying, along the mountainside while the horizon shuts up the day."

Then my lord, as if wondering, said: "Take us, then, where you say we might have joy in resting."

We had gone a short distance when I saw that the mountain was scooped out, in the way that valleys are hollowed out here. The shade said: "We will go there, where the mountainside makes a cradle of itself, and wait for the new day."

The winding track that led us to the side of the hollow, there where the valley's rim more than half-fades out, was neither steep nor flat. Gold and fine silver; crimson and white cloth; bright, clear Indian wood; freshly mined emerald at the moment it is split—all would be surpassed in color by the grass and flowers set inside that fold of ground, as the lesser is surpassed by the greater. Not only had Nature painted there, but had made there one unknown and indefinable perfume from the sweetness of a thousand scents. There I saw souls sitting among the grass and flowers singing *Salve Regina* who could not be seen from outside, because of the valley's depth.

The Mantuan, who had led us aside, began to speak: "Do not wish me to lead you among them before the little sun sinks to its nest. You will see the faces and actions of them better from this terrace than if received among them down in the valley. He who sits highest, and has the look of having left undone what he should have done, and does not move his lips to the others' singing, was the Emperor Rudolph, who might have healed the wounds that meant Italy's death, so that she is helped, too late, by another. The next, who seems to be comforting him, ruled Bohemia, the land where the water rises that the Moldau carries down to the Elbe, and the Elbe to the sea. He was named Ottocar, and, even in his swaddling clothes, was far better than bearded Wenceslas his son, whom lust and sloth consume. And that snub-nosed one, Philip the Third, who seems so deep in counsel with Henry of Navarre, who has so kindly a manner, died fleeing, and withering the lily: look at how he strikes his chest. See the other, sighing, has made a rest for his cheek with the palm of his hand. They are the father and the father-in-law of Philip the Fair, the plague of France: they know his wicked and sordid life, and from that the grief comes that so pierces them. He who seems so stout of limb, Peter of Aragon, who blends his singing with Charles of Anjou, him of the prominent nose, was cinctured with the cord of every virtue. And if the young man who sits behind him had remained king after him, the worth would have flowed from vessel to vessel, which may not be said of his other heirs. James and Frederick have the kingdoms, but no one has the better heritage. Human worth rarely increases through its branches, and this He wills who creates it so that it may be asked for of Him. My words apply to Charles, the large-nosed one, as well, no less than to Peter, the other who sings with him: because of his son, Apulia and Provence now groan. So is that plant more degenerate in its seed, by as much as Constance, Peter's wife, still boasts of her husband, more than Beatrice or Margaret do of the other. See the king of the simple life sitting there alone, Henry the Third of England: he had a better increase in his branches. That one looking up, who humbles himself lower among them, is William, the Marquis of Montferrat, because of whom the town of Alessandria in Piedmont, and its war, made Montferrat and Canavese weep."

It was now that hour which makes the thoughts of those who voyage turn back and melts their hearts on the day when they have said goodbye to their sweet friends, and which pierces the new pilgrim with love when he hears the distant chimes that seem to mourn the dying day, when I began to neglect my sense of hearing and to gaze at one of the spirits who rose and begged a hearing with his hand.

He joined his palms and raised them, fixing his eyes on the east, as though saying to God: "I care for nothing else." *"Te lucis ante"* issued so devotedly from his mouth, and with such sweet notes, that it rapt me from my thoughts. And then the others accompanied him through the whole hymn, sweetly and devoutly, with their eyes locked on the eternal spheres.

Reader, focus your eyes here on the truth, since the veil is now so thin that surely to pass within is easy. I saw that noble troop gaze upwards after that, silently, pale and humble, as if in hope: and I saw two angels come out from the heights and descend with two burning swords that were cut short and blunted. Their clothes were green as tender newborn leaves, trailing behind, stirred and fanned by their green wings.

One came to rest a little way above us, and the other descended on the opposite bank, so that the people were between them. I saw their blond hair clearly, but the eye was dazzled by their faces, like a sense confounded by excess. Sordello said: "Both come from Mary's breast, to guard the valley because of the serpent that will now come." At which I, who did not know which way it would come, turned and, icy cold, placed myself beside the trusted shoulders. And Sordello again said: "Now we go into the valley, among the great souls, and we will talk with them: it will be a great joy to them to see you."

I think I went down only three paces and was down, and saw one who gazed only at me, as though he wished to know who I was. It was now the time when the air was darkening, but not so dark that was what hidden from both our eyes before now grew clear. He approached me, and I said to him: "Noble Judge Nino, how it pleased me when I knew you, and knew that you were not among the damned!"

No kind greeting was left unsaid between us; then he asked: "How long is it since you came over the distant waters to the foot of the mountain?" I said: "Oh, I came from the depths of the sad regions this morning, and I am in my first life, though by this journey I hope to gain the other."

And when they heard my answer, Sordello and he shrank back, like people who are suddenly bewildered. One turned to Virgil, and the other to someone seated there, saying: "Conrad, rise: come and see what God, in his grace, has willed." Then, turning to me: "By that singular grace you owe to Him who hides His first cause so deep there is no path to it, tell my Giovanna, when you are over the wide waters, to pray for me there, where the innocent are heard. I do not think her mother, Beatrice, still loves me, since she has changed her widow's weeds, which, unhappily, she will long for once again. In her is easily known how long the fire of love endures in woman, if sight and touch do not relight it often. The viper that Galeazzo, the Milanese, emblazons on his shield will not gain her as fair a tomb as my Pisan cockerel would have done." So he spoke, his face stamped with the mark of that righteous fervor that with due reason burns in the breast.

My eager eyes were turned towards Heaven again, there where the stars are slowest, like a wheel close to the axle, and my leader said: "Son, what do you stare at up there?" And I to him: "At those three flames that the whole pole here is burning with." And he to me: "The four bright stars you saw this morning are low, on the other side, and these have risen where they were."

As he was speaking, Sordello drew him towards himself, saying: "Look, there is our enemy," and pointed his finger so that he would look in that direction. There was a snake on that side, where the little valley has no barrier, perhaps such a one as gave Eve the bitter fruit. The evil reptile slid through the grass and flowers, now and again twisting its head towards its tail, licking, like a beast grooming itself. I did not see and so I cannot tell how the celestial falcons rose, but I saw both clearly, in flight. Hearing the green wings cutting the air, the serpent fled, and the angels wheeled around, flying as one back to their places.

The shade who had drawn close to the Judge when he called was not freed from gazing at me, for even a moment, during all that threat. He began: "May that lamp that leads you higher find as much fuel in your will as is needed to reach the enameled summit. If you know true news of Valdimagra, or its region, tell it to me, who was once mighty there. I was called Conrad Malaspina: not the elder, but descended from him. I had that love for my own that here is purified."

I said to him: "Oh, I have never been through your lands, but where do men live throughout Europe to whom they are not known? The fame that honors your house proclaims its lords abroad, and proclaims their country, so that he who has never been there knows it. And as I pray that I may go above, I swear to you that your honored race does not impair the glory of the coffer and the sword. Nature and custom grant it such privilege that it alone walks rightly and scorns the evil way for all that a guilty head twists the world."

And he: "Now go, since the sun will not rest seven times in Aries, that couch that the Ram covers and straddles with all four feet, before this courteous opinion is fixed in your brain with a deeper pinning than other men's words, if the course of justice is not halted."

9

Now the mistress of ancient Tithonus was whitening at the eastern terrace, free of her lover's arms, her forehead glittering with jewels, set in the form of the cold creature that stings people with its tail; and, where we were, Night had climbed two of the steps by which she mounts, and the third was already folding its wings when I, who had in me something of the old Adam, overcome by sleep, sank down on the grass, where all five of us were already seated.

At the hour near dawn when the swallow begins her sad songs, in memory, perhaps, of her former pain, and when the mind is almost prophetic, more of a wanderer from the body and less imprisoned by thought, I dreamed I saw an eagle poised in the sky on outspread wings, with golden plumage, and intent to swoop. And I seemed to be there where Ganymede left his own, snatched up by Jupiter to the high senate. I thought to myself: "Perhaps, through custom, he only strikes here, and perhaps he disdains to carry anyone away in his talons from any other place." Then it seemed to me that wheeling for a while, terrible as lightning, he descended and snatched me upwards, as far as the sphere of fire. There he and I seemed to burn, and the flames of vision so scorched me that my sleep was broken.

Achilles was no less startled, turning his waking eyes about, not knowing where he was, when Thetis, his mother, carried him away in her arms as he slept, from Chiron to the island of Scyros, the place from which the Greeks later made him go to the Trojan war, than I was as soon as sleep had left my eyes; and I grew pale, like a man chilled with fear. My comforter was the only one with me, and the sun was already more than two hours high, and my eyes were turned towards the sea.

My lord said: "Have no fear, be assured, since we are in a good position: do not shrink back, but put out all your strength. You have now reached Purgatory: there, see the cliff that circles it, see the entrance, there, where it seems cleft. Before, in the dawn that precedes the day, when your spirit was asleep in you, among the flowers with which it is all beautified below, a lady came and said: 'I am Lucia: Let me take this sleeping man and I will help him on his way.' Sordello was left behind with the other noble forms. She took you, and came on upwards as day brightened, and I followed in her track. Here she placed you, and her lovely eyes first showed me that open passage; then she and sleep vanished together."

I felt changed, as a man in fear does who is reassured, and who exchanges comfort for fear when the truth is revealed to him. When my leader saw me freed from anxiety, he moved up by the cliff, and I followed, towards the heights.

Reader, you know clearly that I must enrich my theme, so do not wonder if I enrich it with greater art.

We drew close and were at a point just there where a break, like a fissure that divides the cliff, first appeared to me. I saw a gate, and three steps of various colors below to reach it, and a keeper, who as yet said nothing. And as I looked closer there, I saw that, seated as he was on the top step, there was something in his face I could not endure. He held a naked blade in his hand that reflected the sun's rays towards us, so that I turned my eyes towards it often, but in vain.

He began to speak: "Tell me what you want, from where you stand; where is your escort? Be careful that coming up here does not harm you!"

My Master answered: "A Heavenly lady who has good knowledge of these things said to us just now: 'Go there, that is the gate.'"

"And may she quicken your steps towards the good," the courteous doorkeeper began again, "come then, towards our stair."

Where we came, the first step was of white marble, so smooth and polished that I was reflected there as I appear. The second was darker than a dark blue-grey, of a rough, calcined stone, cracked in its length and breadth. The third, which is massed above them, seemed like red porphyry to me, fiery as blood spurting from an artery. God's angel kept both his feet on this, seated at the threshold, which seemed to me to be of adamantine stone. My guide led me, willingly, up the three steps, saying: "Ask humbly for the bolt to be drawn." I flung myself devoutly at the sacred feet; I begged him for pity's sake to open the gate to me, but first I struck myself three times on the breast.

He inscribed seven letter *P*'s on my forehead with the tip of his sword, and said: "Cleanse these wounds when you are inside." Ashes, or dry earth, would match the color of his robe, and he drew two keys out from under it. One was of gold, and the other of silver; he did that to the gate that satisfied me, first with the white, and then the yellow. He said: "Whenever one of these keys fails so that it does not turn in the lock correctly, the way is not open. The one is more precious, but the other needs great skill and intellect before it works, since it is the one that unties the knot. I hold them for Peter, and he told me to err by opening it rather than keeping it locked, if people humbled themselves at my feet."

Then he pushed the door of the sacred gateway, saying: "Enter, but let me tell you that whoever looks behind, returns outside again." The doors of the Tarpeian treasury did not groan as harshly, or as much, when good Metellus was dragged from them, so that it remained poor afterwards, as the pivots of that sacred door, which are of strong and ringing metal, when they were turned in their sockets.

I turned, listening for a first sound, and seemed to hear *Te Deum Laudamus* in a voice intermingled with sweet music. What I heard gave me just the kind of feeling we receive when people sing to the accompaniment of an organ, when the words are now clear, and now lost.

10

When we were beyond the threshold of the gate, which the soul's worse love neglects, making the crooked way seem straight instead, I heard it close again, with a ringing sound; but if I had turned my eyes towards it, what could have excused the fault?

We climbed through a broken rock, which was moving on this side and on that like a wave that ebbs and flows. My leader began: "Here we must use a little skill in keeping near, now here, now there, to the side that is receding" And this made our steps so slow that the wandering circle of the moon regained its bed to sink again to rest before we were out of that needle's eye.

But when we were free and in the open, above where the mountain is set back, I, being weary, and both of us uncertain of our way, we stood still on a level space, more lonely than a road through a desert. The length of three human bodies would span it, from its brink where it borders the void to the foot of the high bank that goes straight up. And this terrace appeared to me like that, as far as my eye could wing in flight, now to the left, and then to the right. Our feet had not yet moved along it when I saw that the encircling cliff, which, being vertical, lacked any means of ascent, was pure white marble, and beautified with friezes, so that not merely Polycletus, but Nature likewise would be put to shame by it. In front of us, so vividly sculpted in a gentle attitude that it did not seem a dumb image, the angel Gabriel appeared, who came to earth with the annunciation of that peace, wept for in vain for so many years, that opened Heaven to us, after the long exile. You would have sworn he was saying "Ave," since she was fashioned there who turned the key to open the supreme love. And these words were imprinted in her aspect, as clearly as a figure stamped in wax: *Behold the handmaid of the Lord.*

"Do not keep your attention on one place alone," said the sweet Master, who had me on that side of him where the heart is, at which I moved my eyes about and saw another story set in the rock behind Mary, on the side where he was who urged me onwards. There, on the very marble, the cart and oxen were engraved pulling the sacred Ark of the Covenant, which makes us fear by Uzzah's example an office not committed to us. People appeared in front, and the whole crowd, divided into seven choirs, made one of my senses say "No, they do not sing," another say "Yes, they do." Similarly, eyes and nose disagreed between yes and no over the smoke of incense depicted there. There King David the humble psalmist went, dancing, girt up, in front of the blessed tabernacle; and he was, in that moment, more and less than king. Michal, Saul's daughter, was figured opposite, looking on: a woman sad and scornful. I moved my feet from the place where I stood to look closely at another story, which shone white in front of me, beyond Michal. There the high glory of the Roman prince was retold whose worth moved Gregory to intercession, and to great victory—I speak of the Emperor Trajan—and at his bridle was a poor widow in the attitude of tearfulness and grief. A crowd of horsemen trampling appeared around him, and the gold eagles above him moved visibly in the wind. The poor woman, among all these, seemed to say: "My lord, give me vengeance for my son who was killed, at which my heart is pierced." And Trajan seemed to answer her: "Now, wait till I return." And she, like a person urgent with sorrow: "My lord, what if you do not return?" And he: "One who will take my place will do it." And she: "What merit will another's good deed be to you, if you forget your own?" At which he said: "Now be comforted, since I must fulfil my duty before I go; justice wills it, and pity holds me here." He who never sees anything unfamiliar to him, made this speech visible, which is new to us, because it is not found here.

While I was exulting in seeing the images of such great humility, precious to look at for their Maker's sake, the poet murmured: "You see here many people, but their steps are few; they will send us on to the high stairs." My eyes, which were intent on gazing to find new things willingly, were not slow in turning towards him.

Reader, I would not wish you to be scared away from a good intention, by hearing how God wills that the debt is paid. Pay no attention to the form of the suffering: think of what follows it; think that, at worst, it cannot last beyond the great judgment.

I began: "Master, those whom I see coming towards us do not seem like people, but I do not know what they look like, my sight errs so much." And he to me: "The heavy weight of their punishment doubles them to the ground, so that my eyes at first were troubled by them. But look steadily there, and disentangle with your sight what is coming beneath those stones: you can see already how each one beats his breast."

O proud Christians, weary and wretched, who, infirm in the mind's vision, put your trust in downward steps: do you not see that we are caterpillars, born to form the angelic butterfly that flies to judgment without defense? Why does your mind soar to the heights, since you are defective insects, even as the caterpillar is, in which the form is lacking?

As a figure with knees joined to chest is sometimes seen carved as a corbel to support a ceiling or a roof, which though unreal, creates a real discomfort in those who see it, even so, I saw these when I paid attention. Truly, they were more or less bent down, depending as to whether they were weighted more or less, and the one who had most patience in its bearing seemed to say, weeping: "I can no more."

11

"Our Father, who art in Heaven—not because of Your limitation but because of the greater love You have for Your first sublime works—hallowed be Thy name and worth by every creature, as it is fitting to give thanks for Your sweet outpourings. May the peace of Thy kingdom come to us, since we cannot reach it by ourselves, despite all our intellect, if it does not come to us itself. As angels sacrifice their will to Yours, singing *Hosanna*, so may men sacrifice theirs. Give us this day our daily bread—without which he who labors to advance goes backward through this harsh desert—and forgive us our debts, as we forgive our debtors the evil we have suffered, and judge us not by what we deserve. Lead us not into temptation—which is easily conquered against the ancient enemy—but deliver us from him who tempts it. And this last prayer, dear Lord, is not made on our behalf, since we do not need it, but for those we have left behind."

So those shades, praying godspeed to us and themselves, went on beneath their burdens like those that we sometimes dream of, weary and unequal in torment, all around the first terrace, purging away the mists of the world. If ever a good word is said there for us by those who have their will rooted in the good, what can we say or do for them here? Truly we should help them wash away the stain that they have carried from here, so that, light and pure, they might issue to the starry spheres.

Virgil said: "Ah, that justice and mercy might soon disburden you, so that you might spread your wings that will lift you as you desire, show us now in which direction we might go most quickly to the stairway; and if there is more than one way, tell us which one ascends least steeply, because he who comes along with me is slow in climbing, despite his will, because of the burden of the flesh of Adam he is clothed with."

It was not obvious where the words came from that were returned to those that he whom I followed had said, but this was the reply: "Come with us to the right, along the cliff, and you will find the pass

that a living man can ascend. And if I were not obstructed by the
stone that weighs my proud neck down so that I have to carry my head
low, I would look at him who is yet alive, who does not name himself,
to see if I know him, and to make him pity this burden. I was Italian,
and the son of a great Tuscan: my father was Gugliemo Aldobrandesco:
I do not know if his name was ever known to you. My ancestors' ancient blood and noble actions made me so arrogant that I held all
men in such scorn, not thinking of our common mother, which was
the death of me, as the Sienese, and every child in Campagnatico,
know. I am Omberto, and it is not me alone that pride does ill to,
because it has dragged all my companions to misfortune. And here,
until God is satisfied, I must carry this burden among the dead, since
I did not do so among the living."

Listening, I had bent my head down, and one of them, not he who
was speaking, twisted himself beneath the weight that obstructed him
and saw me, and knew me, and was calling out, keeping his eyes fixed
on me, who all bent down was moving along with them, with difficulty.

I said to him: "Oh, are you not Oderisi, the glory of Gubbio, and
the glory of that art which in Paris they call 'illumination'?" He said:
"Brother, the leaves that Franco of Bologna paints are more pleasing;
the glory is all his now, and mine in part. In truth, I would not have
been so humble while I lived, because of the great desire to excel that
my heart was fixed on. Here the debt is paid for such pride: and I
would still not be here, if it were not that, having power to sin, I
turned to God. O empty glory of human power: how short the green
leaves at its summit last, even if it is not buried by dark ages! Cimabue
thought to lead the field in painting, and now Giotto is the cry, so
that the other's fame is eclipsed. Even so, one Guido has taken from
another the glory of our language, and perhaps one is born who will
chase both from the nest. Worldly fame is nothing but a breath of
wind that now blows here, and now there, and changes names as it
changes direction. What more fame will you have, before a thousand
years are gone, if you disburden yourself of your flesh when old, than
if you had died before you were done with childish prattle? It is a
shorter moment, in eternity, than the twinkling of an eye is to the
orbit that circles slowest in Heaven. All Tuscany rang with the noise of
him who moves so slowly in front of me, along the road, and now
there is hardly a whisper of him in Siena, where he was lord, when
Florence's fury was destroyed, when she was prouder then than she is

now degraded. Your reputation is like the color of the grass that comes and goes, and he through whom it springs green from the earth discolors it."

And I to him: "Your true speech fills my heart with holy humility and deflates my swollen pride, but who is he whom you were speaking of just now?" He answered: "That is Provenzan Salvani, and he is here because he presumed to grasp all Siena in his hand. So he goes, and has gone, without rest, ever since he died: such coin they pay to render satisfaction who were too bold over there."

And I: "If spirits who wait until the brink of death before they repent are down below, and do not climb up here unless holy prayers help them, till as much time has passed as they once lived, how has his coming here been allowed him?" He replied: "When he lived in highest state, he stationed himself in the marketplace at Siena of his own free will, putting aside all shame, and made himself quiver in every vein to deliver a friend from the pain he was suffering in Charles's prison. I will say no more, and I know that I speak darkly, but a short time will pass and your neighbors will act such that you will be able to understand the beggar's shame. That action released him from those confines."

12

I went alongside the burdened spirit, in step like oxen under the yoke, as long as the sweet teacher allowed it. But when Virgil said, "Leave him, and press on, since here it is best if each drives on his boat with sail and oars, and all his strength," I stood erect, as required for walking, although my thoughts remained bowed down and humbled.

I had moved, and was following willingly in my master's steps, and both of us were already showing how much lighter of foot we were, when he said to me: "Turn your eyes downward: it will be good for you to look beneath your feet, to ease the journey." As tombstones in the ground, over the dead, carry the figures of who they were before so that there may be a memory of them, and often cause men to weep for them through that thorn of memory that only pricks the merciful, so I saw all the roadway that projects from the mountainside sculpted in relief there, but of better likeness, because of the artistry.

On one side, I saw Satan, who was created far nobler than any other creature, falling like lightning from Heaven. On the other side I saw Briareus, transfixed by the celestial thunderbolt, lying on the ground, heavy with the chill of death. I saw Apollo Thymbraeus. I saw Mars and Pallas Athene, still armed, with Jupiter their father, gazing at the scattered limbs of the giants. I saw Nimrod at the foot of his great tower of Babel, as if bewildered, and looking at the people who shared his pride in Shinar. O Niobe, with what sorrowful eyes I saw you sculpted in the roadway, between your seven dead sons and seven dead daughters! O Saul, how you were shown there, dead by your own sword, on Gilboa, that never felt rain or dew after! O foolish Arachne, already half spider, so I saw you, saddened amongst the tatters of your work, woven by you to your own harm! O Rehoboam, now your image seems to threaten no longer, but a chariot carries you away, terrified, before chase is given!

Again, the hard pavement showed how Alcmaeon made the gift of the luckless necklace costly to his mother Eriphyle. It showed how Sennacherib's sons flung themselves on him in the Temple, and how they left him there, dead. It showed the cruel slaughter and destruction that Tomyris generated, at the time when she said, to the dead Cyrus: "You thirsted for blood, now take your fill of blood!" It showed how the Assyrians fled in a rout after Holofernes was killed, and also the remains of the murder. I saw Troy in ashes and ruin: O Ilion, how low and debased the sculpture that is visible there showed you.

What master was it, of the brush or the engraving tool, who drew the lines and shadows that would make every subtle intellect gaze at them? The dead seemed dead, and the living, living: he who saw the reality of all the tales I trod on, while I went by, bent down, saw no better than me. Be proud then, children of Eve, and on with your haughty faces, and do not bow your heads, in case you see your path of sin!

Already we had circled more of the mountain, and more of the sun's path was spent than the bound mind judged so when he who was always going on alert in front of me began to say: "Lift your head up, this is no time to go absorbed like that; see an angel there who is preparing to come towards us. Look how the sixth handmaid is returning from her hour's service. Be reverent in your bearing, and in your look, so that it may gladden him to send us on upward: consider that this day never dawns again."

I was well used to his warnings never to waste time, so he could not speak to me unclearly on that matter. The beautiful creature came to us, robed in white, and, in his face, the aspect of the glimmering morning star. He opened his arms and then spread his wings. He said: "Come: here are the steps nearby, and the climb now is easily made." Few are those who do come at this invitation. O human race, born to soar, why do you fall so, at a breath of wind?

He led us to where the rock was cleft; there he beat his wings against my forehead, then he promised me a safe journey. As the ascent is broken on the right by steps, made in the times when the public records and the standard measure were safe, which climb the hill where San Miniato stands, looking down on Florence, that well-guided city, over the Ponte Rubaconte, so is this gully made easier, which here falls steeply from the next terrace, but so that the high rock grazes it on either side.

While we were changing our direction, voices sang, so sweetly no speech could describe, "*Blessed are the poor in spirit.*" Ah! How different these openings are from Hell's: here we enter with songs, and down there with savage groaning.

Now we were climbing by the sacred stair, and it seemed to me that I was much lighter than I seemed to be on the terrace, at which I said: "Master, say, what heavy weight has been lifted from me, so that I hardly feel any effort in moving?" He answered: "When the *P*'s that have remained on your face but are almost invisible shall be erased completely, like that first one, your feet will be so filled with goodness that not only will they not feel it as effort, but it will be a pleasure to them to be urged on."

Then, like someone who goes along with something on their face unknown to them, except when another's gestures make them guess, so that the hand lends its help to make sure, searches, and finds, and carries out the task that cannot be done by looking, I, with the fingers of my right hand outspread, found only six letters of those that he, the key-holder, had inscribed on me over the temples; at which my guide, seeing it, smiled.

13

We were at the summit of the stairway, where the mountain that frees us from evil by our ascent is terraced for a second time. There a cornice, like the first, loops around the hill, except that its curve is sharper. There is no shadow there, or decoration: the cliff appears naked, and the path level, with the livid color of the stone.

The poet was saying: "If we wait here for people to ask our way of, I am afraid our decision may be delayed too long." Then he set his eyes intently on the sun: he made his right side a pivot, and turned his left, saying: "O sweet light, trusting in whom I enter on the new track, lead us on as we would be led within ourselves: you give the world warmth, you shine upon it; if no other reason urges otherwise, your rays must always be our guide."

We, by our eager will, in a short time had already gone as far there as counts for a mile here when we heard, not saw, spirits flying towards us, granting courteous invitations to love's feast. The first voice that passed by in flight said loudly: "*They have no wine,*" and went by, repeating it behind us.

And before it was completely lost to hearing due to distance, another voice passed by, crying: "I am Orestes," and also did not stay. I said: "O father, what voices are these," and as I asked, there was a third voice saying: "Love those who have shown you hatred." And the good Master said: "This circle scourges the sin of envy, and so the cords of the whip are made of love. The curb or bit is of the opposite sound: I think you will hear it, I believe, before you reach the Pass of Forgiveness. But fix your gaze steadily through the air, and you will see people seated in front of us along the cliff."

Then my eyes opened wider than before: I looked in front and saw shades with cloaks of the same color as the stone. And when we were a little nearer, I heard a cry: "Mary, pray for us," and a cry: "Michael, Peter, and all the saints." I do not believe there is anyone on earth so hardened that they would not be pierced with compassion at what I saw then: when I had come near them so that their features were clear to me, heavy tears were wrung from my eyes. They seemed to me to be covered with coarse haircloth: each supported the other with a shoulder, and each was supported by the cliff. Like this, the blind, lacking means, sit near the confessionals, begging for alms, and sink their heads upon one another, so that pity may be stirred quickly in people, not only by their words, but by their appearances, which plead no less. And as the sun does not help the blind, so Heaven's light will not be generous to the shades I speak of, since an iron wire pierces their eyelids, and stitches them completely shut, just as is done to a wild hawk that will not stay still.

By seeing others, and not being seen, I felt I did them a wrong as I went by, at which I turned to Virgil. He knew well what the dumb would say, and so he did not wait for my question, but said: "Speak, and be brief, and to the point."

My counselor was with me on the side of the terrace where one might fall, since there is no parapet surrounding it; the devout shades were on the other side, and were squeezing out tears through the terrible seam so that they bathed their cheeks.

I turned to them and began: "O people, certain to see the light above, the only thing your desire cares for, may grace quickly clear the dark film of your conscience so that memory's stream may flow through it clearly. Tell me, since it will be gracious and dear to me, if any soul among you is Italian, and perhaps it will bring him good if I know it."

I seemed to hear this for answer, some way further on than where I was: "O my brother, we are all citizens of a true city: you mean those who lived as wanderers in Italy." So I made myself heard more distinctly towards that side. I saw a spirit among the others, hopeful in look, and if you ask "How?" its chin was lifted higher in the manner of a blind person. "Spirit," I said, "that does penance in order to climb, if you are the one who replied, make yourself known to me by place or name."

She answered: "I was of Siena, and purge my sinful life with these others here, weeping to Him that He might lend His grace to us. Sapia I was named, though sapient I was not, and I was far happier in others' harm than in my own good fortune. And so that you do not think I mislead you, listen, and see if I was as foolish as I say. Already when the arc of my years was declining, my townsmen were engaged in battle with their enemies, near Colle, and I prayed God for what he had already willed. They were routed there and rolled back in the bitterness of flight, and I exulted above all in watching the chase, so much so that I lifted my impudent face, crying out to God: 'Now I no longer fear you,' as the blackbird does at a little fine weather. I wished to make peace with God at the end of my life, and my debt would not be reduced, even now, by penitence, had it not been that Pier Pettignano remembered me in his holy prayers, and grieved for me out of charity. But who are you who go asking about our state and, as I believe, have your eyes unsewn, and breathing, speak?"

I said: "My eyes will yet be darkened here, but for only a short time, since they did little offense through being turned to envy. My soul is troubled by a far greater fear of the torment just below, since even now the burden there weighs on me."

And she to me: "Who has led you then, up here, among us, if you expect to return below?"

And I: "He who is with me here, and is silent; and I am alive, and so, spirit elect, ask something of me, if you wish me to move my mortal feet for you over there."

She answered: "Oh, this is such a strange thing to hear that it is a sign that God loves you, so help me sometimes with your prayers. And I beg you, by all you most desire, if ever you tread the soil of Tuscany, renew my fame amongst my people. You will see them among that vain race that put their faith in the harbor of Talamone, and will know more lost hopes there than in searching for the stream of Diana; but the admirals will lose most."

14

"Who is this that circles the mountain before death has allowed him flight, and who opens and closes his eyelids at will?"

"I do not know who he is, but I know he is not alone. You, who are nearest, question him, and greet him gently, so that he might speak."

So two spirits talked of me there, on the right, one leaning on the other, then held their faces up to speak to me; and one said: "O soul, still trapped in the body, journeying towards Heaven, out of charity, bring us consolation, and tell us where you come from, and who you are, since you make us wonder greatly at your state of grace as a thing does that was never known before."

And I: "A river runs through the center of Tuscany, rising at Falterona in the Apennines, and is not sated by a course of a hundred miles. I bring this body from its banks. It would be useless to tell you who I am, since my name does not mean much, as yet." Then he who had spoken first answered me: "If I penetrate your meaning clearly with my intellect, you are talking about the Arno." And the other said to him: "Why did he hide the name of the river, as one does with a dreadful thing?"

And the shade who was asked the question replied as follows: "I do not know, but truly it is fitting that the name of such a valley should die, since from its head, where the alpine chain from which Cape Faro in Sicily is separated, is so extensive that there are few places where it exceeds that breadth as far as Pisa, where it yields that which the sky absorbs from the sea, restoring that water that provides the rivers with what flows in them. Virtue, like a snake, is persecuted as an enemy by them all, either because of the evil place, or the evil customs that incite them, so that the people who live in that miserable valley have changed their nature until it seems as if Circe had them in her sty. It first directs its feeble channel among the Casentines, filthy hogs, more fitted for acorns than any other food created for man's use. Then descending, it reaches the Aretines, curs that snarl more than their power merits, and turns its current, scornfully, away from them. On it goes in its fall, and the greater the volume in its accursed ditch the more it finds the dogs grown to Florentine wolves. Having descended then through many scooped-out pools, it finds the Pisan foxes, so full of deceit that they fear no tricks that might trap them. I will not stop speaking even if this other hears me, and it would be well for him if he reminds himself, again, of what true prophecy unfolds to me. I see Fulcieri, his grandson, who is becoming a hunter of those Florentine wolves on the bank of the savage river, and who fills them all with terror. He sells their flesh while they are still alive, then slaughters them like worn-out cattle; he deprives many of life, and himself of honor. He comes out, bloodied, from the sad wood. He leaves it so that, a thousands years from now, it will not regenerate to its primal state."

I saw the other shade, who had turned around to hear, grow troubled and sad after it had heard these words, as the face of someone who listens is troubled at the announcement of heavy misfortunes as to which side the danger might attack him from. The speech of the one, and the look of the other, made me long to know their names, and I asked them, mixing the request with prayers.

At this the spirit who first spoke to me began again: "You want me to condescend to do for you what you will not do for me, but since God wills so much of His grace to shine in you, I will not be reticent with you; therefore know that I am Guido del Duca. My blood was so consumed by envy that you would have seen me suffused with lividness if I saw a man render himself happy. I reap the straw of that sowing. O humankind, why set the heart there where division of partnership must follow? This is Rinier: this is the honor and glory of the House of Calboli, in which no one, since him, has made themselves heir to his worth. And not only is his bloodline devoid of the goodness demanded of truth and chivalry between the river Po and the mountains, the Adriatic shore and Reno, but the Romagna, which is within these boundaries, is choked with poisonous growth that cultivation would now root out with difficulty. Where is the good Lizio, and Arrigo Mainardi, Pier Traversaro or Guido di Carpigna? O you Romagnols, turned to bastards, when will a Fabbro again take root in Bologna; when, in Faenza, a Bernadin da Fosco, scion of a low-born plant? Do not wonder, Tuscan, if I weep when I remember Ugolin d'Azzo, and Guido da Prata, who lived among us; Federico Tignoso, and his fellows, the Houses of Traversari, and Anastagi, both races now without an heir, the ladies and the knights, the toils and the ease, that love and courtesy made us wish for, there where hearts are grown so sinful. O town of Bertinoro, famous for your hospitality, why do you not vanish, since your noble families and many of your people are gone, to escape guilt? It is good that Bagnacavallo produces no more sons, and bad that Castrocaro, and worse that Conio, still trouble to beget such counts. The Pagani will do well when Mainardo, their devil, is gone, but not indeed in that true witness of their lives will remain. O Ugolin de' Fantolin, your name is safe, since there is no more chance of there being any heir to blacken it through degeneration. Now go your way, Tuscan, since it delights me more to weep than talk, our conversation has so wrung my spirit."

We knew that those dear shades heard us leave, thus by their silence they gave us confidence in our road. When we were left journeying on alone, a voice struck us like lightning when it splits the air, saying: "*Every one that findeth me shall slay me*," and vanished like a thunderclap that dies away when the cloud suddenly bursts.

When our hearing was free of it, behold, a second, with such a loud crash that it was like thunder, following on quickly: "I am Aglauros, she who was turned to stone." Then I made a backward step, not a forward one, to press close to the poet.

Now the air was quiet on all sides, and he said to me: "That was the harsh curb that ought to keep humankind within its limits. But you take the bait, so that the old enemy's hook draws you towards him, and the bridle and the lure are little use. The Heavens call to you, and circle around you, displaying their eternal splendors to you, but your eyes are only on the ground—for which He who sees all things chastises you."

15

As much of the sun's course seemed left before evening as we see between dawn and the third hour of the day, on the zodiacal circle that is always skipping up and down like a child; it was Vespers there in Purgatory, and midnight here. And the sun's rays were striking us mid-face, since we had circled enough of the mountain to be traveling due west, when I felt my forehead far more burdened by the splendor than before, and the unknown nature of it stunned me, so that I lifted my hands above my eyes and made that shade which dims the excess light.

Just as when a ray of light bounces from the water's surface towards the opposite direction, ascending at an equal angle to that at which it falls, and traveling as far from the perpendicular line of a falling stone, in an equal distance, as science and experiment show, so I seemed struck by reflected light in front of me, from which my eyes were quick to hide. I said: "Sweet father, what is that from which I cannot shade my sight enough to help me, which seems to be moving towards us?"

He answered: "Do not be amazed if the Heavenly family still dazzles you; it is a messenger that comes to invite us to climb. Soon, seeing these things will not be painful to you but a joy as great as nature has equipped you to feel."

When we had reached the blessed angel, it said in a pleasant voice: "Enter a stairway, here, much less steep than the others."

We were climbing and already leaving while behind us, *"Blessed are the merciful"* was sung, and, *"Rejoice you who conquer."*

My Master and I, the two of us alone, were climbing, and I thought to derive profit from his words while we went, and I addressed him, saying: "What did the spirit from Romagna mean by mentioning 'division' and 'partnership'?"

At which he said to me: "He knows the harm of his great defect, and therefore let no one wonder if he condemns it, so that the harm he mourns for is lessened. Inasmuch as your desires are centered where things are diminished by partnership, it is envy moving the bellows with your sighs. But if the love of the highest sphere drew your desire upward, envious fear would not be at the core of your heart, since each possesses that much more of the good based on how many more say 'ours,' and so much more love burns in that cloister."

I said: "I am hungrier by being fed than if I had kept silent from the start, and I have added more confusion to my mind. How can it be that a shared good makes a greater number of possessors richer by it than if it is owned by a few?"

And he to me: "Because you fix your eyes, again, only on earthly things, you produce darkness from true light. That infinite and ineffable good that is up there rushes towards love as a ray of light rushes towards a bright body. The more ardor it finds, the more it gives of itself, so that, however far love extends, eternal good causes its increase: and the more people there are up there who understand each other, the more there are to love truly, and the more love there is, and, like a mirror, the one increase reflects the other. And if my explanation does not satisfy your hunger, you will see Beatrice, and she will free you completely from this and from every other longing. Only work, so that the other five wounds that are healed by our pain are soon erased, as two have been."

As I was about to say "You have satisfied me," I saw I had arrived on the next terrace, so that my eager gaze made me silent. There I seemed to be suddenly caught up in an ecstatic dream, and to see many people in a temple, and a lady about to enter, saying with the tender attitude of a mother: "My son, why hast thou dealt with us so? Behold thy father and I sought thee sorrowing," and as she fell silent that which had appeared at first now disappeared.

Then another woman appeared to me, with those tears on her cheeks that grief distils, and that well up in someone because of great anger, saying: "O Pisistratus, if you are lord of Athens, the city from which all knowledge shines, and whose naming made such strife between the gods, take revenge on those audacious arms that clasped our daughter." And her lord, kindly and gently, seemed to answer her with a placid look: "What shall we do to those who wish harm to us, if we condemn him who loves us?"

Then I saw people, blazing with the fire of wrath, killing a youth with stones, and calling continually and loudly to each other: "Kill him, kill him!" And I saw him sinking to the ground in death, which already weighed him down, but he made of his eyes all the while gateways to Heaven, praying to the Lord on high, in such torment, with that look that unlocks pity of forgiveness towards his persecutors.

When my spirit returned outwards to find the true things outside it, I understood my visions did not lie. My guide, who could see me acting like a man who frees himself from sleep, said: "What is wrong with you that you cannot control yourself, but have come almost two miles with your eyes covered, and your legs staggering like someone overcome by wine or sleep?" I said: "O sweet father, if you listen, I will tell you what appeared to me when my legs were pulled from under me."

And he said: "If you had a hundred masks on your face, your thoughts, however slight, would not be hidden from me. What you saw was to prevent you having an excuse for not opening your heart to the waters of peace that are poured from the eternal fountain. I did not ask "What is wrong" for the reason one does who only sees with the eye that cannot see when the body lies senseless, but I asked in order to give strength to your feet; thus the slothful, who are slow to employ the waking hour when it returns, have to be goaded."

We were traveling on through the evening, straining our eyes ahead as far as we could against the bright sunset rays, and behold, little by little, a smoke, dark as night, moving towards us, and there was no space to escape it. This stole away our sight and the clear air.

16

The gloom of Hell, and a night deprived of every planet under a scant sky darkened by cloud as far as it could be, did not make as thick a veil for my sight or as harsh a texture to the touch as the smoke that enveloped us there, since it did not even allow the eyes to remain open, at which my wise and faithful escort came near, and offered me his shoulder. As a blind man follows behind his guide in order not to wander and not to strike against anything that may harm him, or perhaps kill him, so I went, through the foul and bitter air, listening to my leader, who kept saying: "Be careful not to get cut off from me." I heard voices, and each one seemed to pray to the Lamb of God, who takes away sin, for peace and mercy. "*Agnus Dei*" was their only commencement: one word and one measure came from them all, so that every harmony seemed to be amongst them. I said: "Master, are those spirits that I hear?" And he to me: "You understand rightly, and they are untying the knot of anger."

A voice said: "Now who are you, who divide our smoke and talk of us as if you still measured time by months?" At which my Master said to me: "You answer, and ask if we should go upwards by this path."

And I said: "O creature, who purge yourself to return beautified to Him who made you, you will hear a wonder if you follow me." He answered: "I will follow you, as far as is allowed me, and if the smoke prevents us seeing, hearing will allow contact between us instead." So I began: "I am traveling upwards with those garments that death dissolves and came here through the pain of Hell, and if God has so far admitted me to his grace that He wills I should see his court in a manner wholly outside modern usage, do not conceal from me who you were before death but tell me, and tell me as well if I am heading straight for the pass, and your words will be our escort."

He answered: "I was called Marco, and I was a Lombard: I knew the world, and loved that worth at the sight of which everyone now unbends their bow; you go the right way to ascend," and he added, "I pray you to pray for me, when you are above."

And I to him: "By my faith, I promise you to do what you ask of me, but I am wrung within by doubt if I cannot free myself of it. First it was simple doubt, and now it is redoubled by your speech, strengthening it in me here, along with that which I couple to it from elsewhere. The world is indeed so wholly destitute of every virtue, even as you say, and covered and weighed down with sin, but I beg you to show me the cause so that I can see it and tell others, since some people place the cause in the sky, and others here below."

He first gave a deep sigh, which grief shortened to "Ah!" and then began: "Brother, the world is blind, and you come from there, indeed. You the living refer every cause to the Heavens, as though they carried all along with them by necessity. If it were so, free will would be destroyed in you, and there would be no justice in taking delight in good, and lamenting evil. The Heavens initiate your movements—I do not say all, but even if I said it, you are given a light to know good from evil—and you are given free will, which gains the victory completely, in the end, if it survives the stress of its first conflict with the Heavens and is well nurtured. Free, you are subject to a greater force, and a better nature, and that creates *Mind* in you, which the sky does not have control of. So if the world today goes awry, the cause is in yourselves; search for it in yourselves, and I will be a true guide to you in this. From His hands, who loves her dearly before she exists, issues the soul, in simplicity, like a little child playing in laughter and in tears, and she knows nothing but that, sprung from a joyful Maker, she willingly turns towards what delights her. At first she savors the taste of childish good, and is beguiled by it, and chases it if her love is not curbed or misguided. That is why it was necessary to create Law as a curb, and necessary to have a ruler, who might at least make out the towers of the true city.

"There are laws, but who sets their hand to them? No one: because the Shepherd who leads his flock may chew the cud, may meditate, but does not have a divided hoof, and confuses spiritual and temporal. So the people, seeing their Guide only aiming at that benefit he is eager for, feed on that, and do not question further. You can see clearly that bad leadership is the cause of the world's sinfulness, and not that nature corruptible within you. Rome, which made the civilized world, used to have two Suns that made the two roads visible: that of the world, and that of God. One has quenched the other, and the sword and the shepherd's crook are joined, and the one linked to the other must run to harm, since, being joined, one will not fear the other. If you do not believe me, look closely at the crop, since every plant is known by its seed. Worth and courtesy used to be found in Lombardy, that land the rivers Po and Adige water, before Frederick faced opposition. Now it can only be crossed in safety by those who, through shame, have ceased to talk to good men, or live near them. True, there are three elder statesmen in whom the ancient times reprove the new, and it feels a long time to them before God takes them to a better life: Corrado da Palazzo, the good Gherardo da Camino, and Guido da Castel, who is better named in the French way, the *honest* Lombard. As of now, say that the Church of Rome, confusing two powers in herself, falls in the mud, and fouls herself and her charge."

I said: "O my Marco, you reason clearly and now I see why the priests, the sons of Levi, were not allowed to inherit. But who is that Gherardo who you say remains as an example of the vanished race, to reprove this barbarous age?"

He answered: "Your speech is either meant to deceive me or to test me, since, speaking in Tuscan, you seem to know nothing of the good Gherardo. I know him by no other name, unless I were to take one from his daughter Gaia. God be with you, since I travel with you no further. See the light, whitening, shining through the smoke: the angel is there, and I must go before he sees me." So he turned back, and would no longer listen.

17

Reader, if a mist has ever caught you in the mountains, through which you saw as a mole does—through the skin—remember how the sun's sphere shone feebly through the dense, damp vapors as it began to melt away, and your imagination will easily understand how I saw the sun again, which was now setting. So, measuring my steps by my faithful Master's, I issued from that cloud to the sunlight, already dead on the low shore.

O imagination, which takes us out of ourselves sometimes so that we are conscious of nothing though a thousand trumpets echo around us, what is it that stirs you, since the senses place nothing in front of you? A light stirs you, which takes its form from Heaven, by itself, or by a will that sends it downwards. The traces of Procne's impiety appeared in my imagination, she who changed her form to a nightingale's, the bird that most delights in singing, and here my mind was so absorbed in itself that nothing from outside came to it, or was received in it. Then in my high fantasy a crucified man, scornful and haughty of aspect, appeared, and it was Haman, so dying. Around about him were the great Ahasuerus, Esther his wife, and the just Mordecai, who was so sincere in speech and actions. And as this imagining burst like a bubble does when the water surface it is made of breaks, a girl, Lavinia, weeping pitfully, rose to my vision, saying: "O Queen Amata, why have you willed yourself to nothingness through anger? You have killed yourself in order not to lose me: now you *have* lost me. I am she who mourns, Mother, for *your* loss, rather than for his."

As sleep is broken when a new light suddenly strikes on the closed eyelids and hovers, brokenly, before it completely vanishes, so my imaginings were destroyed as soon as light struck my face, light far greater than that which we are used to. I was turning about to see where I was when a voice that snatched me from any other intention said: "Here you can climb," and it made me want to see who it was who spoke with that eagerness that never rests till it confronts the other. But my powers failed me there, as at the sun that oppresses our vision and veils his form through excess of light. My leader said: "This is a Divine Spirit that points us towards the path to climb, without our asking, and hides itself in its own light. It does towards us what a man does towards himself, since he who sees the need but waits for the request has set himself malignly towards denial. Now let our feet fit the invitation: let us try to ascend before nightfall, since we cannot then until day returns." I turned my steps with him towards a stairway, and as soon as I was on the first step, I felt something like the touch of a wing, and my face was fanned, and I heard someone say: "*Blessed are the meek* who are without sinful anger."

Now the last rays that night follows were angled so high above us that the stars were appearing on every side. "O my powers, why do you ebb away from me like this?" I said to myself, since I felt the strength of my legs vanish. We stood where the stairway went no further, and were aground like a boat that arrives at the shore; I listened for a while to see if I could hear anything in the new circle, then turned to my Master and said: "My sweet father, say what offense is purged in this circle where we now are? Though our feet are stopped, do not stop your speaking." And he to me: "The love of good that fell short of its duties restores itself just here: here the sinfully lazy oar is plied again. But so that you might understand more clearly, give me your full attention and you will gather some good fruit from our delay."

He began: "Son, neither creature nor Creator was ever devoid of love, natural or rational, and this you know. The natural is always free of error, but the rational may err because of an evil objective, or because of too much or too little energy. While it is directed towards the primary virtues, and moderates its aims in the secondary ones, it cannot be the cause of sinful delight, but when it is turned awry towards evil, or moves towards the good with more or less attention than it should, the creature works against its Creator. Thus you can understand that love is the seed of each virtue in you, and its errors the seeds of every action that deserves punishment. Now, in that love can never turn its face away from the well-being of its object, everything is safe from self-hatred. And because no being can be thought to exist apart, standing separate in itself, from the First Cause, all affection is prevented from hating Him. It follows, if I judge well in my classification, that the evil we desire is due to the presence of our neighbors, and this desire has three origins in your clay. There are those who hope to benefit from their neighbor's downfall, and because of this alone want them toppled from their greatness. This is pride. There are those who fear to lose power, influence, fame, or honor because another is preferred, at which they are so saddened they desire the contrary. This is envy. And there are those who seem so ashamed because of injury that they become eager for revenge, and so are forced to wish another's harm. This is wrath. This threefold desire is lamented below. Now I want you to understand the other desires that aim towards love in an erroneous manner.

"Everyone vaguely apprehends a good where the mind finds rest, and desires it, so everyone labors to attain it. If inadequate love draws you on within sight or attainment of that good, this terrace torments you for it, after just repentance. This is sloth. There is another good that does not make men happy: it is not happiness, it is not the essential good, the root and fruit of all goodness. The love that abandons itself to it excessively is lamented above us, on three terraces; but how it is separated into three divisions, I will not say, in order that you search it out for yourself."

18

The high-minded teacher had ended his discourse and was looking into my face attentively, to see if I was satisfied, and I, who was tormented by a new thirst, was outwardly silent, but inwardly thought: "Perhaps the extent of my questions annoys him." But that true father, who noticed the hesitant wish that did not show itself, gave me courage to speak, by speaking himself.

At which I said: "Master, my vision is so invigorated by your light that I understand clearly what all your reasoning means and describes. I beg you, therefore, sweet, dear father, to define love for me, to which you reduce every good action and its opposite."

He said: "Direct the keen eyes of the intellect towards me, and the error of the blind who make themselves their guides will be apparent to you. The spirit that is created ready for love is moved by everything pleasing as soon as it is stirred into action by pleasure. Your sensory faculties take an impression from real objects, and unfold it inside you, so that the spirit turns towards those objects. And if it is attracted to them, being turned, that attraction is love: that is Nature, newly confirmed in you by pleasure. Then, as fire rises because of its form, whose nature it is to climb to where it can live longest in its fuel, so the mind, captured, enters into desire, which is a movement of the spirit, and never rests until the object of its love gives it joy. Now it may be apparent to you how deeply truth is concealed from those people who say that every act of love is praiseworthy in itself, since love's material may always be good, perhaps, but every seal is not good, even though the wax is good."

I replied: "Your words, and my wits following you, have made love clear to me, but it has made me more pregnant with doubts, since if love is offered to us from outside ourselves, and the spirit has no other foot of her own to walk on, it is no merit of hers whether she walks straight or crooked."

And he said to me: "I can tell you merely what reason sees; beyond this point, wait only for Beatrice, since it is a question of faith. Every living form, which is distinct from matter but is united to it, has a specific virtue contained in it that is not seen except in its operation, or manifest except by what it effects, as life is manifest in a plant in the green leaves. Therefore human beings do not know where knowledge of primary sensations comes from, or attraction to the primary objects of appetite; they are in you, like the drive in bees to make honey, and this primary volition merits neither praise nor blame. Now in order that every other volition may be related to this one, the virtue, which allows judgement, is innate in you, and ought to guard the threshold of assent. This is the source from which the cause of merit in you derives, according to how it gathers and sieves good and evil desires. Those who went to the foundations in their reasoning recognized this innate freedom, and so left their ethics to the world. Therefore, even if you suppose that every love that burns in you rises out of necessity, the power to control it is within you. Beatrice takes free will to be the noble virtue, so take care to have that in mind if she sets herself to speak of it to you."

The moon, almost at midnight, shaped like a burning pail, made the stars appear fainter to us, and her track across the Heavens, in the east, was on those paths in Sagittarius that the sun inflames when in Rome they watch its setting between Sardinia and Corsica. And that noble shade, whose birthplace Pietola is more renowned than any other Mantuan town, had laid down the burden I had put on him, so that I who had gathered clear, plain answers to my questions stood like one who wanders, drowsily. But this drowsiness was suddenly snatched from me by people who had already come around on us from behind our backs. And just as the rivers Ismenus and Asopus saw a furious rout at night along their banks when the Thebans called on the help of Bacchus, so along that terrace, quickening their steps, those were approaching who, by what I saw of them, good will and just desire rode. They were soon upon us, since all that vast crowd was moving at a run, and two in front were shouting, tearfully: "*Mary went into the hill country with haste*," and: "Caesar lanced Marseilles, and then raced to Spain to subdue Lerida in Catalonia." The rest shouted after that: "Hurry! Hurry! Do not let time be wasted through lack of love, so that laboring to do well may renew grace."

My guide said: "O people in whom an eager fervor now makes good, perhaps, the negligence and tardiness shown by you in being lukewarm at doing good, this one who lives wishes to climb, if only the sun shines for us again, and indeed I do not lie to you, so tell us where the ascent is nearest."

One of the spirits said: "Come behind us, and you will find the gully. We are so full of desire for speed we cannot stay, so forgive us if you take our penance as an offense. I was the Abbot of San Zeno in Verona, under the rule of the good Barbarossa, of whom Milan still speaks with sorrow. And one I know, Alberto della Scala, who already has one foot in the grave, will soon mourn because of that monastery, and will be saddened at having held power there, because he has appointed his son there, Giuseppe, deformed in body and more so in mind, and born of shame, instead of a true shepherd."

I do not know if he said more, or was silent, he had raced so far beyond us already, but I heard that and was pleased to remember it. And he who was my help when I needed it said: "Turn this way and see two that come, showing remorse at sloth."

Last of them all, they cried: "The people for whom the Red Sea opened were dead before Jordan saw their heirs," and, "Those who did not endure the labor with Aeneas, Anchises's son, until the end, gave themselves to an inglorious fate."

Then a new thought rose in me after those shadows were distant from us, so far they could no longer be seen, from which many other diverse thoughts sprang; and I wandered so much from one to another that I closed my eyes in wandering, and transmuted thought to dream.

19

In the hour before dawn, when the day's heat, lost by Earth or quenched by Saturn, no longer offsets the moon's coldness, when the geomancers see their Fortuna Major, formed of the last stars of Aquarius and the first of Pisces, rise in the east on a path that is dark only for a little while, a stuttering woman came to me in a dream, her eyes squinting, her feet crippled, with maimed hands, and sallow aspect. I gazed at her, and my look readied her tongue, and straightened her completely, in a few moments, as the sun comforts the cold limbs that night weighs down, and her pale face colored, as love wills. When her tongue was freed, she began to sing so that I could hardly turn my attention away. "I am," she sang, "I am the sweet Siren: I am so pleasing to hear that I lead seamen astray, in mid-ocean. With my song, I turned Ulysses from his wandering path, and whoever rests with me rarely leaves, I satisfy him so completely." Her lips had barely closed when a lady appeared near me, saintly and ready to put her to confusion. She said, angrily: "O Virgil, Virgil, what is this?" And he came, with his eyes fixed on that honest one. He seized the Siren and, ripping her clothes, revealed her front, and showed me her belly, which woke me with the stench that came from it. I turned my eyes away, and the good Virgil said: "I have called you at least three times; rise and come with me, let us find the opening by which you may climb."

I rose, and all the circles of the holy mountain were now filled with the high day, and we went with the new sun at our backs. I was following him, with my forehead wrinkled like someone burdened by thought and who makes half a bridge's arch of his body, when I heard words, spoken in so gentle and kind a voice as is not heard in this mortal world: "Come, here is the pass." He who spoke to us directed us upwards, between two walls of solid stone, with his outspread wings that seemed like a swan's. Then he stirred his feathers and fanned us, affirming that *Blessed are they that mourn*, whose spirits shall be richly consoled.

My guide began to speak to me, both of us having climbed a little higher than the angel: "What is wrong with you that you are always staring at the ground?" And I: "A strange dream that draws me towards it, so that I cannot stop thinking of it, makes me go in such dread." He said: "Did you see that ancient witch, through whom alone those above us now weep? Did you see how man escapes from her? Let that be enough for you, and spurn the Earth with your heels, turn your eyes towards the lure that the King of Eternity spins, in the great spheres."

I became like a falcon that, at first, is gazing at his feet, then turns at the call, and spreads his wings, with longing for the food that draws him towards it, and so I went, as far as the rock is split to allow passage, to him who climbs up to where the terrace begins.

When I was in the open, in the fifth circle, I saw people around it, lying on the ground, who wept, all turned face downwards. I heard them say: "My *soul cleaveth unto the dust*" with such deep sighing the words were hardly understood. "O God's elect, whose sufferings justice and hope make easier, direct us towards the high ascents." So the poet prayed, and so, a little in front of us, there was an answer: "If you come longing to find the quickest way, and are safe from having to lie prostrate, let your right hand be always towards the outer edge." At that I noted what was hidden in the words and turned my eyes towards my lord, at which he gave assent with a sign of pleasure, to what my look of longing desired. When I was free to do what my mind wished, I went forward, standing over that creature whose previous words made me note them, saying: "Spirit, delay your greater business a while for me, you in whom weeping ripens that without which one cannot turn towards God. If you would have me obtain anything for you over there, where I living come from, tell me who you are and why you have your backs turned upwards."

And he to me: "You will know why Heaven turns our backs towards it, but first know that I was a successor of Peter. A fair river, the Lavagna, flows down to the Gulf of Genoa, between Sestri and Chiaveri, and my people's title takes its name from it. For little more than a month, I learnt how the great mantle weighs on him who keeps it out of the mire, so much so that all other burdens seem light as feathers. Alas, my conversion was late, but when I was made Pastor of Rome, then I discovered the false life. I saw that the heart was not at peace there, nor could one climb higher in that life, so that love of this one was kindled in me. Until that moment I was a wholly avaricious spirit, wretched and parted from God; now, as you see, here I am punished for it. Here, what avarice does is declared, in the purgation of the down-turned spirits, and the mountain has no bitterer penalty. Just as our eyes did not lift themselves up to the heights but were fixed on earthly things, so here justice has sunk them towards the earth. Just as avarice killed our love for all good so that our efforts were lost, so here justice holds us fast, taken and bound by hands and feet, and as long as it is the good Lord's pleasure, we will lie here outstretched and unmoving."

I had knelt and was about to speak, but he detected my reverence merely by listening, and as I began, he said: "Why do you bend your knees?" And I to him: "My conscience pricked me for standing, knowing your high office." He answered: "Straighten your legs and rise, brother; do not err: I am a fellow servant of the one Power, with you and the others. If you ever understood the words of the holy gospel 'they neither marry' you will clearly understand why I say so. Now go: I do not wish you to stay longer, since your remaining disturbs my weeping, by means of which I ripen what you spoke of. I have a niece over there, Alagia by name, who is good in herself, if only our house does not make her evil by example, and she is the only one left to me over there."

20

The will fights ill against a finer will; so, to please him, but against my pleasure, I drew the unsaturated sponge from the water. I went on, and my leader went on likewise, through the free space along the rock, as you go by the wall close to the battlements, because those people who distill from their eyes, drop by drop, the evil that fills the whole world were too close to the edge for us to pass on the other side. Accursed be you, Avarice, ancient she-wolf, who, to satisfy your endless hunger, take more prey than any other beast! O Heaven, by whose circling it appears to be believed that conditions down here are altered, when will one come by whose actions Avarice will vanish?

We journeyed on with slow, meager paces, and I paying attention to the spirits that I heard weeping piteously and complaining; and, by chance, I heard one calling tearfully in front of us: "Sweet Mary," like a woman in labor, and continuing with: "you were so poverty-stricken as can be seen by that inn where you laid down your sacred burden." Following that I heard: "O good Caius Fabricius, you wished to possess virtue in poverty, rather than great riches with vice." These words were so pleasing to me that I moved forward to make contact with the spirit from whom they seemed to emerge. It went on to speak of the gifts that Bishop Nicholas gave to the young girls, to lead their youth towards honor.

I said: "O spirit who speaks of good so much, tell me who you are, and why you alone repeat this praise of worthiness? If I return to complete the short space of a life that flies to its end, you words will not be unrewarded."

And he: "I will tell you, not because I expect any comfort from over there, but because so much grace shines in you before your death. I was the root of the evil tree that overshadows all Christian countries so that good fruit is rarely obtained there. But if Douay, Lille, Ghent, and Bruges can, they will soon take revenge on it, and I beg this of Him who judges all. I was called Hugh Capet over there: from me the Philips and Louises derive by whom France is ruled of late. I was the son of a Paris butcher. When the line of ancient kings was ended, except for one who was clothed in the grey robe, I found the reins of the kingdom's government held tight in my hands, and had so much power in new acquisitions and was so rich in friends that the widowed crown was placed on my son's head, he with whom the Capetian dynasty's consecrated bones begin. Before the dowry of Provence took away all sense of shame from my race, the line was worth little, but did little harm. Its rapaciousness began there in force and fraud, and then to make amends, Ponthieu, Normandy, and Gascony were seized. Charles of Anjou came to Italy, and to make amends made a victim of Conradin, and then sent Thomas Aquinas back to Heaven, to make amends.

"I see a time, not far distant from now, that will bring another Charles, of Valois, out of France, rendering him and his people better known. He comes alone, without an army, and with the lance of treachery Judas jousted with, and couches it so as to make the guts of Florence spill. From that he will gather sin and shame, not land, so much the more grave for him because he treats such wrongs so lightly. I see the other Charles, the Lame, who was once taken captive in his ship, selling his daughter Beatrice, and haggling over her as pirates do over other hostages. O Avarice, what more can you do to us since you have so attracted my tribe to you that it does not care about its own flesh and blood? To make the ill that is past and to come seem lesser, I see the fleur-de-lys enter Anagni, and Christ taken captive in the person of Boniface, His vicar. I see Him mocked for a second time, I see the gall and vinegar renewed, and see Him killed between living thieves. I see the new Pilate, Philip the Fourth, acting so cruelly that even this does not satisfy him, but he must carry his sails of greed lawlessly against the Temple. O my Lord, when will I rejoice to see the sweet vengeance that Your anger forms in secrecy?

"What I was saying concerning the only Bride of the Holy Spirit, which made you turn towards me for explanation, such is the burden of all our prayers as long as daylight lasts, but when the night comes, we adopt a different strain instead. Then we rehearse the history of Dido's brother Pygmalion, whose insatiable lust for gold made him traitor, thief, and parricide, and avaricious Midas's misery that followed on his greedy wish, for which he must always be derided. Then each remembers foolish Achan, who stole the consecrated treasure, so that Joshua's anger still seems here to rend him. Then we accuse Sapphira and Ananias, her husband; we praise the kicks from the

hooves that struck Heliodorus; and the whole mountain echoes with
the infamy of Polymnestor, who murdered Polydorus. Last of all, here
we cry out: 'Crassus, tell us, since you know, what does gold taste
like?' Sometimes one speaks high and another low, now with greater
or lesser force, according to the impulse prompting us to speak; so I
was not alone before in speaking of the good, as we do by day, but no
one else was raising his voice near here."

We had already left him and were laboring to conquer the path as
far as it was in our power to do when I felt the mountain tremble, like
something falling, at which a coldness seized me, as it seizes him who
goes to death. Surely Delos was not shaken as violently before Latona
there made her nest give birth to the twin eyes of Heaven. Then a
shout went up on every side, so that the Master drew near me, saying:
"Have no fear, while I am your guide." All were saying: "*Glory to God in
the highest,*" from what I understood of those nearby whose words I
could hear. We stood immobile, still as those shepherds who first heard
that hymn, till it ceased when the quake ended. Then we took up our
holy path again, gazing at the spirits lying on the ground, already returned to their usual laments.

If my memory makes no mistake in this, no lack of knowledge ever
assaulted me with such a desire to know as I appeared to feel then as I
reflected, and because of our haste, I was not keen to ask, nor could I
see any cause for it there myself; so I went on, fearful, and thoughtful.

21

I was troubled by the natural thirst for knowledge that is never quenched except by that water's grace the woman of Samaria asked for, and haste was driving me along the impeded path behind my leader, and I was grieving at the spirits' just punishment, when behold, just as Luke writes that Christ, already risen from the mouth of the tomb, appeared to two who were on the road, so a shade appeared to us, and came on behind gazing at the prostrate crowd at its feet, and we did not see it until it spoke, saying: "My brothers, God give you peace." We turned quickly, and Virgil gave the appropriate sign in reply, then said: "May the true Court that holds me in eternal exile bring you in peace to the Council of the Blessed."

As we went forward quickly, the spirit said: "How is this? If you are shadows that God does not allow here above, who has escorted you as far as this, by His stairways?" And my teacher said: "If you look at the marks this man carries on his forehead, which the angel traced, you will see clearly that it is right for him to reign among the good. But since Lachesis, she who spins night and day, had not yet drawn out the thread fully that Clotho places and winds on the distaff for each of us, his soul, which is sister to yours and mine, coming up here, could not come alone, since it does not understand as we do; so I was sent from the wide jaws of Hell to guide him, and as far as my knowledge can lead, I will guide him upwards. But, if you know, tell us why the mountain shook so much before, and why everyone appeared to shout with one voice, right down to its soft base." So by asking he threaded the true needle's eye of my wish, and my thirst was less fierce through hope alone.

That spirit began: "The sacred rule of the mountain allows nothing without purpose, or beyond what is customary. Here we are free from earthly changes; here, what Heaven accepts from its own self can operate as a cause, nothing else, and rain, hail, snow, dew, and frost cannot fall higher than the brief stair with three steps. Thin or dense cloud does not appear, nor lightning, nor the rainbow, Thaumas's daughter, who over there often changes zone. Dry vapors rise no higher than the top of the three steps I spoke of, where Peter's vicar has his feet. Perhaps it trembles lower down, more or less, because of the winds hidden underground, I do not know; it never trembles here. Here it quakes when some soul feels itself purged so that it can rise, or set out to soar above, and such shouting follows it. The will alone gives evidence of the purging, seizing the soul, completely free to change her convent, and helping her in willing. True, she had will before, but the eagerness that Divine Justice creates for the punishment, where before there was eagerness for the sin, counters the will, inhibiting it. And only now, I, who have undergone this torment for five hundred years and more, feel free will towards a better threshold. So, you felt the earthquake and heard the pious souls around the mountain render praise to the Lord that he might soon send them above." So he spoke to us, and since we enjoy the drink more the greater the thirst we have, I could not convey how much he refreshed me.

And the wise leader said: "Now I see the net that traps you here, and how one breaks through it, why the mountain quakes, and why you rejoice together at it. Now may it please you to tell me who you are, and let me learn from your words why you have been here so many centuries."

The spirit answered: "When the good Titus, with the help of Heaven's King, avenged the wounds from which the blood that Judas sold issued, I was famous with the name of poet, which endures longest and gives most honor, but not yet of the faith. The music of my words was so sweet that Rome drew me from Toulouse to herself, where I merited a myrtle crown for my forehead. The people there still call me Statius: I sang of Thebes and then of great Achilles, but I fell by the wayside with the second burden. The sparks that warmed me from the divine flame, which has kindled more than a thousand fires, were the seeds of my poetic ardor: I refer to the *Aeneid*, which was a mother to me and a poetic nurse, without which I would not have been worth a drachma. And I would agree to endure one sun more than I owe, before coming out of exile, to have lived over there when Virgil was alive."

These words made Virgil turn towards me with a silent look that said: "Be silent." But the virtue that wills is not all-powerful, since laughter and tears follow the passion from which they spring so closely that, in the most truthful, they obey the will least. I merely smiled, like someone who signals, at which the shade fell silent, and looked me in the eyes, where the soul is most present. And he said: "So that great effort might achieve its aim, say why your face just now showed me a flash of laughter?"

Now I am caught on both sides: one forces me to stay silent, the other demands I speak; at which I sigh, and am understood by my Master, and he says to me: "Do not be afraid to speak, but speak and tell him what he asks with such great desire." At which I said: "Ancient spirit, perhaps you wonder at the laugh I gave, but I wish a greater wonder to seize you. He who leads my vision on high *is* that Virgil from whom you derived the power to sing of men and gods. If you think there was any other reason for my laughter, set it aside as untrue, and believe it was the words you spoke about him."

He was already stooping to embrace my teacher's ankles, but Virgil said: "Brother, do not, since you are a shadow, and it is a shadow that you see." And Statius, rising, said: "Now you can understand the depth of love that warms me towards you when I forget our nothingness, and treat shadows as solid things."

22

The angel was already left behind, the angel who had directed us to the sixth circle, having erased the mark from my forehead, saying that those whose desire is for righteousness are blessed, and accomplishing it with the word *sitiunt*, "they thirst," and nothing more. And I went on, lighter than when I left the other stairways, so that I was following the swift souls upwards without effort when Virgil began to speak to Statius: "Love, fired by virtue, has always fired further love when its flame has been revealed. From that moment when Juvenal descended amongst us in the Limbo of Hell and made your affection known to me, my good will towards you has been more than has ever tied anyone to an unseen person, so that this stairway will seem short to me. But tell me now, and if too great a confidence looses the reins, forgive me as a friend, and speak to me as a friend: How could avarice find a place in your heart amongst such wisdom as you were filled with, by your efforts?"

These words at first moved Statius to smile a little, then he answered: "Every word of yours is a precious mark of affection to me. In truth, things often appear that provide false food for doubt, because of the true reasons that are hidden. Your question shows me that you thought *I* was avaricious in the other life, perhaps because of the terrace you found me on. Know now that avarice was too far distant from me, and my excess, in the other direction, thousands of moons have punished. And I would feel the grievous butting where they roll the weights in Hell had I not straightened out my inclinations when I noted the lines in your *Aeneid* where you, as if angered against human nature, exclaimed: 'O sacred hunger for gold, why do *you* not rule human appetite?' Then I saw that our hands could open too far in spending, and I repented of that as well as other sins. How many will rise with shorn heads through ignorance, which prevents repentance for this sin, in life and at the last hour? And know that the offense that counters the sin with its direct opposite, here, together with it, withers its growth. So, if I, to purge myself, have been among those people who lament their avarice, it has happened to me because of its contrary."

Virgil, the singer of pastoral songs, said: "Now, when you sang of the savage warfare between Jocasta's twin sorrows, from the pagan nature of what Clio touches on there, with you it seems that Faith, without which goodness is insufficient, had not yet made you faithful. If that is so, what sunlight or candlelight illuminated the darkness for you, so that after it you set sail to follow the Fisherman?"

And he replied: "You first sent me towards Parnassus, to drink in its caverns, and then lit me on towards God. You did what he does who travels by night and carries a lamp behind him that does not help him but makes those who follow him wise when you said: 'The Earth renews, Justice returns, and the first Age of Mankind, and a new generation descends from Heaven.' I was a poet through you, a Christian through you, but so you may see what I outline more clearly, I will extend my hand to paint it in. The whole world was already pregnant with true belief, seeded by the messengers of the eternal kingdom, and your words, mentioned above, were so in harmony with the new priests that I took to visiting them. Then they came to seem so holy to me that when Domitian persecuted them, their sighs were combined with tears of mine. And I aided them, while I trod the earth over there, and their honest customs made me scorn all other sects, and I received baptism, before I had gotten the Greeks to the rivers of Thebes in my poem, but was a secret Christian out of fear, pretending to paganism for a long while—and this diffidence sent me around the fourth terrace for more than four centuries. Now you, who lifted the veil that hid me from the great good I speak of, when we have time to spare from the climb, tell me where the ancients, Terence, Caecilius, Plautus, and Varro are, if you know: say if they are damned, and in what circle."

My leader answered: "They, and I, and Persius, and many others are with that Greek whom the Muses nursed above all others, in the first circle of the dark jail. We often speak of the mountain that always holds the goddesses, our foster-mothers. Euripides and Antiphon are there with us, Simonides, Agathon, and many other Greeks who once covered their foreheads with laurel. Of the people celebrated in your poems, Antigone, Deiphyle, and Argia are seen, and Ismene, as sad as she was. There Hypsipyle is visible, who showed the fountain, Langia. Tiresias's daughter is there, and Thetis, and Deidamia with her sisters."

Now both the poets were silent, newly intent on looking around, free of the ascent and the walls, and four handmaidens of the day were already left behind, and the fifth was by the pole of the sun's chariot, which still had its fiery tip slanted upwards, when my leader said: "I think we must turn our right shoulders towards the edge and circle the mountain as we did before." So custom was our guide, even there, and we followed the way with less uncertainty, because of the other noble spirit's assent.

They went on in front, and I, alone, behind; and I listened to their conversation, which increased my understanding of poetry. But soon the sweet dialogue was interrupted by our finding a tree in the middle of the road with wholesome and pleasant smelling fruit. And as a pine tree grows so that its branches lessen as the trunk goes upwards, so that did downwards: I think so that no one can climb up. On the side where our way was blocked, a clear stream fell from the high cliff and spread itself over the canopy above.

The two poets went near to the tree, and a voice inside the leaves cried: "Be chary of this food," and then it said: "Mary thought more about how the marriage feast might be made honorable and complete than of her own mouth, which now intercedes for you all. And the Roman women in ancient times were content to drink water; and Daniel despised food and gained wisdom. The First Age was beautiful, like gold: it made acorns tasty to the hungry, and every stream nectar to the thirsty. Honey and locusts were the meat that fed John the Baptist in the desert, and so he is glorious and great, as the Gospel shows you."

23

While I was gazing through the green leaves, like a man who wastes his life chasing wild birds, my more-than-father said to me: "Son, come on now, since the time we have been given must be spent more usefully." I turned my face, and my steps as quickly, towards the wise pair, who were talking; making it no penalty to me to go.

And "O Lord open thou my lips" was heard in singing and weeping, producing joy and pain. I began to speak: "O sweet father, what do I hear?" And he: "Shadows who perhaps go freeing the knot of their debts." Just as thoughtful travelers who pass people unknown to them on the road turn to look but do not stop, so a crowd of spirits, coming on more quickly behind us, passed us by, silent and devout, gazing at us. Their eyes were all dark and cavernous, their faces pale, and so wasted that the skin took shape from the bone. I cannot believe Erysichthon was as withered to the skin by hunger, even when he felt it most. I thought to myself: "See the people who lost Jerusalem at the time when Mary devoured her own child." The sockets of their eyes seemed gemless rings: those who see the letters "omo" in a man's face, would clearly have distinguished the "m" there. Who, if they did not know the cause, would believe that merely the scent of fruit and water had created this, by creating desire?

I was still wondering what famished them, since the reason for their leanness and their skin's sad scurf was not obvious yet, when a shadow turned its eyes towards me from the hollows of its head, stared fixedly, then cried out loudly: "What grace is this shown to me?" I would never have recognized him by his face, but what was extinguished in his aspect was revealed by his voice. This spark kindled the memory in me of the altered features and I recognized Forese's face.

"Oh do not stare at the dry leprosy that stains my skin," he begged, "nor at any lack of flesh I may have, but tell me truly about yourself, and who those two spirits are there who escort you: do not stop without speaking to me."

I replied: "Your face, which I once wept over at your death, gives me no less grief now, even to weeping, seeing it so tortured. Then tell me, in the name of God, what strips you of flesh: do not make me speak while I am wondering, since he talks badly who is filled with another longing."

And he to me: "A power flows down into the water and into the tree we have left behind from the Eternal Will, the cause of my wasting. All these people who weep and sing purify themselves again, through hunger and thirst, for having followed gluttony to excess. The perfume that rises from the fruit, and from the spray that spreads over the leaves, kindles in us the desire to eat and drink. And our pain is not merely renewed once as we circle this road; I say pain but ought to say solace, since that desire leads us to the tree which led Christ to say 'Eli' when he freed us with his blood."

And I said to him: "Forese, less than five years have revolved since the day when you left the world for a better life. If the power to sin ended in you before the hour of sacred sorrow came that marries us again to God, how have you come here? I thought I would still find you below, where time is repaid for time alive."

And he to me: "My Nella, by her river of tears, has enabled me so quickly to drink the sweet wormwood of affliction; by her devout prayers and her sighs she has drawn me from the shores of waiting and freed me from the other terraces. My widow, whom I loved deeply, is the more precious and dear to God the more solitary she is in her good works, since the savage women of mountainous Barbagia in Sardinia are far more modest than those of that Barbagia, Florence, where I left her. O sweet brother, what would you have me say? Already I foresee a time to come, to which this time will not be too distant, when, from the pulpits, the brazen women of Florence will be forbidden to go around displaying their breasts and nipples. When was there ever a Saracen woman, or woman of Barbary, who needed disciplining, spiritually or otherwise, to force her to cover herself? But the shameless creatures would already have their mouths open to howl if they realized what swift Heaven is readying for them, since, if prophetic vision does not deceive me, they will be crying before he who is now calmed with a lullaby covers his cheeks with soft down. Brother, I beg you, do not conceal your state from me any longer; you see that all these people, not just I, are gazing at where you veil the sun."

At which I said to him: "If you recall to mind what you have been with me, and I have been with you, the present memory alone will still be heavy. He who goes in front of me turned me from that life the other day, when the the sister of him" (and I pointed to the sun) "shone full for you. This one has led me through the deep night from the truly dead in this true flesh that follows him. From there his companionship has brought me climbing and circling the mountain, which straightens you whom the world made crooked. He speaks of my being his comrade till I am there where Beatrice is; there I must remain without him. Virgil it is who tells me so" (and I pointed to him), "and this other shade is one for whom every cliff of your region that now frees him from itself shook before."

24

Talking did not slow the journey, nor the journey slow the talking, so we went steadily, like a ship driven by a favorable wind. And the shades, which seemed doubly dead, drew their amazement from me through the pits of their eyes, knowing I lived. And I, continuing my conversation, said: "Perhaps Statius climbs more slowly than he might because of the other. But tell me where Piccarda is, if you know: tell me if I can see anyone of note amongst the people who stare at me."

He said, first: "My sister—I do not know if she was more beautiful or more virtuous—now triumphs, rejoicing in her crown on high Olympus," and then: "It is not forbidden to name anyone here, since our features are so shrivelled by hunger. This" (and he pointed with his finger) "is Bonagiunta, Bonagiunta of Lucca: and that face beyond him, leaner than the rest, is Martin, who held the Holy Church in his embrace: he was from Tours, and purges the eels of Bolsena, and the sweet wine." He named many others to me, one by one, and all seemed pleased to be named, so that I did not see a single black look. I saw Ubaldino della Pila, snapping his teeth on the void out of hunger, and Bonifazio, who was pastor to many peoples with his crozier. I saw Messer Marchese, who had time before at Forlì to drink with less reason for thirst, and yet was such that he was never sated.

But like he who looks and then values one more than another, so I did him of Lucca, who seemed to know me. He was murmuring what sounded like "Gentucca" there where he was undergoing the wounds of justice, which pares them so. I said: "O spirit, who seems longing to talk with me, speak so that I can understand you, and satisfy us both with your speech."

He began: "A woman is born, and is not yet married, who will make my city pleasing to you, however men may reprove the fact. You will go from here with that prophecy: if you have understood my murmuring wrongly, the real events will yet make it clear to you. But tell me if I see here he who invented the new verse beginning: 'Ladies who have knowledge of love.'"

And I to him: "I am one who, when love inspires him, takes note and then writes it in the way he dictates within."

He said: "Brother, oh I see now the knot that held back Jacopo da Lentino, Fra Guittone, and me, from the new sweet style I hear. Truly, I can see how your pens closely follow him who dictates, which certainly was not true of ours. And he who sets out to search any further cannot distinguish one style from the other," and he fell silent, as if satisfied.

As birds that winter on the Nile sometimes crowd into the air, then fly more quickly and in files, so all the people there, turning around, quickened their steps, made swift by leanness and longing. And as someone tired of running lets his companions go by, and walks until the heaving of his chest has eased, so Forese let the sacred flock pass, and came on behind them with me, saying: "When will I see you again?"

I answered him: "I do not know how long I may live, but my return will not be soon enough for my longing not to be before me at the shore, since the place appointed for me there is day by day more naked of good, and seems condemned to sad ruin."

"Now go," he said, "for I see he who is most guilty, Corso Donati, dragged at the tail of a beast towards the valley where sin is never purged. The beast goes faster at every pace, ever increasing, until it smashes him, and leaves his body vilely broken. Those gyres above" (and he lifted his eyes towards the sky) "do not have long to turn before what my words may no longer say is clear to you. Now stay behind, since time is precious in this region, and I lose too much of it matching my pace to yours."

He left us with greater strides, as a horseman sometimes issues at a gallop from a troop riding past, and goes to win the honor of the first encounter, and I was left by the road with the two who were such great marshals in the world. And when he had gone so far in front of us that my eyes chased after him, as my mind did his words, the green and laden boughs of another fruit tree appeared, and not far off, since I had just come around to it. I saw people under it lifting their hands and calling out to the leaves, like spoilt, greedy children begging, and the one they plead with does not reply, but holds up high what they want, and does not hide it to make their longing more acute. Then they went away, undeceived, and now we came to that great tree that denies all those prayers and tears.

"Go on, without coming near: higher up there is a tree that Eve ate from, and this was grafted from it." So a voice spoke among the branches, at which Virgil, Statius, and I went on by the cliffside. It said: "Remember the accursed centaurs formed in the clouds, who fought Theseus with their bi-formed bellies sated with food and wine, and remember the Hebrews who appeared fastidious when drinking, so that Gideon would not have them for his comrades when he came down from the hills to Midian." So we passed, close to one of the two sides, hearing sins of gluttony, followed once by woeful victories. Then a thousand steps or more took us forwards, scattered along the empty road, each reflecting in silence.

"What do you journey considering so deeply, you solitary three?" a voice said suddenly, so that I started, as timid creatures do when scared. I lifted my head to see who it was, and glass or metal was never seen as red and glowing in a furnace as the one I saw, who said: "If it please you to climb, here you must turn: they go from here who wish to journey towards peace."

His face had robbed me of sight, so I turned back towards my teachers, like one who follows the instructions he hears. And as the May breeze, announcing the dawn, moves and breathes, impregnated with herbs and flowers, so I felt a wind on my forehead, and I clearly felt the feathers move that blew an ambrosial perfume to my senses, and I heard a voice say: "Blessed are those who are so illumined by grace that the love of sensation does not fire too great a desire in their hearts, and who hunger only for what is just."

25

It was an hour when nothing prevented our climbing, since the Sun had relinquished the meridian circle to Taurus, while night held Scorpio. So we entered the gap, one behind the other, climbing the stair, whose narrowness separates the climbers, as men do who do not stop but go on, whatever happens to them, when the spur of necessity pricks them. And like the young stork that raises its wing, wanting to fly, and drops it again, not daring to leave the nest, so my longing to question was lit and quenched, getting as far as the movement one makes when preparing to speak. My sweet father did not stop, even though the pace was quick, but said: "Fire the arrow of your speech that you have drawn to the notch."

Then I opened my mouth confidently, and began: "How can one become lean, there, when food is unnecessary?"

He said: "If you recall how Meleager wasted away as the firebrand was consumed, it would not seem so hard for you to understand; or if you thought how your insubstantial image, in the mirror, moves with your every movement, what seems hard would seem easy to you. But in order for you to satisfy your desire, Statius is here, and I call on him, and beg him, to heal your wounds."

Statius replied: "If I explain the eternal justice he has seen, even though *you* are here, let my excuse be that I cannot refuse you anything." Then he began: "Son, if your mind listens to and considers my words, they will enlighten you about what you ask. Perfect blood, which is never absorbed by the thirsty veins but remains behind, like food you remove from the table, acquires a power in the heart sufficient to invigorate all the members, as does the blood that flows through the veins to become those members. Absorbed again it descends to the part of which it is more fitting to be silent than speak, and from that part is afterwards distilled into the partner's blood, in nature's vessel. There one blood is mingled with the other's: one disposed to be passive, the other active because of the perfect place it springs from, and mixed with the former, begins to work, first coagulating, then giving

life, to what is has formed for its own material. The active power having become a spirit, like a plant's, different in that it is developing
while the plant's is developed, now operates so widely that it moves
and feels like a sea-sponge, and then begins to develop organs, as sites
for the powers of which it is the seed. Now, son, the power that flows
from the heart of the begetter expands and distends into human members as nature intends; but you do not yet understand how it becomes
human, from being animal: this is the point which made one wiser
than you, Averroës, err, so that he made the intellectual faculty separate from the spirit, because he found no organ that it occupied. Open
your mind to the truth that follows, and understand that as soon as
the structure of the brain is complete in the embryo, the First Mover
turns to it, delighting in such a work of nature, and breathes a new
spirit into it, filled with virtue, which draws into its own substance
what it finds already active, and forms a single soul that lives and feels,
and is conscious of itself. And so that you wonder less at my words,
consider the heat of the sun, which becomes wine when joined to the
juice of the grape. And when Lachesis has no more thread to draw,
the soul frees itself from the flesh, taking both the human and divine
powers: the other faculties falling silent: memory, intellect, and will
far keener in action than they were before. It falls, by itself, wondrously,
without waiting, to one of these shores: there it first learns its location. As soon as that place encircles it, the formative power radiates
around in quantity and form as in the living members, and as saturated air displays diverse colors by the light of another body reflected
in it, so the surrounding air takes on that form that the soul, which
rests there, powerfully prints on it; and then, like the flame that follows fire wherever it moves, the spirit is followed by its new form.
Since it is in this way that it takes its appearance, it is called a shadow,
and in this way it shapes the organs of every sense including sight. In
this way we speak, and laugh, form tears, and sighs, which you might
have heard, around the mountain. The shade is shaped according to
how desires and other affections stir us, and this is the cause of what
you wondered at."

And now we had reached the last turn, and had wheeled around to
the right, and were conscious of other things. There the cliff hurls out
flames, and the terrace breathes a blast upwards that reflects them
and keeps the path free of them, so that we had to go by the side that
was clear, one by one; and I feared the fire on one side, and on the

other feared the fall. My leader said: "Along this track, a careful watch must be kept, because an error can easily be made."

I heard "*God of supreme mercy*" sung then in the heart of the great burning, which made me no less keen to turn away, and I saw spirits walking through the flames so that I looked at them, and at my steps, with a divergent gaze, from time to time. After the end of that hymn, they shouted aloud: "*I know not a man,*" then they softly recommenced the hymn. At the end they shouted again: "Diana kept to the woods, and chased Callisto away, who had known the taint of Venus." Then they returned to singing, then cried out the names of women and husbands who were chaste, as virtue and marriage demand. And I believe this mode is sufficient for the whole time that the fire burns them: the last wound must be healed, by this treatment, and this diet.

26

While we were going along the brink like this, one behind the other, the good Master often said: "Take care, let me caution you." The sun was striking my shoulder, his rays already changing the whole aspect of the west from azure to white, and I made the flames appear redder in my shadow, and many spirits I saw noted even so slight a sign as they passed. This was the cause that gave them a reason to speak about me, and they began to say, one to another: "He does not seem to be an insubstantial body." Then some of them made towards me, as far as they could, always careful not to emerge to where they would be no longer burning. "O you who go behind the others, perhaps out of reverence not tardiness, answer me who burn in thirst and fire: and your reply is needed not by me alone, since all these thirst for it, more than Indians or Ethiopians do for water. Tell us how it is that you make a wall against the sunlight, as if you were not held in death's net."

So one of them spoke to me, and I would have revealed myself then and there had I not been intent on something strange that appeared, since people were coming through the middle of the fiery road, their faces opposite these people, and it made me pause, in wonder. There I see each shadow hurry to kiss someone on the other side, without staying, satisfied by a short greeting: ants, in their dark battalions, embrace each other like this, perhaps to know their path and their luck. As soon as they break off the friendly clasp, before the first step sends them onwards, each one tries to shout the loudest: the newcomers "Sodom and Gomorrah" and the others "Pasiphaë enters the wooden cow, so that the young bull may run to meet her lust." Then like cranes that fly, some to the northern mountains, others towards the desert—the latter shy of frost, the former of the sun—so one crowd passes on, and the other comes past, and they return, weeping, to their previous singing, and to the cries most suitable to them, and those same voices that entreated me before drew closer to me, showing their desire to listen in their aspect.

I who had seen this desire twice began: "O spirits, certain someday of reaching a state of peace, my limbs have not remained over there, green or ripe in age, but are here, with me, with all their blood and sinews. I go upwards from here in order to be blind no longer: there is a lady there above who wins grace for us, by means of which I bring my mortal body through your world. But—and may your desires be satisfied quickly, and Heaven house you, which stretches furthest, filled with love—tell me who you are, so that I may write it on paper, and who that crowd is vanishing behind your backs."

Each shadow in appearance seemed as troubled as the dazed mountain dweller becomes when he enters the city, staring about speechlessly in his roughness and savagery, but when they had thrown off their amazement, which is soon quenched in finer hearts, the first shade who had made his request to me began: "Blessed spirit, who is gathering knowledge of our borders to achieve the holier life! The people who do not come along with us, offended in that way that caused Caesar to be called 'queen' in his triumph, so they leave us, shouting 'Sodom,' reproving themselves, as you have heard, and helping the burning with the heat of their shame. Our sin was heterosexual, but because we did not obey human law and followed our appetites like beasts, when we part from them, to our infamy we call *her* name that made herself a beast, in the beast-like framework. Now you know our actions, and what we were guilty of: if you perhaps want to know who we are by name, there is not time enough to tell you, nor could I. But I will indeed make your wish to know me wane: I am Guido Guinicelli, and am purging myself already because I made a full repentance before the end."

What in the midst of Lycurgus's sorrow her two sons felt on seeing their mother Hypsipyle again, I now felt, though I cannot rise to those heights, when I heard my "father," and the "father" of others who are my betters, name himself, he who always made use of the sweet and graceful rhymes of love; and without speaking or hearing, I went on, thinking, gazing at him for a long while, and did not move closer there because of the fire. When I was filled with gazing, I offered my services to him, eagerly, with that strength that compels belief in the other. And he said to me: "I hear that you leave tracks so deep and clear that Lethe cannot remove or dim them. But if your words just now expressed truth, tell me why you demonstrate in looks and speech that you hold me so dear."

And I to him: "Your sweet lines, whose very ink is precious, as long as the modern style shall last."

He said: "O my brother, this one whom I indicate with my finger" (and he pointed to a spirit in front) "was the better craftsman of his mother tongue. He surpassed all who wrote love-verses and prose romances, and let those fools talk who think that Giraut de Borneil, he of Limoges, excels. They turn their faces towards rumor rather than truth, and confirm their opinions before they listen to art or reason. So many of our fathers did, with Guittone, shouting praise after praise of him, but truth has won at last, with most people. Now if you have such breadth of privilege that you are allowed to go to that cloister where Christ is head of the college, say a *Pater Noster* there for me, as much of one as is as needed by us in this world, where the power to sin is no longer ours." Then, perhaps in order to give way to another following closely, he vanished through the fire, like a fish diving through water to the depths.

I drew forward a little towards the one Guido had pointed to, and said that my longing was preparing a place of gratitude for his name. And, freely, he began to speak:

> "Your sweet request of me is so pleasing,
> that I cannot, and will not, hide me from you.
>
> I am Arnaut, who weeping goes and sings:
> seeing, gone by, the folly in my mind,
> joyful I hope for what the new day brings.
>
> By that true good, I beg you, that you find,
> guiding you to the summit of the stairway,
> think of my sorrow, sometimes, as *you* climb."

Then he hid himself in the refining fire.

So the sun stood, as when he shoots out his first rays, there at Jerusalem, where his Maker shed his blood; as when Ebro's river falls under Heaven-borne Libra's scales, and Ganges's waves are scorched by midday heat; so there the daylight was fading when God's joyful angel appeared to us. He was standing beyond the flames, on the bank, and singing "*Blessed are the pure in heart*" in a voice more thrilling than ours. Then, when we were nearer to him, he said: "You may go no further, O sacred spirits, if the fire has not first bitten you: enter it, and do not be deaf to the singing beyond," at which, on hearing him, I became like someone laid in the grave. I bent forward, over my linked hands, staring at the fire, and, powerfully conceiving human bodies once seen being burnt alive.

The kindly guides then turned to me, and Virgil said: "My son, there may be torment here, but not death. Remember, remember . . . if I led you safely on Geryon's back, what will I do now, closer to God? Believe in truth that if you lived in this womb of flames even for a thousand years, they could not scorch a single hair; and if you think perhaps that I deceive you, go towards them and gain belief by holding the edge of your clothes out with your hands. Now forget, forget all fear: turn this way, and go on in safety."

And I remained rooted to the spot, my conscience against it. When he saw me standing there still rooted and stubborn, troubled a little, he said: "Now see, my son, this wall lies between you and Beatrice."

As Pyramus opened his eyes on the point of death at Thisbe's name and gazed at her, there where the mulberry was reddened, so my stubbornness softened and I turned to my wise leader on hearing that name that always stirs in my mind. At which he shook his head and said: "What? Do we desire to stay on this side?" Then he smiled, as one smiles at a child won over with an apple. Then he went into the fire in front of me, begging Statius—who, for a long distance before, had separated us—to come behind.

When I was inside, I would have thrown myself into molten glass to cool myself, so immeasurable was the burning there. My sweet father, to comfort me, went on speaking only of Beatrice, saying: "I seem already to see her eyes." A voice guided us that was singing on the far side, and only intent on it, we came out there where the ascent begins. "*Come ye blessed of my father*" sounded from inside a light that shone there, so bright it overcame me, and I could not look at it. It added: "The sun is sinking, and the evening comes: do not stay, but quicken your steps while the west is not yet dark." The way climbed straight through the rock in such a direction that I blocked the light of the already low sun in front of me. And we had attempted only a few steps when I and the wise saw, because of the shadow that vanished, that the sun had set behind us. And before night held all sovereignty, and the horizon through all its immense spaces had become one color, each of us made a bed of a step, since the law of the mountain took the power, not the desire, to climb from us.

As mountain goats that have been quick and wanton on the summits, before they are fed, become tame, ruminating silently in the shade when the sun is hot, guarded by the shepherd leaning on his staff and watching them as he leans: and as the shepherd lodging in the open keeps quiet vigil at night near his flock, guarding it in case a wild beast scatters it: so were we, all three—I, the goat, and they, the shepherds—closed in by the high rock, on both sides. Little could be seen there of the outside world, but through that little space I saw the stars, brighter and bigger than they used to be. As I ruminated like this, and gazed at them, sleep came to me: sleep that often knows the future before the fact exists.

In that hour, I think, when Cytherean Venus, who always seems burning with the fire of love, first shone from the east towards the mountain, a lady appeared to me in a dream, young and beautiful and going along a plain gathering flowers; and she said, singing: "Whoever asks my name, know that I am Leah, and go moving my lovely hands around to make a garland. I adorn myself here to look pleasing in the glass, but my sister Rachel never moves from her mirror, and sits there all day long. She is as happy to gaze at her lovely eyes as I am to adorn myself with my hands: action satisfies me, contemplation her."

And now, at the pre-dawn splendor that grows more welcome to travelers when, returning, they lodge nearer home, the shadows of night were vanishing on all sides, and my sleep with them, at which I rose, seeing the great Masters had already risen.

"That sweet fruit that mortal anxiety goes in search of on so many branches will give your hunger peace today." Virgil employed such words to me, and there were never gifts equaling these in sweetness. Such deep longing, on longing, overcame me to be above that afterwards, I felt my wings growing for the flight at every step.

When the stairway below us was done and we were on the topmost step, Virgil fixed his eyes on me, and said: "Son, you have seen the temporal and the eternal fire, and have reached a place where I, by myself, can see no further. Here I have led you, by skill and art; now take your delight for a guide: you are free of the steep path, and the narrow. See, there, the sun that shines on your forehead, see the grass, the flowers and the bushes, that the earth here produces by itself. While the lovely, joyful eyes that, weeping, made me come to you are arriving, here you can sit down, or walk amongst all this. Do not expect another word or sign from me. Your will is free, direct and whole, and it would be wrong not to do as it demands; and by that I crown you and mitre you over yourself."

28

Now, eager to explore within and around the dense green of the divine wood that moderated new daylight to my eyes, I left the mountainside without delay, crossing the plain, slowly, slowly, over the ground, perfumed on every side. A sweet breath of continuous air struck my forehead with no more force than a gentle wind, before which the branches, immediately shaking, were all leaning towards that western quarter where the sacred mountain casts its first shadow, not bent so far from their vertical that the little birds in the treetops left off practicing their art, but singing, in true delight, they welcomed the first breezes among the leaves that murmured a refrain to their songs such as gathers, from bough to bough, through the pinewoods on Chiassi's shore when Aeolus frees the Sirocco.

Already my slow steps had taken me into the ancient wood so far that I could not see where I had entered; and behold, a stream prevented my going further that with its little waves bent the grass that issued from its shore towards the left. All the waters that seem purest here would appear tainted compared to that which conceals nothing, though it flows dark, dark in perpetual shade that never allows the sun or moonlight there. I rested my feet, and with my eyes I passed beyond the stream to stare at the vast multitude of fresh flowers of May, and just as something suddenly appears that sets all other thoughts aside through wonderment, a lady, all alone, appeared to me, going along singing, gathering flowers on flowers, with which all her path was painted. I said to her: "I beg you, lovely lady, who warm yourself at love's rays if I can believe appearances, so often witness to the heart, may it please you to come nearer to the stream so that I can know what you sing. You make me think of where and how Proserpine seemed when Ceres, her mother, lost her, and she the spring."

As a lady who is dancing turns with feet close to each other and to the ground, and barely placing foot in front of foot, she turned to me among the red and yellow flowers, like a virgin who looks downwards modestly, and satisfied my prayer, drawing so near that the sweet sound and its meaning reached me. As soon as she was there where the grass is already bathed by the waves of the lovely stream, she granted me the gift of raising her eyes. I do not think as bright a light shone beneath Venus's eyelids when she was accidentally wounded by her son Cupid, against his wish. Matilda smiled from the right bank opposite, gathering more flowers in her hands, which the high ground bears without seeds. The river kept us three steps apart, but the Hellespont that Xerxes crossed, a check to human pride to this day, was not hated more by Leander, because of its turbulent wash between Sestos and Abydos, than this stream was by me, because it did not open then, for me.

She began: "You are new, and perhaps because I am smiling here in this place chosen as a nest for the human race, wonderingly, you have some doubts; but the psalm *'You have made me glad'* sheds light that might unfog your intellect. And you, who are in front and entreated me, say if you want to hear anything more, since I came ready to answer your questions, until you are sated."

"The water," I said, "and the sound of the forest are struggling in me with a new belief in something I have heard contrary to this."

At which she said: "I will tell you the cause of what you wonder at, and I will clear away the fog that annoys you. The highest Good, who is His own sole joy, created man good, and for goodness, and gave him this place as a pledge of eternal peace. Through man's fault, he did not stay here long: through man's fault, he exchanged honest laughter and sweet play for tears and sweat. So that the storms caused below this mountain by the exhalations of water and earth, following the heat as far as they can, should not hurt man, it rose this far towards Heaven, free of them, from beyond where it is closed off. Now since the whole of the air turns in a circle with the primal circling, unless its motion is blocked in some direction, that motion strikes this summit, which is wholly free in the clear air, and makes the woods resound because they are so solid; and a plant that is struck has such power that it impregnates the air with its virtue, and the air, in its circling, scatters it around; and the other soil, depending on its quality and its situation, conceives and produces various plants with various virtues. If this were understood over there, it would not seem strange when some plant takes root without obvious seed. And you must know that the sacred plain, where you are, is full of every kind of seed and bears fruit in it that is not gathered over there. The water you see does not rise from a spring, fed by the moisture that the cold condenses, as a river does that gains and loses volume, but issues from a constant, unfailing fountain that, by God's will, recovers as much as it pours out freely, on every side. On this side it falls with a power that takes away the memory of sin; on the other, with one that restores the memory of every good action. On this side it is called Lethe, on that side Eunoë, and does not act completely unless it is tasted first on this side, and then on that. It surpasses all other savors and though your thirst to know may be fully sated, even though I say no more to you, I will give you this corollary, out of grace, and I do not think my words will be less precious to you because they go beyond my promise to you. Perhaps in ancient times, those who sang of the Golden Age and its happy state dreamed of this place on Parnassus. Here the root of humanity was innocent, here is everlasting Spring, and every fruit; this is the nectar of which they all speak."

Then I turned straight back towards the poets, and saw that, with smiles, they had heard the last elucidation. Then I turned my face to the lovely lady.

29

She continued from the end of her words, singing, like a lady in love: "*Blessed is he whose transgression is forgiven.*" And like the nymphs who used to wander alone through the woodland shadows, one wishing to see the sun, another to flee it, she moved then, walking along the bank against the stream, and I across from her, one small step answering the other. Her steps with mine were not a hundred when both banks curved alike, so that I turned eastwards. And our journey was not far yet when the lady turned completely to me, saying: "My brother, look and listen." And behold, a sudden brightness flooded through the great forest on every side, so that I was unsure if it was lightning. But since lightning vanishes as it comes, and that continued and shone brighter and brighter, I said to myself: "What is this thing?"

And a sweet melody ran through the glowing air, at which righteous zeal made me condemn Eve's boldness, a woman who, alone and newly created there, where Heaven and Earth were obedient, could not bear to be under any veil, which if she had borne devoutly, I would have known these ineffable delights earlier, and for longer. While I was moving among such first fruits of the eternal bliss, enraptured and still longing for greater joys, the air turned to blazing fire under the green branches in front of us, and the sweet sound was distinguished as a song.

O sacred, virgin Muses, if ever I endured hunger, cold or vigil for you, the occasion spurs me on to ask my reward. Now I need Helicon to stream out for me, and Urania to aid me with her choir, to put into words, things that are hard to imagine.

A little further on, the illusion of seven golden trees appeared, caused by the great space still between us and them; but when I had come nearer, so that the common object, that can deceive the senses, had not lost any of its details, the power that creates matter for reasoning realized that branched candlesticks were what they were, and the content of the singing was "Hosanna." The lovely pageant was blazing out above far brighter than the mid-month moon at midnight. I turned full of wonder towards the good Virgil, and he replied with a face no less stunned. Then I turned my face back towards the sublime things which moved towards us, so slowly that they would be outpaced by a new bride.

The lady cried to me: "Why are you so ardent only for the sight of the bright lights, and pay no attention to what comes behind them?" Then I saw people dressed in white following as if behind their leader, and there was never such whiteness here among us. The water shone brightly on my left, and reflected my left side like a mirror if I gazed into it. When I was situated on the edge, so that the river alone separated me from them, I stopped to see better, and I saw the flames advance, leaving the air behind them tinted, and they had the appearance of trailing banners, so that the air above remained colored in seven bands, of the hues in which the Sun creates his bow and the Moon her halo. These banners streamed to the rear, way beyond my sight, and as far as I could judge, the outermost ones were ten paces apart. Under as lovely a sky as I could describe came twenty-four elders, two by two, crowned with lilies. They were all singing: "Blessed art thou among the daughters of Adam, and blessed to all eternity be thy beauties." When the flowers and the other fresh herbs on the other bank opposite were free of all those chosen people, four creatures came after them, each one crowned with green leaves, as star follows star in the sky. Each was plumed with six wings, the feathers full of eyes, and the eyes of Argus, if they were living, would be like them. Reader, I will scatter no more words to describe their form since other duties constrain me so that I cannot be lavish here, but read Ezekiel, who pictures them as he saw them coming from the icy firmament in whirlwind, cloud, and fire, and as you will find them in his pages, so they were here, except that John the Divine is with me as to the wings, and differs from him. The space within the four of them contained a triumphal two-wheeled chariot drawn by a Griffin, harnessed at the neck. And the Griffin stretched each wing upwards between the center and three of the banners so that he did no harm by cutting across them. The wings rose so high their tips could not be seen. Its members were golden where he was birdlike, and the rest white mixed with brilliant red. Neither Scipio Africanus nor indeed Augustus ever gladdened Rome with so magnificent a chariot, and the Sun's would be poor by comparison, the one that was consumed when Phaethon strayed, at Earth's devout request, when Jupiter was darkly just. Three ladies came dancing in a circle by the right-hand wheel—

one was so red she would scarcely be visible in the fire; the next was as if her flesh and bones were made of emerald; the third seemed of newly fallen snow—and now they seemed led by the white, and now by the red, and from her song the others took their meter, slow or quick. By the left-hand wheel, four dressed in purple made merry, following the lead of the one with three eyes in her face. Behind the group I have described, I saw two aged men, of similar bearing but dissimilar clothing, grave and venerable: one was Luke, showing himself to be of the school of that supreme Hippocrates, whom nature made physician to the creatures she most cares for; the other, Paul, displayed the opposite role, with a sharp, gleaming sword, so that it made me afraid, even on this side of the stream. Then I saw four, of humble aspect, and behind them all, a solitary old man, John the Divine, coming by, with a visionary face, as if dreaming. And all seven were costumed like the first company, but had no garland of lilies around their heads, rather one of roses and other crimson flowers, so that someone who saw them close up would have said they were all on fire above their eyes. And when the chariot was opposite me, a clap of thunder was heard, and those noble people seemed to have their further progress stopped, and halted there with the first banners.

30

When those seven lights of the first Heaven had halted, which never knew setting or rising, or the veil of any other mist but sin, and which made all aware of their duty, just as the lower seven guide the helmsman towards port, the people of truth who had first appeared between them and the Griffin turned towards the chariot, as if towards their place of peace, and one of them, as if sent from Heaven, lifted his voice, three times, singing: "*Come with me from Lebanon, my spouse,*" and all the others sang after him. As the saints at the Last Judgment will rise, ready, each one, from his tomb, singing Halleluiah with renewed voice, so a hundred rose in the divine chariot at the voice of so great an elder, the ministers and messengers of eternal life. All were saying "*Blessed art thou that comest*" and, scattering flowers above and around, "O give lilies with full hands."

I have seen, before now, at dawn of day, the eastern sky all rose-red, and the rest of the Heavens serene and clear, and seen the sun's face rise, veiled, so that because of the moderating mists, the eye for a long while endured him; and so, in a cloud of flowers that lifted from the angelic hands and fell again, inside and beyond, a lady appeared to me, crowned with olive-leaves over a white veil, dressed in colors of living flame beneath a green cloak. And my spirit, which had endured so great a space of time since it had been struck with awe, trembling in her presence through the hidden virtue that issued from her, and without having greater knowledge through my eyes, felt the intense power of former love. As soon as that high virtue struck my sight, which had already transfixed me before I was out of my childhood, I turned to the left, with that faith with which a little boy runs to his mother when he is afraid or troubled, saying to Virgil: "There is a barely a drop of blood in me that does not tremble: I know the tokens of the ancient flame." But Virgil had left us, bereft of himself, Virgil, sweetest father, Virgil to whose guidance I gave myself; and all the beauties that our ancient mother lost did not prevent my dew-washed cheeks from turning dark again with tears.

"Dante, do not weep because Virgil goes, do not weep yet, not yet, since you must weep soon for another reason." Like an admiral who stands at stern and prow to inspect the crews who man the other ships and to encourage them to brave action, so I saw the lady who first appeared to me, veiled, beneath the angelic festival, directing her gaze towards me on this side of the stream from the left of the chariot, when I turned at the sound of my own name, which I write here from necessity. Although the veil that draped her head, crowned with Minerva's olive leaves, did not allow her to appear clearly, she continued to speak, regally and severely, like someone who holds back the sharpest words till last.

"Look at me, truly: I truly am, I truly am Beatrice. How did you dare to approach the mountain? Did you not know that here man is happy?" My eyes dropped to the clear water, but seeing myself there, I looked back at the grass, so much shame bowed my forehead down. As the mother seems severe to her child, so she seemed to me, since the savor of sharp pity tastes of bitterness. She fell silent, and immediately the Angels sang: "*In thee, O Lord, do I put my trust . . .*" but did not sing beyond the words "*my feet.*" As the snow is frozen among the living rafters along Italy's back, under the blast and stress of Slavonic winds, then, melting, trickles down inside its mass, if the ground, free of shadow, breathes, so that the fire seems to melt the candle, so I was frozen, without sighs or tears, before they sang who always harmonize their notes with the melody of the eternal spheres; but when I heard the compassion for me in their sweet harmony, greater than if they had said: "Lady, why do you shame him so?" the ice that had closed around my heart became breath and water, and issued from my chest in anguish through my mouth and eyes.

She, still standing on that side of the chariot I spoke of, directed her words then to the pitying angels: "You are vigilant in the eternal day, so that night or sleep do not hide one measure of the earth's journey along its way from you: therefore I answer with greater care so that he who weeps there can understand, so that his sorrow and his sin can be measured together. Not merely by the motion of the vast spheres that direct each seed to some objective, according to the stars' attendance, but by the generosity of divine graces that yield their rain from such lofty vapors our eyes do not reach near them, this man, potentially, was such in his new life that every true skill would have grown miraculously in him. But the more good qualities the earth's soil has, the more wild and coarse it becomes with evil seed, and lack of cultivation. For a while I supported him with my face: showing him my young eyes, I drew him with me, directed towards the right goal. But as soon as I was on the threshold of my second age and changed existences, he left me and gave himself to others. I was less dear to him, and less pleasing, when I rose from flesh to spirit, and beauty and virtue increased in me; and he turned his steps to an untrue road, chasing false illusions of good that never completely repay their promise. Nor was it any use to me to gain inspiration to call him back to himself, in dreams or otherwise, he valued them so little. He sank so low that all means to save him were already useless, except that of showing him the lost people. To achieve that, I visited the gates of the dead and, weeping, my prayers carried to him who guided him upwards. God's highest law would be broken if Lethe were passed by and such food was tasted without some tax of penitence that sheds tears."

31

She began again, continuing without delay, directing her speech with its sharp point towards me, whose edge had seemed keen to me: "O you who are on that side of the sacred stream, tell me, tell me if it is true: your confession must meet the charge." My powers were so confused that the voice sounded and was gone before it emerged from its agent. She suffered a pause, then said: "What are you thinking of? Reply to me: the sad memories you have are not yet erased by the water." Confusion and fear, joined together, drove a "Yes" from my mouth, so quietly that eyes were needed to interpret it. As a crossbow breaks, in string and bow, when fired at too high a tension, and the bolt hits the mark with lessened force, so I broke under this heavy charge, pouring out a flood of tears and sighs, and my voice died away in transit. At which she said to me: "In your desire for me that led you to love that good beyond which there is nothing to aspire to, what pits did you find in your path, or chains to bind you, that you had to despoil your hope of passing upward? And what allurements or attractions were displayed in others' faces, to make you stray towards them?"

After heaving a bitter sigh, I had hardly voice to answer, and my lips gave it shape with effort. I said, weeping: "Present things with false delights turned my steps away as soon as your face had vanished."

And she: "If you had remained silent, or denied what you have confessed, your fault would be no less noted, such is the judge who knows of it. But when self-accusation of sin bursts from the mouth in our Court, the grindstone blunts the edge. However, in order that you might be ashamed of your errors and might be more steadfast on hearing the Siren sing next time, stifle the source of your weeping and listen: then you will hear how my entombed flesh should have led you towards the opposite goal. Neither art nor nature ever presented such delight to you as the lovely body I was enclosed by, now scattered into dust; and if the greatest delight was lost to you by my death, what mortal thing should have led you to desire it? Truly, at the first sting of false things, you should have risen after me, who was no longer such.

Some young girl or other vanity of such brief enjoyment should not have weighted your wings to wait for more arrows. The young bird stays for two or three, but the net is spread and the shaft fired in vain in front of the eyes of the fully-fledged." As children stand mute with shame, listening with eyes on the ground, repentant, and self-confessing, so I stood there. And she said: "Since you are grieving at what you hear, lift your bearded face, and you will have greater grief from what you see."

A strong oak tree is uprooted with less resistance by our northern winds, or the southerlies from Iarbas's Africa, than I lifted my face at her command. And when she spoke of my beard, as a man I realized the venom behind her words. And when my head was stretched forward, my eyes saw those primal creatures resting from strewing flowers, and my eyes, not yet quite in my control, saw Beatrice, turned towards the beast with one sole person in two natures. Under her veil, and beyond the stream, she seemed to me to exceed her former self more than she exceeded others when she was here. The nettle of repentance stung me so fiercely that the thing that drew me most to love of it, of all other things became most hateful to me. Such great remorse gnawed at my heart that I fell, stunned, and what I became then she knows who gave me cause. Then, when my heart restored the power of outward things, I saw Matilda bending over me, that lady whom I had found alone, and she said: "Hold me! Hold me!" She had drawn me into the river, up to my neck, and she went along, over the water, light as a shuttle, pulling me behind her. When I was near to the shore of the blessed, I heard "*Cleanse me*" sung so sweetly I cannot remember it, nor can I describe it. The lovely lady opened her arms, clasped my head, and submerged me so that I had to swallow water, then pulled me out, and led me, cleansed, in among the dance of the four lovely ones, and each took my arm, and singing, they began: "Here we are nymphs, and in Heaven we are stars: before Beatrice descended to your world, we were ordained to be her helpers. We will take you within her sight, but the three on the other side, who look more deeply, will sharpen your vision to the joyful inward light."

Then they lead me with them up to the Griffin's breast, where Beatrice stood turned towards us. They said: "See that you do not spare your eyes: we have set you in front of the bright emeralds from which love once shot his arrows at you." A thousand desires hotter than flame kept my eyes fixed on those shining eyes, which in turn stayed fixed on the Griffin. The dual-natured creature was reflected in them, just like the sun in a mirror, with the attributes now of the human, now of the divine. Reader, think how I marveled in my mind to see the thing itself remain unmoving, and yet its image changing. While my spirit, filled with delight and wonder, was tasting that food that satisfies and causes hunger, the other three ladies, revealing themselves to be of highest nobility in their aspect, came forward, dancing to their angelic measure. "Turn Beatrice, turn your sacred eyes to your faithful one," they sang, "he who has trodden so many steps to see you. By your grace, grace us by unveiling your face to him, so that he may see the second beauty that you conceal."

O splendor of eternal living light, who of us is there, grown pale in the shadow of Parnassus, a drinker from its well, whose mind would not seem hampered trying to render you as you appeared there, where Heaven in harmony outlines you, when you showed yourself in the clear air?

32

My eyes were so fixed on satisfying their ten-year thirst that all my other senses were dulled, and there was a wall of disinterest either side of them, so that her holy smile drew my vision in towards itself, into its ancient net, at which my face was turned of necessity to my left to those goddesses, because I heard them say: "Too intensely." And the state of vision the eyes are in, struck just now by the sun, left me sightless for a while, but once my sight adjusted to lesser things (I mean lesser compared to the greater object of perception that of necessity I turned away from), I saw the glorious pageant had turned around on the right and was returning, with the sun and the seven flames in front. As a detachment turns to retreat behind its shields and wheels, with the standard, before it can fully change fronts, that militia of the Heavenly region that led passed us all by before the chariot-pole had turned. Then the ladies returned near to the wheels, and the Griffin moved the holy burden forwards, without ruffling a plume.

The lovely lady who drew me across the ford, and Statius and I, were following the right wheel that made its turn following a tighter arc. An angelic melody accompanied our steps, passing through the tall forest that was empty because of her who believed the serpent. We had gone as far, perhaps, as an arrow would travel in three flights when Beatrice descended from the chariot. I heard them all mutter "Adam!" then they surrounded a tree, with every branch stripped of blossom and foliage. The height of its canopy, which stretches out further the higher it reaches, would be marveled at by the people of India in their forests.

"Blessed, are you, Griffin, who tears nothing sweet-tasting from this tree with your beak, because the stomach is wrenched by it." So the others shouted, around the solid tree; and the creature of two natures said: "So the seed of righteousness is preserved." And turning to the pole he had dragged, he pulled it to the foot of the denuded trunk, and left bound to it the Cross that came from it. As our trees bud when the great light falls, mixed with the light that shines from Aries, following Pisces, the Heavenly Fish, and each is newly dressed with color before the sun yokes his horses under the light of the following constellation, opening tinted more than rose and less than violet, so that tree renewed itself that had naked branches before. I did not understand the hymn the people sang then, nor is it sung here, and I could not withstand its burden to the end.

If I could depict how Argus's pitiless eyes closed in sleep, hearing the tale of Syrinx, those eyes, whose greater power to watch, cost him so dear, I would paint as an artist does from a model how I fell asleep; but who can truly show drowsiness? So I move on to when I woke, and say that a bright light tore the veil of sleep, and there was a cry: "Rise, what are you about?" As at the Transfiguration, Peter, John, and James were brought to behold the blossom of Christ—the apple tree that makes the angels eager for its fruit, and makes a perpetual marriage in Heaven—and came to themselves, having been overcome at the word by which Lazarus's deeper sleep had been broken, and saw that Moses and Elias had vanished, and their Master's white raiment changed, even so I came to myself, and saw the compassionate one, who guided my steps before along the stream, bending over me.

And all bemused I said: "Where is Beatrice?" and Matilda replied: "See her sitting under the new foliage, at its root. See the company that surrounds her: the rest are rising after the Griffin, with sweeter and deeper song." And I do not know if her words went on, because now She was in front of my eyes, whose presence prevented me from attending to other things. She sat alone on the bare earth, left there as the guardian of the chariot that I had seen the dual-natured creature anchor to the tree. The seven nymphs made a ring, encircling her, carrying those lights that are secure from the north and south winds in their hands. Beatrice spoke: "You will not be a forester long here, and will be with me a citizen eternally of that Rome of which Christ is a Roman. So to help the world that lives wrongly, fix your gaze on the chariot and take care to write what you see when you return, over there." And I, completely obedient to her commands, set my mind and eyes where she desired.

Fire never fell so swiftly from dense cloud, falling from that region that is most remote, as I saw Jupiter's eagle swoop down through the tree, tearing its bark, its flowers, and its new leaves, and he struck the chariot with all his power, at which it swayed like a ship in a storm, beaten by the seas, now to larboard, then to starboard. Then I saw a vixen that seemed starved of all decent food leap into the body of the triumphal car. But my Lady put her to flight as swift as fleshless bones could sustain, rebuking her for her foul sins. Then I saw the eagle drop into the body of the chariot from the place where he had first swooped, and leave it feathered with his plumage. And a voice came from Heaven, as it comes from a sorrowing heart, and it said: "O my little boat, how badly you are freighted!" Then it seemed to me that the ground opened between the two wheels and a dragon emerged, pointing his tail upwards through the chariot; and drawing his spiteful tail towards himself, like a wasp withdrawing her sting, he wrenched away part of its base, and slid away.

What was left covered itself with those feathers, just as fertile land is covered with grass, offered perhaps with true and benign intent, and the chariot-pole and both wheels were covered by them in less time than a mouth is open for a sigh. The holy structure, transformed, grew heads above its members, three above the pole and one at each corner. The first three were horned like oxen, but the other four had a single horn on the forehead: such a monster was never seen before. Seated on it, secure as a tower on a high hill, a shameless whore appeared, looking eagerly around her. And I saw a giant standing by her side, so that she could not be snatched from him, and each kissed the other, now and then; but because she turned her lustful, wandering eye on me, her fierce lover scourged her from head to foot. Then full of jealousy and vicious with anger, he loosed the monster, and dragged it so far through the wood that he made a screen between me and the whore and monster.

33

Now as three, then four, alternately and weeping, the ladies began a sweet psalmody, singing "O God, *the heathen are come*," and Beatrice, compassionate and sighing, was listening to them, so altered in aspect that Mary was no less altered at the foot of the Cross. But when the virgins gave way for her to speak, standing upright she replied, coloring like fire: "'A little while, and ye shall not see me,' my beloved sisters, 'and again, a little while, and ye shall see me.'" Then she set all seven of them in front of her, and, merely with a nod of the head, motioned myself, the lady, and the sage who had stayed behind her. So she went on, and I believe that hardly a tenth step touched the ground, until her eyes struck my eyes, and she said to me quietly: "Come along faster, so that if I speak to you you are well placed to listen." As soon as I dutifully was next to her, she said: "Brother, why when you come along with me, do you not venture to question me?"

I was like those who are too humble in speech in front of their elders, who do not raise their voice fully to their lips, and short of full volume, I began: "Madonna, you know my needs, and what is good for them."

And she to me: "I want you to free yourself now from fear and shame, so that you no longer speak like one who dreams. Learn that the chariot that the serpent shattered was, and is not: and let him whose fault it is know that God's vengeance cannot be evaded. The eagle that left its feathers on the car to make it a monster to be preyed on shall not be without heirs forever, since I see with certainty and so I tell you stars are already nearing, safe from all barriers and impediments, that will bring us times in which a five hundred, a ten, and a five sent by God will kill the whore and the giant who sins with her. And perhaps my prophecy, as obscure as Themis and the Sphinx, persuades you less because it darkens the mind after their fashion, but the fact is that the Naiads will solve this difficult question without damage to flocks or harvest. Take note of it, and just as these words carry from me to you, tell them to those who live the life that is a race towards death, and remember when you write not to hide that you have seen the tree, now twice spoiled, here. Whoever robs it and tears at it in a blasphemous act offends God, who created it sacred to his sole use. Adam, the first soul, longed for Him in torment and desire for more than five thousand years; He who punished the bite of the apple in Himself. Your intelligence is asleep if it does not judge that tree to be so high, and widened towards its summit, from some special cause. And if your idle thoughts had not been like the waters of the river Elsa around your mind, petrifying it, and their delights had not stained it as Pyramus's blood the mulberry, you would have recognized in the tree, by these many circumstances alone, that morally God's justice is in the injunction. But since I see your mind is made of stone, and like a stone stained so the light of my words dazes you, I want you to carry my words away with you as well, if not written at least in symbolic form, for the same reason that the pilgrim's staff returns wreathed with palm branches."

And I said: "My brain is now stamped by you, like wax by the seal, whose imprint does not change. But why do your words I longed for soar so far beyond my vision that the more it strains after them, the more they vanish?"

She said: "So you may know the school you followed, and see whether its teachings follow my words, and may see that your way is as far from the divine way as the swiftest Heaven is from the earth."

At which I replied: "I do not remember that I was ever estranged from you, nor does conscience gnaw me regarding it."

She answered, smiling: "And if you cannot remember it, think now how you drank Lethe's water today; and if fire is deduced from smoke, this forgetfulness clearly proves the guiltiness of your desire, intent on other things. But now my words will be naked, as far as is needed to show them to your dull vision."

The sun was holding the noon circle, which varies here and there, as location varies, shining more brightly, traveling more slowly, when, like those who act as escorts for people who stop if they find strange things or their traces, those seven ladies stopped at the edge of a pale shadow, such as the Alps cast over their cool streams, under green leaves and dark branches. I seemed to see the Euphrates and Tigris, welling from one spring, in front of them, and parting like lingering friends. I said: "O light, O glory of humankind, what waters are these that pour from one source here, and separate themselves?" At my prayer, she said: "Beg Matilda to explain," and that lovely Lady answered her, like one who absolves herself from blame: "I have told him about this, and about other things, and I am sure Lethe's water does not hide them from him." And Beatrice said: "Perhaps some greater care, which often robs us of memory, has dimmed the eyes of his mind. But behold Eunoë that flows from there: lead him to it, and as you are used to doing, revive his flagging virtue."

Like a gentle spirit that does not make excuses but forms her will from another's will as soon as it is revealed by outward sign, so that lovely lady set out after taking charge of me and said to Statius in a ladylike way: "Come with him."

Reader, if I had more space to write, I would speak, partially at least, about that sweet drink, which would never have sated me: but because all the pages determined for the second canticle are full, the curb of art lets me go no further. I came back from the most sacred waves remade as fresh plants are, refreshed with fresh leaves, pure and ready to climb to the stars.

PARADISE

1

The glory of Him who moves all things penetrates the universe, glowing in one region more, in another less. I have been in that Heaven that knows His light most, and have seen things, which whoever descends from there has neither power nor knowledge to relate, because as our intellect draws near to its desire, it reaches such depths that memory cannot go back along the track. Nevertheless, whatever of the sacred regions I had power to treasure in my mind will now be the subject of my labor.

O good Apollo, for the final effort make me such a vessel of your genius as you demand for the gift of your beloved laurel. Till now, one peak of Parnassus was enough, but now inspired by both I must enter this remaining ring. Enter my chest and breathe, as you did when you drew Marsyas out of the sheath that covered his limbs. O Divine Virtue, if you lend me your help so that I can reveal that shadow of the kingdom of the Blessed stamped on my brain, you will see me come to your chosen bough, and there crown myself with the leaves that you, and the subject, will make me worthy of. Father, they are gathered, infrequently from it, for a Caesar's or a poet's triumph, through the fault and to the shame of human will: so the leaves of the Peneian frond should light joy in the joyful Delphic god when it makes someone long for them. A great flame follows a tiny spark: perhaps, after me, better voices will pray, and Parnassus will respond.

The light of the world rises for mortals through different gates, but he issues on a happier course, and is joined to happier stars, and molds and stamps the earthly wax more in his manner when his rising joins four circles in three crosses. It had made it morning there when it was evening here, and now that hemisphere was all bright at noon, and this one dark, when I saw Beatrice, turned towards her left, gazing at the sun. No eagle ever fixed its eyes on it so intently. And even as the reflected ray always issues from the first, and rises back upwards, like a pilgrim wishing to return, so my stance took its form from hers, infused through the eyes into my imagination, and I fixed my eyes on the sun, beyond our custom. Much is allowed to our powers there that is not allowed here, through the gift of that place made to fit the human species. I could not endure it long, but enough to see him sparkle all around, like iron poured molten from the furnace. And suddenly, it seemed that day was added to day, as though He who has the power had equipped Heaven with a second sun.

Beatrice was standing with her gaze fixed on the eternal spheres, and I, removing my sight from above, fixed it on her. In that aspect I became inwardly like Glaucus, eating the grass that made him one with the gods of the sea. To go beyond humanity is not to be conveyed in words, so let the analogy serve for those to whom grace alone may allow the experience. Love, who rules the Heavens, You know, who lifted me upwards with your light, whether I was only that which you created new in me. When the sphere, which You make eternal through the world's longing, drew my mind towards itself with that harmony which You tune and modulate, so much of the Heavens seemed to me then lit by the sun's flame that no rainfall or river's flow ever made so wide an expanse of lake. The novelty of the sound, and the great light, lit a greater longing in me than I had ever felt, desiring to know their cause. So that She, who saw me as I see myself, opened her lips, to still my troubled mind, before I could open mine to ask, and said: "You make yourself stupid with false imaginings, and so you do not see what you would see if you discarded them. You are no longer on earth, as you think, but lightning leaving its proper home never flew as quickly as you who are returning there."

If my first perplexity was answered by the brief smiling words, I was more entangled by a second, and I said: "Content and already free of one great wonder, now I am startled as to how I lift above lighter matter."

At that, after a sigh of pity, she turned her eyes towards me with that look a mother gives to her fevered child, and began: "All things observe a mutual order among themselves, and this is the structure that makes the universe resemble God. In it the higher creatures find the signature of Eternal Value, which is the end for which these laws were made that I speak of. In that order, I say, all things are graduated in diverse allocations, nearer to or further from their source, so that they move towards diverse harbors over the great sea of being, each one with its given instincts that carry it onwards. This instinct carries the fire towards the moon; that one is the mover in the mortal heart; this other pulls the earth together and unifies it. And this bow does not only fire creatures that are lacking in intelligence, but also those that have intellect and love. The Providence that orders it so makes the Empyrean, in which the ninth sphere whirls with the greatest speed, quiet with its light, and the power of the bowstring that directs whatever it fires towards a joyful target carries us towards it now, as if to the appointed place. It is true that, as form is sometimes inadequate to the artist's intention because the material fails to answer, so the creature that has power, so impelled to swerve towards some other place, sometimes deserts the track (just as fire can be seen darting down from a cloud) if its first impulse is deflected towards earth by false pleasures. You should not wonder more at your ascent, if I judge rightly, than at rivers falling from mountains to their foot. It would be a marvelous thing in you if, without any obstruction, you had settled below, just as stillness would be marvelous on earth in a living flame." At that She turned her gaze back towards Heaven.

2

O you in your little boat who, longing to hear, have followed my keel, singing on its way, turn to regain your own shores: do not commit to the open sea, since, losing me, perhaps you will be left adrift. The water I cut was never sailed before: Minerva breathes, Apollo guides, and the nine Muses point me toward the Bears. You other few who have lifted your mouths in time towards the bread of angels, by which life up here is nourished and from which none of them come away sated, you may truly set your ship to the deep saltwater, following my furrow in front of the water falling back to its level. The glorious Argonauts who sailed to Colchis, who marveled when they saw Jason turned plowman, did not marvel as much as you will.

The inborn, perpetual thirst for the divine regions lifted us almost as swiftly as you see the Heavens move. Beatrice was gazing upwards, and I at her: and I saw myself arriving, in the space of time perhaps it takes an arrow to be drawn, released, and leave the notch, there where a marvelous thing engaged my sight; and therefore She, from whom nothing I did was hidden, turning towards me, as joyful as she was lovely, said: "Turn your mind towards God in gratitude, who has joined us with the first planet." It seemed to me that a cloud covered us, dense, lucid, firm, and polished, like diamond struck by sunlight. The eternal pearl accepted us into it, as water accepts a ray of light, though still itself unbroken. If we cannot conceive here how one dimension could absorb another, which must be the case if one body enters another, and if I were then a body, the greater should be our longing to see that essence, where we see how our own nature and God's were once unified. There, what we take on trust, will be shown us, not demonstrated, but realized in ourselves, like a self-evident truth in which we believe.

I replied to her: "Lady, I thank Him who has raised me from the mortal world as devoutly as I can, but tell me what are those dark marks on this planet that make the people down there on earth make fables about Cain?"

She smiled a moment, and then said: "If human opinion errs where the key of the senses cannot unlock it, the arrows of amazement should certainly not pierce you, since you see that reason's wings are too short, even when the senses can take the lead. But tell me what you yourself think about it."

And I: "I think what appears variegated to us up here is caused by dense and rare bodies."

And She: "You will see that your thought is truly submerged in error if you listen attentively to the argument I will make against it. The eighth sphere, the Stellar Heaven, shows many lights to you, which can be seen to have diverse appearance in quantity and quality. If rarity and density alone produced that effect, there would be one quality in all of them, more or less equally distributed. Different qualities must be the result of different formal principles, and on your reasoning, only one could exist. Again, if rarity were the cause of those dark nonreflecting patches you ask about, this planet would be short of matter in one part, right through; or, as a body layers fat and lean, it would have alternate pages in its volume. If the first were true, it would be revealed by solar eclipses, when the light would shine through the less dense parts, as it does when falling on anything else that is translucent. That is not so: so we must consider the second case, and if I can show this is false also, your idea will have been refuted. If this less dense matter does not go right through, there must be a boundary beyond which its denser opposite must prevent light traveling on, and from that boundary the rays would be reflected, as colored light returns from glass that hides lead behind it. Now you will say that the ray is darker here than elsewhere because it is reflected from further back. Experiment can untangle you from that suggestion, if you will try it, which is always the spring that feeds the rivers of your science. Take three mirrors, and set two equidistant from you, and let the third, further away, be visible to your eyes, between the other two. Turn towards them, and have a light behind you reflected from the three mirrors back towards you. Though the more distant has a smaller area, you will see it shine as brightly as the others.

"Now, I wish to illuminate you, who are stripped in mind as the surface of the snow is stripped of color and coldness by the stroke of the sun's warm rays, with light so living it will tremble as you gaze at it. In the Empyrean, the Heaven of divine peace, a body whirls, the Primum Mobile, in whose virtue rests the existence of everything it contains. The Stellar Heaven that follows next, within and below it, which shows many lights, divides this existence among diverse essences, which it separates out and contains. The other seven, lower Heavens circling, dispose the distinct powers they have, in themselves, by various differentiations, to their own seeds and ends. These organs of the universe fall, as you can see, from grade to grade, since they receive from above, and work downwards. Now, note well how I thread this pass to the truth you long for, so that afterwards you may know how to keep the ford alone. The motion and power of the sacred lower gyres must be derived from the angels, who are their movers and are blessed, as the hammer's art derives from the blacksmith. And the Stellar Heaven, that so many lights beautify, takes its imprint from the profound mind of the Cherubim that turn it, and from that forms the seal. And as the soul, in your dust, diffuses itself through your different members and melds to diverse powers, so the Divine Intelligence deploys its goodness, multiplied throughout the stars, still turning around its own unity. Each separate angelic virtue makes a separate alloy with the precious body it vivifies, in which it is bound as life is bound in you. Because of the joyful nature it flows from, the angelic virtue, mingled with the body, shines through it, as joy shines through the living eye. From this come the differences between light and light, not from density or rarity; this is the formal principle that, according to its own excellence, produces the turbid and the clear."

3

That sun, which first warmed my heart with love, had unveiled lovely truth's sweet aspect to me by proof and refutation, and I lifted up my head to speak, to confess myself corrected and believing, as was needed. But something appeared that forced me to look at it, so that I stopped thinking of my confession. As the outlines of our faces are reflected from transparent, polished glass, or from clear, tranquil water that is not deep enough for the bottom to be darkened, and are so faint that a pearl on a white forehead is not distinguished more slowly by our eyes, so I saw many faces, eager to speak, at which I fell into the opposite error to that which sparked love between Narcissus and the pool. I was no sooner aware of them than, thinking they were reflected images, I turned my eyes around to see whose they were; I saw nothing, and turned them back again, straight to the light of my sweet guide whose holy eyes glowed as she smiled.

She said: "Do not wonder if I smile in the presence of your childish thought, since it does not trust itself with the truth, but turns, as it usually does, to emptiness. Those you behold are truly substantial, consigned here for failing in their vows. So speak to them, and listen, and believe, since the true light that satisfies them does not allow them to turn their steps away from itself."

And I turned to the shadow who seemed to long to speak to me most, and like someone whom too great a desire seizes, I began: "O spirit, happily created, who feels in the rays of the eternal life that sweetness never understood till it is tasted, it would please me if you would grace me with your name and your story."

At which she replied eagerly, with smiling eyes: "Our love no more closes the gate on a valid request than does that love which would make all its courts like itself. I was a virgin sister in the world, and if your memory is searched deeply, my greater beauty now will not hide me from you, but you will know me again as Piccarda, who am blessed in this sphere that moves the slowest, placed here with these others who are blessed. Our affections that are only inflamed by the pleasure of the Holy Spirit delight to be informed under his guidance. And this fate, which seems so humble, is given us because our vows were neglected and missing certain observances."

At that I said to her: "In your marvelous aspect, something divine shines out again that transmutes you from my previous concept of you. That is why I was slow to recall you to mind: now what you tell me gives me such assistance that I remember you more clearly. But tell me, you who are happy here, do you wish for a higher place, to see further, or to make yourself dearer?"

She smiled with the other shadows first a little, then replied to me so joyously she seemed to be burning with the first fire of love: "Brother, the power of love quiets our will and makes us only long for what we have, and gives us no other thirst. If we desired to be higher up, our wishes would be at odds with His will who assigns us here, and there is no room for that discord in these circles if you think again about love's nature, and that we *of necessity* have our being in love. No, it is the essence of this *being blessed* to keep ourselves to the Divine Will, through which our own wills are unified. So that our being as we are, from step to step, throughout the kingdom, is a joy to all the kingdom, as it is to the King, who draws our wills towards what He wills; and in His will is our peace: it is the sea to which all things flow that it creates and nature forms."

It was clear to me then how every part of Heaven is Paradise, even though the grace of the Highest Good does not pour down to it in only one way. But even as it happens that, if one kind of food satisfies us while the appetite for another kind persists, and giving thanks for that one we ask for the other one, so by word and gesture I learned from her what that warp was through which she had not drawn the shuttle to its end.

She said: "A life perfected, and great merit, set a lady, Saint Clare, higher in Heaven, and there are those in your world who dress and veil themselves according to her rule, so that they might sleep and wake till death with the Spouse who accepts every vow, which love has made conformable with his pleasure. I fled from the world while still a girl to follow her and shut myself in her habit, and promised to pursue the way of her company. After that, men who were more used to evil than good tore me away from that sweet cloister, and God knows what my life became then. And this other splendor, who shows herself to you on my right side, and who burns with all the light of our sphere, says what I say of myself about herself. She was a sister and, in a similar way, the shadow of the holy veil was snatched from her head. But, turned back towards the world as she was, against her will and against right dealings, she was never torn from her heart's veil. This is the light of the great Constance, who by Henry the Sixth, the second stormwind of Suabia, conceived Frederick, the third and final power."

So she spoke to me, and then began singing: "*Ave Maria*," and singing vanished like a heavy weight through deep water. My vision, which followed her as far as it could, turned when it lost her to the mark of a greater longing, and fastened its look wholly on Beatrice; but she flashed into my gaze so brightly that my sight could not at first endure it, and this made me slower with my questioning.

4

Death from starvation would come to a man between two dishes, equally distant and equally appetizing, before a free man set his teeth in either. So a lamb would stand, equally fearful, between the appetites of two fierce wolves, or a dog stand still between two hinds. So I do not blame or commend myself for keeping quiet, caught in the same way, suspended between doubts, because I was forced to. I kept quiet, but my longing was pictured on my face, and my questioning too, in far warmer colors than speech could show. And Beatrice took the part that Daniel took when he lifted Nebuchadnezzar's cloud of anger that had made him unjustly cruel, and she said: "I can see clearly how this desire and that one stirs you, so that your anxiety constricts itself and cannot breathe itself out. You argue: 'If the right intent is still there, how can another's violence lessen my measure of worth?' And you are given further cause for perplexity by the souls returning to the stars in Plato's doctrine. These are the two questions that weigh equally on your will, so I will take that first which contains the more dangerous error.

"He of the Seraphim nearest to God, Moses, Samuel, John, either one you may choose, and Mary, none of them take their places in any different Heaven than the spirits who appeared to you just now, nor do they have more years or less of existence. But all beautify the first sphere, the Empyrean, and share sweet life, but differently, by feeling the eternal spirit more, or less. They have shown themselves here not because this sphere is theirs, but to signify the least steep celestial ascent for you. Such speech needs to match your faculties that can only make fit matter, for your intellect, from what is apprehended by your senses. So the Scriptures also bend to your capacity, attributing hands and feet to God, symbolically, and Holy Church represents Gabriel and Michael, and Raphael who made Tobit complete again, in human form. What Timaeus argues concerning spirits is not what can be seen here, since he seems to believe what he says, and says the soul returns to its star, thinking it was split from it when nature gave it form, though perhaps his meaning is different than the words say and may have an intention that should not be derided. If he means that the honor and the blame ascribed to their influence returns to these spheres, perhaps his arrow hits some mark of truth. This principle, badly understood, almost wrenched the whole world awry, so that it rushed to call upon the names of Jupiter, Mars, and Mercury.

"The other source of doubt that troubles you is less venomous, because its evil influence could not lead you away from me elsewhere. That our justice appears an injustice to mortal eyes is a question for faith, not for heretical error. But since your intellect has the power to penetrate easily to this truth, I will satisfy you, as you desire. If violence occurs when those who suffer it do nothing to contribute to what displays force towards them, well then these souls did not have that excuse, since the will cannot be overcome if it does not will to be, but behaves like nature in the flames, though a thousand times wrenched away by violence. But if it wavers, more or less, it helps the force against it; and they wavered, since they had the power to return later to the sacred place. If their will had remained entire, like that which held Saint Lawrence on the grid, and made Mucius Scaevola treat his right hand with severity, it would have pushed them back towards the path from which they were taken as soon as they were free; but such strong will is all too rare. Now, if you have gleaned what you should have from these words, the difficulty that would have troubled you many more times has been resolved. But now another gulf across your track meets your eyes, which would make you weary before you crossed it alone. I have surely instilled in your mind that spirits who are blessed cannot tell a lie, because they live close to the First Truth; likewise, you might have understood from Piccarda that Constance maintained her devotion to the veil, so that Piccarda appears to contradict me. Brother, many times before things have been done to escape danger that were against the grain, and not fitting: so Alcmaeon, moved by his father's prayer, killed his own mother, and to be pious, rendered himself impious. At this point, I want you to remember that violence is allowed by the will, and they work together, so that the offense cannot be excused. The absolute will does not consent to evil, but it does consent inasmuch as it fears that if it does not, it will encounter worse. So, when Piccarda expresses this, she is speaking of the absolute will, and I of the practical will, so that, together, we both speak the truth."

Such was the flow from that holy stream that rose from the foun-

tain from which all truth derives, and was such that it brought peace
to both my desires. Then I said: "O divine lady, loved by the First
Lover, you whose speech floods through me and warms me so that it
makes me more and more alive, my affections have not the depth to
be able to return grace for grace, but may He who sees it, and has the
power, respond to it. Now I see that our intellect can never be satisfied
unless *the* truth, which no truth goes beyond, shines on it. It rests
there, like a wild creature in its lair, as soon as it has reached it, and it
can, otherwise all longing would be in vain. So inquiry grows, like a
new shoot at the base of truth, a natural thing that rises towards the
summit, from ridge to ridge. That invites me, and gives me confidence, to question you lady, reverentially, about another truth hidden
from me: I wish to know if Man can give you such satisfaction, by
other good intentions, for his broken vows, as not to weigh short on
your scales."

Beatrice looked at me with eyes so filled with divine sparks of love
that my faculties turned away with downcast eyes, overcome, and I felt
lost.

5

"If I blaze at you in the heat of love beyond the degree of what is seen on earth, and in so doing overcome the power of your eyes, do not wonder, since it arises from perfect vision that, as it understands, advances in the good it understands. I note clearly how the eternal light already shines back from your intellect, that which, once seen, always sets love alight, and if anything else seduces your love, it is nothing but a trace of this light, wrongly comprehended, that shines through in it. You wish to know whether reparation may be made for broken vows by means of some other service, great enough as to render the soul secure from disputation." So Beatrice began this canto, and like someone who does not pause, continued the sacred progress, like this: "The greatest gift that God made at the creation out of his munificence, the one that most fitted his supreme goodness and which he values most, is Free Will, with which intelligent creatures all and sundry were and are endowed. Now the high value placed on vows will be clear to you, if they are made such that God consents when you consent, since, in confirming the pact between God and Man, the guilty party is rendered such by this treasure of Free Will, just as I say, and by their own act. What can be done then in recompense? If you thought to make good use of what you once consecrated, you would be doing good with stolen evil. You are now clear on the major point. But since Holy Church grants dispensations that seem to run counter to the truth I have revealed, you must still sit at table for a while, as the tough fibers you have eaten require further help to aid digestion. Open your mind to what I unfold for you, and fix it inwardly, since to understand and not retain is not knowledge.

"Two things appertain to the essence of this self-sacrifice: the first is its content, the second is the vow itself. The latter can never be canceled, except by being kept, and it is about this that my previous discourse is so precise, so it was always necessary for the Hebrews to make sacrifice, though as you ought to know, the thing sacrificed might sometimes be altered. The content, the other aspect of the matter being explained to you, may indeed be such that there is no offense if it is substituted by other content. But let no one shift the burden from his shoulder at his own discretion without a turn of the gold and silver keys. And let him consider any change as foolish unless the thing that is lapsed from bears a proportion of four to six to the thing replacing it. And so whatever weighs so heavily in respect of its value that it exceeds every scale can never be replaced by any other means. Human beings should never take vows lightly: be faithful, and not perverse, as Jepthath was perverse in his first vow, whom it would have been more fitting to have said 'I did wrong' than keep the vow and do worse; and you may accuse the great leader of the Greeks of the same foolishness that made Iphigenia weep that her face was lovely, and made the wise and foolish weep for her, hearing tell of such a rite. Be more cautious in action, you Christians, not like a feather blown by every wind, and do not think that all water purifies. You have the Old and New Testaments, and the shepherd of the Church to guide you: let that be enough for your salvation. If evil greed declares otherwise, be men instead of mindless sheep, so that the Jews among you do not deride you. Do not do as the lamb does that leaves its mother's milk, capricious and silly, sporting with itself for pleasure."

So Beatrice spoke to me, as I have written it: then she turned, all in longing, to that region where the universe is most alive. Her silence, and her changed aspect, demanded reticence from my eager intellect that already had new questions to ask. And like an arrow that hits the target before the bowstring is still, we rose to the second sphere.

There I saw my lady so delighted at committing herself to the light of this Heaven that the planet itself grew brighter. And if the star was altered and smiled, what did I become, who am by my very nature changeable in every way? As the fish in a still, clear pool swim towards whatever falls from above that they consider something to feed on, so I saw more than a thousand radiances draw towards us, and in each one was heard: "Behold someone who will increase our love." And as each one came to us, the shadow seemed filled with delight, judging by the bright glow that came from it.

Reader, think how you would feel an anguished craving to know more if what I have started did not continue and you will see yourself how I longed to hear from them about their state as soon as they were manifested to my sight.

"O fortunately born one, you to whom grace concedes the right to see the thrones of eternal triumph before you abandon the place of militancy, we are fired by the light that burns through all the Heavens, and therefore if you want to be lit by us, satisfy yourself at pleasure." So one of the spirits said to me, and Beatrice said: "Speak, speak in safety, and believe them as you would gods."

Turned to the light that had spoken to me first, I said: "Truly I see how you are nested in your own light, and that you draw it through your eyes, since they sparkle as you smile, but I do not know who you are, noble spirit, or why you are graded in this sphere that is veiled for mortals in the sun's rays," at which it glowed more brightly even than before. Like the sun that hides itself in excess light when heat has eaten away the moderating effect of the thick clouds, so the sacred figure, through greater delight, hid himself in his own rays, and so all enclosed replied to me, as the following canto chants.

6

"When Constantine had turned the Imperial eagle eastwards against the sky's course, which it had followed in the wake of Aeneas, who took Lavinia from her father, the Bird of God held court at the extremity of Europe for two hundred years and more, near to the mountains of Troy that he had first issued from; and there he ruled the world, under the shadow of his sacred wings, from reign to reign, until by the passage of time, rule fell to me. Caesar I was, Justinian I am, who pared excess and ineffectiveness from the law at the wish of the First Love I now feel; and when I first fixed my mind on that labor, I held that Christ had one nature and no more, and I was content in that belief; but the blessed Agapetus, who was pope, pointed me to the true faith by his words. I believed him, and now I see the content of his faith as clearly as you see that in every contradictory pair, if one statement is false the other is true. As soon as I was in step with the Church, it pleased God, in His grace, to inspire me to that high task, and I gave it my all, and committed my weapons to Belisarius, whom Heaven's right hand was so wedded to it was a sign that I should rest from them. Now here is the end, already, of my answer to your first question, who I am; but its context forces me to follow with some additions.

"So you may know how much reason is on the side of those who oppose the sacred banner of Empire, as well as those who embrace it, see how great a nobility has made it worthy of reverence, beginning from the time when Pallas died to ensure its rule. You know it rested in Alba Longa for more than three hundred years, until the end, when the three Horatii and the three Curiatii fought for it. And you know what it enacted, from the wrong to the Sabine women to Lucretia's grief, through the reigns of seven kings who conquered the neighboring peoples. You know what it did, carried against Brennus the Gaul, against Greek Pyrrhus, and against the other princes and powers, from which Torquatus, and Cincinnatus, named for his curling hair, the Decii, and the Fabii, earned the fame that I delight in remembering.

It threw down the Arab pride that followed Hannibal over the Alps, from which the river Po rises. Scipio and Pompey triumphed beneath it while still young, and it was bitter to Fiesole, in those hills under which you were born. Then, near the time when Heaven wished to lead the world to its own peaceful mode, Caesar laid hands on it, at Rome's wish, and the Isère and Arar, the Seine, and every valley filled by the Rhone, know what it achieved then, from Var to Rhine. What it did then, when he left Ravenna and crossed the Rubicon, was so great that tongue and pen could not describe it. It wheeled the armies towards Spain, and then Durazzo, and struck Pharsalia so fiercely that the pain was felt as far as the hot Nile. It saw Trojan Antandros and Simois again, from which it first came, and saw the place where Hector lies, and then, alas for Ptolemy, soared again, and afterwards swooped on Juba in a lightning flash, then wheeled to the west where it heard the Pompeian trumpets. Brutus and Cassius howl in Hell because of its support for Augustus who followed, and it made Modena and Perugia mourn. Miserable Cleopatra still suffers because of it, who, as she fled from the eagle, took dark sudden death from the viper. It ran with Augustus to the coast of the Red Sea, and with him brought the world to such a peace that Janus saw his temple gates closed. But what the Eagle that I speak of did before, what it was yet to do throughout the subject mortal world, becomes a dull and insignificant thing to see if the standard is viewed, with clear eye and pure heart, in the third Caesar's hand, since the living justice that was my inspiration granted it the glory of taking vengeance for his anger, in the hands of which I speak.

"Now see the wonder in the twofold thing I tell you! It rushed to wreak vengeance on that vengeance for the ancient sin afterwards, under Titus. And much later when the Lombard tooth gnawed at the Holy Church, Charlemagne, victorious, sheltered her under its wings. Now you may judge those I accused just now and their sins, which are the cause of all your troubles. One faction opposes the golden lilies of France to the people's Eagle, and the other appropriates it to their party, so that it is difficult to see which one offends the most. Let the Ghibellines deploy their skills under some other banner, since he who divorces it from justice always follows it to disaster. And do not let that new Charles beat it down with his Guelphs, but let him fear the talons that have torn the hide from greater lions than him. Many a time before now the children have grieved for the father's sin, and do not let Charles imagine that God will change his coat of arms for royal lilies.

"This little planet adorns herself with good souls who actively searched for honor and fame, and when desire, swerving, tends towards that, the rays of true love shine upwards with less life. But part of our delight is in the matching of our reward to our merit, because we see them neither magnified nor lessened. By this, the living justice so sweetens our affections that they may never be twisted to any malice. On earth a diversity of voices creates sweet harmony, and in the same way the different degrees in this life make sweet harmony among the spheres.

"And here in this pearl, the light of Romeo of Villeneuve shines, whose fine and extensive efforts were so badly rewarded. But the Provençals who harmed him cannot smile, and he who makes his own ruin out of another's goodness takes a bad road. Raymond Berenger had four daughters, every one a queen, and this was achieved on his behalf by Romeo of Villeneuve, a humble pilgrim wanderer; then muttered words made Raymond demand account from this just man, who gave him twelve for every ten, and Romeo went his way again, old and poor; and if the world knew the heart he had in him, who begged, crust after crust, to stay alive, much as it praises him, it would praise him more."

7

"Hosanna, Holy God of Sabaoth,
Illuminating the blessed fires of these kingdoms
With Your brightness from above!"

So I saw him singing, to whom the double luster of law and empire adds itself, revolving to his own note, and he and the others moved in dance, and like the swiftest of sparks, suddenly veiled themselves from me in the distance. I said, hesitating: "Speak to her, speak," to myself, "speak to my Lady who quenches my thirst with the sweetest drops." But that reverence that completely overcomes me even at the sound of *Be* or *ice* bowed me again, like a man who slumbers.

Beatrice let me be like that only for a moment, than began to direct the rays of her smile towards me that would make a man happy in the flames: "According to my unerring perception, those words about how just vengeance was revenged with justice have set you thinking, but I will quickly relieve your thoughts; now listen closely since my words will grant you the gift of a noble statement. Adam, that man who was not born, condemned his whole race because he would not suffer a rein on his will for his own good. Therefore Humanity lay in sickness down there and in great error for many ages, until it pleased God's Word to descend, when He joined that nature that had wandered from its Creator to His own person, solely by an act of his eternal love. Now turn your vision to what I now say: this nature, joined to its maker, was pure and good, as it was when first created, but it had been exiled from Paradise by its own action, by turning from the way of truth and its own life. Measured by the nature assumed, no penalty was ever exacted so justly as that one inflicted on the Cross, and if we gaze at the Person who endured it, in whom that nature was incarnate, by the same measure no punishment was ever so unjust. So contrary effects came from one cause: God and the Jews were satisfied by the same death, and Earth shook, and Heaven opened at it. Now, it should not seem a difficulty to you to hear it said that just revenge was taken by the Court of Justice. But now I see your mind tangled in knots, from thought to thought, which it greatly longs for release from. You are saying to yourself: Yes, I understand what I hear, but why God only willed this method of our redemption is hidden from me. Brother, this decree is buried from the sight of everyone whose intellect is not ripened in love's flame. But I will reveal why this method was the most valuable, since it is knowledge often aimed at, but little understood.

"The Divine Good that rejects all envy shoots out such sparks from its inner fire as to show forth the eternal beauty. What distills from it, without mediation, is eternal, because the print cannot be removed once it has stamped the seal. What rains down from it, without mediation, is total freedom, since it is not subject to the power of transient things. It conforms more closely to the Good and is therefore more pleasing to it, since the sacred flame that lights everything is most alive in what most resembles it. The human creature has all these advantages, and if one fails, then that creature falls from nobility. Sin is the only thing that disenfranchises it and makes it dissimilar to the Highest Good, so that its light irradiates it less and the creature may never return to dignity unless it fills the place where guilt has made a void, with just punishment for sinful delight. When your nature sinned in totality in the first seed, it was parted from dignity, as it was from Paradise, and they could not be regained, however subtly you search, except by crossing over one of these two fords: either that God out of his grace remitted the debt, or Man gave satisfaction for his foolishness. Now fix your eyes on the abyss of Eternal Wisdom, following my speech as closely as you can.

"Man had no power ever to be able to give satisfaction in his own being, since he could not humble himself by new obedience as deeply as he had aimed, so highly to exalt himself through disobedience. This was the reason why man was shut out from the power to give satisfaction by himself. Therefore God had to return Man to his perfect life in his own way, that is, through mercy or through justice, or both. And since what is done by the doer is more gracious the more it shows us the goodness of the heart it comes from, the Divine Goodness that imprints the world was content to act in both ways to raise you up again. Between the first day and the last, there never was, nor ever will be again, so high and magnificent a progress on either of those roads, since God was more generous in giving of Himself, to make Man capable of rising again, than if He had only granted remission from Himself; and every other way fell short of justice, except that by which the Son of God humbled Himself to become incarnate.

"Now to answer all your longings, I go back to explain a certain passage so that you can understand it as I do. You are saying to yourself: I see the water, fire, earth, and air, and all their mixtures come to corruption, and do not last for long, and yet these things were creatures, and ought to be secure from corruption, if what I have said to you is true. Brother, the angels, and the pure region where you are, may be said to be created as they are, in their total being, but the elements you have named and all the compounds of them have been inwardly *formed* by a created power. The matter that they hold was created; the formative power in those stars which circle around them was created. The life of every wild creature and every plant is drawn from compounds gaining power by the rays and motion of the sacred lights. But your life is breathed into you without mediation by the supreme beneficence that makes life love it, so that it always longs for it. And from this you can deduce your resurrection in the flesh, if you again consider how human bodies were first made, when your first parents were both made."

8

In its pagan days the world used to believe that lovely Cyprian Venus used to beam down fond love, turning in the third epicycle, so that those ancient peoples, in ancient error, not only did her the honor of sacrifice and the votive cry, but honored Dione as well, and Cupid—one as her mother, the other as her son—and told how Cupid sat in Dido's lap; and from her, from whom I take my start, they took the name of the planet that courts the Sun, now setting in front, and now behind.

I had no sense of rising into her sphere, but my Lady's aspect gave me faith that I was there, because I saw her grow more beautiful. And as we see a spark in a flame, and as a voice can be distinguished from a voice if one remains fixed and the other comes and goes, so in that light itself I saw other lamps moving in circles, faster or slower, in accord, I believe, with the nature of their eternal vision. Blasts never blew from a chill cold, visibly or invisibly, so rapidly that that they would not seem slow and hindered to whoever had seen those divine lights coming towards us, leaving the sphere that has its first conception in the exalted seraphim. And among those who appeared most in advance, "Hosanna" sounded in such a manner that ever since I have not been free of the desire to hear it again.

Then one came nearer to us, and began alone: "We are all at your pleasure so that you may have joy of us. We orbit with those celestial princes in one circle, and one circling, and with one thirst, we to whom you from the world below once said: 'You who by understanding move the third circle'; and we are so filled with love that a moment of rest to give you pleasure will be no less sweet to us."

When my eyes had been lifted in reverence to my Lady, and she had herself given them satisfaction and assurance, they turned back to the light that had offered itself so generously, and: "Say, who you are" were my words, stamped with great affection. Oh, how I saw it grow in size and splendor at the new joy, added to its joys when I spoke! Altered in that way, it said to me: "The world held me below for only a little while: if it had been longer, much of the evil that will happen would not happen. My joy, shining around me, keeps me hidden from you, concealing me like a silkworm cocooned in its own silk. You loved me greatly, and with good cause, since if I had stayed below I would have shown you greater love than the mere shoots of it. That left bank that the Rhone washes after its meeting with the Sorgue waited for me to be its lord in time, as did Naples, that stretch of Ausonia, with its cities of Bari, Gaeta, and Catona, down from where Tronto and Verde discharge into the sea. The crown of the land that the Danube waters when it has left its German banks already shone on my forehead, and beautiful Sicily, Trinacria, over the gulf the east wind torments most, which is darkened between Pachynus and Pelorus, not by Typhon but by the sulphurous clouds, would still have looked for its kings born of the line through me from Charles and Rudolph if bad governance, which stirs the hearts of subject peoples, had not caused Palermo to cry out: 'Death, Death.' And if my brother Robert of Calabria had seen it in good time, he would already have avoided the greedy adventurers of Catalonia before they did him wrong, and indeed he or another needs to make provision that a heavier load is not laid on his already laden boat. His nature, meanness descended from generosity, needs soldiers who do not care about stuffing their purses."

I said: "Sir, because I believe you see the great joy your conversation floods me with, as I see it, there where every good has its beginning and end, it is more gratifying to me, and also I value that you see it by gazing on God. You have given me delight, now enlighten me, since in speaking you have stirred me to question how bitter seed can be born from the sweet."

And he to me: "If I can show you a truth, you will have the thing you ask, which is behind your back in front of your eyes. The Good, which turns and makes content the whole kingdom that you climb, makes its providence a power in these great celestial bodies, and provision is not only made for the nature of things but for their welfare too, by that Mind that is perfection in itself. So whatever this bow fires moves towards its destined end, like an arrow fired at the mark. If that were not so, the Heaven you are crossing would bring its effects into being so that they would be chaos and not art, and that cannot be unless the intellects that move these planets are defective, and the First Mover too, who failed to perfect them. Do you wish this truth to be clarified more?"

I said: "No, since I know it is impossible for Nature to fall short of what is needed."

And he again: "Now, say, would it be worse for man if he were not a citizen on earth but left to his own sufficiency?"

"Yes," I replied, "and I do not need to ask the reason."

"And can that be, unless men live various lives below, and with various tasks? Not if your master wrote truly for you." He reached this point, deducing, and then gave the conclusion: "Therefore the roots of your qualities must be diverse, so that one is born Solon, and another Xerxes, one Melchizedek, and another the inventor who lost his son soaring through the sky. Circling Nature, the seal on the mortal wax is a good maker, and does not distinguish between one house and another. So that Esau differs from Jacob in the seed, and Romulus worshiped as Quirinus comes from so lowly a father he is assigned to Mars instead. The nature at birth would always be like its parent, if Divine Providence did not overrule it. Now what was hidden behind you is in front of you, but so you may know I am delighted with you, I will wrap you around with a corollary. Nature makes a poor fist of things if she finds events out of harmony with herself, like any other seed out of its proper soil. If the world below paid attention to the foundation Nature lays, and followed that, it would be satisfied with its citizens, but you drag him born to the sword into a religious order, and make a king of him who should be an orator, so that your path cuts across the road."

9

Lovely Clemence, when your Charles had clarified things for me, he told me about the wrongs his seed was fated to encounter, but added: "Be silent, and let the years turn," so that I can say nothing except that well-justified grief will follow those wrongs. And already the life of that holy light had turned towards the Sun that illuminates it, as towards the Good which is sufficient to everything. O impious creatures! O deceived spirits who twist your hearts away from that Good, turning your minds to vanities!

And see, another of those splendors came towards me and signified its desire to satisfy me by an outer brightening. Beatrice's eyes, gazing at me as before, assured me of happy assent to my wish. I said: "Ah, give quick satisfaction to my will, spirit who are blessed, and show proof that I can reflect what I think from you."

At which the light that was still a stranger to me, from the depths where it was at first singing, continued by speaking, like one happy to do good: "In that region of Italy, the depraved country, which lies between Venice and the sources of the Brenta and Piave, rises a hill raised to no great height, from which a firebrand descended who made a vicious assault on that land. I sprang with him out of the same root: Cunizza I am called, and I shine here because the light of this star conquered me. But I grant myself indulgence for my fate, and it does not grieve me, which perhaps would seem strange to the common man. The great fame of this dear shining jewel in our Heaven, who is my nearest neighbor, remains, and before it dies this centenary year will be repeated five times. See how another life follows the first if a man achieves excellence! The present crew, enclosed by the Tagliamento and the Adige, do not think of that, beaten but still unrepentant. But it will soon come to pass that Paduan blood will stain the water that bathes Vicenza, because the people rebel against their duty. And at Treviso, where the Sile meets the Cagnano, one holds sway and goes with head held high, for whom the net to catch him is already woven. From Feltro a wail of grief will rise yet, because of the sins of its impious pastor, so foul, that no one ever entered the prison of Malta for their equal. The dish that would be needed to receive Ferrara's blood, which this obliging priest will give up to show himself loyal, would be too large and weary whoever had to weigh it ounce by ounce; and such are the gifts that suit this country's way of life. There are mirrors above— you call them Thrones—from which God shines in judgment on us so that these words prove good to us." Here she fell silent, and to me she seemed like one who turns to other things, giving herself to the wheel, so that she was as before.

The other joyful light, which I had already noted as being distinguished, shone to my sight like a fine ruby, illuminated by the sun. Brightness comes from joy up there, as a smile does here on earth, while down below the spirits are dark outside, just as the mind is saddened. I said: "God sees all, and your vision is in him, spirit of the blessed, so that no desire is hidden from you. Why then does your voice, which, with the singing of those devoted fires who make a cowl with six wings of themselves gladdens Heaven endlessly, not satisfy my wishes? If I were in you, as you are in me, I would not have waited for your request till now."

Then he began to speak: "That greatest valley into which water flows from the ocean around the earth extends so far between its opposite shores eastward that its zenith is formed of what was horizon. I was an inhabitant of Marseilles's shore, halfway between the Ebro and the Macra, which, with its short course, separates the Genoese and the Tuscans. The site of Bougia in Algeria is almost alike in sunrises and sunsets to the place I come from, whose harbor Caesar once warmed with that place's blood. Those who knew me called me Folco, and I imprint this Heaven as it imprinted me, since Belus's daughter, wronging Sichaeus and Creüsa, burned no hotter than I, as long as it suited my youthfulness, nor did the girl from Rhodope who was deceived by Demophoön, nor Hercules when his heart enclosed Iole. But this is not a place of repentance; here we smile not at the sin, which the mind does not dwell on, but the Power that ordained and provided. Here we gaze at the art that beautified so great a creation, and discern the good, which returns the world below to the world above. But so that you might fully satisfy all the longings born in this sphere, I must continue. You will wish to know who is inside that light that gleams next to me, like the sun's rays in pure water. Know now that Rahab finds peace there, and when she joined our order, it sealed itself in the highest rank with her. Before any other soul, she

was uplifted at Christ's triumph by this sphere, which is touched by
the shadow your Earth casts into space. It was truly fitting to leave her
in one of the Heavens as a symbol of the great victory achieved by
those two nailed hands, because she favored Joshua's first glorious
campaign in the Holy Land, that land that scarcely touches this pope's
memory.

"Your city, founded by that Satan who first turned his back on his
Maker and from whose envy such great grief has come, coins and
spreads that accursed lily flower that has sent the sheep and lambs
astray, since it has made a wolf of the shepherd. So the Gospels and
the great Doctors are neglected, and only the Decretals are studied, as
can be seen by their margins. On that the pope and cardinals are
intent: their thoughts do not stray to Nazareth, where Gabriel's wings
unfolded. But the Vatican and the other sacred parts of Rome, that
cemetery for the soldiers who followed Peter, will soon be freed from
the bond of adultery."

10

The primal and unutterable Power, gazing at his Son with the love that both breathe out eternally, made whatever circles through mind and space with such order that whoever knows them is not without some sense of Him. Then, reader, raise your eyes with me to the distant wheels, directed to that point where the celestial equator and the ecliptic meet, and begin to view the art of that Master who loves it so much, within Himself, that he never lets His eyes leave it. See how the ecliptic, the oblique circle that carries the planets, slants from that equinoctial point to satisfy the world's call for them; and if their path were not inclined, much of the power of the Heavens would be useless, and every potential dead on Earth; and if the slope from the level was greater or smaller, much would be lacking in cosmic order below and above.

Now, reader, stay on your bench, thinking back on this preamble if you would delight in it before you weary. I have put the food in front of you; now feed yourself, since the matter I have set myself to write of now draws my complete attention to itself.

The Sun, the greatest minister of Nature, who stamps the world with the power of Heaven and measures time for us by his light, was circling on the spiral where he shows himself earlier every day, joined to that equinoctial point I recalled. And I was with him, but I was no more aware of my ascent than a man is aware of his first thoughts approaching. It is Beatrice who leads me from good to better, so suddenly that her action requires no time. How bright in itself must that be that shows itself in the Sun, which I had entered, not by color but by light! Though I might call on intellect, art, and knowledge, I could never express it so as to make it imaginable, but it may be believed and desired to be seen. And if our imaginations are too base for such exaltation, it is no surprise, since no eye could ever transcend the Sun. Such was the fourth house of the supreme Father, who always contents it by showing how he breathes and engenders.

And Beatrice began to speak: "Give thanks, give thanks to the Sun of the angels, who in his grace has raised you to this visible sun." The heart of man was never so disposed to devotion and so eager to give itself to God with all its will as I was at those words, and my love was committed to Him so completely it eclipsed Beatrice from memory. That did not displease her, but she smiled at it so that the splendor of her laughing eyes scattered my mind's coherence amongst many things.

Then I saw many lights, living and victorious, make a central point of us, and a coronet, even sweeter in voice than shining in appearance, of themselves. So we sometimes see Latona's daughter haloed when the air is so damp as to retain the rainbow thread that weaves her zone. There are many jewels so dear and lovely in the courts of Heaven I have returned from that they cannot be moved from that region, and such was the song of these lights that he who does not wing himself to fly up to them may as well look for news of them from the speechless.

When those burning suns, so singing, had circled around us three times, like stars near the fixed poles, they seemed as ladies do: not released from the dance, but resting, silent, listening, until they hear the notes again. And in one I heard a voice begin to say: "Since the light of grace glows in you at which true love is lit, and then by loving is multiplied so as to lead you on that stair that no one descends except to climb again, whoever denied you the wine from his glass to quench your thirst would be as little at liberty to do so as water to refuse to flow to the sea. You wish to know with what flowers this garland is decorated that circles the lovely lady who strengthens your resolve for Heaven. I was one of the lambs, of the sacred flock, that Dominic leads on the path 'where there is good pasture,' if we do not stray. He who is nearest to me on the right was my master and my brother: he was Albert of Cologne, and I, Thomas Aquinas. If you wish to know the rest as well, circling above around the garland, blessed, direct your sight according to my words. This next flamelet issues from Gratian's smile, he who gave such help to the ecclesiastical and civil spheres as is acceptable in Paradise. The fourth that adorns our choir next was that Peter Lombard who, like the poor widow, offered his wealth to Holy Church. The fifth light, which is most beautiful among us, breathes from such a love that all the world below thirsts to have news of it. In there is the noble mind of the one who was granted a wisdom so profound that, if truth be known, no other ever achieved so complete a vision. Next look at that taper's light, one who in the flesh down there saw deepest into the angelic nature and its ministry.

In the seventh little light smiles that pleader for the Christian age whose works Augustine made use of. Now if you run your mind's eye from light to light, following my praise, you are already thirsting for the eighth. In there, seeing every good, the sainted soul rejoices who unmasked the deceitful world to those who give him a careful hearing. The body from which it was chased out lies down below in Cieldauro, and it came from exile and martyrdom to this peace. Next, see the glowing breath of Isidore flame out, of Bede, and Richard, who in contemplation exceeded all men. The one from whom your glance returns to me is the light of a spirit of profound thought who seemed to himself to reach death too slowly: it is the eternal light of Sigier, who, lecturing in the Rue du Fouarre, syllogized truths that brought him hatred."

Then, as the clock that strikes the hour when the bride of God rises to sing her matins to the Bridegroom, so that He might love her, where one part pulls and pushes another, making a chiming sound of such sweet notes that the well-disposed spirit fills with love, so I saw the glorious wheel revolve and answer voice to voice in harmony, and with a sweetness that cannot be known except where joy renders itself eternal.

11

O mindless mortal cares! How defective the reasoning that makes you beat your wings towards the earth! One person was chasing law, another medicine; one following the priesthood, another ruled by force or sophistry; one robbery, another civic business; one was involved in bodily pleasure, and another taking his ease—while I, free of all these things, was received with Beatrice so gloriously in Heaven.

When each spirit had returned to the place in the circle where he was before, he rested, like a candle in its holder. And I saw a smile begin inside the light that had first spoken as it grew brighter, and Thomas said: "Just as I glow with its rays, so as I gaze into the Eternal Light I know the reason for your thoughts. You question and wish to understand my words in such open and extended speech as will match your comprehension, the words I spoke just now—'where there is good pasture' and 'no other ever achieved'—and here we need to draw careful distinctions. The Providence that governs the world with wisdom that defeats every creature's understanding before that creature can plumb its depths ordained two princes to be guides over there and over here, on behalf of the Church, the spouse of Him who wedded Her with great cries in blessed blood, in order that She might go to Christ, her delight, secure in Herself, and more faithful to Him. The one was all Seraphic in his ardor, the other was a splendor of cherubic light on earth. I will speak of the first, because whoever praises either, whichever he chooses, talks of both, since both their efforts were to the same end.

"A fertile slope falls from a high mountain between the Tupino and the Chiascio, the stream that drops from the hill chosen by the blessed Ubaldo, a slope from which Perugia feels the cold and heat, through the eastern gate of Porta Sole, and behind it the towns of Nocera and Gualdo bemoan the Angevin's heavy yoke. From this slope, where it becomes least steep, a Sun was born into this world, even as our sun rises from the Ganges. So that whoever speaks of that place, let him not say *Ascesi* ["I have ascended"], which is inadequate, but

Oriente ["Dayspring"] if he wants to name it correctly. He was not far from rising when he began to make the earth feel a certain comfort from his great virtue, since in his youth he rushed to oppose his father for such a Lady to whom, like Death, no one opens the gate of his pleasure, and he was united to her in the spiritual court that had jurisdiction over him, and in his father's presence, and then loved her more deeply, from day to day. She, deprived of her first husband for eleven hundred years and more, was obscure, despised, until he stood in front of her, uninvited. And the tale that she was found safe with Amyclas when Caesar's voice sounded to terrify the world had not helped her, nor to have been so faithful and unafraid that She mounted the Cross with Christ when Mary remained below. But lest I proceed too darkly, accept in plain speech that Francis and Poverty were these two lovers. Their harmony and their delighted appearance made love, wonder, and tender looks, the cause of sacred thought, so that the venerable Bernard first cast off his sandals and ran to chase after so great a peacefulness, and thought himself all too slow while he ran. O unnoted riches, O fertile good! Egidius casts off his sandals, and Sylvester, following the Bridegroom, as the Bride delights to do. This Master and this Father went his way, together with his Lady, and with that family already wearing the humble cord, nor did lowliness of heart weigh down his forehead, because he was Pietro Bernardino's son, nor that he seemed to be so greatly despised. But he revealed his serious intention to Pope Innocent, and took the seal of his Order from him. When the people of poverty who followed his path increased, his miraculous life sung more sweetly in Heaven's glory, then was this master shepherd's sacred will encircled with a second crown, from Honorious's hands, by the Eternal Spirit. And when, thirsting for martyrdom, he had preached Christ and his followers' message, in the proud Sultan's presence, and, finding the people bitterly against conversion, had returned to avoid a useless stay to gather fruit from the Italian branches; then, on the harsh rock between the Tiber and the Arno, he received the final wounds from Christ that his limbs showed for two years. When it pleased Him, who ordained him to such good effect, to raise him to the reward, which he had earned by humbling himself, he commended his Lady to his brotherhood, his rightful heirs, and asked that they should love her faithfully, and the illustrious spirit willed himself to leave her breast, turning to his own kingdom, yet wished for no other deathbed for his body.

"Now think what he must be who was a worthy colleague to maintain the course of Peter's boat in the right direction! Such was our founder, so that whoever follows his commands, as you can see, freights himself with good cargoes. But his flock has grown so greedy for new food, it cannot do other than stray through strange pastures, and the more his distant, wandering sheep stray from him, the emptier of milk they return to the fold. Indeed there are some of them who fear the loss, and keep close to the shepherd, but they are so few it needs little cloth to make cowls for them. Now, if my words have not been weak, if you have listened closely, and if you recall what I have said, your wish must now be partly satisfied, since you can see the stem they whittle away, and can see the rebuke intended in the words 'where there is good pasture, if we do not stray.'"

12

As soon as the flame of the spirit that was blessed had spoken the last word, the sacred mill began to turn, and had not fully revolved before a second, circling, clasped it, and harmonized movement with movement and song with song—song that is as far beyond our Muses and our Sirens in those sweet pipings as the first glory its reflection. As two rainbows, parallel and identical in color, arch through the thin mist when Juno commands Iris her servant, the outer one born from the inner one, like the speech of Echo, that wandering nymph whom love consumed as the sun the vapor, making people here on earth aware that through the covenant God made with Noah the world should never be drowned again—so the two garlands of those everlasting roses circled around us, and so the outer answered the inner.

As soon as the dance, and the great high festival of song and radiance, of light with light, joyful and gentle, joined in point of time and will, had stilled them, like eyes which must close and open together to the pleasure that stirs them, a voice came from the heart of one of the fresh lights that made me seem like the compass needle to the pole star, turning me towards it, and Bonaventura began: "The love that adorns me brings me to speak of the other leader, on whose account such noble words are spoken of my leader. It is right that wherever the one is, the other should be presented, so that, just as they fought side by side, their glory might shine together. Christ's army, whose re-arming cost so much, followed the standard slowly, fearfully and sparsely, when the Emperor—who reigns forever of His own grace, and not because of that army's worth—made provision for the soldiers who were in danger, and, as has been said, He came to the aid of his Bride with two champions, at whose works and words the scattered ranks regrouped. In Spain, towards that region where sweet Zephyr rises to unfold the new leaves Europe sees herself re-clothed with, not far from the crash of the waves, behind which because of their vast reaches the sun sometimes conceals himself from all people, Calahorra, the fortunate, lies under the protection of the noble shield of Castile, on whose arms, in the left quarters, the lion is below the castle, and on the right above. There the loving servant of the Christian faith was born, the holy wrestler, kind to his followers and cruel to his enemies, and as soon as he was created, his mind was so full of living virtue that in the womb it sent his mother a prophetic dream. When the marriage between him and the faith was completed at the holy font, where they dowered each other with mutual salvation, the lady who gave the assent for him saw in her sleep the marvelous harvest destined to issue from him and his heirs, and so that this might be known in his very name, a spirit from above moved them to call him after the Lord, whose he was completely. Dominic he was named, and I talk of him as I would of a laborer whom Christ chose to nurture His orchard. He showed himself truly a companion and messenger of Christ, since the first love he showed was for the first counsel of Christ, that of poverty. Often his nurse found him on the floor, silent and wakeful, as if to say: *It was for this I came*. Truly his father was Felice, *favoured*, and his mother, Giovanna, *graced by the Lord*, if the interpretation of their names is valid!

Soon, for love of the true *manna* and not of the world, for whose sake men labour after the doctrines of Ostia's bishop and Taddeo, he became a powerful teacher, so that he set himself to a circuit of the vineyard, which soon withers if the vine-dresser is at fault; and from the Apostolic See, that once was more generous to the rightful poor, not because it has altered in itself but because of the one who holds it degenerately, he demanded not a profit of a third or a half, not the grant of the next vacancy, not 'the tithe that belongs to God's poor,' but leave to fight against the heretical world for that seed from which these twenty-four plants enleaf you. Then he went forward, teaching and will as one, with the blessing of the Apostolic Office, like a torrent driven out of a deep fissure, and his force struck the roots of heresy most fiercely where the resistance was most obstinate. Then many streams sprang from his, so that the Catholic garden is watered, and its shrubs achieve a fuller growth.

"If this was one wheel of the chariot in which Holy Church defended herself and won her civil war in open battle, the excellence of the other should be clear to you, about whom Thomas was so courteous before I came to you. But the orbit that touched the highest points of its circumference is derelict, and now there is mold where there was once bread. His family, who walked directly in his footprints, have turned so that their toes strike his heel-prints, and soon the harvest of poor cultivation will be seen, when the tares will bemoan that the barn is closed to them. I accept in truth that those who search page after page of our book might still find one page, reading: 'I am as I was,' but it will not be one of Casale's or Acquasparta's, from whom men come to our discipline by relaxing it, or making it more severe.

"I am the living soul of Bonaventura of Bagnoregio, who in the great offices always placed temporal cares behind. Illuminato and Agostino are here, who were Francis's first poor shoeless brothers, who made themselves friends of God by the cord. Hugh of Saint Victor is here with them, Pietro Mangiadore, and Pietro Ispano, who gave logic light below there in his twelve books; Nathan the Prophet, the metropolitan Chrysostom, Anselm, and that Donatus who deigned to set his hand to the first art of grammar. Rabanus is here, and Joachim of Flora, the Calabrian abbot, imbued with prophetic spirit, shines by my side. The glowing courtesy of brother Thomas and his well-judged speech stirred me to praise of so great a knight, and stirred this company with me."

13

Let him who would grasp correctly what I now saw (and let him retain the image while I speak, as he holds a piece of rock) imagine fifteen of those stars, which, in various regions, vivify the Heavens with such brightness as to pierce the interwoven air; let him also imagine Ursa Major, which rests on the breast of our sky, night and day, so that it is never absent from the polar circle; and let him imagine the mouth of that horn, Ursa Minor, which starts from the axle of the primal circling, all making two wreathes in Heaven such as Minos's daughter made when she felt the chill of death; and one ring of light, to lie inside the other, and both to revolve in such a way that one leads and the other follows, and he will have only the shadow of the real constellation and the twofold dance that circled around the point where I was, since it goes as far beyond what we know, as the movement of the quickest sphere exceeds our sluggish Chiana. There they sang, not Bacchus and the Paean, but three Persons in one Divine Nature, and It, and Human Nature, in one Person.

The singing and circling had completed their measure, and those sacred flames turned their attention to us, rejoicing as they turned, from one care to another. Then amongst the harmonious divinities, the silence was broken by that light in which the wonderful life of the poor man of God had been described to me, saying: "Since the one sheaf has been threshed and its seed already stored, sweet love invites me to thresh the other. You know that whatever light human nature can receive was all infused into that chest from which the rib was taken to form the lovely face for whose taste of the forbidden fruit all the world pays, and into that which, pierced by the lance, gave satisfaction for the past and the future, so as to weigh the scales against all sin by that same Power that made them both. And so you wonder at what I said before when I said the good that was enclosed in the fifth light never had an equal. Now open your eyes to my answer, and you will see your belief and my words hit the truth like the center of a target.

"That which does not die, and that which can perish, is nothing

but the glow of that idea which our Father engenders by loving, since
that living light that goes out from its source—in such a way that it
does not separate from it, nor from the love that makes Trinity with
those two, through its own goodness—focuses its rays, as though reflected in nine emanations, eternally remaining One. So it descends
to the lowest powers, down from act to act, becoming what forms the
briefest of contingencies, by which I mean the things generated from
seed, or seedlessly, by the moving Heavens. The wax there, and what
molds it, is not in only one state, and so is more or less transparent
under the ideal seal, so that it happens that the same kind of tree
fruits better or worse, and you are all born with varying genius. If the
wax was molded precisely, and the Heaven at its supreme point of
power, the light of the seal would be completely apparent; but nature
always makes it imperfectly, acting in a similar manner to the artist
who has the skill of his art, but a trembling hand. Then, if warm love
places and stamps a clear vision of the primal power, complete perfection is attained there. So your clay was once made worthy of utter
physical perfection, and so the Virgin was made pregnant. From this I
sanction your opinion that human nature never was or will be equal
to those two persons. Now if I went no further, 'How then was he
without equal?' would still be your first words.

"But so that you now see what is not obvious, think who Solomon
was, and what the motivation was, when he was told 'Choose' to make
his request. I have spoken so that you may see he was a king who chose
such wisdom as would make him an adequate king, not knowledge of
the number of moving spirits here above; nor if a necessary premise
and a contingent premise can ever give a necessary conclusion; nor
whether we must accept a first movement; nor whether a triangle without a right angle in it can be constructed in a semicircle. So, if you
note this and everything I have said, it is royal prudence, worldly wisdom, that is the unequaled insight that the arrow of my intent strikes.
And if you turn your clear eyes to *achieved*, you will see it only applies
to kings, of whom there are many, and the good ones rare. Take my
words according to these distinctions and then they will agree with
what you hold concerning the first Father, and our Delight. And let
this always weight your feet down with lead, and make you go slowly
like a tired man, approaching the *yes* or *no* you do not grasp, since he
is truly down there among the fools who affirms or denies without
distinguishing between cases, so that it often happens that a quick
opinion leans to the wrong side, and then pride entangles the intel-

lect. He leaves the shore less than uselessly, since he does not even
return as he went, fishing for truth without the angler's skill, and
open proof of this in the world are Parmenides, Melissus, Bryson, and
the crowd who still went on without knowing where. So did Sabellius
and Arius, and those fools who were like gleaming swords applied to
Scripture, in making straight faces crooked. Do not let people be too
secure in their judgments, like those who count the ears of corn in the
field before the crop ripens, since I have seen all winter long the thorn
display itself, sharp and forbidding, and then on its summit bear the
rose; and before now I have seen a ship run straight and sure over the
sea for her entire course and sink in the end, entering the harbor
mouth. Do not let Jack and Jill think that if they see someone steal or
another make offering they therefore see them as Divine Wisdom does,
since the one may still rise and the other fall."

14

The water in a rounded dish vibrates from the center to the rim, or from the rim to the center depending on how it is struck, from inside or out. Just as the glorious spirit of Thomas fell silent, this thought suddenly came into my mind because of the analogy that sprang from his discourse and Beatrice's, whom it pleased to begin speaking, after him: "This man has a need he has not told you with voice or thought, namely to track another truth to its source. Say if the light with which your substance blossoms will remain yours as it is now, and if it will, say whether when you are visible again at the last day it will not cloud your vision." As if pierced and drawn out by excess joy, those who circle in the dance immediately lift up their voices and gladden their aspect, so at this eager and devout request the sacred circles revealed new joy in their whirling and their marvelous sound. Whoever grieves that we must die here in order to live there does not see the refreshment from the eternal rain here. Three times each of those spirits sang that One and Two and Three who lives forever and reigns in Three and Two and One, not circumscribed, but circumscribing all things, sang with such melody as is a just reward for every kind of merit.

And I heard a modest voice, in the most divine light of the smaller circle, perhaps like Gabriel's voice to Mary, replying: "Our Love will cast the rays of such a veil around us, as long as the festival of Paradise exists. Its brightness will match our ardor, our ardor our vision, as great as the grace of it exceeds our true worth. When the cloak of the glorious and holy flesh shall be taken on again, our person will be more pleasing by being fully complete. So that the undeserved brightness which the Supreme Good gives us, that light which allows us to see him, will grow; and then the vision must grow, and the ardor as well, which is lit by it, and the rays that leave it. But like the coal that gives out flame and by its own lively glow shines through it so that its own identity is maintained, so this glow that already veils us will be penetrated by the glow of the flesh, which now the earth covers: and such intensity of light will not have strength to overpower us, since the body's faculties will be strong enough to withstand everything that delights us."

The inner and outer choirs seemed so quick and eager to shout "*Amen*" that they indeed revealed desire for their dead bodies, not only for themselves, perhaps, but for their fathers, mothers, and others dear to them, before they became eternal flames.

Look around! A shining dawn, of equal brightness, beyond what was there, like a whitening horizon. And, as at twilight new things to see begin to appear in the Heavens, so that the vision seems real and unreal, so there I began to see newly arrived beings making a third circle out beyond the other two rims. O true sparks of the sacred exhalation, how sudden and glowing in front of my eyes, which, overcome, could not withstand it! But Beatrice showed herself so lovely and smiling to me, it must be left among those sights that my memory cannot follow. From that my eyes recovered their power to raise themselves, and I saw myself carried, along with my Lady, to a higher fortune. I saw clearly that I was lifted higher, by the burning smile of that planet, which seemed to me redder than usual.

I made sacrifice to God of my heart, and in that speech which is the same for all of us as fitted this newly given grace; and the ardor of the sacrifice was not yet gone from my chest before I knew the prayer had been accepted, and with favor, since splendors appeared to me inside two rays, so radiant and red that I exclaimed: "O Helios, who glorifies them so!" As the Milky Way gleams between the poles of the universe, decked with greater and lesser lights, so white as to set the very sages questioning, so those constellated rays made the ancient sign, in the depth of Mars, that crossing quadrants make in a circle. Here my memory outruns my ability, since Christ flashed out so on that Cross that I can find no fitting comparison. But whoever takes up his cross and follows Christ will forgive me for what I leave unspoken when he sees Christ white within that glow. From cusp to cusp, from summit to base, there were lights moving that sparkled intensely in meeting one another and passing. So we see here motes moving through a ray that sometimes penetrates the shadow people contrive, with art and ingenuity, against the sunlight, straight, curved, fast or slow, long or short, changing in appearance.

And as harp and viol, tuned in many-chorded harmony, make a sweet chime to one who cannot separate the notes, so a melody enraptured me from the lights that appeared, gathered along the Cross, though I could not follow the hymn. I clearly knew it was of high praise, since there came to me the words "*Rise and conquer*," as to one who hears but does not understand. And I was so enamored of it there that there had been nothing till then that tied me in such sweet chains. Perhaps it may be too bold to say so, as if it slighted the joy of those lovely eyes, gazing into which my longing finds rest, but he who recognizes how those living seals of all beauty have ever greater effect the higher the region, and that I had not yet turned towards them, may excuse me from my self-accusation and can see I speak the truth, for that sacred joy is not excluded here that as it climbs grows purer.

15

The benign will, in which the love that truly perfumes always distills itself as greed does in the envious will, imposed silence on that sweet lyre and stilled the sacred strings that the right hand of Heaven plucks and loosens. How can those beings be deaf to just prayers who agreed to silence, so as to give me the will to pray? It is right that they should mourn endlessly who deprive themselves eternally of this love for the love of what does not endure. As a meteoric flame flashes through the pure and tranquil sky from time to time, disturbing steady vision, and seems like a star changing place except that no star is lost from where it flamed, and it itself does not last, so from the horn stretching to the right a star of the constellation that shines there darted to the foot of the cross, and did not leave the arc but coursed along the radial line, like fire shining through alabaster. With such tenderness Anchises's shade came forward when he saw his son in Elysium, if our greatest Muse is to be believed.

"O blood of mine, O grace of God poured into you, to whom was Heaven's gate ever opened twice, as to you?" So the light spoke, at which I directed my attention to him. Then I turned my face towards my Lady, and on this side and on that was stunned, since such a smile was blazing in her eyes I thought with mine I had reached the end of my grace and my paradise. Then, gladdening sight and hearing, the spirit added words to his commencement that I did not understand, his speech was so profound: he hid himself from me, not out of choice but of necessity, since his thought took place beyond the power of mortals. And when the bow of ardent love was so tuned that his speech descended towards the power of our intellect, the first words I understood were: "Blessed be thou, Three and One, who are so noble in my seed," and continued: "My son, in this light where I now speak to you, you have assuaged a dear, long-cherished hunger, induced by the reading of that great volume where black and white never change; thanks be to her who clothed you with wings for this high ascent. You believe that your thought finds its way to me, from the Primal Thought, as the numbers five and six issue from one, if seen correctly, and so you do not ask who I am, or why I seem to you more joyful than others in this festive crowd. You believe rightly, since in this life great and lesser spirits gaze in the mirror where, before you think, your thought is seen. But so that the sacred love, in which I watch with uninterrupted vision, setting me thirsting with sweet longing, can be better fulfilled, let your voice sound out your will, your longing, safely, boldly, and delightedly, to which my answer is already given."

I turned to Beatrice, and she heard me before I spoke, and granted a sign to me that increased the wings of my desire. Then I began: "Love and intelligence became equal in weight to you as soon as the primal equality was visible to you, because the Sun, which warmed and lit you with its heat and brightness has in it such equality that all comparisons fall short. But for mortals, for reasons obvious to you, will and execution are unequally feathered wings. So that I, a mortal, feel the stress of this imbalance and therefore only gave thanks with my heart for your paternal greeting. But I can and do beg you, living topaz who are a gem of this precious jewel, to satisfy me with your name."

"Oh, I was your root, my leaf, whom I delighted in, while only anticipating you," such were the opening words of his reply. Then he said: "He from whom your family takes it name, and who has circled the mountain on the first terrace for more than a hundred years, was my son, and your great-grandfather. It is fitting that you should lessen the long drawn-out labor for him with your works. Florence lived in peace, sober and chaste, behind the ancient circle of wall from which she still hears the *tierce* and *nones*. There were no wreathes and gold chains, no dressed-up women, no sash that set people staring at it more than at she who wore it. The birth of a daughter did not yet dismay fathers, since dowry and bride's age were fitting, the one not too high, the other not too low. There were no empty mansions. Sardanapalus had not yet arrived to show what might be done to make a room luxurious. The first sight of Florence from Ucellatoio did not yet surpass Rome's from Montemalo, which will be surpassed in the fall as well as the rising. I have seen Bellincion Berti dressed in leather, clasped with bone, and have seen his lady come from her mirror with her face unpainted. I have seen men of the Nerlo and Vecchio families, content with only clothing of skins, and their ladies themselves handling flax and spindle. O fortunate women! Each one certain of her burial place, and none deserted in their beds because of France.

One kept watch over the cradle, and spoke in that soothing way that is the first delight of fathers and mothers; another, as she drew thread from the distaff, would tell her family about Troy, Rome, and Fiesole. Then a shrew like Cianghella, or a corrupt lawyer like Lapo Salterello, would have been as amazing then as a Cornelia or a Cincinnatus now. Mary, called on with deep moans, gave me to such a restful, lovely life among the citizens, to such faithful citizenship, such sweet being, and in your ancient Baptistery I became, in the one moment, Cacciaguida and a Christian. Moronto and Eliseo were my brothers: my wife came to me from the valley of the river Po, and your surname was derived from hers. Then I followed the Emperor Conrad, who made me a knight since I advanced myself so greatly in his grace. I marched in his ranks against the infamy of that religion whose infidel people usurp—shame on your pastors—that which is yours by right. There, by those wretched folk, I was disrobed of that deceitful world whose love corrupts many a spirit, and came from martyrdom to this peace."

16

O our little nobility of the blood! If you make people glory in you down here, where our affection languishes, it will never make me wonder again, since I gloried in it there where appetite is uncorrupted—I mean in Heaven. Yet, you are indeed a cloak that shrinks, so that if nothing is added, day by day time circles it with its shears. I began again with that *you* that Rome first allowed for Julius, which her families persevere with least, at which Beatrice, who was a little apart from us, smiled and seemed like the Lady of Malehaut who (it is written) coughed at Guinevere's first indiscretion.

I began: "You are my father, you give me full authority to speak, you lift me so that I am greater than myself. My mind is filled with joy from so many springs, it delights in itself that it can suffer it and not be destroyed. Tell me then, dear source of me, what was your ancestry, and what did the years record in your youth. Tell me about the sheepfold of Saint John, how great Florence was then, and who were the people worthy of highest places there."

As a coal bursts into flame at a breath of wind, so I saw that light shine out at my flattering words, and even as it grew more beautiful to my sight, so, in a voice sweeter and gentler but not in this current dialect of ours, he said: "From the day that *Ave* was first spoken to the day of my birth when my mother, now a saint, unburdened herself of my weight, this burning planet returned to his own constellation of the Lion five hundred and eighty times to relight itself under his feet. My predecessors and I were born in the place where he who runs in your annual race first encounters the last ward of Saint Peter. Let that be enough about my ancestors; silence about who they were and where they came from is more fitting than speech. At that time, between the statue of Mars and the Baptistery, all who were capable of bearing arms were only a fifth of those living now. But the citizenship saw itself as pure in blood, down to the humblest worker, now contaminated by the blood of Campi, Certaldo, and Fighine. Oh how much better it would be to have these people as your neighbors, and your boundary south at Galuzzo, and north at Trespiano, than to have them inside and bear the foulness of that villain from Aguglion, or him of Signa whose eye is keen for abuse of office! Had that race, the most degenerate on earth, been benign, like a mother to her son, and not been a hostile stepmother to Caesar, one of those who is a Florentine now, merchant and moneychanger, would have been sent back to Simifonte where his grandfather was a beggar. Montemurlo would still house the Conti, the Cerchi would still be in Acone's parish, and the Buondelmonti perhaps still in Val di Greve. Confusion of people was always the source of the city's sorrows, as mixed food is of the body's. And a blind bull falls more heavily than a blind lamb, and one sword often cuts keener and deeper than five. If you look how the cities of Luni and Urbisaglia are done for, and Chiusi and Sinaglia following them, it will not seem strange or difficult to understand how families destroy themselves, since even cities have an end. Everything of yours comes to an end, as you will, but it is not noticed in things that last a while because your lives are short. And as the turning of the lunar sphere covers and uncovers the shoreline endlessly, so Fortune handles Florence, so that it should not seem remarkable when I speak of the noble Florentines whose fame is buried by time.

"I have seen the Ughi, seen the Catellini, the Filippi, Grechi, Ormanni and Alberichi, illustrious families already on the wane. And with Sannella, as great as ancient, I have seen Arca, Soldanieri, Ardhingi and Bostichi. Over the gate of Porta San Piero, which is now heavy with the Cerchi's new crimes that will soon lead to shipwreck, the Ravignani lived, from whom the Conti Guidi are descended, and those who have since taken noble Bellincioni's name. The Della Pressa already knew how to govern, and Galigaio, in his house, already had the gilded hilt and pommel of knighthood. The vair column of the Pigli was already great, the Sacchetti, Giuochi, Fifanti and Barucci, the Galli, and the Chiaramontesi who blush for falsifying the measure. The stock the Calfucci sprang from was great already, and the Sizii and Arrigucci were already civic dignitaries. Oh how great I have seen them, those Uberti, now destroyed by pride! And the Lamberti's device of the golden balls adorned Florence in all her great actions. So did their fathers, who now, whenever the Bishop's See is vacant, stand guzzling in the consistory. The outrageous race, the house of Adimari, which is a dragon to those who flee it and is as quiet as a lamb to those who show their teeth, or purse, was rising already, but from humble people, so that Ubertino Donati was not pleased when his father-in-law made him a relative of them by marriage. Caponsacco had already come down from Fiesole to the marketplace, and Giuda and Infangato were already good citizens. I will tell you something unbelievable but true: the little circle of walls was entered by a gate named after the Della Pera. Everyone who carries any of the fair device of the great baron whose name and worth is kept alive by the festival of Saint Thomas derived knighthood and privilege from him, though the Della Bella who fringes it with gold has now joined the party of the people. There were Gualterotti and Importuni already, and the Borgo Santi Apostoli would be a quieter place if they did not have the Buondelmonti for new neighbors. The house from which, O Buondelmonte, your grief sprang, because of righteous anger which murdered you and put an end to your joyful life, was honored, it and its associates. How wrong you were to reject its marriage rite at another's prompting! Many would have been happy who are now saddened if God had committed you to the Ema the first time you crossed it to reach the city. But it was fitting that Florence should sacrifice a victim to that mutilated stone of Mars that guards the bridge in her last time of peace. I saw Florence in such calm repose, with these men and others like them, that she had no reason for grief. I saw her people, so glorious and just, with these men to serve them, that her arms of the white lily were never reversed on the standard, nor the lily dyed red by division."

17

As Phaethon, he who still makes fathers give grudgingly to their sons, came to Clymene to receive reassurance of what he had heard thrown back at him, so I: and so did I seem to Beatrice and that sacred flame who had already changed his position for my sake. At which my Lady said: "Emit the heat of your desire so that it may flow truly stamped with the internal seal, not so that our knowledge increases by your speaking, but so that you may learn how to speak of your thirst so that men may quench it."

"Dear ground of myself in which I am rooted, who are lifted up so high that, gazing on that point to which all time is present, you see contingent things before they themselves exist, as earthbound minds see that two obtuse angles cannot exist in one triangle, heavy words were said to me, about my future while Virgil accompanied me, descending through the dead world, and around the mountain that purifies souls, though I feel well set to resist Fortune's blows, so that my mind would be content to hear what fate comes towards me, since the arrow seen in advance arrives less suddenly." So I spoke to that same light who had addressed me previously, and confessed my wish as Beatrice wanted.

That paternal love, revealed or hidden by its own smile, did not reply in dark prophecies that misled the foolish ancients before the Lamb of God who takes away sin was killed, but in clear words and with precise statements: "Contingent things, which do not extend beyond your world of matter, are all outlined in the eternal gaze, though predetermination does not follow from this, no more than a boat slipping downstream is driven by the eye in which it is reflected. From that, what is in store for you is visible to me, as a sweet harmony comes from an organ. You must be exiled from Florence, as Hippolytus was exiled from Athens through the spite and lies of his stepmother. It is already willed so, and already planned, and will be accomplished soon by him who ponders it in that place where every day Christ is sold. The cry will put the blame on the injured party, as is usual, but truth will bear witness to itself by the revenge it takes. You will lose every-thing you love most dearly: that is the arrow that exile's bow will fire. You will prove how bitter the taste of another man's bread is, and how hard it is to descend and climb another man's stair. And what will bow your shoulders down will be the vicious and worthless company with whom you will fall into this abyss, since they will all be ungrate-ful, fierce, and disrespectful to you; but not long after, their cheeks, not yours, will blush for it. Their fate will demonstrate their brutish-ness so that it will be to your credit to have formed a party of one. Your first refuge and first lodging will be by courtesy of the great Lombard whose arms are the sacred eagle atop a ladder, since he will cast such a friendly gaze on you that, between you, in request and fulfilment, that will be first which between others comes last. With him will be the one who was so marked at birth by this potent planet that his actions will be notable. People have not yet taken due regard of him because of his age, since these spheres have only revolved around him for nine years. But before the Gascon has deceived the Emperor Henry, the gleam of his virtue will be apparent in his indifference to money or to hard labor. His generous actions will eventually be known so that even his enemies will not be able to stay silent about them. Look to him and to his gifts. Many people will be changed by him, their conditions altered, the wealthy and the poor, and you will carry it inscribed in your memory of him but will not speak it"—and he told me many things incredible even to those who shall see them. Then he added: "Son, these are my comments on what has been said to you: see the difficulties hidden by a few rotations. But I would not want you to be envious of your neighbors, since you will live far beyond the punishment that will fall on their infamies."

When the sacred soul showed by his silence that he had finished passing the weft through the warp I had stretched out ready for him, I began like a man who, doubting, longs for advice from one who sees straight, wills the right, and loves: "My father, I see clearly how time comes spurring at me to give me such a blow, one heaviest to those who lose themselves, so that it is best for me to arm myself with fore-sight so that if the dearest place is denied me, I do not lose all other refuge because of my writings. Down in the world, endlessly bitter, and around the mountain from whose summit my Lady's eyes raised me, and afterwards through the Heavens from light to light, I have learnt things that, if I tell them again, will savor of acrid pungency to many; and if I am a shrinking friend to truth, I fear to lose life among those who will call this time ancient."

That light in which my treasure that I had found there was smiling, first coruscated like a golden mirror in the sun's rays, then answered: "A conscience darkened by its own shame or another's will truly find your words harsh, but reveal all your vision nonetheless, avoid all lies, and let them scratch if they find a scab, since though your words may be bitter at first tasting, they will still be vital food afterwards when they digest them. This outcry of yours will do as the wind does that strikes the highest summits hardest, and that will be no small cause of honor. Thus, only spirits known for their fame have been shown to you in these spheres, along the mountain, and in the sad depths, since the souls of those who hear will not be content with or truly believe in examples that have unknown and hidden roots, nor any other obscure argument."

18

That mirror of the blessed was already joying only in his own discourse, and I was tasting mine, tempering the sweet with the bitter, when that Lady who was leading me to God said: "Change your thoughts: remember that I am near to Him who disburdens us of every wrong." I turned to the beloved voice of my comfort, and I forgo speaking here of what love I saw in those sacred eyes, not merely because I am diffident about my words, but because my memory cannot climb again so far beyond itself unless another guides it. I can only say this much about that moment: that as I gazed at her, my affections were free of any other desire, while the eternal joy that shone directly on to Beatrice contented me with its reflection from her lovely face. Overcoming me with the light of her smile, she said to me: "Turn now and listen, for my eyes are not the only Paradise."

Just as here we sometimes read affection in a face if it is so great that the whole mind is seized by it, so in the flaming of his sacred glow to which I turned, I knew the desire in him to speak to me still. He started: "In this fifth canopy of the tree, which takes life from its crown and is always in fruit, never shedding leaves, are spirits who are blessed, who had great names below before they came to Heaven, so that every Muse would be made richer by them. So look at the horns of the cross, and he whom I will name will there enact the lightning in a cloud."

I saw a light traced along the cross as Joshua was named, and the word was not complete for me before the action. And at the name of the great Maccabeus, I saw another light move, revolving, and delight was like the whip to the spinning-top. So for Charlemagne and Roland, two more followed by my keen gaze, as the eye follows a hawk in flight. Then William, Renard, Duke Godfrey, and Robert Guiscard. At that the soul who had spoken with me, moving to mingle there with the other lights, displayed the quality of his art to me among Heaven's singers.

I turned to my right to know my duty from Beatrice, indicated either by speech or sign, and I saw her eyes, so clear, so glad, that her appearance exceeded all previous form, even the last. As a man sees that, day by day, by feeling more delight in achieving good things his virtue increases, so I saw that my circling with the Heavens had increased its orbit while I watched the miraculous vision becoming more adorned. And the change that quickly crosses a lady's pale face when she throws off a weight of shame was offered to my eyes when I turned, because of the white radiance of the sixth, temperate planet that had received me. In that torch of Jove I saw the sparkle of the love inside it, signing letters of our language to my eyes. And as birds rising from the riverbank make flock in wheeling or extended shapes as if they were delighted by their pastures, so the sacred beings in the lights sang, flying, and formed now **D** or **I** or **L**. First they moved to the note they were singing, then, as they shaped one of these letters, would stop for a moment and stay silent. O Muse, goddess of the fount of Pegasus, who makes intellect glorious and gives it enduring life, as it with your help does cities and countries, illuminate me with yourself so that I can show their figures in relief as I hold them in mind: let your power be shown in these brief words. Then they showed themselves in thirty-five vowels and consonants, and I took note of the letters, as they appeared one by one to me: **DILIGITE IUSTITIAM** [love righteousness] was the first verb and noun of the whole vision, **QUI IUDICATIS TERRAM** [you judges over earth] was the last. Then they remained ordered in the **𝕸** of the fifth word so that Jupiter seemed silver in that region, pricked out with gold; and I saw other lights descending where the summit of the **𝕸** was and come to rest there, singing, I think, of the good that moves them towards Himself.

Then, as innumerable sparks rise from a blow to a burning log, from which foolish people make auguries, more than a thousand lights rose, it seemed to me, and some ascended steeply, some a little, just as the Sun that lit them ordained; and when each one had come to rest in place, I saw an eagle's neck and head outlined by that pricked out fire. He who depicts it has no one to guide Him, but He Himself guides, and from Him that power flows into the mind that builds the eagle's nest: the other blessed spirits, who seemed at first content to entwine the **𝕸** with lilies by a slight motion, filled in the outline.

O sweet planet, how great the quality and quantity of jewels, which made clear to me that our justice is an effect of that Heaven you bejewel! Thus I beg the Mind in which your motion and your power has source to gaze at the place from which smoke rises to vitiate your light, and that the anger be roused once more against the buying and selling in the Temple, whose walls were built by miracle and martyrdom. O soldiers of Heaven, whom I see, pray for those who have gone awry on earth, following bad examples. It was custom once to war with the sword; now it is done by holding back spiritual bread, here and there, that the tender Father denies to no one. But you that write only to cancel out the lines, think that Paul and Peter are living still, who died for the vineyard you destroy. Though indeed you may say: "I have so fixed my desires on him who lived a solitary life and was dragged by dance to martyrdom that I do not know Paul or the Fisherman."

19

The marvelous image that those entwined spirits made, joying in their sweet fruition, appeared in front of me with outstretched wings. Each soul appeared like a ruby in which the sun's rays burn, so lit as to refract light to my eyes. And what I must tell now pen never wrote, voice never spoke, nor was it ever known by imagination, since I saw and heard the eagle's beak speaking, saying in its voice *I* and *mine* when in its form it was *we* and *ours*. And it began: "I am exalted here to this glory, which does not allow itself to be overcome by longing through being just and pious, and I have left a memory on Earth, so constituted that even the evil approve it, though they do not follow its path." As we feel one glow from many coals, so there came a single sound out of the image from those many points of love.

At which I said quickly: "O perpetual flowers of eternal delight, you who make all your perfumes seem like a single one to me, relieve as you breathe the great fast that has kept me hungering for a long time because I found no food to eat on Earth. I know in truth that whatever other realm of Heaven Divine Justice takes as its mirror, your realm comprehends it without a veil. You know how eagerly I ready myself to listen: you know what the question is that has caused my fast to endure so long."

As the hawk divested of its hood shakes itself and beats its wings, demonstrating its will and beautifying itself, so I saw that symbolic eagle, woven from the praise of Divine Grace, with the songs that are known to whoever rejoices there. Then it began: "He who drew the compass around the edges of the universe, and marked out inside it so much that is shown and hidden, could not impress His greatness on all the universe without His word being infinitely beyond us. And this is attested by Lucifer, that first proud being, who was a pinnacle of creation, falling abortive because he could not wait for enlightenment; and so it appears that every minor nature is too small a vessel to hold that good which is endless and measures itself by itself. So our vision, which must be one of the rays of that Mind by which all things are filled, cannot have such great power without its origin seeing far beyond that which it itself can see. Therefore such perception as your world has is lost with depth as our vision is in the ocean, since though it sees the seafloor by the shore, it cannot reach it in the open water, even though it is there, and the depth has hidden it. There is no light unless it comes from that serenity that is never troubled: the rest is darkness, or the shadow of the flesh, or its poison. Now the labyrinth is open enough for you, that labyrinth that hid the living justice from you, which you have questioned so incessantly since you said: 'A man is born on the banks of the Indus, and there is no one to speak to him about Christ, or read or write of Him, and all that man's will and action are good, as far as human reason can tell, without sin in speech or life. He dies unbaptized and without the faith. Where is the justice in condemning him? Why is it his fault that he is void of faith?' Now, who are you to sit on the judge's seat, a thousand miles away, with sight that sees a short span? Certainly, to him who trades subtleties with me, it would be wonderful if there were no doubts, if the Scriptures were not set above them. O earthly creatures, O coarse minds! The Primal Will, which is goodness itself, never abandons its own self, which is the supreme good. All that is in harmony with it is just: no created goodness draws it to itself but it, by shining out, gives rise to it." As the stork sweeps over her nest when she has fed her chicks, and as the ones she fed look up at her, so did that eagle-form of the blessed, which moved its wings powered by so much wisdom, and so I raised my forehead. Wheeling, it cried and said: "As my cries are to you, who do not understand them, such is eternal judgment to you mortals."

When those glowing lights of the Holy Spirit were still, though still in the form of that insignia which gained the Romans the world's reverence, it began again: "No one ever rose to this region who did not believe in Christ, not before He was nailed to the tree, nor after. But see, many call out: 'Christ, Christ' who shall be further from Him at the Judgment than those who do not know of Christ: and the Ethiopians will condemn such Christians when the two crowds part, the one rich in eternity, the other naked. What would the Persians say to your kings when they see that volume opened in which all their ill deeds are recorded? Amongst the actions of Albert, that one will soon set the pen in motion that will make Prague's kingdom of Bohemia a desert. There will be read the sorrow that he who will die by a wild boar's wound is bringing to the Seine by falsifying the coinage. There the pride will be seen that parches, and makes the Scots and English so mad they cannot keep the proper borders. The lechery and effeminate life of the ruler of Spain will be seen, and that of Bohemia who never knew or willed anything of worth. For the Cripple of Jerusalem will be seen marked with a 1 for virtue, whereas a 1000 will tally the contrary charge.

"The baseness and avarice of he who holds the Isle of Fire where Anchises ended his long life will be visible, and in order to understand the magnitude of his baseness, his record will be kept in tiny writing, to fit a great deal in a little space. And the foul deeds of his uncle and his brother will be shown clearly to all, who have bastardized a great nation and two crowns. And the kings of Portugal and of Norway shall be recorded there, and he of Serbia who sadly saw the coin of Venice only to counterfeit it. O happy Hungary if she no longer allows herself to be mauled, and happy Navarre if she could protect herself with the Pyrenees that border her! And all should know, as a warning, that Nicosia and Famagusta already moan and cry by reason of their beast who cannot be separated from the rest."

20

When the Sun that illumines all the world descends so far below our hemisphere that day vanishes on every side, the sky that was only lit by him before now reappears in many lights, in which the one light shines. And this effect in Heaven came to mind when the insignia of the world and its leaders closed its eagle's beak, because all those living lights, shining far brighter, began to sing things which must slip and fall from my memory. O sweet Love, mantled in a smile, how ardent you seemed in those flutings, breathed out only in sacred thoughts!

When the dear, lucid stones with which I saw the sixth Heaven gemmed had rendered silent those angelic chimes, I seemed to hear the murmuring of a river that falls from rock to rock and reveals the abundance of its source. And as the sound takes form from the lute's neck, or the wind that enters from the unstopped pipe, likewise, the delay of anticipation over, the eagle's murmur rose through its neck as if it were hollow. There it became a voice and issued out of its beak in the form of words that the heart waited for, and on which I wrote them.

It began to speak to me: "That part of me that sees and in mortal eagles endures the sun must now be gazed at intensely, since the fires with which the eye in my head sparkles are the most important of all the crowd of those from which I construct my shape. He who shines in the middle, as the pupil does in the eye, was the singer of the Holy Spirit, who carried the ark from city to city. Now he knows the value of his song, inasmuch as it was produced by his own judgment through the reward that matches it. Of the five who make the arch of the profiled eyebrow, he who is closest to the beak is he who consoled the widow for her son: now he knows how dearly it costs not to follow the Son from his experience of this sweet life and its opposite. And he who follows on the arch I speak of, on its upper arc, is the one who delayed death by his true penitence; now he knows that the eternal judgment is not altered when a pious prayer seems to delay today's event until tomorrow. The next who follows, with a good intention that produced evil consequences made himself, the laws, and my Imperial self all Greek, in order to give way to the Shepherd; now he knows that the evil flowing from his good action does not harm him, even though the world is destroyed by it. And him you see on the downward slope of the arc is William, whose country deplores his loss while grieving that Charles and Frederick are alive; now he knows how Heaven loves a righteous king, and he makes it visible still by the appearance of his radiance. Who would believe, down in the world of error, that the Trojan Ripheus is in this sphere, fifth of these holy lights? Now he knows much about the Divine Grace the world cannot see, although his sight does not reach the end of it."

Like the lark ascending in the air, first singing and then silent, content with the final sweetness that sates her, so that image of the imprint of eternal pleasure seemed to me by which, in longing for it, each thing becomes what it is. And though I was to my doubt like the transparent glass is to the color it surrounds, it would still not wait and bide its time in silence, but it thrust "What are these things?" from my mouth by its own pressure, at which I saw great sparkles of joy. Then immediately the insignia, blessed and with its kindling eye, replied to me so that it would not keep me in amazed suspense: "I see you believe in these things because I tell you, but do not see the *how*, so that they are obscure, though still believed in. You are like him who knows the thing by name, but cannot see its *quiddity* unless someone else brings it to light. The Kingdom of Heaven suffers the force of ardent love and living hope, which overcomes the Divine Will, not in the sense in which man overcomes man, but overcomes that Will because it wishes to be overcome, and once overcome, in turn overcomes with its own kindness. The lives of the first and fifth lights along the eyebrow cause you to marvel because you see them decking this region of the angels. They did not leave their bodies as Gentiles but as Christians, with firm belief in those pierced feet that to the first *would* suffer and to the other *had already* suffered. Since the first came back to his bones from Hell, where no one ever returns to the true will, this was the reward for living hope, the living hope that added power to the prayers to raise him, so that His will might have the power to be moved. That glorious soul of which we speak, returning to the flesh where it lived a while, believed in Him who had the power to help, and believing kindled so great a flame of true love that it was worthy of coming here, to this rejoicing, on its second death. The other set all his love below on righteousness, by that grace which wells from so deep a fount that no creature ever set eyes on its last depth, so that God, going from grace to grace, opened his eyes to our redemption yet to come; and he believed in that, and from that time did not suffer the mire of paganism, and reproved the stubborn peoples. Those three ladies whom you saw at the right wheel of the chariot stood as sponsors at his baptizing, more than a thousand years before baptism. O predestination, how remote your roots are from our vision that cannot see the First Cause *completely*! And you mortal creatures, keep yourselves from judging, since we who see God do not yet know all those who will be elected, and such defective sight is sweet for us because our good is refined by this good: that what God wills we also will."

So sweet medicine was given me by this divine image to correct my short sight. And as a good harpist matches the quivering chord to a good singer so that the song gives added pleasure, so while he spoke I remember that I saw those two sacred lights make their fires quiver at the words, just as two eyes blink together.

21

My eyes were already fixed on my Lady's face once more, and my mind with them, free of every other intent; she did not smile but said: "Were I to smile, you would be like Semele, turned to ashes, since my beauty—which burns more brightly, as you have seen, on the steps of the eternal palace, the higher we climb—if it were not moderated, glows so much that at its lightning flash your human powers would be like the leaves the thunder shatters. We have risen to the seventh planet, which beams downwards in the breast of the fiery Lion, mingling with its power. Fix your mind in your eyes and make them mirrors to the figure that will be shown to you, in this mirror."

Whoever knows how my sight was fed by her blessed aspect when I changed to a different concern would know how great a joy it was to me to obey my Heavenly guide, weighing contemplation's joy against the joy of obedience. Inside the crystal planet, which as it circles the world carries the name of its illustrious ruler in whose age every wickedness died, I saw a ladder colored like gold that reflects the sunray erected so far upward my sight could not follow it. And I saw so many splendors descending the rungs that I thought every light that shines in Heaven had been poured downwards there. And as according to their nature the rooks set out in a flock at dawn to warm their cold feathers, and then some flap away without returning, others come back to where they started, and the rest wheel in flight, it seemed to me that was also the way among that glittering of spirits that came in a crowd as soon as they reached a particular rung, and the spirit that landed nearest to me became so bright in my thoughts that I said: "I clearly see the love you signal to me. But She from whom I wait for the how, and when, of speech and silence pauses, and therefore I ask no questions, countrary to my own wishes." At which She who sees everything saw my silence in his look and said: "Let free your burning desire."

And I began: "My lack of worth does not make me worthy of a reply, except for her sake who allows me to make the request: O blessed soul life, who lives hidden in gladness, tell me the reason why I am placed near you, and say why the sweet symphony of Paradise is silent here when it sounded below through the other spheres so devotedly."

He replied: "You have mortal hearing, as you have mortal sight; there is no song here for the same reason that Beatrice does not smile. I have descended so far on the steps of the sacred ladder only to give you joy with words, and with the light that mantles me, nor did greater love make me swifter, since more and greater love burns higher there, as the flaming made clear to you, but the deep love that keeps us as ready servants to the wisdom that controls the world assigns me here, as you see."

I said: "Yes, I see how love, freely given in this court, is sufficient to make you follow the eternal providence, but it is this which seems hard for me to understand: why you alone among your peers was predestined to this role."

I had not reached the last word before the light made a center of its midpoint and whirled itself around like a rapid millstone. Then the love that was inside it answered: "Divine Light focuses itself on me from above, penetrating that in which I am involved, which power, joined to my vision, lifts me so far beyond myself that I see the supreme essence from which it is extracted. From there comes the joy I glow with, equaling the clarity of my sight with the brightness of my flame. But neither the most illuminated soul in Heaven, nor the seraph with eyes most fixed on God, can satisfy you as to your question, because the thing you ask lies so deep in the abyss of the Eternal Law that it is hidden from created sight. And when you return to the mortal world, report this: that it should no longer presume to set its feet towards so great a goal. The Mind that shines here on earth is clouded, so think if it could have that power there below if it does not when Heaven takes it to itself." His words put such constraint on me I left the question, and restricted myself to asking, humbly, who he was himself.

"Between Italy's two coasts, not far from your native place, the mountains rise so high that the thunder sounds far lower down, and make a hump called Catria, beneath which a monastery was consecrated, which used only to be given over to prayer." So he began his third speech to me, and then continued: "There I became so rooted in God's service that I treated heat and cold lightly, ate Lenten-fare cooked with olive oil, and was satisfied with contemplative thought. That hermitage once yielded fruit to Heaven but now is barren, so that before long it must be exposed. I was Peter Damian in that place, and was Peter the Sinner in the house of Our Lady on the Adriatic shore. Little of mortal life was left to me, when I was called and drawn to the cardinal's hat, which passes now from bad wearer to worse. Cephas came, and the great vessel of the Holy Spirit, lean and unshod, taking their food from any place. Now the modern shepherds have to be buttressed on both sides and have someone to lead them, they are so fat and heavy, and someone to support them from behind. They cover their ponies with cloaks so that two creatures go under one hide: O patience that endures so much!"

At his voice I saw more flames descend, gyring from rung to rung, and every gyration made them more beautiful. They came and rested, and made a sound so deep that there is nothing here to compare it to, and I did not understand its meaning, its thunder overcame me so.

22

Oppressed by stupor, I turned to my guide, like a little child who always goes for help where he has most confidence, and She, like a mother who, with her voice that sets him right, quickly aids her pale and breathless child, said to me: "Do you not know you are in Heaven? And do you not know that Heaven is wholly sacred, and that which is done here is done from righteous zeal? Now you can understand how the song, and my smiling, have transmuted you since that cry has so moved you, in which the vengeance you shall see taken before you die would already be known to you had you understood their prayers. The sword from above does not strike hastily or reluctantly, except to his perception who waits for it with longing, or in fear. But turn now to the others, since you will see many renowned spirits if you direct your look according to my words."

I turned my eyes, as her wish commanded, and saw a hundred smaller spheres, which were made more beautiful by their collective rays. I stood like someone who represses the stirrings of desire in himself, who does not presume to ask because he fears to exceed due bounds. And the greatest and most lustrous of these pearls came forward to satisfy my wish about him. Then I heard inside there: "If you could see as I can the love that burns among us, your thought would have been spoken, but so that you do not miss the goal by delay, I will answer only the thought you were so cautious about. That mountain on whose slopes lies Monte Cassino was once populated by deceived and perverse worshipers of the pagan gods. And I am the one who first carried His name up there, He who brought that Truth that raises us up so high, and such great grace shone over me that I weaned the surrounding villages from the impious cults that seduced the world. These other flames were all contemplatives, lit by the warmth that bears sacred fruits and flowers. Here is Maccarius, here is Romoaldus, here are the brothers who stayed inside the cloisters and kept their hearts intact."

And I to him: "The love you show by speaking with me, and the benign aspect I see and note in all your fires, has increased my confidence as the Sun expands the rose, when it opens as far as is within its power, so that I beg to know, assure me father, as to whether I might receive such grace as to see your unveiled form."

At which he said: "Brother, your noble desire will be fulfilled in the last sphere, where I and all the rest find fulfilment. There every desire is perfect, full and ripe: in it alone every part is where it always was, since it is not in space and has no poles, and our ladder reaches it at last, vanishing out of sight. The patriarch Jacob saw its upper rungs stretch up there when he saw it filled with angels. But no one leaves Earth to climb it now, and my rule, down there, remains a waste of parchment. The walls that used to be a House of Prayer are dens, and the cowls are sacks full of moldy grain. But even gross usury is not as contrary to God's wishes as the fruit that maddens the monks' hearts, since what the Church holds in its keeping belongs to the people who pray to God, not to kin, or to other viler uses. The flesh of mortals is so easily seduced that down there, a good beginning does not last the time from the oak's sprouting to the acorn harvest. Peter began his flock without gold or silver, I mine with prayers and fasting, and Francis his with humility. And if you gaze at the beginning of each order, and look again at where it has failed, you will see the white darken. But Jordan being rolled back and the Red Sea separating when God willed would be a less marvelous sight than alteration here." So he spoke to me, and then returned to his companions, and the companions drew close together, then were all gathered upwards in a whirlwind.

The sweet Lady drove me behind them up the ladder merely with a gesture, her power so conquered my nature, and motion was never so quick down here, where we climb and fall by nature's law, as to match my flight. O Reader, I swear by my hopes of ever returning to that sacred triumph, for which I, many a time, regret my sins and beat my breast, you would not have put your finger in the fire and drawn it back in so short a time as it took me to see the sign that follows the Bull and to be inside it. O glorious stars, O light pregnant with great power from which I derive all my genius, whatever of it there is, He who is father of every human life was rising and setting in your sign when I first felt the air of Tuscany, and then, when grace was granted me to enter the distant sphere where you revolve, your region was assigned to me. To you my soul breathes devoutly, to gain the strength for the difficult passage that draws her towards itself.

Beatrice began to speak: "You are so near the highest blessedness that your eyes should be sharp and clear. So, before you make your way deeper into it, look down and see how great a world I have placed under your feet in order that your heart may be presented as joyfully as it can to the triumphant crowd that comes delightedly through this ethereal sphere."

I turned my gaze back through each and every one of the seven spheres and saw this globe so that I smiled at its pitiful appearance, and I approve that wisdom best that considers it least, since he whose thoughts are directed elsewhere may be called truly noble. I saw the daughter of Latona lit without that shadow which gave me reason before to consider her rare or dense. I endured the face of your son Hyperion, and saw how the offspring of Maia and Dione move around and near him. Next, Jupiter appeared, moderate between his father's cold and his son's heat, and the changes in their position were clear to me. And all the seven were revealed to me: how large, how fast they are, and how distant from each other in orbit. The threshing-floor that makes us so fierce appeared to me from mountains to river-mouths as I revolved with the eternal Twins. Then I turned my eyes to the lovely eyes again.

23

Like a bird among the beloved leaves that has brooded over the nest of her sweet chicks in the night that hides all things from us, and that prematurely takes to the open branch, eager to see their longed-for aspect and to find food to feed them, awaiting the sun with ardent love, watching fixedly for the dawn to break, so was my Lady, standing erect and ready, turned towards the region of the south where the sun moves slowest, so that as I looked at her in her anticipation and longing, I became like the desiring soul who wishes for something new, and delights in hope. But the time between one *when* and *then*, for fixing my attention I mean, and for seeing the Heavens grow brighter and brighter, was short. And Beatrice said: "See the procession of Christ's triumph, and all the fruits gathered by the wheeling of these spheres." Her face seemed alight, and her eyes so full of joy, that I have to pass it by without description.

As Trivia in the calm of full moons smiles among the eternal nymphs who clothe the Heavens in every space, I saw one Sun above a thousands lights firing each and all, as our own sun does the things we see above, and the glowing substance shone so brightly through the living light that my vision could not endure it. O Beatrice, sweet, dear guide! She said to me: "Nothing has defense against what overpowers you. Inside are the wisdom and the power that opened the path between Heaven and Earth, for which there had been such great desire before." Even as fire is released from cloud, because it expands so that there is no space inside, and rushes down to earth against its nature, so my mind, expanded by these feasts, issued out of itself, and cannot remember what it became. "Open your eyes and look at what I am: you have seen things that have made you strong enough to endure my smile."

When I heard that gift, worthy of great thanks that can never be erased from the book that records the past, I was like someone who returns to himself from an unremembered dream and tries vainly to recall it to mind. If all of those tongues sounded that Polyhymnia and her sisters enriched with their sweetest milk, the sound would not reach to a thousandth part of the truth in helping my singing of the sacred smile, and how it brightened her sacred face. And so the sacred poem must take a leap in describing Paradise, like someone finding his way obstructed. But whoever thinks about the weighty theme, and the human shoulder that has burdened itself with it, will not cast blame if the shoulder trembles beneath it. It is not a little boat's path that my bold keel cuts as it goes, nor a pilot who spares himself.

Beatrice spoke: "Why does my face so entrance you that you do not turn to the lovely garden that flowers below the rays of Christ? There is the rose, in which the Divine Word made itself flesh; there are the lilies, within whose perfume the good way was taken." And I, who was eager for her wisdom, surrendered again to the struggle of my weak vision.

As I have seen, before now, a meadow filled with flowers, under the sun's rays, shining pure through broken cloud, themselves covered in shadow, so I saw many crowds of splendors, shone on from above by ardent rays, not seeing the source from which the glow came. O benign Power that so forms them! You had risen yourself to make space for my vision that lacked strength. The name of that lovely flower I invoke always, morning and night, drew my mind to gaze at the greatest flame, and when the quality and might of the living star, which overcomes there as it did down here, had been pictured in both my eyes, an encircled flame, shaped like a coronet, fell from the Heavens and clothed her and surrounded her.

Whatever melody sounds sweetest here, and draws the spirit most towards itself, would seem the thunder from a torn cloud compared to that lyre to whose sound the lovely sapphire was crowned, who ensapphires the brightest Heaven. The circling melody named itself: "I am the angelic love who circles the noble joy that takes breath from the womb that was the inn of our longing, and Lady of Heaven I will circle you until you follow your Son, and render the Highest Sphere more divine, by entering it." Then all the other lights rang out with the name of Mary.

The royal mantle of all the folds of the universe, which burns brightest and is most alive with the breath and manner of God, had its inner shore so far above us that its appearance was not yet visible to me. Thus my eyes had not the power to follow the crowned flame as She climbed after her own Child. And like the babe who stretches his arms up towards his mother when he has suckled, because his mind flames out in external gesture, so each of those fires tapered its flame, so that the deep love they had for Mary was made clear to me. Then they rested there, in my sight, singing *Regina Coeli* so sweetly that the delight has never left me.

O how great the wealth is filling those rich coffers, spirits that on earth were good sowers of its seed! Here they have life and joy, even from that treasure that was earned weeping in exile in Babylon, where gold was rejected. Here he who holds the keys to such great glory triumphs, with the ancient and the new synod, under the noble Son of God, and Mary.

24

"O company elected to the great feast of the Blessed Lamb, who feeds you in such manner that your hunger is always sated: if by the grace of God this man tastes what falls from your table before death has determined his time, take heed of his immeasurable yearning and sprinkle him a little, you who always drink at the fountain from which flows that on which his thought is fixed." So Beatrice spoke: and those joyful souls made spheres of themselves, with fixed axes flaming out like comets. And as wheels in harmonious clockwork turn so that the first seems still to whoever inspects it but the last to fly, so these dancers with their various gyres, fast or slow, made me consider their riches. I saw a blissful flame shoot from the one I thought most beautiful, such that none brighter remained, and it swept three times around Beatrice with a song so divine that my imagination cannot repeat it, so my pen passes on and I do not write, since our thought and speech is too grossly colored to trace such folds. "O my holy sister, who begs us so devotedly, you free me from this lovely sphere by your glowing love."

As soon as the blessed flame had rested, the breath that spoke the words I wrote turned to my Lady, and she replied: "O eternal light of that great man to whom our Lord left the keys of this marvelous joy that he brought to earth, test this man here on the points of faith, lesser or greater as you choose, the faith that enabled you to walk upon walker. Whether he loves well, and hopes truly, and believes is not hidden from you, since you have sight of that place where everything is brought to light. But since this kingdom has made its citizens from those of true faith, it is fitting that he should be allowed to speak of it, to give it glory."

Even as the student equips himself but does not speak until the master sets out the question—to discuss it, not to decide it—so I armed myself with every thought while she spoke so that I might be ready for such questioning and response.

"Speak, good Christian, reveal yourself: what is faith?"

I raised my forehead to the light that breathed those words, then turned to Beatrice, and she eagerly signed to me to pour out the water of my inner fountain. I began: "May the grace that allows me to confess myself to the noble forerunner, make my thought achieve expression!" And I went on: "As the true pen of your dear brother, who with you set Rome on the better path, wrote for us, 'Faith is the substance of things hoped for, the evidence of things not seen,' and this I take to be its essence."

Then I heard: "You understand it truly, if you understand why he placed it among the substances, and then cited it as evidence."

And I to that: "The deep things that grant me the privilege of appearing in front of me here are hidden from the sight of those below, so that their existence is only a belief down there, on which is built a high hope, and so it justifies the meaning of substance. And from this belief we need to reason, without any further insight, so it satisfies the meaning of evidence."

Then I heard: "If everything that is learnt down there by teaching were understood so clearly, there would be no room left for sophistry." So it breathed out from that burning love; then it added: "This coin's weight and alloy has been well tried; but tell me if you have it in your purse."

At which I said: "Yes, I have it there, so bright and round that there is no *perhaps* for me in its stamp."

Then this issued from the deep light that was burning there: "From where did that dear gem, on which all virtue is founded, come to you?"

And I: "The profuse rain of the Holy Spirit, which is poured over the Old and the New pages, is the reasoning that brought it to so clear a conclusion for me, so that compared with it, all argument seems coarse to me."

Then I heard: "That Old and New proposition, which leads to your conclusion: why do you take it for divine discourse?"

And I: "The proof that reveals the truth to me is in the miracles that followed, which nature never heated the iron for, or struck the anvil."

The answer was: "Tell me, who assures you that these miracles took place? The writing, which seeks to be the proof of itself, no other attests to them."

I answered: "If the world turned to Christianity without miracles, that would be such a miracle that the others would not rate a hundredth of it, since you entered, poor and hungry, on the field, to sow the plant that was once a vine, and is now a thorn." So ending, the high sacred court rang out a "Praised be God" through the spheres, with that melody that is sung up there.

That spirit who had drawn me from branch to branch with his questioning, now that we were near to the topmost leaves, began again: "The grace that holds loving speech with your mind has opened your mouth till now, as was appropriate, so that I sanction what emerged, but now you must say what *you* believe, and how it was offered to your belief."

I began: "O holy father, you spirit who see now what you once so believed that you outstripped younger feet in entering the sepulcher, you would have me declare the form of my eager faith, and also ask the source of it, to which I answer: I believe in one God, sole and eternal, who moves all the Heavens with love and desire, Himself un-moving. And I do not merely have physical and metaphysical proofs for such belief, but it is shown me also by the truth that flows from it through Moses, the Prophets and the Psalms, through the Gospel, and through you, who wrote when the ardent Spirit had made you holy. And I believe in three Persons, eternal, and I believe they are One essence *and* Threefold in such a way as to allow *are* and *is* to be joined. My mind is stamped more than once by the evangelic teaching with the profound Divine condition of which I speak. This is the Source: this is the spark which then expands to living flame, and shines in me like a star in Heaven." Like the master who hears what pleases him and so clasps the servant, thanking him for his news when he falls silent, so the apostolic light at whose command I had spoken circled me three times, blessing me as it sang, as soon as I had ceased, I pleased him so with my words.

25

If it should ever come to pass that the sacred poem to which Heaven and Earth have set their hand, which has made me lean through many a year, conquers the cruelty that bars me from the lovely fold where I used to sleep as a lamb, enemy of the wolves that war on it, I will return a poet, now, with altered voice and fleece, and will assume the wreath at my baptismal font, since it was there I entered the faith which makes souls visible to God, and afterwards Peter, for its sake, so encircled my brow. After which a light moved towards us from the sphere out of which the first fruits of the vicars left by Christ on earth came. And my Lady, full of joy, said to me: "Look! Look! Behold the saint for whose sake down there they travel to Galicia."

As a dove, taking his perch next to his companion, pours out his love for the other, billing and cooing, so I saw one great and glorious prince received by the other, praising the food that feasts them there. But when the greeting was over, each one rested silently *coram me* [in my presence], so fiery that they overcame my gaze. Then Beatrice, smiling, said: "Noble life, by whom the generous gifts of our court were recorded, let hope be sounded in this altitude; you know it who described it all those times when Jesus gave greater light to you three."

"Lift your head, and reassure yourself, since whatever comes here from the mortal world must ripen in our rays." Such comfort came to me from the second flame, at which I lifted up "mine eyes unto the hills," which had been bowed before with excessive weight. The second light continued: "Since our Emperor, by his grace, wishes you to be confronted with his saints in His most secret court before you die, so that having seen its truth, you might increase the hope in yourself and others, which makes people on earth love the good, explain what hope is, and how your mind is enflowered by it, and say from where it comes to you."

And that gentle one who guided my feathered wings to so high a soaring anticipated me in speaking, saying: "The Church Militant does not have a child more full of hope, as it is written in the Sun who shines on all our host; so it was granted to him to come out of Egypt to Jerusalem, to gaze on her, before the proper end of his struggle. Those two points, of hope and love, asked about not so that you might learn anything but so that he can take back word of how much they give pleasure to you, I leave to him, since they will not be difficult for him, or a chance to boast: so let him answer to them, and may God's grace allow him this."

Like a pupil following after his teacher in what he is expert in, pleased and eager for his knowledge to be shown, I said: "Hope is the certain expectation of future glory, the product of Divine Grace and previous worth. This light comes to me from many stars, but the highest singer of the highest leader first distilled it in my heart. Let those who know your name, hope in you, he says in his divine song, and who does not know it, if they have my faith? You then rained it on me with his rain, in your epistle, so that I am drenched and pour your shower again over others."

While I was speaking, a sudden flash like lightning trembled in the living heart of that flame. Then it breathed out: "The love with which I am still on fire for virtue, and that followed me to the palm of martyrdom and the leaving of the field of life, wills me to breathe on you who delight in her, and it is my further wish that you tell of what it is hope promises to you."

And I: "The Old and the New Testaments display the sign that points me once more to the thing itself. Isaiah says that, of the souls that God has made his friends, each one will be robed with double robes in its own land, and its own land is this sweet life. And your brother John sets out this revelation for us, more clearly worked through, where he treats of the white robes."

And not long after the ending of these words, "They hope in you" rang out above us, to which all the singers responded; then a light flashed out from among them, so that if the Crab contained a star like it, winter would have one month with unbroken daylight. And as a joyful virgin rises and goes to join the dance, not from wrong motives but only to honor the bride, so I saw that illumined splendor join the other two who were turning in a ring in such a manner as fitted their ardent love. There it entered their song and its words, and my Lady fixed her gaze on them like a bride, silent and motionless; then my Lady said: "This is the one who leaned on the breast of the Pelican, who chose him from the cross and committed Mary to his care." So she spoke, but no more moved her eyes from their fixed intent afterwards than before.

Like one who strains and gazes at the sun's brief eclipse and loses his sight by looking, so was I at this last flame, until a word came: "Why does it dazzle you to see that which has no place here? My body is earth in the earth, and there it will be with the others until our time suits the eternal purpose. Only the two lights that ascended wear both robes in this blessed cloister, and this you can take back to your world."

The inflamed circle quieted itself at this voice, together with the sweet harmony made by the sound of that triple breath, as oars, striking the water until then, all pause at the whistle's sound so as to stave off weariness or danger. Oh how I was stirred in my mind, turning to search for Beatrice, whom I was blind to, though I was near her, and in the world of bliss!

26

While I was doubtful of my darkened sight, I was made attentive by a breath that came from the glowing flame that had darkened it, saying: "Until you regain the sense of sight you have spent on me, it would be well to compensate for it by speaking. Begin then, and say on what your mind is focused, and be assured that your vision is dazzled and not destroyed, since the Lady who leads you through this divine region has the same power in her gaze that Ananias had in his hands."

I said: "Let help come sooner or later, at her wish, to these eyes that were the gates where she entered with the fire I always burn with. Love, the good that satisfies this court, is the alpha and omega of all the scriptures Amor reads to me, shallowly or deeply." The same voice that had erased my fear at the sudden dazzling set my mind again to speech, and said: "Truly, you must strain through a finer sieve: you must tell me what it was that aimed your bow at such a target."

And I replied: "Such love must stamp itself on me by philosophical arguments, and by authority that descends from them, since good, as good, in my understanding, lights the fire of love, and the more so the more excellence it finds in itself. So the mind of whoever sees the truth on which this proof depends, must move in love towards that essence, which has such advantage that whatever is found good outside it is nothing but a ray of its own light. And this same truth is made known to my intellect by he who showed me the primal love of all eternal beings. It is made known to me by the voice of that true Author who says to Moses, speaking of himself: 'I will make all my goodness pass before thee.' It is made known to me by you as well, where your prelude cries out the secrets of this place to Earth beyond all other speech."

And I heard: "Keep the highest of your loves for God, as urged by human reason, and by the authorities that concur with it, but tell me if you feel other strings drawing you towards Him, and say how many teeth this love grips you with."

The sacred purpose of Christ's eagle was not hidden but rather I saw in which direction he wished to lead my statements. So that I began again: "All those bitings that have power to make the heart turn towards God work together on my love, since the world's existence and my own, the death that He suffered so that I might live, and what each believer hopes, as do I, together with the living consciousness I spoke of have all drawn me out of the sea of the perverse and set me on the shore of true love. I love the leaves with which the whole garden of the eternal Gardener is leafed, as greatly as good has been offered to them by Him."

As soon as I fell silent, the sweetest song resounded through the Heavens, and my Lady cried: "Holy, Holy, Holy," with them all. And as a man wakes from sleep at a bright light, because his spirit of sight runs to meet the glow that pierces veil after veil of the eye, and he, waking, confuses what he sees, his sudden vision being so clouded, until thought comes to its aid, so Beatrice made the scales fall from my eyes with the rays from hers that would cast their glow a thousand miles, so that I saw more clearly afterwards than before, and, almost stupefied, I questioned as to a fourth light that I saw with us. And my Lady said: "In those rays, the first soul that the primal Power ever made holds loving converse with his Maker."

As the branch bows its head when the wind passes over it, and then lifts itself by its own strength that holds it up, so I did, all dazed while she was speaking, and then was recollected by a desire to speak with which I burned, and I began: "O ancient father, who has a daughter and a daughter-in-law in every bride, you, the only fruit of the harvest created fully mature, I beg you, devoutly as I can, to speak to me: you see my wish, and I do not say it so that I can hear you even sooner."

Sometimes a creature struggles under a cloth, so that its intent is visible because what covers it follows its movement, and similarly that primal soul made the joy with which it came to serve my pleasure apparent through its surface. And from it breathed: "Though you do not say it, I see your will more clearly than you see what you are most certain of, because I view it in the true Glass, who makes Himself the Mirror of all things, and makes nothing which completely reflects Him. You wish to know how much time has passed since God set me in the exalted Garden in which She prepared you for this long stairway, and for how long its delights endured my presence, and the true cause of the great wrath, and about the language that I used, and made myself. Know, my son, that it was not the eating of the Tree that was the cause in itself of such harsh exile, but solely the going beyond the bounds set. In that place from which your Lady sent Virgil to you, my longing for these courts lasted four thousand, three hundred and two revolutions of the sun, and I had seen him pass through all the stars along his track nine hundred and thirty times while I was on Earth. The language I spoke vanished long before the tower that was never completed was built by Nimrod's people, since the products of reason never last forever because of human taste that alters with the movement of the skies. It is nature's doing that man should speak, but nature allows you to do it this way or that, as seems best to you. Before I went down to infernal anguish, *Jah* was the name on earth of that Supreme Good from which the delight comes, that clothes me: He was called *El* thereafter, and that is fitting, since mortal usage is like the leaf on the twig that falls and another opens. In life, pure and then disgraced, I was on the mountain rising furthest from the sea from the first hour to that which follows the sixth hour, when the sun changes quadrant."

27

"Glory be to the Father, to the Son, and to the Holy Ghost," began through all of Paradise, so that the sweet song intoxicated me. I seemed to see the universe's smile, so that my intoxication came from sight and sound. O joy! O ineffable happiness! O life of love and peace combined! O safest riches that are beyond longing! The four torches stood burning in front of my eyes, and the first one, which had neared me, began to grow more intense, and became like Jupiter if he and Mars were birds and exchanged plumage.

The Providence that assigns roles and offices there had imposed silence on the choir of the blessed on every side, when I heard: "Do not wonder if I transform the color of my light, since you will see all these others do the same as I speak. He who on Earth usurps my place—mine, mine, vacant in the presence of the Son of God—has made my burial ground a sewer for that blood and filth whereby the perverse angel who fell from above is placated down there." Then I saw Heaven tinged with that color which paints the clouds at dawn or evening, from the opposing sun, and like a modest woman who is certain of herself but feels fear only at the hearing of another's fault, so Beatrice changed in appearance, and such, I take it, was the eclipse in Heaven when the Supreme Power suffered.

Then his speech continued, in a voice so far altered from itself that even his appearance had not altered more greatly, saying: "The spouse of Christ was not fed on my blood and that of Linus and Cletus so that she might be used to acquire gold, but it was to gain this joyful life that Sixtus, Pius, Calixtus, and Urban gave their blood after many tears. It was not our purpose for one part of Christianity to sit on the right side, and the other on the left of our successors; or that the keys given in trust to me should become the insignia on a banner making war on the baptized; or that I should become the head on that seal that stamps false and mercenary privileges, at which I often blush and shoot out flames. From here above the ravening wolves are seen, dressed as shepherds, in all the pastures. O succor God, why do You rest?

Gascons and Cahorsines prepare to drink our blood. O good beginning, what evil end must you fall to! But the high Providence that defended the glory of the world for Rome in Scipio will soon bring aid, I think. And you, my son, who will return below because of your mortal heaviness, open your mouth, and do not hide the things I do not hide."

As our air snows down frozen moisture in flakes when the horn of the Heavenly Goat is touched by the sun, so I saw the ether clothe itself and snow the flakes of the triumphant lights that had rested with us upwards. My vision was tracing their form and followed them until excess of space inhibited its power to see further. At which the Lady who saw me free now of straining upwards said to me: "Look down, and see how you have orbited." I saw that since the hour when I had first looked down, I had moved through the whole quadrant the first clime makes from noon to evening, so that I could see beyond Cadiz that foolish path Ulysses took, and, on this side, at evening, the near shore where Europa became the bull's sweet burden. And the sight of the threshing-floor would have been unfolded further to me except that the sun was in advance under my feet, separated by a sign and more from me.

My enamored mind, which always held loving speech with my Lady, burned more than ever to bring my eyes back to her, and whatever food, art or nature makes to captivate the eyes and so possess the mind, whether in human form or in paintings, all brought together would seem nothing compared to the divine delight which shone on me when I turned towards her smiling face. And the power which that look bestowed on me plucked me out of Leda's fair nest and thrust me into the swiftest Heaven.

Its regions, highest and most alive, are so alike that I cannot say in which one Beatrice chose to place me. But She, who saw my longing, began to speak, smiling so delightedly that God seemed shining in her face: "The nature of the universe, which keeps the center fixed and moves the rest around it, begins here, as if from its goal. And this Heaven has no other place than in the Divine Mind, in which the love that moves it is fired and the power that it disperses. Light and love clasp it in one circle, as it does all the other spheres, and only He who embraces it understands this embrace. Its movement is not measured by any other, but all the rest are measured by it, as ten by halves and fifths. And it may now be clear to you how time has its roots in this same sphere, and its leaves in the rest.

"O greed, which so corrupts mortals below that not one of them
has strength enough to draw his eyes away from your depths! It is true
that human will is still strong, but the continuous rain turns ripe plums
to cancerous growths. Faith and innocence are only found in little
children, then both vanish before the cheeks are downy. Many a lisping babe keeps the fast who, when his tongue is free afterwards, eats
any food in any month, and many a lisping babe loves and listens to its
mother who, when his speech is perfected afterwards, longs to see her
buried. So, at the first appearance, the white skin blackens of the
lovely daughter of Him who brings the dawn, and leaves us evening.
And you, lest you wonder at it, consider there is no one governing on
earth, so the human household wanders from the path. But before
January abandons winter by that hundredth of a day in the calendar
year ignored on earth, these upper spheres shall roar, so that the fated
season, long awaited, will reverse stem to stern, so that the fleet can
sail true, and ripe fruit will follow the flower."

28

When the truth had been revealed by her who imparadises my mind, a truth in opposition to the present life of miserable humanity, my memory recalls that, gazing on the lovely eyes from which love made the noose to capture me, I looked—as a candle flame lit behind a man is seen by him in a mirror before it is itself in his vision or thought, so that he turns around to see if the glass spoke true, and sees them agreeing, as song lyrics to their meter—and when I turned, and my own eyes were struck by what appears in that space, whenever the eyes are correctly fixed on its orbiting, I saw a point that beamed out a light so intense that the eye it blazes on must be closed to its fierce brightness, and whatever star seems smallest from down here would be a moon if it were placed alongside it, as star is placed alongside star. Perhaps as near as a halo appears to be to the light that generates it when the vapor in which it glows is thickest, at such a distance as that, around that point, a circle of fire revolved so quickly it exceeded the speed of the fastest sphere that surrounds the universe, and this circle was surrounded by another, that by a third, the third by a fourth, the fourth a fifth, the fifth a sixth. After it the seventh followed, already so broad in its reach that if Juno's rainbow messenger were complete it would be too small to contain it. And so the eighth and ninth, and each one moved more slowly as its number was further from unity; and the one from which the pure light source was least distant had the clearest flame, because, I believe, it is more embedded in the light's truth.

My Lady, who saw me laboring in profound anticipation, said: "Heaven and all nature hangs from that point. Look at the circle that is most nearly joined to it and learn that its movement is so fast because of the burning love that it is pierced by."

And I to her: "If the universe was ordered in the sequence I see in these circlings, then I would be content with what I see in front of me. But in the universe of the senses, we see the spheres as more divine the further they are distant from Earth, the center. So, if my desire is to find its goal in this marvelous, angelic temple, which has only love and light as its limits, I must hear why the copy and the pattern are not identical in form, since, I myself cannot see it."

"And if your fingers are not skilled in untying such a knot, it is no wonder: it has become so difficult to achieve from never being tried." So my Lady spoke, and continued: "If you wish to be satisfied on this, take what I tell you and wrap your mind around it. The earth-centered circles are wide or narrow according to how much virtue spreads through their region. Greater excellence has power to work greater benefit, and greater benefit is conferred by the largest sphere, if all parts of it are equally perfect. So the sphere that sweeps with it all the rest of the universe, corresponds to the circle that loves and knows most. Therefore, if you take your measure from the virtue, not the appearance, of the substances that appear to you in these circles, you will see a marvelous correspondence between greater and more, smaller and less, between every Heaven and its angelic intelligence."

As the hemisphere of air shines serenely when Boreas blows a north-easterly from his gentler cheek so that the layer that covered it is purged and dissolved and the sky laughs with the beauties of all its regions, so was I after my Lady had replied to me with her clear answer and the truth was seen as clearly as a star in the sky. And when her words ceased, the circles glittered as iron shoots outs sparks when it is poured, and every scintillation followed their fire, and the quantity of sparks were thousands more than the doubling of the chessboard at every square.

I heard Hosanna sung from choir to choir towards the fixed point, which holds, and will hold them forever, to the *where* in which they have ever been; and She who saw the questions in my mind, said: "The first circles have shown you the seraphs and the cherubs. They follow their loops so fast so that they can identify themselves as closely with the point as possible, and they succeed according to their sublimity of vision. Those other Loves that circle around them are called Thrones of the divine aspect, because they bring the first triplet of circles to completion. And you must know that they all take delight according as their vision sinks more deeply into the truth where every mind is stilled. So you can see how being blessed is founded on the act of seeing, not of loving, which follows from it, and the extent of vision is measured by the merit that grace, and the right will, create, and so it goes from rank to rank. The second triplet that flowers like this, in this eternal spring that Aries does not despoil by night as it does in

our autumnal and wintry skies, perpetually sing spring's Hosannas
with three melodies that sound in the three ranks of joy, by which it is
triply formed. In that hierarchy are the three divinities, the Domina-
tions and Virtues, and the third order, Powers. Then in the two
penultimate dance-circles the Principalities and Archangels whirl, and
the last consists all of angelic play. These orders all gaze upwards, and
have such all-conquering power downwards that all are drawn towards
God, and in turn draw. And Dionysius set himself to contemplate
these orders with such longing that he named them and separated
them as I do. But Gregory afterwards differed from him, such that
when he opened his eyes in this Heaven, he smiled at himself. And if
such hidden truth was uttered by a man on Earth, do not wonder at it,
since one who saw it here revealed it to him, with other truths about
these circles."

29

When the children of Latona, one in the Ram, the other in the Scales, make the horizon their circle, and the zenith is the point from which both hang till one rises, the other sets, removing themselves from that zone's scales, both changing hemispheres, that long did Beatrice keep silent with a smile pictured on her face, gazing intensely at the point whose light overcame me. Then she began to speak: "I do not ask, I say what you wish to hear of, since I have seen the point of Creation, on which every *where* and *when* is focused. In his eternity beyond time, past all others' understanding, the eternal love showed Himself, in new love, as He desired: not to gain any good for Himself, since that cannot be, but so that His reflected light, shining, might say: *I am*. He did not lie there, as if sleeping, before Creation: God's movement over these waters was not a process of before or after. Form and matter, pure and conjoined, issued into being without flaw, like three arrows from a triple-strung bow, and as a ray of light shines in glass, amber, or crystal, so that no time passes between its entry and the illumination, so the triple effect of the Lord shone out instantly into being, without a separate beginning. Order was co-created, and interwoven with substance; and they were the crown of the universe in whom pure act was produced: potentiality held the lowest place; in the middle potentiality formed such a knot with act as can never be untied. Jerome wrote for you about the vast stretch of time in which the created angels existed, before the rest of the universe was formed, but the contrary truth I speak is written on many pages of the writers of the Holy Spirit, and you will become aware of it if you look closely; and reason also sees it in some degree, which cannot allow that the movers of the spheres should exist so long without their spheres' perfection. Now you know where and when these loves were elected, and how, so that three flames of your longing are quenched already. Before one could count to twenty, some of the angels fell, stirring the foundation of your elements. The rest remained, and began the art you see, with such delight that they never leave their circling. The

source of the fall was the cursed pride of Satan, him you saw imprisoned by the whole weight of the universe. Those you see here were
humble, recognizing themselves as being from that same excellence
that made them so quick in understanding, so that their vision was
exalted by illuminating grace and their own virtue, so that they have
their will free and entire. And I want you to be certain, and not doubtful, that it is a virtue to receive grace by opening the affections to it.

"Now, if my words have been absorbed, you can contemplate much
of this court without further help. But I will go on, because in your
schools it is taught that the angelic nature is such as understands,
remembers, and wills, and I wish you to see in its purity the truth that
is confused down there by the equivocations in such lectures. These
angelic substances, since they first gathered joy from God's face, have
never turned their eyes from that from which nothing is hidden, so
that their vision is never disturbed by any new object, and there is no
need to recall anything to memory because of divided thoughts. So
humans dream down there, when not asleep, certain that they speak
the truth, or uncertain: and there is greater error and shame in the
latter. You do not follow a single track when you philosophize down
there, love of display and the thought it produces delights you so. But
even this is tolerated here with less indignation than when Divine
Scripture is twisted or discarded. They forget how great the cost was in
blood to sow its seed in the world, and how much he pleases who
keeps it by him in humility. Everyone strains his wits to make a display
and show his inventiveness: the priests discuss these things, and the
scriptures are left silent. One says the moon reversed when Christ
suffered, and blocked the sun's light from shining below, and others
that the light vanished by itself, so that the same eclipse occurred for
Spain and India as it did for the Jews. Florence does not have as many
Lapos and Bindos as these sorts of story, proclaimed year after year
from the pulpits here and there, so that the sheep, knowing nothing,
return from the pasture fed on air, and not to know their loss is no
excuse. Christ did not say 'Go and preach nonsense to the world' to
his first gathering, but gave them the true foundation: that, and only
that, was on their lips, so that they made the Gospels lance and shield
in their fight to light the faith. Now a man goes to preach with jokes
and grimaces, and if there is loud laughter, his cowl swells, and nothing else is needed. But such a devil is nesting in the hood that if the
crowd could see it, they would know what remission they were trusting in, and from this the foolishness has increased so much on Earth

that people would go with any promise, without proof of evidence. Thus the pigs of Saint Anthony, and others more swinish than they, are fattened by the gains of this false coinage.

"But since we have wandered enough, turn your eyes back now to the true path, so that our time and journey may shorten. This angelic nature has such deep-numbered ranks that mortal speech and thought have never extended so far, and if you look at what Daniel reveals, you will see that determinate number is lost among his thousands. The primal light that shines above it all is received by it in as many ways as the reflected splendors, with which it pairs. And since affection follows the act of conception, the sweetness of love is warm, or hotter in them, in various ways. See, now, the breadth and height of eternal value, since it has made so many mirrors of itself, in which it is reflected, remaining itself One, as it was before."

30

Noon blazes some six thousand miles from us, and this world's shadows already slope to a level field when the center of Heaven, high above, begins to alter, so that, here and there, a star lacks the power to shine to this depth; and as the brightest handmaiden of the sun advances, so Heaven quenches star after star till even the loveliest are gone. In the same way, that triumph that always plays around the point that overcame me, appearing to be embraced by that which it embraces, faded little by little from my vision, so that my seeing nothing, and my love, forced me to turn my eyes towards Beatrice. If that which is said of her above were all condensed into one act of praise, it would be too little to answer to this case: the beauty I saw is beyond measure, not only past our reach, but I truly believe that only He who made it joys in it completely. At this point, I consider myself more utterly vanquished than ever his theme's weight overcame comic or tragic poet, since, like the sun, in trembling vision, so the memory of the sweet smile cuts off my memory from my deepest self. From the first day in this life when I saw her until this present vision, my song has never failed to follow, but now my way must cease the tracking of her beauty through poetry, as every artist must at his furthest reach. So as I leave her to a greater fanfare than my tuba, which sounds the close of its arduous subject, she began again to speak with a leader's alert gestures and voice, saying: "We have issued from the largest sphere into the Heaven that is pure light, intellectual light, filled with love, love of true goodness, filled with joy, the joy that transcends every sweetness. Here you will see the redeemed and angelic soldiers of Paradise, and the former in their forms that you will see at the Last Judgment."

As a sudden flash of lightning destroys the visual powers so as to rob the eye of strength to make out even the clearest objects, so a living light shone around me, leaving me bathed in such a veil of its brightness that nothing was visible to me. "The love that stills Heaven always accepts spirits into itself with such a greeting, to fit the candle for its flame."

As soon as these few words entered me, I felt I surmounted my normal powers, and blazed with such newly created sight that there is no unalloyed light that my eyes could not hold their own with. And I saw brightness in the form of a river pouring amber between banks pricked out with miraculous spring. Living sparks flashed from this river and fell into the blossoms on all sides, like gold-set rubies. Then they plunged themselves again into the marvelous vortex, as if drunk with the perfumes, and as one entered, another issued out.

"The high desire that burns and urges you now to acquire knowledge of the things you see pleases me more the more it intensifies. But you must first drink of this water before so great a thirst in you can be satisfied." So my eyes' sun spoke to me, then added: "The river and the topazes that enter it and exit, and the smile of the grasses, are the shadowy preface to their reality. Not because the things are crude in themselves, but the defect is in you, because you do not have such exalted vision yet."

Never did infant waking much later than usual turn so quickly towards the milk as I did then, bending to the waters that are formed so that we may better ourselves, to make still truer mirrors of my eyes. And my eyelids' rims no sooner felt it than their length seemed to alter into roundness. Then the flowers and the sparks changed in front of me into a fuller joyousness—just as masked people seem other than before if they remove the image that hid them, not their own— and I saw both courts of Heaven made manifest.

O splendor of God, through which I saw the high triumph of the kingdom of truth: give me the power to say what I saw.

There is a light up there that makes the Creator visible to the creature, who only in seeing him finds its peace, and it extends so far in a circle that its rim would loosely contain the sun's light. It whole appearance is formed of rays reflected from the surface of the *Primum Mobile*, which draws its life and power from them. And as a hillside reflects itself in the water at its foot, as if to view its own beauty, rich in grass and flowers, so rising above the light, around, around, I saw all of us who have won their way back up there, casting their reflection in more than a thousand ranks. And if the lowest level attracts so great a light inside it, what of the intensity of the rose's outer petals? My sight was not lost itself in the height and breadth, but grasped the quality and quantity of joy. Near and far do not add or subtract there, since where God rules without mediation the laws of nature have no relevance.

Beatrice drew me, a man silent who would speak, into the yellow glow of the eternal rose that rises, layer on layer, and exudes the perfume of praise towards the Sun that makes eternal spring, saying: "Marvel at the vastness of the white-robed gathering! Our city, see how wide its circle! See our thrones, filled, so that few spirits are still awaited there. The soul of Henry, an imperial one on Earth, shall sit on that high seat that you fix your eyes on because of the crown you already see placed over it before you yourself dine at this wedding feast: he, who will come to set Italy straight before she is ready for it. Blind greed that bewitches you has made you like a little child that chases away its nurse while dying of hunger: and he who will be pope then in the court of divine things will be such as will not tread the same path as him, openly or in secret. But God will not suffer him long in that sacred office, since he will be forced down where Simon Magus is for his reward, and push him of Anagna lower still."

31

That sacred army that Christ espoused with his blood displayed itself in the form of a white rose, but the angelic one that sees and sings the glory of him who inspires it with love, as it flies and sings the excellence that has made it as it is, descended continually into the great flower, lovely with so many petals, and climbed again to where its love lives forever, like a swarm of bees that now plunges into the flowers, and now returns, to where their labor is turned to sweetness. Their faces were all of living flame, their wings of gold, and the rest of them so white that snow never reached that limit. When they dropped into the flower, they offered to tier after tier the peace and ardor that they acquired with beating wings, and the presence of such a vast flying swarm between the flower and what was beyond it did not dilute the vision or the splendor, because the Divine Light so penetrates the universe to the measure of its value that nothing has the power to prevent it. This kingdom, safe and happy, crowded with ancient peoples and the new, had vision and love all turned towards one point.

O triple Light that glitters in their sight, a single star, and so contents them: look down on our tempest! If the barbarians coming from those countries that the Bear spans every day, orbiting with her son whom she longs for, if they were stupefied on seeing Rome and her great works at the time when her palaces exceeded mortal things, what then of me, who had gone to the divine from the human, to the eternal from time, and from Florence to a true and just people? With what stupor must I be filled! Truly, what with it and with my joy, my wish was to hear nothing and say nothing.

Like a pilgrim who renews himself by gazing in the temple of his vows and already hopes to retell how it looks, so I led my eyes, crossing the living light along the levels, up and down, and then around them, circling. I saw faces persuasive of love, graced by another's light and their own smile, and with gestures adorned with all honor. My gaze had already taken in the general form of Paradise in its completeness, and my sight had not rested on any one part, and I turned, with reillumined will, to ask my Lady about things with which my mind was concerned. I intended that, but another sight answered mine: I thought that I would see Beatrice, but I saw an old man dressed like the glorious folk. His eyes and cheeks were full of gentle joy, with kindly gestures as befits a tender father.

"Where is She?" I said quickly, at which he replied: "Beatrice brought me from my place to lead your desire to its goal, and if you look up at the third circle from the highest level, you will see her again, on that throne her merit has marked out for her." I raised my eyes without answering, and saw her making a crown for herself by reflecting the eternal light from her person. No human eye is further from the highest vaults of the thunder, though plunged to the sea's depths, as my sight was from Beatrice, but that did not affect me, since her image came to me undiluted by any medium. "O Lady, in whom my hope has life, and who, for my salvation, suffered to leave your footprints in Hell, I recognize the grace and virtue of all I have seen through your power and your goodness. You have brought me from slavery to freedom, by all those paths, by all those ways that you had power over. Guard your grace in me, so that my spirit, which you have made whole, may be acceptable to you when it leaves my body." So I prayed, and she, far off though she appeared, smiled and gazed at me, then turned towards the eternal fountain.

And the holy man said: "Let your eyes fly around this garden so as to consummate your journey perfectly, the mission for which prayer and sacred love sent me, since gazing at it will better fit your sight to climb through the divine light. And the Queen of Heaven, for whom I burn wholly with love, will grant us all grace, because I am her loyal Bernard."

Like one who comes from Croatia perhaps to see our cloth of Veronica, and is not sated with looking because of its ancient fame, but as long as it is visible says in thought: "Lord Jesus Christ, true God, was this then your face?" such was I gazing at the living love of him who in this world tasted of that peace in contemplation.

He began: "Son of grace, this joyful being will not become known to you merely by keeping your gaze down here at the foot, but look at the circles, to the very farthest, until you see the enthroned Queen of Heaven, to whom this kingdom is subject and devoted."

I lifted my eyes and, as at dawn the eastern space of the horizon conquers that space where the sun declines, so, as if raising my eyes from a valley to the mountain, I saw a space at the edge exceed all the rest of the ridge in light. And as down here that place where we expect the chariot that Phaethon failed to guide is most glowing and the light is cut away on either side, so was She, that flame of peace, quickened in the center, tempering the blaze on all sides. And at the midpoint I saw more than a thousand angels joying with outstretched wings, each angel distinct in glow and function. I saw there a beauty that was delight in the eyes of all the other saints, smiling at their dances and their songs. And if I had words as rich as my imagination, I would still not dare to attempt the smallest part of her delightfulness.

Bernard turned his eyes to her with so much love when he saw my eyes, fixed and attentive, gazing towards the source of his own light that he made mine more eager to gaze again.

32

The contemplative, with his love fixed on his delight, freely assumed the office of a teacher, and began these sacred words: "The wound that Mary sealed and anointed is that which the lovely one at her feet opened and pierced. In the order made by the third level, Rachel with Beatrice sit below her, as you see. Even as I go down the rose, petal by petal, naming their proper names, you can see, descending from level to level, Sarah, Rebecca, Judith, and Ruth, her from whom came the singer, third in descent, who cried out from grief at his sin: 'Pity me!' And down from the seventh, and beyond, again the Hebrew women, separating the flower's tresses, since they are the wall that parts the sacred stairway, according to how faith in Christ was realized. On this side, where the flower is full-blown in all its petals, those who believed in Christ to come are sitting; on the other side, where there are empty seats among them, are the semicircles of those whose eyes were turned towards the Christ who had come. And as the glorious throne of Heaven's Lady, and the seats below her, make such a partition, so, next to her, does that of the great John, who, ever holy, suffered the desert and a martyr's death, and then Limbo for two years' space, until Christ came there, and below him, the separating line, assigned to Francis, Benedict, Augustine, and the others from circle to circle, down to here. Now marvel at the depth of Divine provision, since both aspects of the faith will fill this garden equally. And know that, down from the level that cuts across the two divisions, the spirits have their places not because of their own merit, but another's, given certain conditions, since these are all souls freed before they had exercised true choice. You can see it by their faces, and their voices, those of children, if you look carefully and listen.

"Now you doubt and are silent in your doubting, but I will untie the difficult knot for you in which your subtle thoughts are entangling you. No chance point has place in all this kingdom, no more than sadness, thirst, or hunger do, because what you see is established by Eternal Law, so that the ring corresponds exactly to the finger. The ordering of these children, swiftly come to the true life according to greater or lesser excellence, is not *sina causa* [without reason]. The King, by whom this kingdom rests in such great love, such great delight, that the will dares nothing more when He creates minds in his joyous sight of His grace and at His pleasure, grants them diversity, and let the effect suffice as proof. And this is marked clearly and expressly in Holy Writ concerning those twins who struggled in anger in their mother's womb. So the Supreme Light must wreathe them worthily, according to the color of the tresses of such grace. Therefore they are placed at different levels without regard for the externals, differentiated only by their primal keenness in seeing Him. So, in ancient times, the parents' faith alone, combined with innocence, was enough to reach salvation. When those first ages were complete, males needed to gain power in their innocent wings through the rite of circumcision. But when the time of grace came, then, lacking Christ's perfect baptism, such innocence was held there below. Now see the face that is most like Christ's, since its brightness, and no other, has the power to equip you to see Christ."

I saw such gladness borne in the sacred angelic minds created to fly through that altitude rain down on that face that nothing I had seen before seized me with such dumb admiration, or so revealed the semblance of God. And that love which first came down to Her, singing: "Hail, Mary, full of grace," now spread his wings in front of her. The Divine Canticle was responded to on every side by the court of the blest, so that every face found peace in it.

"O holy father, you who accept being here below for my sake, leaving that sweet place where you sit by eternal sanction, who is that angel who looks our Queen in the eyes with such joy, so enamored he seems all on fire?" So I turned again to his teaching, he who gathered beauty from Mary as the morning star does from the sun.

And he to me: "The greatest exultation and chivalry that exists in angel or in spirit is all in him; and we would wish it so, since it is Gabriel who brought the palm down to Mary when the Son of God willed that He should take on our burden. But now let your eyes come travel, even as I speak, and note the great noble souls of this most just and pious empire. Those two who sit up there, most blest by being nearest to the Empress, are like two roots of this Rose. Her neighbor on the left is that father through whose audacity in tasting the fruit the human race tastes such bitterness; on the right is that ancient father of Holy Church to whom Christ entrusted the keys of this beloved flower. And he sits by his side who, before he died, saw all the dark prophetic seasons of that fair Bride, who was won with lance and nails; and by Adam's side, that leader rests under whom the ungrateful, fickle, and mutinous people were fed with manna. See Anne sitting opposite Peter, so content to look at her daughter that she does not remove her gaze to sing Hosanna. And opposite the greatest father of our family sits Lucy, who stirred your Lady when you were bending your brow downwards to ruin. But since the time of your vision is fleeing, here let us stop, like the careful tailor who cuts the garment according to the cloth, and let us turn our eyes towards the Primal Love, so that gazing at Him you might penetrate as far as possible into His brightness. Truly grace needs to be acquired by prayer (so that you do not by chance fall back as you beat your wings), grace from Her who has power to help you, and follow me with such affection that your heart is not separated from my words." And he began this sacred prayer:

33

"Virgin mother, daughter of your Son, humbled and exalted more than any other creature, fixed goal of the Eternal Wisdom: you are She who made human nature so noble that its own Maker did not scorn to become of its making. The love, beneath whose warmth this flower has grown in eternal peace, flamed again in your womb. Here you are the noonday torch of love to us, and down there, among mortal beings, you are a living spring of hope. Lady, you are so great and of such value that if any who wishes for grace fails to resort to you, his longing tries to fly without wings. Your kindness not only helps those who ask it, it often freely anticipates the request. In you is tenderness, in you is pity, in you is generosity, in you whatever excellences exist in the creature, combined together. Now he who has seen the lives of souls, one by one, from the deepest pool of the universe even to here, begs you, of your grace, for enough strength to lift his eyes higher, towards the final bliss; and I, who was never so on fire for my own vision as I am for his, offer you all my prayers, and pray they may not be wanting, asking that for him you might scatter every cloud of his mortality with your prayers, so that supreme joy might be revealed to him. And more I beg of you, Queen, who can do the things you will: after he has seen so deeply, keep his affections sound. Let your protection overcome human weakness; see Beatrice, with so many saints, folding her hands to pray with me."

Those eyes, loved by God and venerated, fixed on the speaker, showed us how greatly devout prayers please her. Then they turned themselves towards the Eternal Light, into which, we must believe, no other creature's eye finds its way so clearly. And I, who was drawing near the goal of all my longing, quenched as was fitting the ardor of my desire inside me.

Bernard made a sign to me and smiled, telling me to look higher, but I was already doing as he asked me because my sight, as it was purged, was penetrating deeper and deeper into the beam of the Highest Light, which in itself is truth. My vision then was greater than our speech, which fails at such a sight, and memory fails at such an assault. I am like one who sees in dream, and when the dream is gone an impression, set there, remains, but nothing else comes to mind again, since my vision almost entirely fails me, but the sweetness, born from it, still distils inside my heart. So the snow loses its impress to the sun, so the Sibyl's prophecies were lost on light leaves in the wind.

O Supreme Light, who lifts so far above mortal thought, lend to my mind again a little of what you seemed then, and give my tongue such power that it might leave even a single spark of your glory to those to come, since by returning to my memory, in part, and by sounding in these verses, more of your triumph can be conceived.

I think that I would have been lost, through the keenness of the living ray that I suffered, if my eyes had turned away from it. And so, I remember, I dared to endure it longer that my gaze might be joined with the infinite goodness. O abundant grace, where I presumed to fix my sight on the Eternal Light so long that my sight was wearied! In its depths I saw gathered and bound by love into one volume all things that are scattered through the universe, substance and accident and their relations, as if joined in such a manner that what I speak of is One simplicity of Light. I think I saw the universal form of that bond, because, in saying it, I feel my heart leap in greater intensity of joy. A single moment plunged me into deeper stillness than twenty-five centuries have the enterprise that made Neptune wonder at the *Argo*'s shadow. So my mind gazed, fixed, wholly stilled, immoveable, intent, and continually inflamed by its gazing. Man becomes such in that Light that to turn away to any other sight is beyond the bounds of possibility, because the Good, which is the object of the will, is wholly concentrated there, and outside it, what is perfect within it is defective.

Now my speech will fall further short of what I remember than a baby's who still moistens his tongue at the breast. Not that there was more than a single form in the Living Light where I gazed, which is always such as it was before, but by means of the faculty of sight that gained strength in me, even as it altered, one sole image quickened to my gaze. In the profound and shining Being of the deep Light, three circles appeared, of three colors and one magnitude; one seemed refracted by the other, like rainbows, and the third seemed fire breathed equally from both. O how the words fall short, and how feeble compared with my conceiving! And they are such, compared to what I saw, that it is inadequate to call them merely feeble. O Eternal Light, who only rest in yourself, and know only yourself, who, understood by yourself and knowing yourself, love and smile! Those circles that seemed to be conceived in you as reflected light, when traversed by my eyes a little, seemed to be adorned inside themselves with our image, in its proper colors, and to that my sight was wholly committed. Like a geometer who sets himself to square the circle but cannot find by thought the principle he lacks, so was I at this new sight: I wished to see how the image fitted the circle, and how it was set in place, but my true wings had not been made for this, were it not that my mind was struck by lightning, from which its will emerged. Power, here, failed the deep imagining, but already my desire and will were rolled like a wheel that is turned equally by the love that moves the Sun and the other stars.

BORDERS. CLASSICS

AMERICAN LITERATURE

Louisa May Alcott, *Little Women*
Kate Chopin, *The Awakening and Selected Stories*
James Fenimore Cooper, *The Last of the Mohicans*
Stephen Crane, *The Red Badge of Courage* and *Maggie*
Emily Dickinson, *Selected Poems*
Frederick Douglass, *Narrative of the Life and Other Writings*
F. Scott Fitzgerald, *This Side of Paradise*
Robert Frost, *Collected Early Poetry*
Nathaniel Hawthorne, *The Scarlet Letter*
Washington Irving, *The Legend of Sleepy Hollow and Other Tales*
Jack London, *The Call of the Wild* and *White Fang*
Herman Melville, *Moby-Dick*
Edgar Allan Poe, *Major Tales and Poems*
Upton Sinclair, *The Jungle*
Harriet Beecher Stowe, *Uncle Tom's Cabin*
Henry David Thoreau, *Walden* and *Civil Disobedience*
Mark Twain, *Adventures of Huckleberry Finn*
Mark Twain, *The Complete Adventures of Tom Sawyer*
Mark Twain, *The Mysterious Stranger and Other Stories*
Edith Wharton, *Ethan Frome* and *Summer*
Walt Whitman, *Leaves of Grass*

BRITISH LITERATURE

Jane Austen, *Emma*
Jane Austen, *Pride and Prejudice*
Jane Austen, *Sense and Sensibility*
J. M. Barrie, *Peter Pan*
Charlotte Brontë, *Jane Eyre*
Emily Brontë, *Wuthering Heights*
Lewis Carroll, *Alice in Wonderland*
Joseph Conrad, *Heart of Darkness and Other Tales*
Daniel Defoe, *Robinson Crusoe*

Charles Dickens, *A Christmas Carol and Other Holiday Tales*
Charles Dickens, *Great Expectations*
Charles Dickens, *Oliver Twist*
Charles Dickens, *A Tale of Two Cities*
George Eliot, *Silas Marner*
Kenneth Grahame, *The Wind in the Willows and Other Writings*
Thomas Hardy, *Tess of the d'Urbervilles*
Rudyard Kipling, *The Jungle Books*
William Shakespeare, *The Sonnets and Other Love Poems*
William Shakespeare, *Three Romantic Tragedies*
Mary Shelley, *Frankenstein*
Robert Louis Stevenson, *Dr. Jekyll and Mr. Hyde and Other Strange Tales*
Robert Louis Stevenson, *Treasure Island*
Bram Stoker, *Dracula*
Jonathan Swift, *Gulliver's Travels*
H. G. Wells, *The Time Machine* and *The War of the Worlds*
Oscar Wilde, *The Picture of Dorian Gray*
Oscar Wilde, *Selected Plays*

WORLD LITERATURE

Sir Robert Burton, *Tales from the 1001 Nights*
Miguel de Cervantes, *Don Quixote*
Dante Alighieri, *The Divine Comedy*
Fyodor Dostoevsky, *Crime and Punishment*
Alexandre Dumas, *The Count of Monte Cristo*
Alexandre Dumas, *The Three Musketeers*
Gustave Flaubert, *Madame Bovary*
Homer, *The Iliad*
Homer, *The Odyssey*
Victor Hugo, *The Hunchback of Notre-Dame*
Victor Hugo, *Les Misérables*
Gaston Leroux, *The Phantom of the Opera*
Guy de Maupassant, *The Necklace and Other Stories*
Michel de Montaigne, *Selected Essays*
Ovid, *Metamorphoses*
Virgil, *The Aeneid*
Voltaire, *Candide* and *The Maid of Orléans*

ANTHOLOGIES

Four Centuries of Great Love Poems

The text of this book is set in 11 point Goudy Old Style,
designed by American printer and typographer
Frederic W. Goudy (1865–1947).
This serif font was chosen for its readability
and beautiful characteristics.

The archival-quality, natural paper is composed of recyclable products
made from wood grown in sustainable forests;
the manufacturing processes conform to the
environmental regulations of the country of origin.
Binder's boards are made from 100% post-consumer waste.

The finished volume demonstrates the convergence of Old World
craftsmanship and modern technology that exemplifies
books manufactured by Edwards Brothers, Inc.
Established in 1893, the family-owned business is a well-respected
leader in book manufacturing, recognized the world
over for quality and attention to detail.
In addition, Ann Arbor Media Group's editorial and design services
provide full-service book publication to business partners.